Elf Rock

An epic Romance
Inspired by an Icelandic saga

Sella Páls

A former version of this book was published in eBook form on Amazon under the title Arctic Lust. Copyright © 2020 by Sella Pals U.S. Library of Congress 1-10026333291

Elf Rock Copyright © 2023 by Sella Pals
Library of Congress 1-12790969207

First paperback edition September 2023

Editor: Simon Coury
Cover design: Betty Martinez

ISBN 978-9979-72-873-3 (paperback)

~~~

Sella Páls is a playwright and novelist who divides her time between Iceland, United States and Spain
www.sellapals.com

~~~

See the appendix for a list of characters and maps

In memory of my uncle
Professor Hermann Pálsson, (1921-2002)
scholar, author, and translator of the Icelandic Sagas,
who in 1999 encouraged me to embellish
on the saga of Skáld-Helgi

"My bounty is as boundless as the sea,
My love as deep;
the more I give to thee,
The more I have,
for both are infinite."

    -William Shakespeare, In *Romeo and Juliet*

1
Iceland in the year 1000
Katla

The promise of spring is never broken.
The promise of new life.
The promise of change.

Katla did not understand how people could sleep when the sun shone, the plover piped with joy and the sheep bleated for their wandering lambs.

Her father snored like a neighing horse in his bed. If Katla dressed in a hurry, she could sneak outside before he awoke and badgered her about whatever she enjoyed doing, be it cuddling lambs, running with calves, or singing in gibberish.

She put on a knee-length linen frock, tied a woven belt around her waist and a matching band around her forehead and unruly hair. She grabbed her sheepskin shoes and tiptoed by the sleeping workers into the corridor. Her mother stood by the door to the bath house, struggling to comb her thick and curly hair.

"Don't go outside in a girl's frock," her mother whispered. "Wear a long one like a proper fourteen-year-old woman."

"Dear mother," whispered Katla as she slipped on her shoes and tied them around her ankles, "my feet get caught on the hem when I run."

Oddlaug sighed. "Your father expects you to behave like a

noble woman."

"But I have to run."

"Run along then before your father sees you."

Katla kissed her mother on the cheek. "I think Ljóma is giving birth."

Oddlaug waved her comb. "Go on. I'll wake Jónsi."

Katla walked down the corridor to the shed where Ljóma stood writhing in pain with her tail in the air, two calf's legs stretched out of her rear end.

"My poor Ljóma. Giving birth must be painful."

She clasped the calf's legs, pulled slightly, as she had seen Jónsi do, and sang like the old Celtic maid had done to calm the animals.

Little by little, the calf slid out, along with a gush of water and slime. She hugged the calf to prevent him from dropping to the floor, but they both fell. Ljóma turned towards her calf and licked him, as if he were covered in butter.

Jónsi the workman came in and wrinkled his brow when he saw her. "Good job, but you're a mess."

Katla went outside, grabbed an old rag, ran to the creek and tried to wash the slime and blood off her frock, but to no avail. She did not care, but climbed the hill above the farm, careful not to crush the blueberry and crowberry bushes. Midway up, she stopped and sat down on a mossy mound to enjoy the view. Blooming dandelions smiled at her from the meadow and the bleating of sheep in the field echoed over the valley. She could see where the Hvítá river joined the sea. Katla wanted to climb as high as she needed to in order to see all the farms in the valley that she longed to visit, but was not allowed to until she was married. "Unmarried maidens should stay at home," her father would say, but Katla preferred to be on the move.

Four workmen were gathering their tools by the workshop below. Her father had hired them to build the biggest longhouse in the Thverárhlíd valley, where he intended to hold large gatherings, in particular the wedding festivities for his two daughters. Katla did not know when those weddings would take place, as neither she nor her older sister were betrothed.

What was the rustling in the hollow on her left?

She lifted the hem of her tunic, fell to her knees and crawled towards the sound. If ptarmigans were hiding there, she had better not scare them.

Before Katla reached the hollow, she heard a young woman say, "I love you."

"I love you just as much," whispered a young man. "It's coming." Then he sighed with contentment.

She crawled closer. From the bank of the hollow, she gazed at the white bare buttocks of a young man who lay on top of a woman. He rolled over on his back and his penis looked like an expanded worm. Oh, it was Thórmundur the workman, Jónsi's son. The sun danced about Hrefna's naked body, making her moist breasts and black pubic hairs glisten.

"Love is the only reason to keep going," whispered Hrefna.

Thórmundur raised himself up on one elbow and licked Hrefna's breasts, while she stroked his hair. He kissed her on the mouth for a long time before he said, "Kissing you is delightful."

Katla crawled backwards, stood up, and tiptoed towards the elf rock perched on the hill above, careful not to rip her shoes on the sharp stones. She was tired of being scolded for wearing out her sheepskin shoes. Her cheeks burned, her nipples rubbed against her undershirt and she felt warm below her belly.

Earlier in the spring, blood had started gushing from her crotch and trickled down her thighs. Then, she hurried to the creek where no one could see her, removed her underpants, rolled up her tunic, squatted over the creek and splashed the stinging cold water on her bottom and thighs. Afterwards she bathed in the hot spring west of the farmhouse. This daunting ritual went on for five days until the bleeding stopped.

Her mother had noticed and said, "Instead of washing until your skin is raw you should put a rag in your underpants and change when it is drenched. Then wash it."

"How long does the bleeding last?"

"A few days every month."

"Every month?"

"Except when you're with a child, then you'll not bleed until after the child is born."

"When can I make a child?"

"When you're married, you'll lie in bed with your husband and mate. Nine months later a child is born."

"Can only married couples mate?"

"It's indecent and against the law to mate outside the marriage. If you allow a man to entice you to lie down with him, you'll run the risk of having an illegitimate child and be ousted from society."

On her way uphill, Katla decided to keep secret what the maid Hrefna and Thórmundur had been doing, naked in the hollow. They could lose their jobs. If they had a child, it could be snatched from them and maybe killed.

Katla was puzzled by Thórmundur and Hrefna's reckless behaviour, but she found it enchanting.

When she reached the elf rock she sank to the ground. Her underwear was drenched with sweat. Could she remove all her clothes and let the sunshine play with her body like Hrefna did? She resisted the urge, closed her eyes, caressed her lips with her index finger and imagined a young man was kissing her softly. Was one of the elves playing with her? Kissing her? She reached out and touched the elf rock and whispered, "Vonadís, Vonadís, who's playing with me? You elves understand all secrets and I'll tell you mine." She took a deep breath. "I wish a young and handsome man would say to me 'I love you,' and then lie on top of me." She grasped the soft moss to get the elves' attention. Something tickled her hand. She opened her eyes and saw a blooming buttercup next to her. She picked it up and secured the flower in her headband.

Katla danced around the rock and sang like the famished priest who had once visited the farm. She gave him a sack full of food for teaching her songs. Unlike the Celtic maid, he sang in Latin, words she did not understand and forgot as soon as he left. She made up her own. Now she sang "I love you" many times, and ended with "kissing you is delightful."

When would her betrothed whisper in her ear, "I love you"?

Katla jumped up when she heard her father's thundering

voice yelling, "Katla, come home immediately!"

She stood up and rushed down the hill, humming all the way. She quit singing when she approached the farmhouse. Why run the risk of upsetting her parents, who argued about Christ, God, Thór and all the strange men who did not matter at all? Instead, her parents should kiss on the lips.

Halldór ignored her when she walked into the quarters. He stood like a giant by a wooden column, stroking his thick fingers over the images of Thór he had carved himself.

Katla's mother wore an embroidered frock and her thick braided hair looked like a crown of gold on top of her head.

Thórdís, Katla's sister, looked elegant in a sky-blue frock tied with a silver belt around the waist. Her straight fair hair reflected the light, but her frosty blue eyes gazed at Katla.

Katla removed the flower from her hair and handed it to her mother. "The buttercups by the elf rock are blooming. Vonadís gave me this one."

Oddlaug sighed. "My dear Katla, you're a grownup. You should restrain yourself from time to time."

Halldór shook his money pouch which hung from his belt and stared at Katla with stone-grey eyes, sending a chill down her back. "How feeble-minded you are." He turned to Thórdís and gave her an adoring look. The thick beard on his cheeks rose and from between his lips a few teeth appeared: an indication of a smile.

"Why are you dressed up like this?" Katla said.

Oddlaug pinched Katla's cheek. "It's time for you to wash up and change clothes. Our guests would be shocked to see you dressed as a pauper."

"And you stink," Thórdís said.

"Guests! How exciting. What guests?" Katla said.

Halldór straightened his back. "Thórdur from Hofdi and his son, Helgi."

Thórdís looked at her father with a cunning glint in her eyes, then glanced at Katla and said, "He's a poet."

"A poet!" Katla said, and clapped her hands. "Oh, I hope

he'll entertain us."

"Don't you dare insult the guests by asking them to entertain us," Thórdís said, and walked to Finnbjorg, the maid who sat by the fire, stirring the ale pot.

Was Finnbjorg stirring ale or a witches' brew? She came from Finnmark and some suspected her of sorcery.

Halldór thundered, "Any decent man can recite Hávamál or Voluspá the Prophecy in my house."

"Hávamál!" said Katla. "I know Hávamál is supposed to reflect the ultimate wisdom, but it says women are betrayers."

Halldór's laughter made his large stomach wobble "Unfaltering wisdom."

Oddlaug gave her husband a harsh look. "Christian women don't betray their vows, unlike heathen men."

Thórdís lifted her chin to show her disapproval, as was her custom. "And those married men even pay for their concubines." She looked at her mother. "I don't understand why married women tolerate such infidelity."

"You'll understand once you're married," Oddlaug said, not flinching.

Katla knew nothing about concubines, but they could all use some cheer. "Shall we ask Helgi to recite love poems?"

"Don't shame us with shallow chatter," Thórdís said.

"Katla. While the guests are here, listen carefully and speak sparingly," Halldór said, and stroked Thórdís's hair. "How gorgeous you look today, my dear Thórdís."

Oddlaug patted Katla on the rear end and said, "Hurry to the spring and bathe. Then put on your light linen tunic."

Katla lifted her eyes to the ceiling and called out, "Honour the poet! Honour the one who knows!"

"Katla frolics like an untamed colt," Thórdís said.

Katla stopped by the door, turned around and said, "In spite of her sister's whining, Katla is full of joy."

She walked out singing at the top of her lungs, imagining what a poet looked like.

2
Helgi

When Helgi finished saddling Sleipnir, the horse pushed his head into Helgi's armpit to let him know it was time to dart off.

Helgi grasped the bridle. "Why be impatient, my friend? Do you think a willing mare awaits you where we're going?" He smiled and stroked Sleipnir's neck. "Spring infuses us with boundless energy, my dear Sleipnir. Like you, I would rather dash about the valley and visit willing maidens than go to Holl, where the old fogeys want to saddle me with a wife." Sleipnir neighed. "Calm down. We must wait for Father."

Helgi looked over the wide valley below, where the Thverá river wound its way through the lava and the bush on its way to the sea. The valley was scattered with farms and Helgi wondered why the farmers had become so docile, settled down like old mares, seldom budging from their barns. Had they not inherited their ancestors' thirst for exploration? Unlike valiant Vikings, the leaders of the country were obsessed with securing land, accumulating livestock and passing laws.

They had lost their passion. Helgi swore to never lose his.

Despite the cloudless sky, the ocean Helgi longed to cross was out of sight. If he could only jump on board a ship with spirited men headed for distant lands. He sighed. Instead, he was about to be chained to one woman and a dreary farm.

His father Thórdur appeared beside him with his horse in tow and slapped Helgi on the shoulder. Thórdur looked dignified, dressed up in a blue embroidered mantle, his beard trimmed, his brown hair combed straight and tied at the nape of the neck.

"Father. You look exuberant," Helgi said.

"My lucky son is betrothed only once in a lifetime."

"You like to see me shackled," Helgi said.

Thórdur smiled with a glint in his eyes. "You should be

grateful to acquire a superior farm by marrying Thórdís."

"With it come obligations, children and isolation. Father, why can't I travel to Norway for a bit before the wedding?"

Thórdur snapped, "I sent you abroad once and you didn't mature much. I doubt that another trip will render you more prudent."

"Everyone was fighting then in Saxony, and I had to hide in a monastery."

"I didn't expect you to be stuck with Christians. Still, you managed to learn Latin."

"Dear father, I can't compose poetry worthy of kings when I'm surrounded by wailing women and crying infants."

"It's futile to go to Norway now because King Olafur Tryggvason is hostile to Icelanders. He wants to force independent landowners in Iceland to kneel before wretched foreign priests in praise of a new god. The god of swarthy foreigners."

"Gunnlaugur Serpent-Tongue got to sail abroad when he was twelve and he's going again with his father's support."

"Gunnlaugur is reckless and pompous. I would not be surprised if his audacity got him killed."

"He and I are expert swordsmen whom few men defeat. But now he'll be famous for his poetry and sportsmanship, while I'll fade into obscurity."

"You would be wise to follow in the footsteps of Gunnlaugur's brother, Hermundur. He's industrious and will prosper."

Thórdur jumped on his horse as if it were a tiny mound. Helgi mounted Sleipnir. "Do I have a choice?"

"Halldór and I agreed to the engagement years ago, and if you honour me, you must abide by it. Our prosperity depends on keeping our commitments."

"Kinsmen. Prosperity. Friendship. Honour. Commitments. Farm. Land. Loyalty. Simple words, often uttered," Helgi said and let Sleipnir gallop down the road.

When Helgi was far ahead of his father, he stopped, dismounted and stroked Sleipnir's sweaty neck. "I'm just as skittish as you are, my friend. What is a spirited young man of eighteen to do with a wife and a farm? You and I have yet to explore enchanting places." Sleipnir neighed in agreement.

How could he persuade his father and Halldór to delay the wedding so he could sail abroad for two years before settling down?

Colourful wildflowers caught Helgi's eyes. Ah! Women adore men who bring them flowers. He picked enough for a large bouquet, sure to melt the heart of his future fiancée.

3
Thórdís

Thórdís was relieved when Katla left the living quarters. Her younger sister resembled an untamed beast, running incessantly, bathed in sweat, and bellowing nonsense wherever she went. Her gaiety was nothing but sheer arrogance and pretence.

Few things scared Thórdís, but now she feared Katla could overshadow Helgi's visit by demands for attention and childish requests for love poems.

Halldór beamed and said, "Helgi is lucky to gain such a beautiful and wise young woman."

Thórdís stretched up to kiss her father on his bearded cheek and said, "Thank you for selecting a well-bred young man for me." She whispered in her father's ear, "After the guests are gone, we should thank Ódinn and Freyja for our good fortune."

Halldór smiled. "Devoted you are, my dear daughter."

Oddlaug approached them. "What are you two scheming?"

"I was telling father how grateful I am," Thórdís said. "People say Helgi is reserved, has good command of Icelandic and looks knightly."

"Knightly is hardly an asset, and I've heard he prefers amusement to farming," Oddlaug said.

A horse neighed outside, indicating the arrival of strangers. Halldór and Oddlaug headed outside.

Thórdís walked to Finnbjorg, who was polishing drinking horns with a linen rag.

"All is not in order," Finnbjorg said, and sniffed the air around her as if she were trying to detect an evil odour. "I smell deceit. "

Only Thórdís knew of the herbs Finnbjorg had slipped into the ale. "What do you mean? The engagement shall take place. What's there to do?"

"You're never baffled, dear girl," Finnbjorg said, and flipped a black braid behind her shoulder. "If you never waver from your intention, your wishes will come true – in time." She pointed her index finger at Thórdís as if scolding her. "Stay resolute, in spite of obstacles."

The door opened and Oddlaug walked in, smiling widely, carrying a bunch of colourful wildflowers. Thórdís could not remember seeing her mother this jovial. Did it take only common weeds to cheer her mother up?

Thórdur and a young man, undoubtedly Helgi, walked in. Helgi's hair was dark brown and wavy, and he held a bunch of wildflowers. He stared at Thórdís and smiled widely, exposing his glistening white teeth. Thórdís felt a wave of victory warm her body. She tilted her chin downward and attempted a demure smile. Helgi handed her the flowers, which she took against her inclination. She sneezed. Instead of thanking him for the bouquet of weeds, she handed it to Finnbjorg.

Without asking Thórdís permission, Helgi seized the drinking horn she had been engraving, examined it and grinned. "Your hands look too delicate to damage by inscribing runes. Have you studied the secret arts of the sorceress?"

Oddlaug laughed. "We are Christian and Thórdís does not practise sorcery."

"What is she engraving then?"

Thórdís snatched the horn from Helgi. Her future husband would never get away with questioning her. "It's my secret until the gift is finished." She smiled and hoped he did not detect her hostility.

"We shall make merry," Halldór said.

Finnbjorg poured ale into a horn and handed it to Thórdur. He took a sip and passed the horn to Halldór.

Thórdís observed the men, careful to avoid Helgi's stare. She feigned joy, but she was disappointed in Helgi, who seemed cocky. He told funny stories and laughed at them himself. His dark unruly hair indicated mixed blood. Their children would have dark hair.

Why was she contemplating what their unborn children would look like? She had decided long ago that bearing children and cuddling them was a waste of her time, and she would find ways to avoid such slavery.

As if Helgi detected her reservations, he said, "How disrespectful of me to be dusty in the presence of beautiful women." He moved towards the door. "I'll step outside and wash myself. I promise to be as quick as a cat catching a mouse." He laughed once more, bowed his head to the women, and left.

"My son likes to be clean and presentable," Thórdur said, and took another swig from the horn.

Oddlaug asked Thórdur about the rumour the national assembly might agree to adopt Christianity at Althing.

"They say we have to become Christian if we're going to keep peace with King Olafur Tryggvason," Thórdur said.

"Preposterous!" Halldór bellowed. "Independence is paramount to Icelanders." His nostrils flared. "Our ancestors fled bloodthirsty dictators to settle here and run their own affairs. Only fainthearted men succumb to the king's demands. Olafur, with the aid of bishops, is forcing people to believe fairy-tales from foreign lands. Christianity is pure nonsense."

Thórdís felt suffocated by the air in the room. Was the aroma from the ale pot or her disappointment with her future husband the reason for her queasiness? She could not afford to let him ruffle her. Although Helgi was a self-absorbed fool, she was determined to marry him, sooner rather than later. Then she could seize the power she deserved.

4
Helgi

Helgi took a deep breath when he stepped outside into the sunshine.

If he was reluctant to marry before, he was even more so after meeting his bride-to-be. Despite her beauty and her dignity, she lacked feminine softness, and he was sure her cunning smile reflected a calculating temperament. She rejected the flowers on purpose and evaded eye contact, as if she were safeguarding her thoughts. Snatching the horn from his hand revealed her obstinacy. Could she be trying to hide her objection to their marriage?

Helgi walked deep in his thoughts across the farmyard, past the workshop, horses, the cowshed, and headed towards a murmur from a stream. He agonised over his foreseeable lacklustre future as a prisoner of his wife, his children and a farm.

He looked up when he detected the sulphur smell of a hot spring. Ahead, steam floated up from the ground. How convenient; he could wash himself there. He crossed damp moss mounds, trying to avoid slipping on the rusty brown mud around the hot spring.

When he looked up, a naked young girl, surrounded by mist, was stepping out of a hot spring.

Was this an hallucination?

He closed his eyes and rubbed them, but when he reopened them, he imagined the girl was a fairy, so bewitching was the vision. The maiden's wet blonde hair fell in waves over her shoulders and over her plump breasts, down to her waist. She lifted her arms, danced around in circles and sang with an enchanting voice. Her celestial singing reminded him of the nuns raising their voices to their Christ in the cloister in Saxony. The tune sounded familiar, but the maiden did not sing the Latin lyrics. Instead, she sang over and over again, "I love you. I love you."

He approached her as if hypnotised.

When she saw Helgi she stopped dancing. She skipped over the rocks to a grassy patch, leaned over, took a large piece of cloth and wrapped it around herself. They stared at each other and Helgi found his manhood rising under his garments. For a moment he was bewildered.

She smiled and a deep dimple formed in her rosy cheek.

He said, "Are you a fairy?"

She walked towards him laughing. The brightest laugh there ever was. "The elf fairy lives in the rock over there." She pointed up the hill. "My name is Thórkatla but everyone calls me Katla."

"Katla!" He drank in the smiling lips and the flashing sky-blue eyes. A poem formed in his mind and he recited it out loud.

> "Like stars that sparkle, bright and lush,
> your taunting smile, it makes me blush.
> Katla, you're like the loveliest queen
> this simple lad has ever seen."

Katla laughed wholeheartedly and said, "Delightful!" She shivered a little. "You're very daring, but I have to get dressed before they scold me."

He turned around. "I'll wash while you get dressed." When he walked by her, the aroma of fresh flowers overpowered him, as if he were immersed in a fairy tale. He washed his hands, splashed warm water on his face, and composed a poem. Without turning around, he stood up and called out with sheer joy:

> "As Katla egressed from the spring,
> And naked commenced to sing
> The amour's arrow flew to me,
> and bit my heart with eternal glee."

When he turned around, he expected to see Katla fully dressed, but in her place stood Thórdís, looking hostile.

"Do you recite poems to all the girls you meet?" she said.

"Only to the most beautiful and I'm fortunate to have beheld two today." He looked past Thórdís and saw Katla wearing a light frock approach the farmhouse.

"It's inappropriate for the man I'm to marry to seduce my fourteen-year-old sister."

"I didn't know Katla was your sister. But you and I are not betrothed yet."

"Do you intend to betray your father?"

"How could I marry one woman when I have designs on another?"

"Most marriages are arranged. To honour one's parents is paramount."

"How can we ignore the flames of love that flare up between a man and a woman, as if inspired by a primal force?"

"Such flames flare from lust, and all fires turn to ash." She turned around and continued, "It's rude to keep our parents waiting." She strode towards the farmhouse.

Helgi walked by her side. "Thórdís, my dear beautiful Thórdís. I'm a blithesome poet and my heart will be crushed if I'm to restrain the joyous force of love. How could we, you and I, bed together and bring up children in a loveless house?"

"Our fathers' arrangement is not governed by rashness, but by reason."

"Please spare us both the misery of a marriage based on reason."

They had reached the farmhouse. Thórdís stopped and turned to him. She stared at him with a steady gaze, and said with an iron will Helgi knew would be impossible to sway, "A wise man tames his lust." She walked inside.

The ecstasy Helgi felt moments before had evaporated. A chill went through him as if he were naked in an ice-storm. He prayed quietly to Jesus Christ and to Thór to remove the shackles his father and Halldór had placed on him.

He was about to enter the farmhouse when Katla stepped out. She looked like an angel in her white frock. The blooming flower in her hairband smiled at him, as its alluring owner did.

Katla laughed with glee and said, "Helgi, please come inside."

Helgi looked to the sky and said, "How quickly you answer my prayers, dear Christ. I'm forever grateful."

"Are you talking to the saviour, Jesus Christ?"

"You heard right. How lucky the flower is to be planted in your hair. No meadow is as enchanting."

She blushed and said, "No man has talked to me this openly before."

"I shall forever tell you what my heart perceives."

"And I shall listen to you and believe you above all other men."

"As long as I live, I shall compose poems about you with the most eloquent words the Icelandic tongue has to offer."

"Do you compose love poems?"

"Only to you."

She jumped. "How lucky I am! Icelandic poets don't compose love poems. My father and other men only appreciate poems about battles and heroes."

"Men fight for riches, men fight for land, men fight for prestige, but who is a more deserving hero than the one who fights for the woman he loves?"

The door opened and their fathers, Halldór and Thórdur, stepped out.

As Halldór pinched Katla's cheek, her smile faded. "My dear Katla, I know you prefer to piddle in a blooming field or to race around the pasture like a colt, but now you must come inside and greet the guests."

"I've not been ignoring the guests. I've used the time to get to know Helgi."

Helgi's father looked grim and said, "Helgi, go inside. It's time we voiced our errand."

Helgi said, "Father, can I have a word with you in private."

Katla's father grasped her elbow and pushed her inside, ahead of him.

When they were out of sight, Thórdur said, "How rude you are, my son, to ask to talk to me alone while our hosts await us inside."

"Dear father, I want to honour your wish. But I can't betray my heart by marrying Thórdís. Therefore, we shall abandon our errand."

"How could you have changed your mind faster than the eagle flies?"

"I'm in love with Halldór's younger daughter, and I must have her instead of her sister."

"Are you mad? It's out of the question." Thórdur's face turned pale.

"My happiness depends on you. Please convince Halldór to switch the brides. If he doesn't agree, I'll obey you, albeit with a heavy heart."

Thórdur asked him to wait. He went inside to fetch Halldór.

After they came outside, Thórdur said, "Some kind of savage has captured my son's mind. I don't agree with his unreasonable whim."

"What whim?"

"As we had agreed upon, it was my plan to request the hand of Thórdís on behalf of Helgi."

"Have you changed your mind?" Halldór expanded his stomach and pulled on his red beard.

"The boy now wants the hand of Thórkatla instead."

With a thundering voice, Halldór said, "Katla!"

Damn, this man had a violent temper. Helgi was not prepared for such a hostile reaction. He stammered, "If I marry Thórdís much unhappiness will befall us."

"Happiness! What do you think marriage has to do with happiness?" Halldór said.

"Happiness is superior to unhappiness," Helgi said.

Halldór looked at Helgi with disdain. "Happiness is a state of mind."

"I agree," Thórdur said.

Halldór looked at Thórdur. "These Christian proclamations of love and such nonsense are poisoning rational minds and undermining the splendour of noble Icelandic men. It's pure insanity."

"True," Thórdur said.

"Katla is fourteen years old, and I will not give her away until she's seventeen. Besides, I have already picked out a husband for her."

"I'll wait until she's seventeen," Helgi said, and tried to sound meek although he was angry.

Halldór spoke to Thórdur, ignoring Helgi. "Rich and promising sons of leaders have asked for Thórdís's hand, but I have refused them all because I promised you, my friend, she should marry Helgi." Halldór's face was now close to Thórdur's. "Are you backing out of our agreement?"

"It's not my intention. Our friendship is precious to me."

"Then bring the boy to his senses. Helgi will never get my Katla, as long as the rivers run," Halldór said, and stamped his foot down. "I'll never go back on my word."

His eyes looked like they were about to pop out of his head.

Thórdur patted Halldór on the shoulder and said, "Rest at ease, my friend. Helgi will come to his senses."

Halldór's shoulders dropped slightly. "Then we'll make peace. Let's go inside, have a drink and let the whims of youth breeze by our ears like a gust of wind."

Helgi was too upset to follow them inside. To his father he said, "I regret having angered you, and I shall weigh my options."

"Don't forget the consequences of your choices," Thórdur said, and followed Halldór inside.

Even though they had made a contract years ago, how could they ignore Helgi's wishes when his happiness was at stake? Halldór himself looked unhappy. Had he been forced to marry a woman he did not love?

As a rule, Helgi could persuade his father to see matters his way, but he sensed Halldór's will was as inflexible as the iron sword the gigantic man wore as if he were a king.

5
Katla

Katla sat on a bench next to her sister in the living room, staring at the front door, dangling her feet and humming. Thórdís, who was carving her horn with precision, shushed Katla to stop.

Soon Thórdur and Halldór entered and sat down. Finnbjorg brought them a horn filled with ale.

Where was Helgi?

Katla jumped up and rushed outside. She found Helgi sitting by the spring where they had first met, throwing pebbles into it. She ran to him and said, "Everyone inside is so gloomy. We're not like them. Let's be jolly. Please recite the poem, the one you wrote about me."

Helgi stood up and walked towards her – so close she could hear him breathe. He lifted her chin with one hand, looked deep into her eyes and said with a thrilling voice, "Like stars that sparkle, bright and lush," and he never let his eyes wander from hers. After he was done, he kissed her on the forehead and lowered his hand.

Blood rushed to Katla's face. She sat down and said, "Have you composed many love poems?"

Helgi laughed. "Love poems do not befit court poets."

"Court poets! Are you a poet of the king's court?"

"I wanted to be one, and learned the original skaldic language from my mother's father, Einar the Bowltinkle."

"Teach me skaldic language."

"Women don't learn the skaldic language."

"I want to understand all you say and do. Give me an example."

"Sight-rocks. Guess what that means?" Helgi said. "Is it eyes?"

"You're smart. Yes, sight-rocks are eyes."

Helgi continued with fervour. Even though Katla could not decipher the words, she listened spellbound. He explained to her the various metaphors used in skaldic poetry. The word combinations and the symbolic names sounded alien, but hilarious. They began a game, playing with unusual word combinations. They continued making fun of poetic synonyms, until Thórdís called, "Your fathers are waiting for you inside."

They stood up. Helgi brushed the moss from Katla's cream-coloured frock and said, "I'm the costly warrior."

"Costly warrior. What does it mean?"

"Uncontrollable man." He threw his hands up and laughed. "I cannot help it." They held hands as they walked to the farmhouse.

Thórdís stood in the doorway. She stepped aside to let Helgi pass but, before Katla could follow him, Thórdís grasped her elbow and said, "I must talk to you."

Katla was still jubilant and said, "Helgi is the most extraordinary young man I have ever met."

"Are you too dumb to grasp the purpose of Thórdur and Helgi's visit?"

"What purpose?"

"They're on an important errand."

Katla was baffled, and guessed, "Discussing Christianity or Althing?"

Thórdís laughed, no doubt to make fun of Katla's ignorance. "Our fathers made a pact a long time ago about Helgi marrying me." Now she smiled slyly.

Katla's heart stopped. "You're lying because you want to hurt me."

"I don't give a damn about your feelings, but don't you dare ruin their plan."

"Helgi loves me. I know it."

"Loves you! Rubbish. He doesn't know you. Did he tell you about the marriage match?"

"It didn't come up."

"There you are. He's dishonourable and devious."

"In spite of that, you want to marry him?"

"It's my destiny." Thórdís raised her chin.

Thórdís was wrong, Katla thought. She was certain love

could conquer all adversity. She entered the farmhouse smiling, looking forward to seeing Helgi again. But Thórdur and Helgi were preparing to leave.

Once the guests were gone, her father was angry and told his wife, "You've failed to teach Thórkatla to respect her parents. She embarrasses us on a whim." To Katla he said, "You're to stay by your mother the rest of the day and learn how to be useful."

Oddlaug stared at her husband and said, "If I have failed to teach her so far, how am I to teach her to be useful now?"

Katla could not help but giggle.

Her father grabbed Katla by the front of her frock, lifted her up so her face was close to his, and said, "How dare you disrespect me? Don't ever forget you're my property and I control your future." He let her go and stormed out.

Oddlaug said, "Dear Katla, if you want a good life, don't provoke your father."

"But you provoke him," Katla said.

"I'm his wife and I have a right to respond when he shows me disrespect."

How unfair. No one cared how she felt. Except Helgi. He cared, she was sure.

Katla sneaked out of the house early the next morning to avoid her father's wrath. As she climbed the hill, she saw Halldór and four farmhands saddling horses and riding down to join Thórdur and other men by the main road.

As soon as the group of men rode away, Katla hurried down to the farmhouse, changed into a long, clean frock, and tied a colourful belt around her waist. Once outside, she walked gracefully up the hill to the elf rock, lifting the hem of her dress slightly, as a full-fledged woman would.

Soon she heard the sound of hoofs approaching the farm, and turned around. A man was riding towards the main house with a package tied to his saddle. He held the reins with one hand and a large bundle of flowers with the other. Flowers! Who other than Helgi would bring flowers? She pulled up the hem of her dress, ignored her resolution to behave like a grown-up woman, and ran down the hill.

Helgi jumped off the horse about the time she stepped on her dress and fell flat on the ground in front of him. He reached out his hand, helped her to her feet, handed her the flowers and said, "You run faster than a young colt."

"I'm overjoyed to see you." She blushed when she looked into his shining warm eyes. She wanted to cover his face with kisses but she restrained the urge, and smiled and laughed instead until tears ran down her cheeks.

Her mother approached and said, "Good day, Helgi."

"Good day, Mistress Oddlaug." Helgi untied a big bundle from his saddle. "I brought you a present."

The salmon he brought melted Oddlaug's heart.

Katla said, "Can I show Helgi the elf rock?"

"You can, but I must be able to see you from the yard at all times."

Katla kissed her mother on the cheek. "Thank you, dear Mother."

"I adore Katla, and I respect Halldór too much to engage in any improper behaviour," Helgi said.

On the way up the hill they continued their poetic wordplay and laughed often.

When they reached the elf rock, Katla kissed it and said to Helgi, "Vonadís knows about our love."

Helgi took Katla's hand. "May all elves and other beings bear witness that my heart belongs to Thórkatla Halldórsdóttir until the end of time."

Katla put Helgi's hand on her chest by her heart and said, "And my heart belongs to you until the end of my life."

"In Saxony we read a Latin text by Plato."

"Who is Plato?"

"He was a Greek wise man who wrote about love and other subjects."

"A wise man who knew love? Is it true?"

"According to him, love was created in heaven when one

soul split in half. One half was placed in a man's body and the other in a woman's body. When their souls were near each other, they yearned to combine, to become one again."

"This Plato was a wise man indeed."

They speculated about when Helgi should ask Halldór for Katla's hand in marriage. Helgi wanted to wait until later in the summer after the conflict concerning the adoption of Christianity was resolved. Katla agreed to all he said, as he was older and educated, but discussing boring political matters did not interest her. "Tell me about Saxony. I want to know all about the funny people there."

Helgi told her amusing stories and she laughed and laughed.

"Your laughter reminds me of a twirling brook," he said, waving his hands in the air.

At midday, the maid Hrefna walked up the hill to them and said with a smile, "Katla, you're to come home and Helgi is supposed to leave." Hrefna turned around and lifted her frock, exposing her ankles and calves, and swung her hips in a carefree manner as she walked down the hill.

Helgi watched Hrefna strutting downhill. As if she could feel it, Hrefna turned around and smiled at Helgi. Then she ran the last bit.

"She's uninhibited," Helgi said.

Katla felt Hrefna was too daring. "Yes, and she lies naked in the hollow with a young man who says 'I love you' to her."

Helgi laughed. "As we will do when we are married."

"Yes." Her dream of love would come true, no matter what her father said.

~~~

After Helgi rode away, Thórdís asked Katla what they had talked about.

"The Bible," Katla said. What Helgi told Katla belonged to her alone.

"You lie. If you don't want to be called a whore, then you should leave an engaged man alone, unless of course you intend to become a concubine."

"I'm only doing what my mother permits. Helgi is not engaged yet." Katla began singing to calm herself down, and to irritate her sister.

"Our father decides whom we marry." Thórdís removed the carving knife which hung from her belt and held it up in the air, as if it was a weapon. "And no one shall prevent me from becoming the lady of the house at Hvammur."

Katla liked to avoid Thórdís's domineering attacks by singing loudly and helping her mother with chores. Thórdís only showed affection towards Finnbjorg, and she pretended to be devoted to her father. Unlike her parents, Katla knew Thórdís's motivation for marriage was to become rich and powerful. Thórdís needed Helgi to realise her ambition. Katla was determined to get in the way.

Katla found her mother in the food supply hut rearranging provisions.

"Helgi is gone, as you wished," Katla said.

"The boy prefers amusement to work. Not a desirable trait in a husband."

"But he's a poet. Isn't it a sign of intelligence?"

"Fancy words often hide dubious intentions," Oddlaug said, and put an onion on the shelf.

Katla wanted to flee, to run up the hill again and talk to Vonadís, her only ally on the farm. "I'm a grown-up woman and not a child any more. Tell me, how do I become a desirable match for an honourable man?"

Oddlaug was usually serious but now she smiled to one side, deepening the dimple in her cheek. "Due to your beauty and your lineage, you are already a superb match."

"I want to be like Thórgerdur Egilsdóttir."

"But she's temperamental."

"No man wins an argument with her," Katla said.

"Because she's a well-educated woman of reason and has an excellent memory, despite her age."

"Maybe I'm not temperamental enough to be a woman of substance, but I'm a quick study. Who other than Thórdís can teach me how to carve runes?"

"Finnbjorg."

"But she loves Thórdís and she doesn't care for me."

"Then I'll teach you, although I'm short of time."

"You must teach me how to manage a household and how to weave. Then I can be of more help to you."

Even though her mind was preoccupied with her love for Helgi, Katla did not want him and her parents to be ashamed of her. Perhaps she should be less impulsive – although cautious people were often deceptive, like her sister. She wished everyone could be more spontaneous and sincere, like Helgi.

The next morning, she awoke full of anticipation, wrapped herself in linen, walked to the spring, bathed, dressed in her finest long frock and tucked a fresh flower in her hair.

She was a woman. A woman in love.

Again, Helgi showed up early in the day with fresh salmon for Oddlaug and flowers for Katla.

Oddlaug received the salmon with gratitude, yet she welcomed Helgi with reserve. "Helgi, when you are with Katla, I must be able to see you from the farmhouse. You are not to touch Katla nor recite love poetry to her. Such behaviour is against the law. You can teach Katla the holy text, but please abstain from telling her barbaric Southern tales that glorify violent men."

"I revere Katla as if she were a queen, and I shall teach her respectable Christian scriptures," Helgi said, and smiled sweetly.

"Then you'll be useful. Maybe you should also teach Thórdís."

Helgi looked surprised and said, "If she is interested."

Oddlaug called Thórdís, who seemed offended and said, "I have more productive things to do," turned around and walked away.

Helgi visited daily and brought to life a foreign and exotic world for Katla. He imitated monks, the abbess of the cloister and his fellow students in Saxony. She shook with laughter, which inspired him to keep going.

When he quit, he said, "Your joy delights like the sun and has the power to cure every malady on this earth."

Later, Katla sat by her mother's side in the weaving room. While they wove and spun, Katla related to her mother the stories from the Bible Helgi had told her. Oddlaug welcomed the opportunity to learn about "goodness, peace and love".

When Thórdís accused Katla of seducing Helgi, Oddlaug told Thórdís she was better off learning the words of Christ than sneaking off with her father to hold heathen rites in honour of violent gods.

Three days before Halldór was due to return from his trip, Helgi and Katla, who were at the elf rock, spotted him approaching Holl on Hreidfaxi. They rushed down the hill.

Despite Halldór's immense weight, Hreidfaxi trotted rapidly up the road with steaming nostrils. When Halldór dismounted, he was as sweaty as Hreidfaxi and snorted like a horse.

Halldór approached Helgi with raised fists, and yelled, "Your audacity is insulting!" He towered over Helgi. "The rumour flies across the land that you have defamed my daughter in plain sight."

Helgi looked furious. "It's a blatant lie. I would never defame Katla."

Halldór screamed, "Go! Go! Go! Get out of my sight and off my property, you lunatic."

Katla feared her father would attack Helgi and wished Helgi would stay quiet, but he yelled, "I have not disgraced your daughter in any way."

"I alone decide who Katla spends time with. She has been promised to a better man than you'll ever be." Halldór spat on the ground in front of Helgi. "You shall abide by my wishes and never again defile Katla's purity with your insulting presence."

Oddlaug stepped outside and said, "How little you trust me, my husband. Nothing disrespectful has happened here. Helgi has taught Katla the words of Christ, which I appreciate since you don't permit a priest to set a foot on these premises."

"The words of Christ! Relaying rubbish for halfwits is reason enough to keep them apart. After Althing, we the descendants of the settlers of this land, will ban fairy tales concocted by Southern simpletons to expunge rational thought." He glared at his wife. "Also, we will not tolerate gullible women rehashing the priests' hogwash."

Helgi's furious eye seemed to be on fire. He straightened his back and put one hand on the handle of his sword. Katla feared he would raise it.

Then Helgi said what he should have left unsaid. "I alone dictate my comings and goings, here as to other farms."

Helgi's audacity did not intimidate Halldór. "If you disregard my order, I will separate you and Katla forever."

The more Halldór insisted, the more stubborn Helgi became. "You don't scare me, and I promise to visit Katla wherever she is."

"Katla is my property and I'll never allow you to diminish her worth."

Halldór's entourage arrived, dismounted and rushed to Halldór's side. Helgi did not budge.

Katla stepped in front of her father and said, "Honourable father, I hold you in high esteem, but I'm the one who invited Helgi here. You'll regret keeping us apart."

"How defiant and blind you are, my child. The closer you want to be to this numbskull, the farther you shall be from him." Halldór grabbed Katla's hand and dragged her to the farmhouse. Katla escaped from his grip and ran up the hill. She heard Halldór order Helgi off his property.

Katla ran past the elf rock and up the bush-covered hill. She had to catch up with Helgi. When she could not be seen from Holl, she headed west towards Hofdi. She did not care if her best frock ripped, and the sharp rocks tore holes in her sheepskin shoes. She feared her father would send her far away, where Helgi could not visit.

Down below, she spotted Helgi sitting with stooped shoulders on Sleipnir, who walked slowly up the road. Katla skipped on the mossy mounds down the hill. When Helgi saw her, he jumped off the horse and embraced her. They promised to be loyal to each other, whatever obstacles they were to face. "Hurry home and tell them I'm innocent, and I never defiled you," he said.

On her return, she met two farmhands, whom her father must have sent to find her. She ran by them, crying uncontrollably.

6
Nidbjorg

Helgi's mother stood by the front door at Hofdi and watched her friend Maefa as she rode away with two escorts. They turned west on the Thverárhlíd road until the fog swallowed them. Despite her soaked mantle, Nidbjorg was too numb to move.

On Maefa's arrival, Nidbjorg was bedridden with a painful backache, and led others to believe it was caused by sitting for long hours sewing. When Maefa told her of Helgi's argument with Halldór, Nidbjorg suspected the source of her pain was Helgi's conduct at Holl.

Nidbjorg turned around, grimaced with pain, removed the soaked mantle, handed it to her maid Jóhanna, asked her maid to light the fire and to bring Helgi to her as soon as he came home.

She sat down at the centre of the living room in the seat of honour, her husband's seat. When he was away, she was the one in charge. Besides, she was better at solving disputes than her congenial husband.

Nidbjorg suspected something was amiss when Helgi rushed to Holl each morning and was gone most of the day. After two such trips, Nidbjorg asked her son to stay home and supervise the building of a rock wall around the farmhouse. Idleness was at the root of most ills. He fooled her by claiming he was helping the family of Holl by giving them salmon he had caught himself and by teaching them scriptures. Since he did not mention Thórkatla, Nidbjorg assumed he went to Hofdi to visit Thórdís.

Her son was guilty of deceit, a vice she despised.

While Jóhanna lit the fire, Nidbjorg pondered what had gone wrong in Helgi's upbringing. The answer was simple. Thórdur was too lenient with Helgi. He indulged him. In addition, Nidbjorg's father had tricked Helgi by romanticising poetic fame and encouraging his grandson to join the courts of battling kings across the ocean.

Even though Einar was famous, and she was fond of her father, she did not revere him. How could she forget her mother's struggles in Saelingsdalur while her father was busy glorifying kings and earls with convoluted poems? Einar's wealth never made it to his wife and children in Iceland. In fact, Nidbjorg's mother was the true hero, running the farm and bringing up the children in the poet's absence.

Helgi arrived with a sour look on his face.

She ordered him to sit down beside her and said, "Your father is a wise man, but he indulges you beyond reason. He has allowed you to go as you please because of your poetic wit and fencing ability. But you lack prudence."

"What is ailing you, dear mother?"

"It breaks my heart to hear you have brought disgrace upon us by arguing with Halldór, your father's best friend. How could you tarnish his daughter's reputation by seducing her?"

"Halldór is a pathetic loudmouth."

"What! He's the most powerful landowner in Borgarfjordur. Both Halldór and Oddlaug descend from heroic men and women."

"He's as stubborn as a bull."

"The more stubborn he is, the more humble you should be," she said firmly.

"He acts as if he owns Katla like a cow."

"Halldór has the right to protect his daughter. In Iceland three things matter most: land ownership, friendship, and family ties. It's time you showed loyalty to your father's friends and to your parents."

"I love Katla and I dislike and distrust Thórdís. I refuse to marry her."

"Fondness develops in time with mutual trust and loyalty. Do you realise how your father suffers when he hears friends mock his lovestruck son for belittling the daughter of his best friend?"

Helgi stood up. "These accusations are without merit."

"Sit down, my son," she ordered. "As you know, there are

penalties for seducing honourable girls.

He yelled, "Katla and I talk in plain view of her mother. No one would dare sue me."

"Halldór will exercise his rights. Your father and he cannot afford to be at odds. Together they established an alliance of powerful landowners who are opposing the Icelanders' adoption of Christianity."

"What do my marriage matters have to do with politics?"

"When you marry Thórdís you'll receive a prosperous farm. Should you marry Katla, you'll get nothing from her father or from us."

"Land ownership doesn't matter to me."

"Land is paramount. With it you receive the right to attend parliament meetings and to be involved in law-making. Thórdur and Halldór will never alter the marriage contract."

"I'll not be happy until Katla and I are betrothed. It's useless for friends and family to insist on me marrying Thórdís. Although she smiles when prompted, she looks at me like an angry cat. It makes my heart freeze."

"She respects her father and will abide by their contract."

"This contract will result in nothing but hostility. Thórdís's heart is too cold to melt, even by bearing children. I want to go to Norway and return when Katla is seventeen."

"To Norway! You'll accomplish nothing there."

"I'll become a court poet."

"I knew it was a bad idea to allow you to stay with my father in Saelingsdalur."

"Why don't you honour your father? He's the famous Einar the Bowltinkle, and he taught me the intricacies of poetic language. Once you were proud when my grandfather called me a gifted poet."

"We're proud of your ability to learn. But it appears he has taught you arrogance and irresponsibility. You are not to receive any privileges from us until you apologise to Halldór and Oddlaug for your disrespectful behaviour."

Nidbjorg stood up briskly, not letting her considerable weight and backache bother her. "Go and fetch my horse and two companions, immediately. I'm going to Holl to assess matters."

"Mother, what do you hope to accomplish?"

"Angry men are incapable of resolving disputes." She stroked her frock and called to Jóhanna to bring her travelling mantle.

"I'll not change my mind, no matter what," Helgi said.

"Loyalty is a virtue."

"But my dear mother. It is raining outside."

"It rains heavier in your mother's heart."

7
Katla

How could Katla throw away the flowers Helgi gave her? Pitch gifts from her lover into the wind? If wilted flowers indicated wilted love, she needed to find a way to retain the flowers' vibrancy. What if she dried them? The day after Helgi's last visit, she spread old linen on the ground on the south side of the house and covered the cloth with yellow, pink and blue flowers. Later in the day, she spread another piece of linen over the flowers and secured it with rocks. In the evening, Katla was overjoyed to see the cloth was speckled with colours, and she hid it under her bed.

The next day it rained but she went up the hill to the elf rock anyway. When she reached the rock, she turned around to inspect the valley, as was her custom. A heavy-set woman was riding towards the farm, accompanied by two men. Katla's mother greeted her in a friendly manner and they went inside. Even though Katla was curious about the visitor, she did not want to be scolded by her father in front of the woman, so she stayed put.

The woman did not stay long and rode away in the pouring rain. Katla hurried down the hill and walked through the cowshed attached to the house, intending to sneak straight into the sleeping quarters. But when she approached the entrance to the living room she heard her parents talking. She lingered and eavesdropped.

"Our honour and prosperity are at stake," Halldór said. "I'll make sure no one reduces my assets."

Oddlaug said, "I regret Nidbjorg is upset about her son's impertinence. But Helgi did not misbehave in Katla's presence."

"What do you know about his conduct? You dawdle in the pantry while the braggart strokes Katla's hair as if she were his bitch. An honourable man will not pay a decent dowry for a tarnished girl."

"Then we won't allow him to visit her."

"How does he dare to argue with me? With me!"

"Nidbjorg agreed her son was disrespectful," Oddlaug said.

"Helgi is cunning. I'll send Katla up north where no one can approach her."

"Where to?"

"To Eyjafjordur – to relatives."

"We don't know how proper they are," Oddlaug said.

"Relatives protect their kin."

"It's better to send them to Garpur and Gróa at Saudafell in Dalir."

"Garpur? – Possibly."

"They're childless, diligent and respected. Garpur will uphold your wishes regarding Katla."

To avoid being seen, Katla turned around, walked back through the cowshed, around the house to the front door, into the sleeping quarters, picked up her coloured cloth, climbed the hill again to the elf rock, and said to Vonadís, "My father is evil. I'll never be able to see Helgi."

A plover sat on the next rock, stared at Katla and sang with a beautiful voice. Katla heard, "You'll meet again. Be patient."

Vonadís was right. Katla's heart filled with joy for an instant, but her mood changed when Thórdís called for her.

Katla wrapped the coloured linen around her head to shield her hair and to absorb Helgi's love. She removed the linen before going inside, and laughed when she noticed the colourful spots on her frock. How spectacular! She could wear the frock every day and imagine Helgi embracing her with flowers.

Katla walked into the room, holding her head high.

Thórdís sat by her parents, engraving her horn. She sneered when Katla walked by. "How shabby you look. Are the rags supposed to appeal to Helgi?"

Oddlaug said, "It's unkind to ridicule your sister."

Halldór spat into the fire before turning his gaze to Katla. "The imbecile has poisoned your mind. We're giving you a chance to come to your senses. You'll be staying with prudent people on another farm."

"Are they more prudent than the people here at Holl?"

Katla said.

With frosty eyes her father said, "What audacity! Pack your clothes. We'll travel as soon as the weather clears."

Two days later, when the rain had abated but the sky was still covered with clouds, Katla said a reluctant farewell to her mother, mounted her horse and rode from Holl with her father and six men. Thórdís stood outside smiling and holding her horn in the air. Was it a sign of victory?

Halldór did not address his daughter until they reached the North River, when he said, "Go in peace and make your parents proud." He turned around and rode off with four men.

Dark grey clouds covered the sky, and a gust of wind blew her hood off her head.

Under different circumstances Katla would have welcomed travelling this far from home. She would have been delighted by the colourful landscape, been curious about who lived on each farm, learned the name of each river and mountain and admired the moss-covered lava. But each moment brought her farther from Helgi. She lowered her chin, grasped her hood with one hand and held it close to her face.

The rain kept pounding on her as they rode up the rocky path through Bjarnardalur. Katla's hood filled with wind. She could only glimpse her horse's drenched red mane. Although her clothes were soaked through, she tried to stay warm by reciting Helgi's love poems in her mind.

By Thórolfsstadir she started sneezing. Her nose was stuffed and she strained to breathe. The road turned to mud and the horses slid in it. The rain did not let up until they arrived at Saudafell after dinner time.

Garpur welcomed them. He was a strongly built man about her father's age, but bald – and he flashed a warm smile. The farmhands helped Katla's companions while Garpur lifted her off her horse and walked with her to the farmhouse.

Once inside, Garpur put Katla down on a bed. Gróa met them by the door and said, "Let's go straight to the bath house. It's hot there." Her face was freckled and her eyes small and light brown. She took Katla's hand and led her through the narrow corridor. A lock of Gróa's bright red and voluminous hair kept tickling Katla's face as they walked. The bath house was roomier than the one at Holl. In the corner, a fire burned, and steam escaped from the bathtub. "You're in terrible shape," Gróa said. "Go to the fire immediately."

Katla sneezed constantly and could barely utter a word.

At first Katla thought Gróa was temperamental, judging by her quick movements and her authoritarian way with the maids. But her hands were gentle as she squeezed the water from Katla's hair and wrapped it in linen. A maid brought a delicious fish soup that warmed her through to the bones.

While Katla sat in the hot tub, Gróa said, "If you enjoy hearing stories, I shall tell you how we managed to buy Saudafell."

With a hoarse voice, Katla said, "I relish stories."

"Garpur was brought up in Saudafell. When his father joined the Vikings he sold Saudafell without knowing the buyer Thorbjorn was a double-dealer who had been ousted from all four corners of Iceland for evil deeds. Rannveig, his wife, was a tyrant, who provoked her husband to do wicked things like letting the sheep roam on Kvennabrekka, the farm next door, without getting permission from the widow who lived there with her lazy son Refur. People thought Refur was ignorant, but to their surprise he manned up and killed Thorbjorn for letting his sheep graze on Kvennabrekka's land. Refur then sailed abroad and became known as an expert trickster, called Refur the Sly. Rannveig, the dim-witted widow, could not stay at Saudafell any longer and sold the farm to Garpur."

"What became of Refur's mother?"

"Thórgerdur still lives next door at Kvennabrekka and is our friend."

Katla laughed until she had another coughing fit.

"How delightful it is to hear your cheerful laughter and watch those dimples deepen," Gróa said. "How can anyone resist returning your smile?"

Katla blew her nose. She felt better. Why not take advantage of her stay at Saudafell and enjoy it?

Nothing would prevent her from becoming as valued and as resolute as her sister.

8
Helgi

Helgi felt lost after Katla was gone from Holl and he wanted to flee. His parents' pride in him had vanished and they looked gloomy. He took to riding down to the Thverá river in the morning, staying there for the day, and watching the salmon struggle to swim upstream. He shared the salmon's strife. Life was like a strong current surging at him, but the salmon were more successful than he was in reaching their goal, their destination.

He tied a rope to a big rock, tied the other end of the rope to his spear, and practised throwing the spear at the salmon. He aimed at a resting fish and threw the sharp spear as fast as he could. The salmon escaped most of the time, but eventually he managed to kill a couple by first holding the shaft steadily in position, and focusing on the spear's point and the salmon's midsection. If he could learn to be as agile as the salmon and avoid the traps set for him, he would accomplish his goals.

One evening his mother said, "You can save your father's honour by becoming engaged to Thórdís. Do it. The sooner, the better."

"If fulfilling other men's wishes is all there is to life, I might as well be dead," Helgi said, and rushed outside.

On a cloudy day, Thórdur came to the iron forge where Helgi was sharpening his spear points and said, "Your idleness is making you miserable. It's time for you to join us in making hay."

"The workmen take care of haymaking. I'll catch salmon."

"We have enough salmon until next spring."

Helgi forced a smile. "I wish you and my mother would forget me, enjoy life and laugh once in a while."

"It's no laughing matter when friends and family ridicule our only son."

"I'm going to visit Hermundur at Gilsbakki."

Thórdur cheered up. "Maybe he can bring you to your senses."

"I should not be scorned for choosing the woman I want to marry."

"Hermundur is betrothed to the woman his parents chose."

"Ambition matters most to him."

"He's sensible. He and you could run Borgarfjordur in due time," Thórdur said. "Hermundur can run things alone, I have no interest in power struggles."

Helgi rushed outside, caught Sleipnir, saddled him, mounted him, and let the horse gallop down the hill. Sleipnir crossed the rivers with ease and still had plenty of energy to trot at a rapid pace up the hill below Hnausar. Sleipnir passed Sidufjall mountain with his head raised and his mane floating in the air, as if he knew his master was in a hurry.

On the way they passed Hvammur, the farm he would receive as part of Thórdís's dowry if they got married. Even though the farm was prosperous, he did not intend to live there with Thórdís.

They turned at the fork in the road which led to Gilsbakki. The farmhouse and outhouses sprawled across the hillside like an estate Helgi had seen in Saxony. Two men came riding towards them. Illugi the Black of Gilsbakki was a rich chief who permitted only his friends to enter his land. The men recognised Helgi and led him to Hermundur, who was working on constructing a longhouse. Hermundur was carrying an enormous rock, and he placed it on the wall as if it were a piece of dried manure. He was tall and muscular like his brother Gunnlaugur, but calmer and more handsome.

Hermundur slapped Helgi on the shoulder and said, "Why the sour face?"

Helgi briefed him on his struggle with Halldór. "Our fathers insist on tying me to Thórdís, but I love her sister. What shall I do?"

Hermundur burst out in a laugh. "Am I supposed to feel

sorry for you for the gift of a beautiful woman and a profitable farm? What have you accomplished to deserve this honour, aside from entertaining people?"

Helgi felt ashamed for expecting Hermundur to commiserate with him. He blushed. "The marriage will be unhappy."

"What nonsense is this – coming from you, who flirts with all the young women in the district? You, who have declared that the keys to happiness are not tied to one woman's belt?"

"Everything has changed since I met Katla."

"Nothing has changed." Hermundur gave Helgi a determined look. "One woman, superior to others, possesses the keys to power. She is rare – and the one you should snare." He smiled mischievously. "Some young women offer affectionate embraces – ones you enjoy for the moment and then forget. Katla would never be any man's mistress."

Hermundur continued to stack rocks while Helgi described to him Katla's many assets and his hope to seek fame and fortune in Norway.

"If you want me to listen to your wails you must earn my ear. Idleness breeds cowardice."

Helgi worked alongside Hermundur for the rest of the day, and they made huge progress. The conversation was minimal.

After supper they fenced. Hermundur was sharper and won this time around.

Afterwards Hermundur said, "Peace between your fathers is more precious than fame. You will gain a fortune by marrying Thórdís, and you will gain freedom. If you cannot find peace within the marriage, you can divorce her."

"Really? Then I could marry Katla."

"If she'll wait. But I suspect you'll be satisfied with Thórdís. Katla will be married off quickly."

"Unthinkable," Helgi called out.

"I thought you were a brave lad. How could you let a young girl unsettle you like this? Lovesickness is poison."

"I thought you were my friend."

"Only a good friend is as frank as I am."

On his way home Helgi thought of his grandfather, who was his only ally. Einar Bowltinkle was one of Iceland's most venerated living heroes. If his grandfather talked to Halldór on his behalf, how could Halldór refuse Helgi Katla's hand? Unfortunately, his grandfather lived far away.

The next day Helgi informed his parents he was going up north to Saelingsdalur to visit his grandfather.

Thórdur said, "I hope he'll bring you to your senses."

"I doubt it," Nidbjorg said. "While my father was in Norway, he expected my mother to manage the farm and feed his children."

"Experienced men know a marriage based on lust is ill advised," Thórdur said. "Why don't you ride with me to Althing? It's the most crucial gathering since the settlement of Iceland. Perhaps Einar will be there."

"Grandfather is too old and has no interest in current disputes," Helgi said.

For the first time in his life, Helgi felt lonely and misunderstood. He could not imagine living without Katla's laugh, her beauty, her curiosity, her warmth. How could he disappoint her? He had to visit her at Saudafell.

9
Katla

Garpur and Gróa offered room and board for payment in the guest lodge at Saudafell. In the evening Garpur and guests told tales of brave soldiers and high-spirited knights. Katla was allowed to sit in the corner and listen.

One night, Garpur asked Katla if she would sing for the guests. While she sang, one young man gazed at her with passionate eyes. It made her uncomfortable. After she was done, he said, "I've never seen such a beautiful girl – and with such a voice. Are you betrothed?"

Garpur jumped in and said, "Halldór at Holl, one of the most powerful men in Borgarfjordur, is her father. She's engaged to a noble man, and no one is allowed to approach her."

After the incident, she sang only for respected married men in Garpur and Gróa's presence.

Katla wondered when Helgi would visit her. If he loved her as deeply as he claimed, he would not let any man or storm prevent him from seeing her. Maybe he would abduct her, as the knights did in the Southern tales.

To visit Katla, Helgi would either travel through the valley from Borgarfjordur or sail into Hvalfjordur. In either case, he would arrive late at night. When weather permitted, she climbed up the shrub covered Saudafell mountain, high enough to see riders travelling on the Middalur valley road. Rivers and creeks curved through the valley and lowlands, then combined in Hvammsfjordur bay. One day Helgi and she would unite like the rivers did.

Midsummer, groups of horsemen rode from the north to the south, heading to Althing, where heathen and Christian chieftains and their devotees would choose whether Christianity should become the national religion. At Saudafell, daily life calmed down and few travellers passed by.

Finally, late in the evening of a cloudless day, a lone rider darted down the valley on a horse resembling Sleipnir. When he approached Saudafell he slowed down. It had to be Helgi. She ran down the hill, slipping twice on the way.

They met in the front yard. His eyes looked moist when he said, "My dear Katla, you're even more beautiful than before."

Katla wanted to lock her arms around Helgi's neck, even though he stank a little. She resisted her impulse when Gróa approached. Katla introduced Helgi to Gróa.

Helgi said to Gróa, "Your hair is magnificent. It reminds me of autumn colours and Irish women."

"It's not surprising since my grandmother was an Irish slave girl." Her laugh was warm. "Unfortunately, I cannot invite you inside. We promised Halldór the headstrong to keep you two apart."

Katla pulled Gróa by the arm. "My dear Gróa, please let us chat for a short while right here? He won't touch me."

"Oh, just for a moment, even though Garpur will scold me for it." Gróa shrugged her shoulders.

Katla said, "My dear Helgi, why do you look so upset?"

"I have terrible news."

"Have our fathers not changed their minds?" Katla's heart filled with despair.

"My father accuses me of betrayal when I insist I will marry only you," Helgi said.

"It's Thórdís's fault."

"After my mother visited Holl, she declared Thórdís was the best catch in Borgarfjordur."

"I'm sure Finnbjorg gave your mother a potion to make her adore Thórdís."

"Even my best friend Hermundur makes fun of me and calls me a lovesick idiot."

"What shall we do?"

"We cannot give in or lose heart. Promise me you'll never lose hope and keep smiling."

"I promise you with all my heart."

"My beloved Katla, don't worry. I'll solve this problem." He looked proud. "I'm on my way to see my grandfather. He understands me and he could persuade our stubborn fathers to allow us to marry."

"Who is he?" said Gróa.

"Einar the Bowltinkle Helgason."

"In the Saelingsdalur valley?" Gróa looked pensive. "Are you sure he's not on his way to Althing like all our leaders?"

"He is sixty and reluctant to travel far."

Gróa was friendlier towards Helgi after hearing who his grandfather was. She allowed them to speak alone for a moment.

Helgi looked deep into Katla's eyes. "I promise not to give up before we're engaged."

Katla smiled and she felt the blood rush to her cheeks. "Helgi, you are my hero, my poet and the only one I shall love forever."

"In the end we'll prevail," Helgi said.

"Einar is a poet and he'll understand how exceptional our love is," Katla said.

"If he disagrees, I'll be forced to honour my father's wishes or leave the country penniless."

Gróa came closer and said, "Helgi, you must leave right now. You'll never resolve your plight in our front yard. Why don't you stay at Kvennabrekka overnight?"

"I shall."

Katla said, "I'll never lose hope."

"I'm Einar's favourite grandson and I trust he'll sway our fathers' will."

When he rode off Gróa said, "The boy is short-sighted."

"He's a poet."

"It's foolish to admire poets for glorifying powerful men and seducing young women with fancy words. You're an exquisite young woman. I encourage you to think about your priorities."

"My happiness depends on being with Helgi."

"Not if you decide it doesn't," Gróa said, and kissed her on the cheek.

"I'll never change my mind," Katla said, and smiled.

10
Helgi

Thórgerdur, the famous mother of Refur the Sly, met Helgi in the yard when he rode up to Kvennabrekka. After learning who he was, she slapped her thigh, stroked his cheek and said, "Einar's grandson. Of course you can stay in my humble house." She took his hand and led him into the farmhouse.

After dinner, Helgi told her stories from the cloister in Saxony. She was thrilled to meet "such an educated and handsome young man", dried all his clothes, and ordered a farmhand to feed Helgi's horse. She refused payment and said storytellers seldom visited and no one dared to recite the Voluspá prophecies, afraid to offend the new God.

Early the next morning Helgi mounted Sleipnir and rode up Middalur valley to Hvammsfjordur. The trail by the seashore was smooth, and a heavy mist hung over the sea and shore. He stopped at a creek between Hjardarholt and the bay to let Sleipnir drink and rest. There he eyed an elderly man who was struggling to drag his boat onto the beach. Helgi walked to him. The old man had a gaunt face, thin white hair, and wore a grey cloak, tied around the waist with a worn rope. Helgi grabbed the boat's gunwale, and they dragged it onto the beach, while a few haddock wriggled on the bottom of the boat. One fish jumped out and both men laughed.

"This one is as lively as you are, young lad," the old man said, and examined Helgi's face and clothes. "You don't work with your hands, I see. What do you do then?"

"My name is Helgi and I'm a poet and an athlete."

The old man smirked and said, "My name is Narfi, and I'm a fisherman and a small-time farmer."

"Then you won't starve."

Narfi grabbed a haddock, chopped its head off, and said, "Last year I listened to two rich farmers argue at the top of their lungs about Christianity. What they said sounded comical, but I could not grasp what all the fuss was about. If you know anything

45

about Christ, I'd enjoy hearing a tale or two while I gut a fish or two."

"I heard this story in Saxony," Helgi said.

"In Saxony. What did you do there?"

"It's south of Denmark. I learned Latin there and some stories about Jesus Christ."

The old man passed a fish to Helgi and said, "They say a child who has not ventured far from home is a stupid child, but I've stuck to this region all my life and I've not missed a thing."

Helgi could not waste the day in useless chatter. "This story comes from the Bible of Christian men. — One day Jesus walked to a lake called Galilee. It's down south where it's hot outside and men have dark skin." Helgi took a bite from the fish and chewed. "There, by the shore, Jesus noticed two brothers, Andrew and Simon, who were fishermen. As the brothers were casting nets into the water, Jesus asked them to follow him and said, 'I will show you how to catch men.'"

"Catch men?" The old man wiped his face with the bottom of his cloak and said, "Should they catch men in their nets?"

"Jesus meant to gather men, not catch them."

"I get it. They who gather up men are catching them in their net." Narfi giggled. "Jesus went on to gather twelve men who followed him and became his apostles or messengers."

"Ha ha. Just like the fancy chiefs who get together to make up new rules they expect us to follow. Next thing you know, you can't ride your horse in your own pasture."

Helgi smiled. "Thank you for the fish. You're a wise man."

"I've never met a man whose words were so wise I would abandon all my belongings to serve him. — But where are you headed?"

"To visit Einar the Bowltinkle. He's my grandfather."

A cloud came over Narfi's face. "I heard Einar is lost."

"Lost?"

"A fisherman said Einar went out rowing before the last storm hit and has not been seen in three days."

Helgi was shaken by this news. He stood up and mounted Sleipnir. On his way to Saelingsdalur he wondered if he was like

Jesus, needing to gather supporters, but unlike Jesus he was not offering salvation.

He rode along the river Saelingsdalsá until he arrived at the sprawling farm, Laugar. His uncle Ósvífur, Einar's brother, lived there with his family. Ósvífur had many children. The second youngest, Vandrádur, met him in the yard. He was muscular, but aloof.

"My father and brothers all went to Althing," he said, as if he resented their absence.

"Where is my grandfather Einar?"

"The Bowltinkle is going crazy. He insisted on rowing alone when he knew a storm was approaching. He must have run his boat onto a rock, capsized it or something." Vandrádur spat on the ground as if he did not care whether his uncle was dead or alive.

Blood rushed to Helgi's cheeks. "Has anyone looked for him?"

"Who wants to go out in a storm? Look how foggy it is now."

"Where can I get a boat?"

"It's too late today." Vandrádur turned around and walked away.

Helgi mounted Sleipnir again and rode further down the valley to Einar's farm. He tied Sleipnir by a creek and walked into his grandfather's modest cabin where Einar's maid was lighting a fire in the stove. He came closer and said, "Good day, Kolfinna. Are you expecting Einar?"

She looked at him with mournful black eyes. "Greetings, Helgi. I was hoping you would come to look for Einar. I have lost faith in Ósvífur's sons. They look brawny, but they lack bravery. I trust you have inherited your grandfather's courage." She walked out with stooped shoulders.

Einar's ornate sword, a gift from Earl Hakon, hung above his bed. Helgi lifted it from the wall and said, "Show me where your owner is." He raised the sword and began reciting the famous poem Vellekla his grandfather had composed about Earl Hakon: "Hark all high-minded…"

"I hear well and people call me high-minded," said a female standing in the doorway.

He recognised Gudrun, the daughter of Ósvífur, and walked towards her. "You are indeed high-minded, my lovely cousin."

"And you swing the sword as nimbly as a knight."

They laughed and he returned his grandfather's sword to the wall.

Gudrun and Helgi were the same age. As all Icelanders knew, she was twice married, once divorced, now a widow, and recently engaged to the heroic Kjartan Olafsson, who was in Norway. She was beautiful indeed, with big blue eyes, thick flowing hair and a quick wit, but she looked sad. "I'm delighted you came, as few quick-witted men visit us," she said.

"Most have gone to Althing."

"What brings you here?"

"I wanted to get advice from my grandfather, but he has gone."

"In my father's absence, no one is willing to look for Uncle Einar. I'm left here with a handful of cowards."

"I'm willing to go, but I need a boat and a rower to assist me."

"You shall have a boat and two rowers."

"Will your brother Vandrádur agree?"

Gudrun blushed and her eyes flashed as she said, "Follow me to Laugar," and hurried outside.

She mounted her horse and they rode to Laugar. There she asked her escort to find Vandrádur and summon him to the living room without delay. With an erect spine and brisk steps she strode into the farm. Helgi followed her and they sat down on a long bench next to the seat of honour.

Vandrádur appeared and said, annoyed, "Sister, what do you want?"

"If our father had disappeared, what would you do?"

"Look for him, of course."

"Would you look for him if he disappeared during a storm."

Vandrádur shrugged his shoulders. "Of course."

"If our father were here, he would have demanded his

brother be sought."

"So?"

"Then you shall loan Helgi a boat and two rowers without delay." She stood up, marched by her brother without looking at him, and left.

When she was gone Vandrádur laughed sarcastically and muttered, "Women! They know nothing about going to sea." He walked towards the door.

"Thank you anyway for the favour," Helgi said. Later, when Helgi told Kolfinna he was setting out to sea the next morning, she kissed him on the cheek and brought him sausage and milk to eat. He slept well in his grandfather's bed that night.

The sea was calm and light clouds floated in the blue sky as Helgi and two oarsmen rode south to Asgardssund at Hvammsfjordur where Ósvífur kept his boats. They pushed the most solid boat to the water, climbed in, and the two men rowed out into the fjord towards Flatey island, staying clear of visible reefs. Einar was last seen by the Svefneyjar islands.

At the north end of a cluster of small islands, they spotted what looked like the keel of Einar's boat. Near it they found the brass bowls Einar took with him wherever he went because he felt they brought him good fortune.

Helgi was grief-stricken and close to tears when he carried the bowls into the boat.

On their return, the younger oarsman asked, "What was special about these bowls?"

Helgi said, "Einar was once the court poet of Hakon, Earl of Lade in Norway. The earl used balance scales when he needed to make decisions. The scales contained two bowls and two weights, one made of gold, the other one of silver. After he put the weights into the bowls, he asked the bowls if they agreed with his intention. If the weights made the bowl chime, the earl assumed the powers of nature agreed with him. When my grandfather was going to leave Hakon's court, the earl objected, and he asked the bowls if Einar should stay with the earl. The weights swirled around in the bowl, making it vibrate and tinkle.

Due to the bowl's emphatic response, Einar remained with the earl and was called Einar the Bowltinkle.

"But what happened to the weights?"

"I gather they sank to the bottom of the sea," Helgi whispered.

They returned to Laugar after sunset, and Kolfinna met Helgi at his grandfather's farmhouse. She looked as if she knew Einar had drowned. She stroked the brass bowls and said, "Einar was a kind and modest man."

That night Helgi dreamed about his grandfather walking on water.

Helgi went to Laugar the next morning. Vandrádur was nowhere in sight but Gudrun and Helgi walked up the hill and discussed his grandfather and his rise to fame in Norway. They stopped by a rounded pool built with rock walls where spring water, both hot and cold, combined to make an ideal bath. The view was spectacular. Gudrun removed her outer garments and stepped into the pool in her underclothes. Helgi followed her lead. The warm water soothed his sore muscles and aching heart.

Gudrun said, with a glint in her eye, "Einar said you were as nimble a poet as he was."

"He did?" Tears flooded Helgi's eyes. "How happy it makes me. I want nothing more than to follow in his footsteps."

"But don't be tempted to go to Norway before we have adopted Christianity. King Olafur abhors heathen men and he thinks most Icelanders are heathen." She stroked the water with her fingers. "You said you wanted to ask Einar for advice. Does it concern the matter of your marriage?"

"Have people in Dalir heard of my problems?"

"Vagabonds travel widely. Your crimes of passion are even greater fodder for gossip than mine." She giggled. "I should thank you because I get a break."

"Thórkatla Halldórsdóttir is life to me: my ray of sunshine; the brightest star in the sky; the reason my heart beats. She is a vision to behold, but Halldór has promised her to someone else."

The smile disappeared from Gudrun's lips. "Beauty limits

our choices. Fathers cherish us as they do their gold, and by marrying us to wealthy men they expect to increase their own power." She tilted her head and said, blushing, "But now my fortune is about to change because I shall marry Kjartan, whom I will love until I die."

"As I will love Katla to the end of my life, and I suspect she'll love me the same."

"Two things I know," Gudrun said. "As painful as it is to carry on in a loveless marriage, it's better than to deceive your father. You'll be cut off. Think about the consequences before you act."

Helgi stayed in Einar's cabin for a few days, hoping to be inspired by his grandfather's surroundings, but he was still in a state of despair.

On his return home, Helgi stopped at Saudafell. How could he ride by without seeing Katla?

Gróa stood outside the farmhouse talking to a muscular, bald man. Helgi dismounted and walked to the couple, holding Sleipnir's reins. Gróa introduced Helgi to Garpur.

"Helgi himself, famous for lovesickness and stubbornness!" Garpur said, and laughed.

"Is it an illness to love one woman above others?" Helgi said. "Were you at Althing?"

Garpur frowned. "I was."

"What news do you have?" asked Helgi.

"Heathen men were short changed. We trusted Thórdur, the chief of Ljósvetningar, to protect our rights to Heathen beliefs. But at the last minute he betrayed us and yielded to pressure from the King of Norway and Christian Icelanders."

"Do all Icelanders have to become Christian then?" Helgi said.

Gróa said, "Oh, it'll be impossible to force it upon the men who prize their independence."

"I expect my father and Halldór will continue to put their faith in the Nordic gods, even if they have to hide it," Helgi said. He did not care whether Icelanders were Christian, heathen or without beliefs, but he suspected this turn of events had angered his father and Halldór.

"Did you meet your grandfather?" Gróa said.

Helgi told them of his grandfather's boat wreck.

"He was a true hero," Garpur said.

"May I see Katla and tell her myself of this disaster?"

Gróa looked at her husband and said, "He's safe. I'll get her." She rushed inside.

Garpur said, half smiling, "I cannot invite you inside without disobeying Halldór's orders. But you are welcome to sit here in the yard for a moment."

Soon, Katla came running out of the farm to Helgi. How beautiful she was, with her bouncing hair and pink cheeks. She flashed a wide smile and the bottom of the dimple disappeared into her cheek.

When they were seated on a rock, she said, "Tell me, what did Einar say? Is he going to persuade our fathers?"

A lump formed in Helgi's throat, and he whispered, "I'm sorry, Katla. I have bad news." As he told her of his disheartening trip, her joyful smile faded. Could he do nothing but disappoint her? He longed to draw her into his arms to console her, but he resisted the temptation.

Katla said, with quivering lips, "Dearest Helgi, you lost your beloved grandfather. What heartbreak."

"He taught me poetry." Helgi scratched his beard. "I feel defeated. As if I've lost my troops and the war."

Katla straightened her back, raised her chin and said with determination, "We must carry on. If you want to marry me you have to ask for my hand, as our traditions dictate."

He admired her tenacity. "You're right. I shall not be defeated due to lack of courage."

She smiled. "Now go home and beg your father to ask for my hand instead of my sister's."

"My father is unyielding, and your father's mind is as inflexible as his sword. It does not help our cause that Thórdís is heathen like Halldór, and you're Christian."

"My love for you will always surpass my belief in God,

Christ and Freyja."

Garpur called, "Your time is up."

"I promise to ask for your hand," Helgi said, and stood up.

"You're strong and steadfast," she said, and smiled. "How can anyone deny you anything?"

But when he mounted Sleipnir he wondered if he could ever be resolute enough to measure up to Katla's expectations.

~~~

The rain poured on Helgi all the way to Borgarfjordur. Einar's brass bowls, which were tied to his saddle, tinkled now and then as if to soothe his troubled mind.

When he passed Holl he reflected on the delightful moments he had shared with Katla. How full of hope she was. Now he had caused her to suffer and robbed her of her dream.

Helgi could barely breathe, and coughed as if his despair was strangling him. Sleipnir must have sensed the urgency to deliver his owner home, as he hastened his pace and galloped home.

When Helgi dismounted in front of Hofdi, he stumbled and fell. His father met him at the door and helped him into the sleeping quarters where he undressed and climbed into bed. His mother sat by him and pressed a cold cloth to his burning forehead.

After Helgi told her of her father's death, Nidbjorg said, "I'm glad you searched for your grandfather, and you found the bowls."

"The bowls are yours, my beloved mother. You did not inherit anything else from your father."

She looked sad. "Instead of returning to Iceland to take care of his family, my father remained with the earl. I hated the earl when I was a little girl."

"You must be proud of his poem Vellekla." Helgi said.

"Vellekla made him famous, but did not benefit us. The earl repaid him with a fancy shield decorated with gemstones. Father could have sold the shield but gave it to Egill Skallagrímsson. Instead of thanking him, Egill announced he was going to kill him for the gift. What an ungrateful bastard Egill was. On top of the insult, he threw the shield into a pot full of acid. Of course, he removed the twelve gold coins and the jewels first. Mother could have used the money for our sustenance."

"Grandfather was farsighted. He maintained his friendship with Egill," Helgi said.

"To keep peace, he often sacrificed." She kissed Helgi on the forehead. "Well, we can console ourselves with these bowls. They were considered supernatural. Maybe we can ask them for advice like Earl Hakon used to."

"But we need the weights. And they're at the bottom of the sea."

"The bowls contain wisdom. The earl's weights were made of gold and silver, but some men used different weights without diminishing the bowls' power. I shall find other weights so we can consult the bowls."

~~~

Helgi stayed in bed most of the autumn, either soaked with sweat or shivering from cold. His grandfather Einar often appeared in his dreams. In one dream, his grandfather sat by Earl Hakon, telling the earl and his courtiers a story about a young boy named Wildcat. When Einar was finished, the earl said, "The best poets possess the skill to entertain with captivating stories." In another dream his grandfather told Helgi, "Insight, skill and tenacity mould a poet."

If his grandfather was prodding him to keep going, Helgi should heed his words. He began rehearsing the metaphors found in the dictates of skaldic poetry and attempted to compose a court poem.

On a dark morning before Christmas, Helgi woke up early and breathed easier than he had done for weeks. He bathed, dressed in a clean cloak and walked into the sitting room, where his parents and the farm workers were gathered after the evening meal.

Nidbjorg looked up from her sewing and said, "I'm pleased

to see my son healthy again."

"My dear mother, I regret having caused you misery. I would like to bring joy to you and others by telling stories and reciting poems."

Nidbjorg slapped her ample thigh, producing a loud clapping sound. "And we shall listen with glee." She laughed with her infectious laugh. Her shoulders shook like they used to before Helgi's feud with Halldór at Holl.

Helgi stepped up on a bench and told the story of a boy called Wildcat, a hardy boy who was left to die, but a poor peasant picked the boy up and brought him home to the peasant's caring wife. "The boy was strong and massive like a bear." Helgi kept the suspense going so no one could guess who Wildcat's parents were until the end. The audience gazed at him in awe until the story ended. Then they laughed and argued about whether the parents should be allowed to claim the boy after the good woman raised him, and so forth.

Helgi felt like a new man. Instead of being treated as the worthless son, he was popular and encouraged to tell new stories. He made up stories where the women were as noteworthy as the men, which caused a heated discussion afterwards. Often the household members wanted to hear the same story over and over.

He never mentioned Katla or Thórdís to his parents – or to anyone – to discourage gossip about his womanising.

Guests came and went and listened to his stories with enthusiasm. Later, Helgi learned men had spread the word, calling Helgi a skilled poet fit for kings and earls.

It was time he made plans to become a court poet. First, he had to make sure Katla was not promised to another man.

11
Katla

Since the day Helgi told her of his grandfather's death and of his intent to ask for her hand, Katla made the best of her stay at Saudafell, confident that Helgi would arrive soon bearing good news.

On clear days she climbed up the hill above the farm to be on the lookout for Helgi. On the way she noticed enchanting flowers strewn about the hill. She picked a bunch and carried them downhill, where she sorted them by colour.

A few days later Gróa asked her, "What are you going to do with all these wilted flowers?"

"I'm going to learn to colour linen and wool with them."

"When I was a child in Ireland my mother coloured cloth. I don't remember much but I'll teach you."

"Will you! I'm thrilled. Maybe I can be useful in some other way than just singing."

"If you can colour and sew as well as you can sing, you'll be all set."

The rest of the summer and into autumn, Katla and Gróa picked dandelions, potentillas, bedstraw, marigolds, and whatever plants and shrubs they thought would produce colour. They removed the dirt and moss from the roots and dried the flowers and herbs inside. Katla boiled the plants and experimented with the length of time they sat in the pot until she obtained the colours she wanted. Then she soaked the fabric in the solution and rinsed it in cow urine to seal in the colour. She dropped some fresh flowers in the pot, others she boiled when they were dry. After numerous attempts with rare flowers, Katla obtained the bright yellow colour of the dandelion. Her next colour challenges were bright blue and bright red. In her mind she named the colours after someone's eyes. The chestnut she named Helgi's eyes; the stone grey became Father's eyes; the pale blue she named Thórdís's eyes, but after that colour became popular, she changed the name to Infant's eyes.

Garpur built a special loom for her. As it was big and heavy, Garpur put it in the corner of the guest quarters. At night Katla stood behind the loom under a window, weaving; she listened to the guests and peeked at them through her stretched yarn. As few noble women wove, the guests ignored her.

Gróa made a point of asking the guests for news from Borgarfjordur, as she knew Katla was curious to hear about Helgi. One night a farmer from Hamar in Thverárhlíd said Helgi was ill, not just from lovesickness – at which point most men laughed. But Helgi was suffering from a high fever and a cough and did not leave the house.

After hearing of Helgi's illness, Katla left the room, crawled into bed and cried. She envisioned Helgi's face, his flashing chestnut eyes and half-smiling lips. She quit crying and imagined kissing him on the lips to make him feel better. She recalled one of their conversations when he came to visit her at Holl.

Helgi had said, "All Gods and men have designated stars in the sky."

"Me too?"

"You have the brightest star in the heavens. I'll name her Katla Star."

"And I shall name the next brightest star Helgi Star."

"When we're together on a starlit night I'll show you the stars of Odin, Thór and Freyr."

"And Freyja."

Now Katla was sure the stars could help her to cure Helgi. The next night when the sky was starlit, Katla sneaked out into the moonlight with two sheepskins, laid one on the ground, lay down on top of it, and wrapped the other one around her.

She stared at the sky. Some of the stars appeared to move more than others. The stationary stars must be the ones watching out for her. She named the brightest ones Freyja, Jesus, Helgi and Katla. She asked Helgi Star to make him healthy. She asked Freyja Star to protect their love. The Jesus Star was also the star of peace. She prayed to it for fathers, mothers and all men to quit arguing. When the bright northern lights stretched in waves of green and purple from the sky to the ground, Katla knew the stars were discussing things in their own distinct language.

The snow covered fields and roofs in a matter of days. Even then, on starry nights, Katla lay outside and prayed to the stars. But after a few nights she began coughing. Her forehead and whole body felt like they were burning. She assumed she now had Helgi's sickness and he would therefore be recovering.

Gróa forbade her to lie outside, and she soon recovered. In her bed at night, Katla closed her eyes and visualised the sky. Sometimes she dreamed the stars transformed into flying elves who delivered her prayers to the northern lights. Then she woke up full of hope. During the day she sang quietly to remind the stars and Helgi to fulfil their obligations.

Few wayfarers or vagabonds stopped at Saudafell during the snowy winter and no news arrived from Borgarfjordur. Katla was eager to know if Helgi had recovered. One day a guest from Borgarfjordur stopped by, and said people in the valley were talking about how joyous the household at Hofdi in Thverárhlíd was, where Helgi the poet entertained people with absurd tales and fanciful arm gestures.

Katla was elated to hear this good news and she spread her joy by singing more sweetly than ever.

At Christmas time she stood at the loom weaving, and during the day she coloured yarn and cloth. Her woven fabric grew into piles. To use it she sewed frocks, pants and shirts for the household members. Katla clapped with delight when she watched the workers stroking their clothes and smiling with pleasure.

In late winter Gróa said, "If you continue colouring and weaving, you will become the most popular seamstress in the country."

"Can we sell the cloaks and the mantles?" Katla said.

"Why not?" Gróa said. She stacked Katla's finished garments in the corner of the guest quarters and a maid sold the clothes to guests. Katla got to keep half of the silver coins for her work. In the trunk she kept underneath her bed, she stored the most colourful fabric for future use.

She turned fifteen years old in early spring. Now she was the same age as Gudrun when her father Ósvífur gave her away for the first time. She told Gróa on her birthday, "The lambs, the flowers and I are born in spring," and she secured a flower in her hair. "In two years, I'll be married to Helgi."

"Your father is not known for changing his mind."

"Helgi is now a famous poet. He'll change my father's mind."

12
Helgi

When the road down Thverárhlíd had turned from ice to mud, Helgi asked to speak to his father in private, and they sat down in the living quarters.

"Dear father, don't you think my reputation has improved since last summer?"

"Perhaps."

"Has Halldór at Holl heard of my storytelling and poetic mastery?"

"Why does that matter?"

"Of course it matters whether he accepts me as his son-in-law."

"Have you changed your mind?"

"Not at all. I still want to marry Katla."

Thórdur looked at him with grieving eyes. "Haven't you come to your senses yet? You would be lucky if Halldór still agreed to you marrying Thórdís."

"My dearest father, why would you insist on me marrying a woman who is sly as a vixen?"

"Thórdís is the best catch in the district. — Your lust for Thórkatla Halldórsdóttir is nothing but impertinence."

Helgi jumped to his feet. "Lust! It's pure love. I love her and I'll be like a wingless falcon roaming around the highlands if I cannot marry Katla."

"Don't you realise how you're ridiculed for your defiance?"

"Katla and I have always behaved properly."

"Men report otherwise."

"I promise you I'll resolve my dispute with Halldór in a peaceful way. Please come with me to Holl. We'll approach Halldór together."

"I cannot support this impulsive madness."

"Then I'll go alone."

"And be ridiculed once more? It's insane."

"Am I insane for wanting to marry one woman, a particular

woman? And go to any length to secure her?"

"Without funds, you are," Thordur said, and walked out.

Helgi went to the bath house, groomed his hair and beard, and dressed in his most ornate cloak and mantle. His mother appeared with his grandfather's brass bowls and weights similar to those Earl Hakon gave Einar.

"Wait for a moment while I consult the bowls," Nidbjorg said.

He laughed. "My dear mother, I'm surprised to learn you're superstitious."

"I'm not, but I trust in the wisdom found in the bowls."

Helgi smiled as his mother asked the bowls if he should go to Holl and ask for Katla's hand. Helgi and Nidbjorg stared at the weights for a while, but they did not move.

"The bowls imply your trip to Holl will be unsuccessful, so you should stay at home."

Helgi patted his mother on her shoulder. "Your weights are different from the earl's."

"Bitter is the truth," Nidbjorg said, picking up the weights and returning them to the bowls again. Then she asked the bowls if Helgi should seek Thórdís's hand. The weights moved around and the bowls tinkled. "There, you see. The weights work."

"In spite of the tinkle, I will ask for Katla's hand." He kissed his mother on the cheek, mounted Sleipnir and rode down the trail.

When he arrived at Holl he greeted Dagur, the foreman on the farm, and asked to speak to Halldór. Dagur took him to the living quarters. There, Halldór sat in the seat of honour polishing his sword, paying no attention to Helgi. How was he supposed to start a conversation with a preoccupied chief? Helgi felt awkward.

"Good day, chief Halldór," Helgi said.

Halldór stroked his sword and said, "The day was fine until you arrived."

"Last time when I was here I spoke in haste. I should have been more respectful. I want to make it up to you."

"How do you propose to make up for your impertinence?"

Halldór said, and stared at him.

Halldór's bluntness took Helgi off guard, and he blurted out, "I'm going to compose a tribute to you. A poem."

"A tribute. What for?"

"Your reputation and your nobility."

"Why not for my tenacity?"

"Tenacity? — Why not?"

"It's futile to compose a poem about my reputation, nobility and tenacity. Important men know I don't change religions as I do my underpants, and I don't break agreements like a traitor. — On the other hand, no one knows what kind of a man you are. Men tell absurdities about you, standing on a bench, wriggling about, spewing worthless tales."

Helgi felt his blood rush to his cheeks but stayed calm. "I'm a poet. People are entertained by my poetry and stories."

"A thespian." Halldór must have smirked because his cheeks rose slightly. "When I was in Gardariki I saw a fool trotting around with a mule's head to entertain the Vikings. Brave men laughed at the fool and paid the idiot with copper coins. Tell me, do men throw coins at your feet in return for the laughter?"

"Of course not. — I'm the son of a noble landowner."

"A nobleman's traits seldom pass to their offspring." He examined the reflection of himself in the sword and grinned. "How do you intend to get rich and famous?"

"I intend to follow my grandfather Einar's example."

"I understand. Like Einar Helgason, you intend to glorify power-hungry foreign earls, neglect your home, and give your most valuable assets to unjust men."

"I don't intend to neglect my wife and my children."

"Who'll be the fortunate wife of this famous poet?"

Helgi wiped the sweat from his forehead. He was still standing because Halldór had not offered him a seat. He straightened his spine and said, "I cannot imagine living without your daughter Thórkatla and want to ask you for her hand."

Halldór sniggered. "What an idiot! You propose to make up a poem about my nobility and tenacity." He waved the sword he was polishing. "Go ahead. Compose your poem. You must add that I'm so tenacious you'll never – I say never – be betrothed to my Katla."

"Katla does not want anyone but me."

"I'll not donate my daughter to a shiftless man who betrays his father."

Helgi could not control his temper any longer and said, "If you oppose our union with cruelty and rage, we will suffer and so will you."

"Threats do not weaken my resolve." Halldór's nose turned red, and he raised his sword towards Helgi. "I shall crush your will if you don't heed my orders. You shall never see or touch Katla as long as I live. Get out of here!"

Helgi turned around and rushed outside, found Sleipnir, and mounted him. Thórdís was standing by the food shack. She waved to him in a friendly manner and smiled. He did not return the gesture.

"I'm going to kill Halldór, the stubborn fool," Helgi said to himself, and made Sleipnir gallop down the road.

The proposal had to wait, but he vowed never to let this unjust brute insult him again. In order to marry Katla, Helgi must become a hero.

13
Thórdís

While Thórdís watched Helgi's hasty departure from Holl, she debated what steps she should take to ensure her plans would take shape. She had eavesdropped on Halldór and Helgi's conversation with glee. Katla would never be given to Helgi. Nonetheless, she disliked the grim treatment her father had given Helgi. Her father's hostility could prevent him from keeping the agreement with Thórdur about her marriage to Helgi.

How could she persuade her father to honour the contract?

From the time Katla was born and began smiling and laughing without cause, she was the jewel in her mother's eye, but a thorn in Thórdís's heart. Although Thórdís resented her mother's aloofness towards her, she pretended it did not bother her, and set out to gain her father's favour. He alone ruled her destiny anyway. As time went by, she made a point of understanding his views on all matters. Whenever the opportunity arose, she complimented him. In turn, he praised her for her dignity, reserve, wisdom and knowledge. She only spoke to suit her needs and only did what served her goals.

Thórdís had schemed to have her little sister sent away to Saudafell where she could not interfere with Thórdís's plans. This so-called love between Katla and Helgi was merely impetuous lust bound to fade soon. Although Katla might suspect her of malice, she was not defeated yet, and she was still sure of her victory.

Finnbjorg was like a mother to her, and Thórdís trusted the old prophetess above all others. Together they could devise a way to direct Helgi's adoring gaze towards her. Without anyone hearing, the women discussed magic and love potions.

Thórdís collected the grasses and roots Finnbjorg needed and brought them to her in a large sack. The sorceress cut thick roots from the grasses, dried them and hid them for later use.

How could Thórdís entice Helgi to visit Holl before autumn? She should persuade her father to send an invitation to

Hofdi. But it presented a challenge as Halldór had forbidden the people at Holl to utter Helgi's name.

One rainy summer day Halldór came home tired and dirty, walked into the bath house and said, "Arngeir at Steinar is the most obnoxious man in the valley. My horses slid around in his muddy yard and I had to wade in the slime to his front door."

"What humiliation!" Thórdís said. "I'll fetch some refreshing ale." She hurried to the kitchen, picked up a horn of relaxing ale from Finnbjorg, returned to the bath house, handed her father the horn and said, "Dear father, sit in front of the fire and drink the ale while I remove your muddy boots and wash your feet."

He sat down and began drinking. She fetched linen and put warm water with herbs in a tub, ordered a maid to bring it to her father, told the maid to leave and removed her father's shoes. The stench filled her nostrils. She wanted to vomit, but how could she lose heart at such a fateful moment? She stood up, put the socks and the boots by the door, took a deep breath, knelt in front of her father again and placed his feet in the fragrant tub.

"Dear Thórdís, how good you are to me. — Your husband will be a lucky man."

"If Helgi only knew how tender and tolerant I am." Thórdís looked up at her father, smiling.

"Helgi! He's crazy and not deserving of you. I'll find you a better man."

"It seems like such an unnecessary hassle when Thórdur and you have already made a binding contract." She stroked her father's swollen legs. "I suspect Helgi is regretting his impulsive behaviour."

"Even if he has regrets, I don't want a deceitful son-in-law."

"Temporary defiance in a young man is not unusual, and should not upset us." She smiled. "Thórdur is an honourable and trusted friend. You two deserve your mutual dreams to come true. — Or am I wrong?"

"Our discord saddens me." Halldór sighed.

"You've often said intolerance prevents understanding."

Halldór stroked his beard as if to straighten it. "Thórdur is a true friend and a wise man."

"Father, the surest way to improve your and Thórdur's reputation is if I marry Helgi."

She dried her father's feet with care. If Thórdís was honest, which she was only to herself, the reason for her wanting to marry Helgi was simple. The farm Hvammur would be hers, and she intended to rule the farmland and the household by herself. If she were the eldest son, no one would be opposed to her running the farm. Why should she let the fact she was a woman keep her from reaching her goal? In reality, she was lucky. She did not have to raise a sword and behead men in order to get what she wanted.

She stood up and kissed her father on his hairy cheek. "Isn't it time we invited Thórdur and Helgi to make peace? Ask them to visit?"

"I don't want to entertain that bouncing buffoon in my house."

Thórdís smiled. "You are a distinguished chief and above letting an impetuous youth keep you from honouring your agreements. In any case, I'm going to follow your advice."

Halldór glanced at his daughter. "What advice?"

"It's pointless to lose heart over a done deed."

"True."

"Helgi is just impulsive, but not an idiot."

"Perhaps."

"If Helgi and I discuss matters in private, I'm confident we'll come to an equitable conclusion." Thórdís was aware of her father's greed and added, "I think it would be a mistake to allow this much wealth to escape our grip." She stroked her father's elbow. "Even though you and I reject the Christian faith, peace must reign in Borgarfjordur."

"True, my dear daughter."

"Thorgeir, the chief of Ljósvetningar, and King Ólafur Tryggvason are both dead and the future of Iceland is now determined by the remaining chiefs in the country, like you." Thórdís beamed.

Halldór returned to stroking his beard, deep in thought.

"Harmony and the independent spirit should reign in the country." He took a big gulp from the horn, smiled and stood up. "I shall invite Thórdur for a visit."

Halldór sent a messenger to Hofdi with an invitation to Thórdur to come with Helgi for a visit the next day.

Thórdís hurried to the kitchen to tell Finnbjorg the news.

The sorceress was stirring a steaming pot. She said, "The brew is ready."

The next day, Thórdís washed in the warm spring and rinsed her hair in a perfume from Finnbjorg. Then she walked into the kitchen and punctured her index finger with a needle until it bled, rubbed the blood inside the horn tucked in her belt, and murmured, "Carve runes in a horn, smear deceit with blood."

She held out the horn towards Finnbjorg, who spooned brew into it.

Thórdís turned the horn in three circles above the pot, then lifted it to the sky to honour the Nordic gods, before drinking the sweet brew. "Thank you, dear Finnbjorg, for improving the taste of the brew with honey."

Her lips formed a triumphant smile, but Finnbjorg stroked her forehead and sighed.

14
Helgi

Helgi could not shake off his anger toward Halldór for treating him like a belligerent child. Poor Katla. What was he to do? Unable to focus on projects at home, Helgi roamed on Sleipnir around Borgarfjordur, sometimes sitting by the ocean where the Hvítá river ran into the sea, watching the waves splash onto the shore and thinking about his predicament. He had been a fool to visit the cunning Halldór alone and unprepared. The humiliation Helgi experienced was insignificant compared to how disappointed Katla would be with her father's refusal.

Who in Iceland appreciated Helgi's poetry? Only Katla, who preferred romantic poems. The heathen gentry valued poems about their gods, heroes and battles. But Christianity was taking hold in Iceland. What should the subject matter of Helgi's poems be? Poems of strength and high morals still reigned, and Hávamál was the most popular such poem among Icelanders. Helgi had no desire to improve on that.

His recent poems glorified Katla's beauty: her glistening blond hair, her sky-blue eyes, and a mouth he longed to kiss night and day. If anyone heard these poems, he would be further fodder for ridicule.

Helgi sighed. A good poet seeking acclaim needed to go abroad and become a court poet. He should sail to Norway and earn enough money to buy a farm in Iceland for Katla and himself.

One day Helgi came upon a ship at the mouth of the Hvítá river. A watchman told him the ship would be sailing to Norway soon, and his friend, Gunnlaugur Serpent-Tongue, the son of Illugi the Black at Gilsbakki, owned half a share in the ship, a present from his father.

The next day Helgi rode to Gilsbakki and found Gunnlaugur by the food hut selecting provisions for his overseas trip.

Gunnlaugur hugged Helgi, gave him mead and said, "Come with me to Norway."

"My father will not support my trip to Norway now."

"What of it? Just bring your sword. I'll feed you. Earl Eirikur is a good man, unlike the tyrant Olafur Tryggvason. Eirikur appreciates skaldic poetry. Besides, our fencing skills are unparalleled. You and I are the best.

"I want nothing more than to sail with you, but my marriage matters must be resolved first," Helgi said.

"What nonsense," Gunnlaugur laughed. He was not handsome, but his confidence made him look formidable.

"Tell me, Gunnlaugur. How did you get the father of Helga the beautiful to agree to your betrothal despite your leaving Iceland?"

"Simple matter. My father talked to Helga's father and all agreed that if I returned within three years, the betrothal would take place. — Don't buckle under." He slapped Helgi's arm jokingly. "Obviously, you're not as brave as I am."

"But I'm better looking," Helgi said, and grabbed Gunnlaugur by his waist, as if he wanted to wrestle. "A hero doesn't abandon his beloved Helga for three years."

They wrestled, rolling around on the dusty and muddy ground, and stood up again dirty from head to toe. Men gathered around them and watched. Among them was Hermundur, Gunnlaugur's brother. In time, Gunnlaugur got the better of Helgi, tripped him and pinned him to the ground.

Gunnlaugur stood up and said, "You and I are sportsmen, witty and popular. Why let girls throw us off balance?"

Helgi jumped to his feet. "I should sail with you."

"A man without deeds of valour might as well be dead," Gunnlaugur said with a grin and looked at Hermundur. "Here, a man's greatest deed is building a longhouse bigger than his neighbour's."

Hermundur turned serious. "There are greater deeds to be done here – to nurture family and friends, keep peace and increase the prosperity of those who till the earth. To acclaim foreign kings and earls is neither heroic nor brave, but arrogant."

69

Gunnlaugur slapped Hermundur on the back. "No worthy woman wants a faint-hearted man. Beautiful women want heroes, virile and brave men who fight villains. Those men are only found in the court of kings, and they become rich and famous."

Hermundur laughed. "A man who fights for fame risks losing his head."

Helgi contemplated Gunnlaugur's offer on his way home to Hofdi. He longed to sail, to fence, to be in the king's court and to receive treasures as compensation for unforgettable skaldic poems. But could he survive in Norway without Katla? He had to, otherwise he would never be allowed to marry her.

When Helgi returned to Hofdi he found his father tying a bundle of hay to a horse. Helgi dismounted Sleipnir and helped his father tighten the knots.

"Why are you this dirty?" Thórdur said.

"I was wrestling with Gunnlaugur Illugason."

"Who won?"

"Gunnlaugur. He wins everything. He's sailing to Norway while Helga the beautiful waits for him for three years. He invited me to go with him."

"The boy is a daredevil. — If you're sailing to escape your responsibilities, the journey will be counterproductive."

Helgi was too exhausted to try to sway his father's opinion.

He finished securing the ropes to the horse in silence, mounted Sleipnir and rode to the farmhouse. A three-month-old colt was attacking other horses in the corral. With whip in hand, Helgi separated the colt from the other horses and tethered him, relieved to have an outlet for his frustration.

Helgi yelled into the colt's ear, "They shall see I don't fear anyone or anything and I shall tame you even if others think you can't be broken."

That evening, Helgi sat deep in thought in the living quarters, carving runes on a whalebone. Thórdur dashed in and said smiling, "Halldór at Holl has invited us over. We're leaving at noon tomorrow. Bathe and be neat." He turned around and left.

Why? The ogre could hardly have changed his mind.

Thórdur was cheerful on their way to Holl the next day, looking forward to seeing his close friend. Helgi did not want to change his father's mood by mentioning Katla.

Halldór was standing in the yard when they arrived. He ignored Helgi, reached his right hand toward Thórdur and said, "Welcome, my dear friend. I wish you had come earlier." He put his left hand on Thórdur's shoulder, turned him toward the horse barn where a mare stood with a newborn foal by her side, and said, "Isn't this foal splendid?"

Helgi was relieved that Halldór had ignored him. A cool breeze played on his face. He looked up the hill towards the elf rock as if he expected to see Katla come running towards him. He stroked Sleipnir's neck, trying to restrain his tears.

"Welcome, Helgi," a soft woman's voice said behind him. He turned around. There stood Thórdís. Her hair glistened in the sunshine, and the brightness of her visage made his eyes blink.

She smiled as if he were a dear friend. "The breeze is cool. Let's go inside. The freshly brewed ale awaits you."

Helgi glanced towards his father, who was in deep conversation with Halldór.

"They'll come inside soon," Thórdís said, and walked to the guest lodge.

He followed, not taking his eyes off her. When she walked, her straight hair floated in the breeze and her fragrance reminded him of seductive women from southern lands.

Three fires burned in the lodge's pits. They sat down by the innermost fire, close to a large tub of ale.

"I'm delighted to get to know you better," Thórdís said, and looked at him with sparkling light-blue eyes. They reminded him of the early morning sky.

Helgi said, "I regret having disappointed you. It was not due to your lack of beauty or substance."

"It fills me with joy to hear you still think of me with

affection."

"I hope to call you my sister-in-law before long."

The smile left Thórdís's lips. "I'm sad to say our fathers object to such an arrangement. — May I offer you some ale?"

"Why not?"

Thórdís removed the walrus tusk from her belt, poured ale into it with a ladle and handed the tusk to him.

The aroma from the ale tickled his nostrils. "A generous serving of ale."

"For a thirsty man."

"As I am." He took a big gulp of the sweet-tasting ale, swallowed it and said, "I thirst for Katla's laugh, her blue eyes and her skin as soft as down."

Thórdís smiled warmly. "I understand."

Helgi drank more and felt a warm wave wash over his body. "I cannot look up the hill here at Holl without remembering how Katla came running to greet me."

"She amused herself like a child at play."

Helgi examined the tusk. "Why am I going on like this? Am I not holding the drinking horn you carved with runes last summer?"

"How observant you are."

"Did you say this tusk was a gift?"

"The tusk was intended for you, and I want you to accept it as a gift to commemorate the first day you met Katla."

"You surprise me." He drank. "I'll be grateful to you forever for this gift, for your patience and your understanding."

Helgi was dazzled by Thórdís, watching her round bosom rise with each breath she took. He thought of undressing her, stroking and kissing her magnificent breasts. He took another sip of ale. "How gorgeous, noble and kind you are."

"Thank you for the compliments. You're enchanting yourself."

Helgi's penis swelled, pushing his codpiece forward. "Do you think Katla could be happy without me?" he said.

"Katla is young and impressionable. She claims to love all she sees, newborn lambs, awkward calves and blooming flowers." Thórdís winked one eye. "Not to mention the first young man she laid her eyes upon. Of course, most people are infected by Katla's perpetual gaiety. I know my sister. She lusts for the new, but her affection for the old wilts like flowers in the autumn. I have never seen her grieve for a slaughtered lamb." She smiled and tilted her head to one side. "I understand she's happy at Saudafell, entertaining guests with songs."

"Could I have been blinded by her youthful gaiety and beauty?" He sipped. "Impetuous, they say." Thórdís's eyes shone like the light blue pebbles he had once picked up at the shore. "You and Katla are alike in many ways. Delicate face and blushing cheeks. I bet countless young and rich men would like to marry you."

"It's what they say."

"Why does your father not betroth you to another man since I was rather naughty?" He drank.

"Even though my father has a quick temper, he's a wise man and keeps his word. I suspect your father is equally honourable."

"It saddens me to cause my noble father disappointment." Helgi drank again and the ale was gone. "This ale delights me, as you do."

When Thórdís stood up to pick up the tusk, he held it close to him, and her breasts stroked his face. He took a deep breath and loosened his grip on the tusk.

Thórdís laughed with a deep and tantalising tone which reminded him of Mediterranean dancers he had seen in Saxony. She filled the tusk once more. "Your father is fond of you and proud of your poetic skills and sportsmanship."

Helgi drank again and stroked the carved runes on the tusk. "But now he's disappointed in me because I did not honour his agreement – about us."

"Few men are wiser than our fathers are." She stroked her lips as if she were making them softer for kisses. "I trust they have made the correct choice for both of us." She took a deep breath, and her bosom rose.

"Perhaps they have made the wisest choice." He could no longer control his urge to touch her. He lifted his hand and

73

stroked her lips with his fingertips.

Thórdís opened her lips and licked his finger. Helgi stood up but she sat still, reached her hand out, and fondled his codpiece where it bulged.

"My mother objected to me marrying a seducer of women. — On the other hand, I can appreciate the source of delight concealed below the belt."

Helgi was hot with longing and could only think of how beautiful Thórdís would be naked. "I should have agreed to our fathers' contract without delay."

"Together we could save their reputation."

"We should."

"I'll be an indulgent wife."

The voices of their fathers approached, and Thórdís walked over to another pot of ale.

Halldór, Thórdur and Oddlaug entered.

Thórdur looked perplexed at his son and said, "It's started raining."

Thórdís filled a drinking horn, handed it to Thórdur and said, "You must be ready for a refreshment."

"No storm is brewing in here. Harmony hovers over us," Helgi said, and patted his father on the shoulder.

Thórdur drank, handed the horn to Halldór and said to Helgi, "What is new?"

"I deeply regret having caused you anguish, my dear father." He turned to Halldór. "And I apologise to Halldór for my past outbursts. I was blind. Now I see how wise you and my father were when you agreed that I should marry your precious daughter, Thórdís." He sent Thórdís an admiring glance. Her pink cheeks glowed, her heavenly eyes sparkled, and he was overcome by desire. "Therefore, my beloved father, I wish you would ask for Thórdís's hand in marriage."

Thórdur lifted his eyebrows in surprise and put his hand on Helgi's shoulder. "I'm proud of you, my son, for recouping your wits. I hope my friend Halldór will accept you as a son-in-law, despite the lack of respect you have shown him."

Thórdís walked to her father and took his hand in hers.

"Helgi and I respect our fathers' wishes."

Halldór assumed a noble look and patted Thórdís's hand.

Thórdur said, "On behalf of my son Helgi, I would like to ask you, noble Halldór, for the hand of your daughter Thórdís in marriage."

"As long as Helgi will not seek to be near Thórkatla, I'll be a loyal father-in-law to him," Halldór said. "The profitable farm and land of Hvammur in Hvítársída will be Thórdís's dowry."

Thórdur straightened his back. "And I will provide one hundred silver coins, twenty healthy cows, one bull and one hundred sheep."

"Generous, and agreed." Halldór winked at Thórdís, who looked elated. "Although there are few witnesses, we can seal their engagement. Now let us drink to the good fortune of all present."

Helgi took the horn. "The ale soothes my senses."

"Only the best for my dear friends," Halldór said, and sipped.

This ale was not as sweet as the ale Thórdís had served him earlier, but it was still delicious.

Oddlaug said, with a reproachful tone, "Finnbjorg flavours the ale with rare herbs."

Helgi could not understand why Oddlaug sounded hostile but said, "She's resourceful."

Oddlaug ignored his words and said, "Is this engagement what you desire, Thórdís?"

"Indeed. I have been honoured." Thórdís said, and smiled.

Helgi was spellbound. "How could I have refused such an enchanting woman?"

Oddlaug stared at Helgi. "Your will changes faster than the wind in the Westfjords. I pray to God you won't change your mind when the next storm hits." She turned around and left.

When she was out of sight, Halldór said, "My wife has a sharp tongue on occasion. It's a Christian affliction." He laughed until his belly shook.

The others returned to merriment and drank until evening.

A storm prevented Helgi and Thórdur from riding home.

Helgi lay in a bed wrapped in Thórdís's aroma. In his mind he played with her breasts until he fell asleep.

15
Katla

Katla worried about Helgi. Why didn't he come to Saudafell? Was he ill? Had he gone to Norway?

One overcast day when she was picking mountain grass on the hill above Saudafell, she noticed about a dozen horsemen turn from the road onto the path to Saudafell. The leader was huge. Sure enough, it was her father. She walked down the hill as two men helped her father dismount. He was talking to Garpur when Katla reached him.

"Good day, father," Katla said.

He patted her cheek. "My dear Katla, I hear you have flourished here at Saudafell."

"The people are good, and I have learned to dye fabrics."

"Remarkable. And you are still one of the most beautiful women in Borgarfjordur and in Dalir."

"Helga the beautiful is more enchanting," Katla said.

"She's betrothed to Gunnlaugur, the son of Illugi," her father said.

"I thought Gunnlaugur had sailed abroad."

"I'm not surprised. He thrives on captivating large audiences."

"Did Helgi Thórdarson go with him?"

Halldór straightened his back and smiled. "Far from it. He's getting ready to take over Hvammur in Hvítársída."

"I thought Hvammur belonged to you."

"After Thórdís and Helgi's wedding, Hvammur is theirs."

She called out, "Their wedding! — Impossible! — Are you telling the truth or making fun of me?"

"Why would I lie to you?"

Katla shouted, "Helgi loves only me. He'll never marry Thórdís."

"Quit your childish squealing. Helgi must have some sense because he asked for her hand and they're already betrothed."

Katla stared at her father. "When is the wedding?"

"Late summer, when haymaking is over."

"Did you make this trip just to tell me this dreadful news?"

"But this is joyful news." He grinned. "I thought you had matured while staying here with sensible people."

"How did their engagement come about?"

"As all men are, Helgi was spellbound by your sister's beauty and charm."

"Was she alone with him before he asked for her hand?"

"They weighed their options and agreed their marriage would delight all concerned. You should share in their joy."

Katla pointed her index finger at her father and said, "Spellbound is right. She put a spell on him, and it will not last long. Wait and see."

Halldór grunted and said, "Spell?" He laughed sarcastically. "What nonsense!"

Gróa stepped in and said, "Can I invite you inside for refreshments?"

Halldór turned to her and said kindly, "Thank you, but I cannot stay as I came to fetch Katla."

"Fetch me?"

"Thórdís heard you've turned into a skilled seamstress, and she wants you to make her wedding garments."

Katla trembled with anger. "If I sewed her wedding dress, I would shed tears with every stitch. On her wedding day Thórdís would be draped in her sister's tears."

"You insult me."

"If you want me to come to Holl, I shall do all I can to induce Helgi to break the engagement."

"You have taken leave of your senses."

"Your greed is more precious to you than your concern for my wellbeing."

"What nonsense."

Katla yelled, "You refused to allow me to marry Helgi because of a selfish agreement you made years ago. No one else cared about it but you. — I promise I shall be as stubborn as you are." She ran back up the hill.

When the hill got steep, she turned around and watched her

father at the bottom of the hill. He was having problems walking. When he dropped to the ground, two men helped him stand and then walked him to the farmhouse. There he turned, looked towards Katla, and raised his clenched fist in the air. She was unable to decipher what he yelled, and she did not care. She kept walking uphill until she was too winded to continue.

She would not despair. Helgi was her sister's victim. He must have swallowed a love potion Finnbjorg had brewed. If Katla could entice Helgi to visit, she could convince him to call the wedding off, and elope with her.

16
Helgi

The day after Helgi returned home, the realisation of what he had done hit him, and he was crushed by regret. How could he have promised to marry Thórdís when he loved Katla? He was a doomed man. Again, a black cloud shrouded his mind.

He was unable to get out of bed, and he saw no reason to.

Helgi stayed in bed for two days, refusing to speak. His father came to his bedside, grabbed his shoulders, shook him and spoke in an angry tone, "How could you disgrace me like this? Instead of gathering the sheep and cattle to herd them to Hvammur before the wedding, you hide under covers, sulking like a child. Two hundred guests from all over the country plan to attend your wedding and pay us respect. How can any man or king trust you if you don't possess the courage to stand by your word?" Thórdur stormed out.

His father was right. Even if Helgi felt tricked, sulking did not change the situation, and it was time he took responsibility for his actions. He went outside to gather livestock.

What kind of a coward was he to promise Halldór and his father he would stay away from Katla? How could he have broken his promise to his beloved Katla? How could he tell her?

After the fateful engagement day, Helgi had never visited Thórdís. One day he summoned the courage to tell his mother he wanted to ride to Saudafell to see Katla.

Nidbjorg answered, "Did you know Halldór went to fetch her, and she refused to come home with him to sew her sister's wedding dress?"

"She is angry at me. I must ride to Saudafell to explain to Katla how the betrothal came about."

"Stay put, and don't complicate matters. Whatever you and Katla discuss is irrelevant, because the wedding will take place."

"Thórdís and I will never feel affection for each other."

"So be it. Remember, a marriage is a family affair, not based on your selfish desire. Nevertheless, nothing should prevent you from being practical and discussing your marriage terms with your father."

Helgi asked his father to ride with him to Holl to negotiate with Halldór the terms of Helgi and Thórdís's marriage agreement.

The next day a jubilant Halldór received them, and proudly showed off the now-finished guest lodge, with the three fire-pits and the carved thick columns made of wood shipped in from Norway. It was the most opulent lodge in the valley and could house 150 people.

Halldór sat down in the seat of honour and said, "What brings you here?"

Thórdur scratched his cheek, looked down and said, "Helgi wanted to talk to you before the wedding—"

Helgi cut him off. "I wish to come to an understanding, an agreement about what would happen if our cohabitation did not go well."

Halldór stared at Helgi with cold grey eyes. "The cohabitation will only fail if you neglect your duty."

Helgi looked away. "If Thórdís and I find our temperaments clash and I want a divorce, I want to be able to return Thórdís to Holl and divide our property."

Halldór stamped his foot down. "Return Thórdís! Absurd. Thórdís is the only owner of Hvammur in Hvítársída, and you are not entitled to a straw in the field should you choose to escape."

"I agree, as long as I will not be sued for divorcing her."

Thórdur said, "You must be wed for at least two years before you entertain thoughts of divorce."

They agreed, and Finnbjorg brought them ale which they drank with delight and Helgi was somewhat relieved. But would Katla wait for him?

~~~

The day before the wedding Helgi decided to act jolly and be playful. The wedding was a perfect opportunity for him to demonstrate his poetic skills. He should adopt the poise of a court poet and entertain people without using mimicry and other pretences. He would prove to Halldór that his new son-in-law had nothing in common with the clowns he had pitched coins at in the past.

The wedding was to last for four days. As tradition dictated, the kinsmen of the bride arrived first at Holl. Helgi would not see them until the second wedding day. Among them were Hermundur and his father, Illugi the Black.

Helgi's kinsmen met at Hofdi. Thórdur greeted the guests one by one and invited them into the guest lodge, where Nidbjorg greeted them. Sixty kinsmen, women and friends stayed there the first night. Some chose to go to the bath house and clean up, others sat down and indulged in mead. Ósvífur, three of his sons and his daughter Gudrun made the trip from Saelingsdalur. Helgi greeted them with reverence, and his mother with glee.

Oddlaug said, "Dear Ósvífur, thank you for coming and bringing your family."

"I grieve for the drowning of your father Einar, who was a hero, a loyal brother, a close friend, but an absent father to you," Ósvífur said.

Oddlaug's eyes filled with tears. She squeezed Ósvífur's hand and said, "Thank you, dear uncle."

Later Helgi spoke to Gudrun, Ósvífur's daughter, who said, "You were wise to honour your father's wishes and marry Thórdís."

"But my heart is crying," he said.

"The heart's time will come," she said, and smiled.

In the evening, most of the guests ate well and drank modestly as they wanted to have their wits about them on the day of the wedding.

The next day the guests mounted the horses and waited for Helgi, Thórdur and Nidbjorg to lead the way to Holl. Helgi called his kinsmen the scarlet troupe, as many men and women wore red mantles.

At Holl Helgi played the happy bridegroom when he

greeted Thórdís's kinsmen and Halldór's friends, including Hermundur and his father Illugi. Even though Ósvífur and Illugi were known adversaries, they were both gentlemen, and Thórdur did not expect any friction between them during the wedding.

Halldór's many workmen led the horses to an out-of-the-way corral where the horses could rest and be fed without soiling the yard.

When Helgi saw Halldór walking among the guests, hugging them, slapping their shoulders, laughing and exchanging niceties, he realised that Halldór needed this wedding to impress his allies. Heathen chiefs like Halldór were accustomed to hosting large gatherings two or three times a year, where men worshipped their heathen gods. Since Christianity had become the country's religion, heathen assemblies were illegal.

Helgi laughed. By marrying Thórdís he was reinforcing Halldór's stronghold.

Most young men played ball, but Helgi did not take part and felt relieved when the evening meal was served. Oddlaug and Nidbjorg decided where the guests sat and were careful to avoid conflicts. As tradition dictated, the father of the bridegroom occupied the first seat of honour and Halldór the second one.

Despite the meticulous seating arrangement, Helgi knew that ambitious men were likely to argue about where they sat. To minimise the guests' potential displeasure, once everyone was seated, Helgi asked for silence.

He grinned and yelled, "Honoured chiefs and women, men with broad shoulders, muscular arms and wide bottoms may find their seat a little too tight for their size. The solution is to rise from your seat and hug the person next to you now and then." He stood up, pulled his father to his feet and hugged him. Laughter rang out. "We shall fill this magnificent lodge with songs and witty poetry and remember that humble giants can huddle up."

"Who is wittier than you?" someone yelled, and many laughed.

Helgi laughed and called out, "Do you want merriment or to waste your time tattling?"

"Merriment!" called Gudrun Ósvífursdóttir.

"Merriment!" echoed in the longhouse.

Halldór stood up. "Kinsmen, friends and women, welcome to Holl. Here you shall not starve any more than I do." He patted his fat belly. "I promise to take no more room than a humble giant." He sat down and wiggled in his seat, so his belly shook. Loud laughter followed.

Helgi feigned joy, recited poetry and drank to excess. He was not a target of ridicule; at least, he did not hear a sarcastic comment.

~ ~ ~

The next day Helgi woke up with a pounding headache, shivering and confused. A fly buzzed above his nose. He attempted to slap the fly, missed it, and his hand landed on something rock-hard. He moaned in pain, sat up with difficulty and examined his bleeding hand. Where was he? He looked around and realised he was on the hill above Holl. He had injured his hand on Katla's elf rock.

He murmured to the rock, "Vonadís, oh Vonadís. Losing Katla is painful."

What had brought him there? He vaguely recalled being drunk, needing to vomit, and rushing outside. After spewing on the north side of the lodge, he had looked up the hill and seen a glowing light. As if under a spell, he walked towards the light. When he reached the elf rock the light vanished. He recalled Katla whispering, "Rest here." He lay down next to the rock and fell asleep. Had Katla saved him from making a fool of himself in the lodge?

The wedding itself took place later in the day. Every time Helgi felt pain in his hand, he thought of Katla.

Several men seated in the guest lodge looked as lifeless and tired as Helgi felt, but not Halldór, who governed with glee.

Thórdís sat at the centre of the bride's bench, dressed in a white gown with a golden silk veil on her head. She glittered all over and Helgi thought that gold sparkled even when surrounded by debris.

Halldór led Thórdís to the seat of honour where Helgi sat. The guests rose to their feet. The wedding contract was read out loud and six men bore witness.

"Hail to the couple!" Halldór said and lifted his drinking horn.

Helgi stood as if nailed to the floor and had no idea what he should do.

"Kiss the bride," Thórdur whispered.

Helgi leaned over and kissed Thórdís on the lips. Halldór handed him a horn. He took a sip and passed it on to his bride. Thórdís lifted her horn, turned to the benches where the women sat, and said, "Hail to Freyja and to all women!" The women and some men laughed.

Helgi felt relieved when Thórdís left his side and walked to where the women sat.

Thórdur hugged Helgi and said, "May your marriage bring you prosperity."

Good wishes from others followed. Helgi paid little attention to what was said, but made a point of smiling. After the ceremony Helgi sat and drank with his friends and did not attempt to speak to his wife.

Halldór called out, "Time to sing!"

Helgi felt he was suffocating and walked outside with Hermundur.

"Now you're married and a rich farmer," Hermundur said.

"My only consolation is you'll be my neighbour."

"Don't forget, the ceremony is not over until you bunk down with your bride."

Halldór called, "Come on in! It is time to auction off the bride."

Helgi had forgotten the custom where several men bid for the bride, and that the groom should bid higher.

They walked inside and the bidding started. While Thórdís stood smiling by the bride's bench, men called out, "One white lamb," "Five silver coins," "Two fat calves," and so on. After

Helgi offered an ornate gold brooch, the bidding stopped, and Thórdís was led to him.

The couple walked to Thórdís's bed in the sleeping quarters. Hermundur and others followed. Helgi and Thórdís undressed, leaving on their underpants, and crept under the covers.

"Nothing will happen until you're naked," Oddlaug yelled.

"We want to be grandmothers next spring," Nidbjorg called out.

Helgi and Thórdís undressed under the cover. When he felt her soft skin his penis rose, but she whispered, "Wait to put it inside until tomorrow night when we're alone and can enjoy each other properly. Let's pretend we're making love."

They kissed and he rubbed his penis in circles around her pubic area until he came. He sighed and heard clapping. He rolled over to the side and looked at Thórdís, who turned on her stomach. He guessed she wanted his fluid to seep into the linen. They dressed in their undergarments and rose from the bed; he was serious, but she was smiling. The onlookers clapped as the couple finished putting on their clothes, and Nidbjorg removed the linen with the wet spot and held it up for all to see. Helgi was surprised to see a faint residue of blood mingled with the fluid. He looked at Thórdís and lifted his brows. She winked with one eye, turned around and walked outside with the triumphant air of a conqueror.

~~~

Helgi and Thórdís rode to Hvammur the next day with twelve men. Hrefna, the daughter of Finnbjorg, was already there and brought a cup of water to Thórdís and then handed it to Helgi, making eye contact and tilting her head as if she were flirting. He stared at the pearls of sweat trickling down between her breasts.

Later, when Thórdís and Helgi were alone in their sleeping quarters, Thórdís called Hrefna and asked her to dance for them. She swung her hips and lifted the hem of her frock, exposing her knees. Thórdís joined in and together they danced around him in an alluring manner. He assumed they had practised the dance ahead of time. How flattering and unusual! He clapped and he laughed.

Thórdís said to Hrefna, "Thank you for the dance. Now I will entertain my husband."

Hrefna left and Thórdís undressed in front of him, dropping the garments one by one onto the floor. He reached out to touch her milk-white breasts, but she turned around and asked him to undress. He removed his clothes quickly. She lay down on the bed on her back and opened her knees wide. Helgi knelt down and stroked her breast, but she did not touch him. He climbed on top of her and let his penis go where it wanted. But when he was about to come, Thórdís pushed him aside. The fluid spilt on her stomach for the second time. Why?

She sat up quickly, rolled over him and said, "Our marriage is now legal. I have made plans for improving the farm and it does not suit me to be pregnant at this time." She called out, "Hrefna, bring the warm water!"

Helgi stayed in the bed, too exhausted to move. When he lifted his head to see what was going on, Hrefna was washing Thórdís's stomach and pubic area. They glanced at Helgi and laughed. He felt ridiculed. So what? He turned to the wall, closed his eyes and thought of Katla.

From then on, Thórdís slept in another bed. When he tried to touch her, she turned away. All her considerable energy went into running the farm. She never consulted him or asked him to do anything. Why should he let it bother him? Hvammur was hers anyway.

Since he was treated as a trespasser in his own home, he made a habit of riding to Gilsbakki to visit Hermundur. One day when Helgi complained about the lack of affection in his marriage, Hermundur laughed and told him to get a concubine, as other rich men did. "And never be cowed by a woman."

When Helgi was back at Hvammur he started to pay more attention to Hrefna and to flirt with her. She laughed easily, moved close to him as if infused by passion, and he caught the whiff of blooming flowers. One day when Thórdís was away, and he was sitting alone in bed trying to compose a poem, Hrefna came to him, took his hand and laid it on her breast. He was overcome by longing and lifted her frock. She was not wearing underpants and he touched her moist groin. He pulled down his pants and lifted her on top of him. She moved around, moaned and seemed to enjoy it as much as he did. Then she laughed and left.

When Thórdís came home he overheard the two women whispering to each other outside. When they saw him approaching, they quit talking. Had Thórdís hired Hrefna to satisfy his masculine needs?

One day after he finished having his way with Hrefna in the barn, Thórdís entered and said, "Never seduce Hrefna so others can see, and never dishonour me in my home."

"So be it," he said, got dressed, walked outside, mounted Sleipnir and went to visit Hermundur.

Most days he found a way to corner Hrefna when no one could see, and played with her, wishing she were Katla. His yearning for Katla herself did not diminish.

17
Katla

Katla knew some of her father's wedding guests would stop by Saudafell on their way south from Dalir. To avoid them, and curious glances from members of the Saudafell household, Katla stayed away from the guest lodge. During the days of the wedding she woke up early, packed a meal, climbed up the hill above Saudafell and collected plants. She was too angry with her sister and father to cry. Poor Helgi. He had been tricked, captivated by Thórdís, and was now confined at Hvammur.

One sunny autumn day she was laying down flowers on an old cloth outside Saudafell when two dark-skinned vagabond women walked up the path towards her. Their black braids fell down to their waists. Feathers, bones and other oddities dangled on their clothes and purses. Katla smiled and greeted the twins with kindness. Tvinna-One and Tvinna-Two could not be told apart by their faces, only by the location of their dangling decorations. If one mistreated these roaming women, they would retaliate by inventing gossip about the culprit.

Katla asked the twins if they were hungry and they said they were. She fetched Gróa, who invited them into the kitchen. The twins ate lamb and porridge with milk until they were full. Then Gróa asked them if they had any interesting news.

"News from where?"

"From Hvammur in Hvítársída."

Tvinna-One looked at her sister. "Life there goes as it goes."

"We'll pay well," Gróa said.

Tvinna-One rocked in her seat and glanced at the coin Gróa had put in front of her, then she stared at Katla and said, "The wife of the house, your sister, runs the household with rugged workers."

"And controls the husband with a notorious maid," Tvinna-Two said.

The twins laughed, exposing their yellow teeth.

"Is Helgi happy?" Katla asked.

"He is morose and useless around the farm," Tvinna-One said.

"And flees to Gilsbakki to play with his toys, swords and such," Tvinna-Two said.

The twins were generous with information and gossip. Katla was not surprised to hear Hrefna was the notorious maid. Thórdís must have hired Hrefna to avoid her wifely duties.

The following day, Katla and Gróa walked up the hill to pick the last of the blueberries.

On the way, Katla said, "I want to know about men. I cannot understand why they want mistresses when they're married."

Gróa laughed. "Many men are like stallions, especially the young ones who want to have frequent sex. The wives are not as needy unless they enjoy the closeness. After babies are born, the women often turn their attention from the husband toward the children and the husbands seek intercourse elsewhere."

"If I have to marry someone other than Helgi, will I have to have intercourse with my husband?"

"Only once. If he's rough you don't have to accommodate him. Wives with abusive men want their husbands to have mistresses." Gróa smiled. "If the mistress is not demanding."

"If I dislike my husband, can I have sex with another man?"

"Only in secret. Husbands are often afraid lovers undermine their dominance over their wives."

"How about Garpur? — Do you enjoy having sex with him?"

"We love each other."

"Does he have a mistress?"

"Not as far as I know."

When they were high up on the hill, Katla said, "Please teach me how to be with a man, in the way men and women enjoy it most."

"I'll show you." Gróa led Katla to a hollow where they both undressed. Gróa touched herself on different parts of her body, inside her thighs and on her nipples which changed shape. She instructed Katla to do the same with her own body. Katla felt moist down below. Gróa pointed to a small node located above the opening. Katla found one on her own body. Gróa told her to play with it with her fingers. Katla did, and she felt warmer and breathed faster. She thought about Helgi while moving her finger. Soon, a delightful wave made her body quiver and she felt she would explode with joy.

"Let him do this to you first and then allow him to insert his limb inside you. Afterwards, you'll both be ecstatic."

"Oh, this feels so good." Katla could barely move from sheer bliss.

"Never allow a man to enter you unless he pleases you," Gróa said, and tickled Katla's foot. "Let's get dressed."

They laughed like little girls all the way down the hill.

Later, and many times a week, when Katla was alone on the mountain, she played with her bump, imagining how it felt to make love to Helgi. Afterwards, she felt closer to him. She regained her joy and resumed singing with delight for the guests at Saudafell.

In the evening, she sat in the guest quarters at Saudafell, watched the men, listened to their conversations, and wondered whether their wives were happy. She decided that the men who spoke of revenge, adventures and battles were unhappy at home. On the other hand, the men who were pleasant, reserved, and talked about cultivating their land must be happily married.

One day she asked Garpur if he knew the identity of the man her father wanted her to marry.

"I heard he is one of Ósvífur's sons."

"Oh. Gudrun's brother. Is he fond of fencing and sailing with Vikings?"

"He certainly is. But then don't all young men want to fight with kings and earls?"

"Did you want to be a knight?"

Garpur smiled. "Before I married Gróa. After the wedding, I became a happy farmer."

Human nature became less of a mystery to Katla. Men who sailed abroad wanted to prove how tough and fearless they were to other men. Women mattered less to them than weapons, chiefs and allies. Why had Gunnlaugur Serpent-Tongue abandoned the beautiful Helga and gone abroad for so long? He was the restless sort and would never be happy on an Icelandic farm. Katla felt sorry for Helga the Fair. Beauty and love were not enough to keep a swordsman at home.

Katla never doubted that her sister's marriage to Helgi would end in divorce. Until then, Katla needed to prevent her father from marrying her off. Could she learn from her sister to use deceit to get what she wanted? Thórdís married Helgi to obtain ownership of Hvammur and her independence.

If Helgi left Thórdís, he would be poor.

Katla decided to become rich of her own accord. At sixteen, she figured out that men became rich from owning land, trading goods or receiving gifts. To buy a farm was not within her reach, but she could buy linen and wool, dye it, sew garments and sell them. Rich men who were enchanted by her singing often wanted to give her valuable presents like brooches, necklaces or coins. She refused the gifts, as she did not want to be indebted to any man. But why not accept the gifts as payment, as poets welcomed gifts for their poetry?

When she married Helgi, she would not receive a dowry. To secure her financial future, she would fill her trunk with all the presents and payments she received for her singing and sewing. The locked trunk was secured under her bed.

Helgi and she would never be poor.

18
Helgi

Helgi was not needed at Hvammur. Thórdís hired all the workers and ordered them about. If one of them should, by chance – or rather, due to ignorance – ask Helgi for instructions, he referred him to Thórdís. He and Thórdís behaved like two rams who had no sheep to fight over, and avoided each other.

He wanted to be respected for his poetry and storytelling, so he had to polish his skills. He took to entertaining the household members in the evening with stories of kings and battles he heard when he was in Saxony, and embellished them as needed. Thórdís never attended and he did not miss her.

During the day, he attempted to compose love poems. How did Katla smile, laugh, run, hug? He struggled to form a fresh stanza. Each line lacked inspiration and he was too restless to search his unquiet mind for new words.

When the snow melted in the spring Helgi heard a trade vessel was moored at the mouth of Hvítá river. He rode down there with a couple of farm workers to buy supplies. When he spotted a bow he cheered up. The bow was not for sale, but Helgi talked the boatman into selling it to him, along with a few arrows, for a handsome amount.

The bow ignited a new passion in Helgi. Even though the bowmanship of the fallen Gunnar from Hlídarenda was legendary, few men owned a bow. Helgi built a hut he called his workshop and gathered sprigs on the hill to make arrows. For hours every day, he sat in his workshop carving arrows. At last he succeeded in composing poems about adventures and heroism, thus making use of his isolation.

One day Thórdís appeared in the doorway of the workshop and said, "Maybe you can be of some use with the bow."

"How so?"

"The foxes are killing sheep. Are you skilled enough to shoot a running fox or two?"

"Of course."

"I'll believe it when I see it," she said, turned around and left.

The disrespectful vixen! He would show her how skilled he was. He gathered up his bow and arrows, hid himself in the bushes above the farm and waited for a fox to pass by. A few passed, or maybe the same ones. With each miss, Helgi's frustration increased. Damn them! He grabbed an arrow and snapped it over his knee in anger. Damn it all! He fell to the ground and pounded it with his fists.

Damn Thórdís! Damn Halldór! Damn all the self-righteous swine who had robbed him of his freedom! He kept pounding until his hands ached. Then he sat up and cried.

Halldór, Thórdís and his father were right. At the farm he was unproductive. He took a deep breath, picked up his bow and an arrow, drew the bow slowly and let the arrow fly into a branch. It hit right where he wanted it to. With more practice, he could develop patience and be useful.

When he killed his first fox, Helgi's chest filled with pride. In time, he became a better marksman and brought home one slain fox after another for the workers to skin. Despite his usefulness, he did not intend to be a fox hunter all his life. Instead, his longing to travel abroad intensified.

The next summer, Helgi was invited to the wedding of Bera Ormsdóttir and Skúli Thorsteinsson at Borg. Skúli had fought for Earl Eirikur Hakonarson and composed a famous poem in honour of the earl, who now ruled over a large section of Norway.

Helgi wanted to attend the wedding to gather support for a trip to Norway. In anticipation of his trip, Helgi sat in his workshop, carved arrows and practised his skaldic poetry.

Two years after they were married, Helgi rode without Thórdís to Skúli's wedding at Borg.

On the last day of the wedding, Helgi managed to talk with Skúli in private. Skúli was a tall man with a huge nose and penetrating eyes. They walked along the shore below the new church at Borg.

"What's troubling you, Helgi?" Skúli said.

"I want to travel to Norway and join Earl Eirikur's court."

"You're a skilled sportsman and a good poet, but are you seasoned at sea?"

"I don't fear a heaving wave or two," Helgi said, trying to appear confident.

"When do you intend to sail?"

"Perhaps next spring. Could you recommend me to Earl Eirikur?"

Skúli wrinkled his nose. "I introduced Gunnlaugur Serpent-Tongue to him. It turned out to be a mistake."

"I'm more modest than Gunnlaugur and I intend to be loyal to the earl." Helgi smiled. "I want to keep my intention to sail a secret until I'm ready to leave."

"I shall not extol you to the earl until I'm assured your wife, Halldór and your father agree to your departure."

"You have my word." Helgi shook his hand.

Helgi felt rebuked by Skúli, and did not want to rejoin the festivities. He fetched Sleipnir and rode to Hvammur, calculating his assets on the way. Thórdís would get the farm and the land, but he should get at least half of the livestock and most of the coinage. He needed enough to buy a share in a ship, provisions and gifts for Earl Eirikur. It was too late in the summer for him to sail, and he should make preparations for his divorce.

From that day on, he made a note of how many lambs were slaughtered at Hvammur and how many calves were sold.

During the winter he composed poems in praise of Earl Eirikur. He would not arrive in Norway as unprepared as he had been when he asked Halldór for Katla's hand in marriage. Then he was mocked and humiliated.

Helgi spent the winter in his workshop. Hrefna came once a day. She brought food, put it on the bench, lay down on the bed and lifted her frock without uttering a word. Sometimes he wanted to cuddle with her after he withdrew his penis and to feel the warmth of her body, but she pushed him aside and left.

In early spring he told Thórdís of his intention to leave for Norway.

Thórdís grinned and looked him in the eyes. "Where are you going to find a ship and the funds for the trip?"

"I intend to divorce you, return you to Holl and sell my half of our possessions."

"I've been waiting for you to flee and I shall not miss you. But your intention of returning me to Holl is absurd. I have created a home here and according to our fathers' agreement I will own Hvammur alone." She smiled. "I'm not going anywhere."

"Then I own the livestock."

"You get only what you came with. What I have added with my hard work belongs to the farm and belongs to me. It's absurd for you to expect to be rewarded for my diligence and fortitude."

His desire to flee was too strong to delay the trip by arguing with Thórdís. No one could budge her, any more than they could her father. "Then I agree."

"Go to our fathers and tell them about the divorce and our agreement. I'll stay here at Hvammur."

Intending to get the coins his father had contributed as part of the marriage settlement, he pulled the trunk out from underneath Thórdís's bed. Half of the coins were not there.

"Where is my silver and gold?" he asked Thórdís.

"You squandered the coins on buying weapons, horses, hay, and on your wasteful trips for pleasure."

Helgi was too angry to speak. Aware he would gain nothing by debating with a master manipulator, he turned around to leave.

Thórdís called out to him, "What do you intend to do with your mistress?"

He stopped and turned towards her. "You two are collaborators so Hrefna can stay here with you."

She walked up close and stared at him with cold eyes. "I don't intend to house your whore."

"I'll find Hrefna a place to stay. "

"Where?"

"Somewhere with a farmer who accepts concubines."

Thórdís glanced to the ceiling as she did when she was

inventing some ploy. "Arngeir at Steinar needs money."

"He's a drunkard."

"What options do whores have?"

"I'll talk to him."

Helgi hurried outside. In the brisk air he could taste the freedom he was about to gain.

~~~

Helgi rode straight to Hofdi and told his parents about the divorce and the settlement.

"Rumours have it Thórdís's diligence in running Hvammur equals your indolence," his mother said.

"Running Hvammur is her passion," Helgi said.

"And she excels. Is your passion loftier?" his father said.

"Poetry is my passion. I plan to sail to Norway and join Earl Eirikur's court."

"So be it," Thórdur said. "I'll not support you."

Helgi was sorry for his father. "Dear father, you have given a fortune to ensure a solid future for me in Iceland, and I have disappointed you." His eyes filled with tears. "I don't intend to be a burden to you any longer, and I don't expect assistance from you, but I will not sail if you object to my departure."

"I doubt if this journey will bring you the accolades you expect."

"But are you at peace with me leaving?"

"I shall pretend I am," Thórdur said.

"Will you ride with me to Holl to tell Halldór of the divorce?"

"Your mind has never been swayed by reasonable men, so you shall face the consequences of your selfish choices alone."

When Helgi arrived at Holl, Halldór was sitting on a rock by the longhouse. His father-in-law was even wider around the middle than Helgi remembered. Halldór did not stand up, took a gulp from his horn, and did not offer Helgi a sip.

"Helgi, salmon killer and fox hunter, what prey are you now

seeking?"

Helgi dismounted Sleipnir and said calmly, "Good day, Halldór. I came to tell you Thórdís and I have made an agreement to divorce."

Halldór laughed. "I expected so, and I'm confident you've made a fair agreement. Thórdís is shrewd and does not fear any mendicant."

"I married her to honour your contract with my father. I now consider myself released from all obligations."

"And released from Thórkatla also. As long as I live, you can neither seduce Katla nor marry her. For her, I'll receive far more than your puny satchel contains."

Helgi wanted to kill this arrogant bull with a blow to his chest, where his heart was supposed to be. Instead, he ran to Sleipnir, jumped on his back, rode up to Halldór and called out, "You shall regret keeping us apart. Katla will not marry anyone but me."

He rode down the plateau towards Steinar in a frenzy. Never again would a man humiliate him without revenge. He would show this loudmouth he could indeed become rich and famous in Norway. Earls and kings across Norway and beyond would value his poetic skills and his sportsmanship. Would Halldór then give Katla to him?

Arngeir at Steinar was a rude brute with a swollen, sweaty face. After hearing Helgi wanted to house his mistress with him, he grinned and said, "Lucky me. The poetic womaniser wants to ask me for a favour."

Helgi did not let Arngeir's rant affect him, and paid the beast to board Hrefna for one year.

Even though Arngeir was a swine, Helgi did not fear for Hrefna in his house. Hrefna knew men and could defend herself if needed.

19
Katla

When Garpur told Katla of Helgi's divorce, she kissed him on the cheek, danced with joy and said, "Now I can marry Helgi."

"Your father has made it clear you'll never marry Helgi."

"In spite of my father's objection, Helgi and I will be married."

Garpur shook his head and Gróa said, "Poor child."

"I must prepare for his visit," Katla said, and looked at her plain frock.

"We promised you father you would not see Helgi," Garpur said.

"No man on this earth has the power to destroy a union dictated by the stars in heaven." She sang on her way to the bath house.

Each morning Katla rubbed oil from flowers into her hair and dressed in her prettiest frock. Her trunk contained enough gold, silver and valuable garments to buy her freedom, even from her greedy father.

A month passed and Helgi never came.

One evening, when she was standing at her loom in the corner of the guest lodge, a guest said Helgi Thórdarson had bought a share in a ship and was sailing to Norway. She rushed outside so no one would see tears flooding her cheeks. Could Helgi be more interested in seeking fame and fortune than settling down with her? Impossible. He was not one of those callous men who valued sportsmanship above love.

Six days later, Helgi arrived at Saudafell looking like a knight from a fairy-tale, dressed in a white tunic tied with a silver belt, and a moss-green mantle. A large bow was strapped on his back.

As he dismounted, Katla ran to him. He picked her up and swung her around before planting her on the ground. People stared. Katla led him up the hill above the farm. No one followed them.

When they had reached a point where no one could hear them, they sat on a ledge with a view of the farm below. Helgi took her hands, looked deep into her eyes and said, "Dear Katla, you are even more beautiful. How I have missed you."

"And you're more splendid than ever. Is it true you're going to Norway?"

"My vessel is tied up at Borgarfjordur, ready to sail." He described the ship in detail, as if it were an object of love. But to Katla it was his escape vessel.

"When are you returning?"

"After I have earned a stellar reputation and enough gold to secure our future together."

"My dear Helgi, I sit in the guest quarters and listen to men describe their pointless odysseys, year in and year out. I know one thing: wealth and reputation change. Everything fluctuates, except the essence of a man's heart." She laid her hand over his heart. "Your heart is the only thing I want from you."

"I gave you my heart a long time ago, and it shall be yours as long as I live."

"When we unite again, I want your heart to be as pure as it is today." She stroked his wavy hair. "A soldier protects himself from attacks with a shield, but once he has killed a man, the shield of regret casts a shadow over his heart," Katla said.

His eyes filled with tears and he kissed her hand. "I promise to avoid killing men."

"You don't have to wait to return until you're rich because I have enough funds to pay my father for my hand."

"Why are you rich?"

"I weave cloth, sew garments and sell to guests, and they pay me for singing." She laughed and took his hand. "You see, we both enjoy entertaining people."

He did not look pleased. "I shall never accept your charity. I'll be wealthy on my own."

His words stung her heart. "If you sell your share in your ship we could buy a farm."

He jumped to his feet. "Please understand my need to go to

Norway to salvage my reputation. My skills will not be valued in Iceland until I return with a splendid reputation and a trunk full of treasures." He sat down and squeezed her hand. "Then we'll marry, and we'll be the envy of all."

"While you sail and fence with foreign men, I'll wilt from worry."

"My lovely Katla, you should never quit laughing and smiling. I cherish your liveliness and pure spirit as much as your beauty."

She smiled through her tears. "I promise to act cheerful."

"I'll return within two years and marry you."

"Could we be intimate before you go?"

"In spite of my deep desire for our union, I'll never dishonour you because you're my virgin."

"Are you baptised? Have you taken the Christian faith?"

"I have."

"To please Earl Eirikur?"

"Not to please him, but my rise to fame requires me to serve only one God."

"Then I shall also be baptised."

When Katla watched Helgi ride away she envied all men who could gallop at will around the country and sail to foreign lands while women stayed in place. Why was he abandoning her? Why didn't he take her with him, despite what her father said or did? Why did men value their reputation more than love?

Perhaps she could find answers and solace if she sought the grace of Jesus Christ and his mother Mary.

That evening she found a star for the Virgin Mary and prayed to all the stars for love to be treasured above heroism and pride.

~~~

The day after Helgi's quick visit, Katla was deep in thought about God's will as she and Gróa sorted dried flowers.

"Did you want Helgi to stay?" Gróa said.

"He wanted to go. He'll be back. How can I get instruction

from a priest?"

"A priest? Why do you need him?"

"I want to be christened."

"Your father would disapprove."

"I have never pleased him. My mother is Christian and Helgi has been baptised."

"So be it. I've met a pitiful but handsome young priest called Pétur. He learned in Norway and now wanders around the district christening people."

Katla laughed. "Isn't it better to be christened by a handsome priest than an old sceptic?"

A few days later Pétur arrived riding an old mare. Two housemaids who also wanted to be christened were waiting for him by the door.

When his clear blue eyes saw Katla's face, he blushed and stammered, "Where would you like to be christened?"

"In the living quarters. What do you need?"

"A bowl with clean water," he said, avoiding her gaze.

The maids fetched the water as Katla asked him to follow her inside.

One maid put the water on the bench. Pétur made a cross over the water with his hand and said something in Latin. He asked Katla to stand in front of him.

Peter said in a ceremonious tone, "Do you promise to believe in one God, the father, the son and the holy spirit, and to be christened with water in his name?"

"I promise," Katla said.

He poured a little water on her head. It was ice cold and she jumped.

After the maids were christened, they hurried outside to go to work.

Katla said to the priest, "Can I talk to you for a little bit?"

Pétur blushed and said, "Why not? — In the name of God."

"It's about the man I love and am going to marry."

Pétur stammered, "Is he a Christian?"

"He has been baptised and is on his way to Norway. I think

he sinned – before."

"He did?"

"He is divorced and he has had a mistress."

"I see. A big sinner."

"But isn't it true God and we should forgive all missteps?"

"Has he dishonoured you?"

"He would never do that. He's too fond of me."

"I understand." He looked away and stammered, "You cannot let him destroy your purity before you have a Christian wedding."

"I don't know if I've sinned," Katla said, and sat down on the bench.

"You? A sinner? I didn't expect it from such a well-bred young woman." He clasped his hands, did not look at her but said, "If you have sinned, you must confess your sins to me. I shall then forgive you in the name of God, because you are immature. Then you'll be cleaned of all sins and be pure again." He smiled but never looked at her.

"What is sin?"

"There are many kinds of sin. To kill, to steal, to desire other people's things, to dishonour your parents, curse and tell a lie."

"Can you sin by thinking about a man?"

"If you desire the man, it's a sin."

"Can you sin in your dreams?"

"If you dream something impure, something physical."

"Do you ever dream about something sensual?"

"I?" He blushed again. "I cannot control my dreams."

"Are you then innocent?"

"If I confess my dreams to another servant of God, and he forgives my sins on behalf of God, then I'm forgiven. Absolved."

"Does the same go for daydreams? The things I wish for when I'm alone?"

"Such sin is more severe because you have decided to sin yourself."

"But I feel so good afterwards. Does God not want us to be happy?"

"We're born to make up for the sins of man, the sins Jesus Christ died for on the cross."

"Can we never be happy then?"

"According to God's will, happiness is gained by living a chaste life and never sinning."

Katla played with a lock of her hair. "Then I could be a sinner, although I've never lain down with a man."

"Why don't you tell me why you think you've sinned so I can ask God to forgive you."

"I think of Helgi, the man I love."

"It's not a sin unless it is... is a carnal thought."

"Then I touch myself."

"Touch yourself?" The priest opened his eyes wide. "Where?"

"It's difficult to explain because I don't know names for these body parts, so I'll show you if you promise to forgive me."

"God forgives everything."

Katla lay down on the bench where the priest sat, with her feet turned towards him. She bent her knees, lifted up her frock, slipped her hand into her underpants and stared at the ceiling while she moved the tip around until the pleasure moved like a hot wave all through her body. Then she was immobile and closed her eyes.

When she heard the priest sigh, she looked at him. His head hung down, soaked in sweat and his right hand was underneath his robe. Katla pulled her frock down and sat up while the priest cried. Someone yelped by the door. It was Hallbjorg, the head housekeeper.

Hallbjorg said, "I expected to find a priest here, a holy man, but he's defiled like all other men." She turned around and left.

The priest hunkered over as if he'd been whipped, looked up at the ceiling, clasped his hands in front of his chest and said, "Holy father, forgive me because I've sinned."

Katla was baffled, but then she suspected the priest had also touched himself and released his man-water. "Have I sinned?"

"You're a big sinner," the priest sobbed. "You tricked a chaste priest, as the whores did when they tried to seduce the

104

innocent Jesus Christ."

"You said God forgave all sins."

The priest stammered, "Did I?"

"Were the whores in the Jesus story not forgiven?"

He blew his nose on his sleeve. "Only after they confessed regret and promised to be chaste thereafter."

"Should I repent?" She knelt like the priest and said, "Holy father, forgive me because I've sinned."

The priest stood up, wiped the sweat and the tears from his face with his sleeve, and stood in front of her where she knelt. Words in Latin poured from his mouth while he laid his hand gently on the top of her hair. She stared at the wet spot on his frock, in front of his manhood, and wondered what she should regret.

After the priest finished and was leaving, Katla asked, "Am I now free of all sins?"

"If you promise not to sin again, God will then forgive you, I think."

He rushed outside.

When Katla went outside, Pétur the priest was riding away on his skinny mare. An assembly of household workers watched as Pétur attempted to speed up his mare by kicking his heels into her side. The mare took her time and tottered along, unaffected by the abuse.

Hallbjorg looked at Katla and said, "How do you feel being christened by a horny priest?"

Someone laughed and Katla ran inside crying.

Katla quit talking to anyone but Gróa and Garpur – to avoid being ridiculed for Helgi deserting her and for playing with herself in private. She had promised Helgi to be cheerful, but she felt punished for her joy. Did anyone laugh in the Bible stories? Maybe laughter was a sin.

Gróa and Garpur did not care whether she was Christian or heathen, but she was a believer, and recalled the words of God: "For I know the plans I have for you, plans to prosper you and not to harm you, plans to give you hope and a future." She thanked the Lord.

20
Helgi

Helgi stood in the hull of the ship watching Snaefellsnes disappear. On the other side of the peninsula, Katla the beautiful waited for his return. Why had he wasted precious time with her, babbling about skaldic poetry and fencing, instead of entertaining her with funny stories?

Thorsteinn slapped him on the back and said, "You look like a doomed man. Be careful. Men who brood over leaving their women behind are prone to putting themselves in harm's way."

Helgi smiled and said, "Nonsense. Now Iceland is behind us, and I shall labour like a madman. The sooner we reach Norway and become rich, the sooner I can return and marry Katla."

In spite of his regrets, Helgi was confident glory awaited him on the other side of the ocean.

Thorsteinn taught Helgi how to manoeuvre the rudder, and during calm periods Helgi worked on his skaldic skills.

When they were about to moor at Halogaland in Norway, they learned that Earl Eirikur was at Nidaros. The oarsmen rowed the ship south, along the winding and rocky Norwegian coast. Thorsteinn directed the oarsmen with skill, avoiding craggy islands and narrow peninsulas.

Nidaros sat at the mouth of a fjord covered with trees on both sides. Where the river Nid joined the sea they found a safe landing and moored their ship there.

As they disembarked, several merchants offered their wares for sale. Thorsteinn and Helgi bought six horses and headed to Earl Eirikur's camp at Hladir, located on a cape a short distance north-east of Nidaros.

The camp included a large longhouse and several smaller buildings. Labourers had constructed wood cabins, laid stone walls and skinned dead animals. Blacksmiths were hammering loudly on rocks. Two guards with ornate swords stopped Helgi and Thorsteinn and asked why they were there.

The recommendation from Skúli Thorsteinsson worked, and Helgi was led to the earl. Eirikur was a handsome man, with broad shoulders and light hair and beard. He paced back and forth as if he were planning the next battle. Helgi presented the earl with woollens, walrus tusks from Greenland and seal meat. Eirikur smiled and summoned his master carver, who carried the walrus tusks away as if they were gold.

The earl looked Helgi square in the eye and said, "What do you want from me, dark-haired Icelander?"

"I want to join your court and I shall recite for you a skaldic poem I composed in your honour."

"About me?"

"About your conquests and bravery."

The earl called his court poet and asked him to hear Helgi's poem. Both the earl and the court poet liked the poem.

"Now, I'll give you a chance to show your sportsmanship by fencing with me. Do not shy away from winning."

They raised their swords and began. The earl was nimble, but Helgi felt lithe and applied more skill than aggression, winning in the end.

"I shall call you Skáld-Helgi from now on. Tell me about your ancestors, Skáld-Helgi."

"Einar the Bowltinkle is my grandfather and I learned skaldic skills from him."

"Your language is as lithe on your lips as your sword is in your hand. You'll overcome many hurdles and become famous."

Helgi did what he could to please the earl; he fenced, played games, laughed often, told stories and composed poems. Earl Eirikur sought his company and within two months he made Helgi a member of the court. Helgi should have been thrilled, but despite the praise and coins he received, he was dissatisfied. None of his accomplishments could be classified as heroic. Heroes conquered the enemy. Here, danger did not lurk anywhere close. When the earl, Helgi and a ship full of men sailed back and forth along the shores of northern Norway, an enemy was nowhere in sight.

In the autumn, trees turned orange and red before shedding their leaves. Soon it snowed day after day. Helgi was compelled to quell his roving spirit and succumb to immobility.

Between snowstorms, restless courtiers rushed outside and waded through the snow down to a frozen bay nearby. There they tied polished bones to the bottom of their shoes and made a game of gliding on the thin ice. The first man to reach the other side without falling was the winner. Helgi soon mastered skating and won most of the races. The activity helped him forget his troubles, but winning games was not a heroic feat.

Hladir was not without charming and beautiful women, many of whom were captured in foreign lands. Helgi did not seek their company, as none equalled Katla in beauty or manner.

The earl held a big Christmas gathering offering plenty of meat, ale and southern fruit. The delicious food and the gay singing failed to instil joy in Helgi's heart. The best songstress could not sing with the exhilarating tone of Katla's voice.

When Helgi attended church, he stared at a statue of Virgin Mary which resembled Katla. The priest's sermon centred around faith, hope and love. The priest said, of those three, love was the most important. Though the priest indicated that love meant devotion to Christ, Helgi believed his love for Katla was a purer love.

Earl Eirikur summoned Helgi to his quarters and said, "Helgi, I never see you content. What ails you?"

"My heart is filled with longing for a beautiful Icelandic maiden. Her father refuses to give me her hand. Therefore I suffer."

The earl laughed and said, "Compose a masterly poem about her virtue and then forget your sorrow." He gave Helgi a crimson cape.

After Christmas and into the new year, Helgi composed various poems about Katla's beauty and virtues. With each poem, Katla became even more vivid to him. Yet a dark wave descended on his thoughts, drenching his mind in hopelessness.

When the snow thawed, but slippery leaves were still

embedded in the mud, Earl Eirikur sent a message to Helgi to come to the earl's private maidens' quarters. Eirikur sat in front of a table piled with food. Twenty beautiful slave women, dressed in colourful silk caftans, sat on floor pillows by the earl. Some looked Celtic, others darker, and a few were fair with golden hair.

The earl pointed to the seat next to him and Helgi sat down.

Eirikur said, "It's enfeebling for a handsome and robust man to be sick with longing for one woman. Chiefs and clever men report that the best cure for lovesickness is to clear the mind by bedding many women. Hence, I have selected these twenty beautiful girls to amuse you. You will lie down with a different girl each night for twenty nights. Then you'll be cured."

What could Helgi say but thank the earl and obey?

The earl bade the women to rise. Some picked up lutes and played, others sang enchanting songs from exotic lands. Each girl was beautiful in her way.

The earl left Helgi alone with the concubines. One led him to a tub filled with perfumed water. Three naked maidens undressed him and giggled with delight at his manhood, which pointed straight as a spear. He stepped into the warm water and two girls rubbed him with soap all over, not shy to caress his erect limb. Helgi was dazzled by how enticing and amiable they were to him. He soon relaxed, sat in the tub and enjoyed himself. Several girls stood around the tub, sang and played. Others fed him pieces of fruit.

After a while they asked him to stand up and the naked girls dried him off with soft linen and wrapped him in a silk caftan, which caressed him like soft hands. All his muscles relaxed except one. They led him to a table, gave him wine to drink and fed him flavoured lamb and potatoes. The women appeared to be enjoying themselves, and one kissed him on the back of the neck while he ate. Another one blew in his ear. A tall woman with voluminous red hair appeared to be in charge. She introduced herself as Signa. She led him to a small room with a large bed covered with silk, asked him to lie on the bed, and three dark-skinned girls with black hair entered. They rubbed him all over until he was sleepy. Signa lit a candle, asked the dark girls to leave, and removed her clothing. The scent from the candle was so bewitching his only thought was to play with Signa's naked body.

Every night for twenty nights he played with and enjoyed a different girl. Even though they were delightful, the earl's plan failed. Helgi thought as much about Katla as before and no activity could relieve his longing for her.

He had to sail for Iceland as soon as he could.

Helgi went to a priest and confessed having intercourse with the earl's twenty slave girls. The priest said, "Those are not sins. You are a single man and his excellency the earl offered the maidens to you as a cure for your illness. You are free of all sins and should count yourself a lucky man."

Even though Helgi was absolved of his sins, he had violated Katla's trust.

In the spring, the earl called Helgi to his quarters and said, "I've never seen a man so lovesick." He shook his head. "Twenty beautiful maidens could not lift your spell."

"I still want to marry Katla."

"Even if you're a valiant young man and a good poet, you can't suppress your lust for this Icelandic farmer's daughter. I've never come across anything like it." He laughed. "I would not mind meeting her."

"If you heard her contagious laughter and celestial singing, you would be as captivated as I am."

"Then you must sail to Iceland."

The earl gave Helgi a gold ring with his emblem and said, "Have a safe journey."

Helgi prepared his ship and hired oarsmen, an easy task since many men had lost their land to chiefs in Norway and wanted to sail west to seek fortune.

Nothing but Halldór, Katla's father, could prevent Helgi from marrying Katla.

21
Katla

Not long after Katla's christening, more guests sought food and shelter at Saudafell. Men were eager to see the bold temptress who led the priest astray. Gróa was baffled and asked Katla in private, "Tell me exactly what happened."

Katla told her the story and then added, "I wanted the priest to tell me if playing with my body was a sin. I didn't know how to explain it with words because I didn't know all the words. I had to show him."

Gróa laughed so hard that Katla had to join in. She gave Katla a hug and said, "What you were doing is not a sin. The idea of sin was made up by the men. Because priests claim to represent Jesus and God, they have assumed the power to declare who sins and who should be forgiven. Thus, they manipulate simple people."

"The priest also said he himself had sinned, as if it were my fault."

"This relentless talk of sin is nonsense. The horny and deprived priest took it upon himself to let off steam."

"I'm trying to be Christian by making an account of everything I do."

"Quit it. Don't believe what men say. You have the right to develop relationships with your gods, whatever you call them. God, Jesus, Virgin Mary or Freyja. Keep your prayers to yourself. Be careful how you act around men and how you talk about Helgi. Then people won't be making fun of you for being gullible and lovesick."

"So this is the reason all these men want to see me?"

"I expect so."

"What shall I do?"

Gróa kissed her on the cheek. "Your mother believes in Christ. It's time you went home to Holl and stayed there until you're given to a man."

"My father hates Helgi."

"Your father is your custodian. You'll never marry Helgi unless he agrees."

"I don't want to leave. You're my best friend." Tears ran down Katla's cheeks.

Gróa put her arms around her and stroked her hair. "You're needed at home. You're stronger than you think."

Later, Katla walked up the hill and prayed to the stars to help her reason with her father.

Katla wrapped all the coins and jewellery in her favourite linens and placed the bundles at the bottom of her trunk. On top of it she arranged folded woven cloth and garments.

On a clear and cold day in autumn, Katla rode away from Saudafell accompanied by Garpur and two men. Her trunk was tied to a sled pulled by two hefty horses. A thin layer of ice covered the road. The horses managed to keep the sled on the road by adjusting their gait.

Katla's heart leaped with joy as they descended into Borgarfjordur. The valley was spotted with vivid colours. "Look." She pointed at the vegetation. "Yellow, green, brown and red – what a delight!" The moss covered the lava like a torn blanket.

The travellers followed the Nordurá river until Garpur found a suitable crossing. The workmen untied the trunk, lifted it and waded across the river. Their trousers were soaking wet up to their thighs. Katla felt sorry for them even though the men never complained.

The sun had set by the time they ascended the hill by Thverárhlíd. They rode the rest of the way in complete darkness.

Her mother met her inside the doorway of Holl. Katla hugged her tightly and said, "Forgive me, mother, for having disappointed you." Then she looked into her mother's sorrowful eyes.

"Such a beautiful woman deserves more than mockery," her mother said, and walked down the hallway with stooped shoulders. Her hair had turned grey.

After Katla's trunk was secured under her bed, she changed

clothes and went to the kitchen to chat with her mother. What a relief that her father was not home.

"It's time you forgot about Helgi," Oddlaug said.

"Mother, you're asking me to do the impossible."

"My dear Katla, your father has promised you to another man. But now he fears he'll break their contract because of your indecent behaviour."

"Excellent news. Maybe the mockery is a blessing."

"A respectable man does not pay a fortune for a disgraced woman, even though a priest has forgiven her."

"Mother, please don't think of your daughter as disgraced. Although I pleasured myself, I'm a virgin." She kissed her mother on the cheek. "Why don't we get a priest to come here to teach us Christian scriptures?"

Her mother clasped her hands, looked up to the ceiling and said, "Thank God you want to be the servant of our Lord." Her face lit up. "I'll send for the only priest in the valley."

"Thank you, my beloved mother."

The next morning, Katla hurried up the hill to the elf rock she had missed for five years.

She described her stay at Saudafell to Vonadís and ended, "My dear Vonadís, I'm now a Christian woman and we're not supposed to believe in elves, but you'll be my best friend until I die." She kissed the rock.

Halldór was away for two weeks. When he returned he was even thicker around the waist than before, his movements slower, and his belly shook when he walked. His speckled beard reminded Katla of a ptarmigan in the spring. He told Katla to come to the living quarters and talk to him.

He stood by his seat of honour and said to Katla, "You've managed to damage our reputation. The wealthy young man you were promised to has refused to marry you, in spite of your great beauty."

"I regret having damaged your reputation, my father. — It would have served us better to give me to Helgi in the first place. Now Thórdís is alone and childless."

Oddlaug said, "Thórdís is a free woman and handles it well."

Halldór said with a thundering voice, "I shall marry Thórdís off soon. She's beautiful, the farm is profitable, and many respected men desire those assets." He plopped down on the bench so it creaked.

"Do they know Thórdís uses sorcery to get her way?" Katla said.

Halldór slammed his fist on the bench. "Thórdís is too intelligent for sorcery and does not waste her time wailing about Jesus."

Oddlaug interrupted him. "Have you found a noble man in Iceland deserving of Thórdís, if she agreed to marry?"

"What she agrees to is irrelevant. The one who buys a woman owns her."

"They say a good woman is more valuable than gold," Oddlaug said.

"True," Halldór said.

"Is your concubine so valuable her embrace lightens your purse with each visit?" Oddlaug said.

Katla was surprised. Now she understood why her mother was so bitter towards her husband. She said, "Isn't it against the law to have concubines?"

"Some men think they are above the law," Oddlaug said.

"Even your so-called holy men have concubines." Halldór's nose was bright red.

"And men who seduce every other woman like Helgi Thórdarson," Oddlaug said.

"Helgi is with Earl Eirikur and his concubine Hrefna is in safekeeping at Steinar. He does not love her," Katla said.

"I hear Arngeir at Steinar is using Hrefna himself," Oddlaug said.

Katla smiled and said, "Then Helgi is free of her."

"Helgi is a wimp. He lets women ruin his reputation and allows men to use his possessions," Halldór said, and laughed sarcastically.

Oddlaug stared at her husband with cold eyes. "I thought a woman belonged to the man who's in charge of her household."

"It's futile to bicker with a bitter woman." Halldór turned to Katla. "Helgi may never be mentioned in my household. You understand?"

"Then I'll tell you once and for all, I'll never marry another man."

"You belong to me and you'll not ignore my orders. Instead of making me proud, you have dishonoured me."

"I honour you because you're my father, as the Bible stipulates. — I'm innocent in the eyes of Christ."

"This hideous Bible is senseless foreign flummery devised to undermine our independence. I'll stay with reality. No powerful man will pay for a blemished bride. Are you aware how you're making me poorer?" Halldór said.

"You pretend to be a Christian man. So what of your independence?" Oddlaug said.

"A weak, gullible woman is worthless," Halldór said.

"Your aversion to Helgi has poisoned your mind. — Would you not be better off to make peace with him?" Katla said.

"I'll never allow a sloth to own my daughter or to lead her astray."

Katla kissed her father on the cheek and said, "Dear father, hate fosters discord and wars, but love will cure all grievances."

"You are too uninhibited, daughter."

Oddlaug laughed. "Katla is carefree and cheerful by nature. It used to make you happy."

"I'm hungry. Where's Finnbjorg?"

"Every woman in my home shall be Christian. — Finnbjorg has gone to Thórdís at Hvammur."

"You're more cunning than most Christians."

"I only honour one lord," Oddlaug said proudly.

Katla had to prevent her father from marrying her off without making him angry. She made it known to the rest of the household she was going to marry Helgi when he returned from Norway. If all men knew her intention, no man would ask for her hand.

~~~

On a sunny day in late autumn, when Katla was outside combing her mother's tangled hair, a priest rode up to Holl. He was a middle-aged man. Everything about him was brown: his horse, his beard, his eyes, his skin, his cloak, and even the rope which held his cloak together at the waist.

He dismounted and said, "God be with you. My name is Lodmundur."

"God be with you, Lodmundur," Katla said without thinking, and laid the comb down.

Oddlaug's hair pointed in all directions and Lodmundur stared at her with adoration. Oddlaug seemed to enjoy the priest's attention because she smiled.

"What brought you here?" Oddlaug said.

"The bishop has entrusted a few priests to teach the holiest of scriptures to all household chiefs. I am obliged to teach Halldór Kolsson."

Katla laughed with joy. "I want to be there when you do."

Oddlaug gave Katla a stern glance and said to the priest, "Halldór is confined to his bed due to an ailing back and does not permit visitors."

"Can't he learn the words of Christ while lying down?" Lodmundur said.

"Thórkatla will teach him," Oddlaug said.

"Thórkatla... But does she know—?"

Oddlaug cut him off. "She knows scriptures."

Lodmundur glanced back and forth at them with raised eyebrows and said, "Well then, I'll go now and return in a month." He mounted his horse and rode off.

After he was gone, Katla braided her mother's hair while they laughed.

Oddlaug said, "Let's go in together and bring Halldór the celestial news."

As anticipated, Halldór was incensed when he learned of Lodmundur's errand and yelled, "An ignorant blockhead will never sway me to believe in one fallacy or another. Even if these slaves of the bishop hit me over the head with their Bible, decapitate me and toss my head into hell, I shall never betray Thór, Ódinn and the truth. I'm outraged that the brave men who settled this land, and fought for their independence, should succumb to the king, the bishop, and all those pillagers of freedom."

"Well then," Oddlaug said with a calm tone, "expect to be punished by the bishop and ousted by powerful men." She walked out.

"Father," Katla said, "you only need to know the simplest things and they're virtues you already believe in."

"Like what?"

"Friendship, loyalty, patience, tolerance and forgiveness."

"Forgiveness?"

"As when you do your friend wrong—"

Halldór cut her off. "I never do my friend wrong."

"If unintentionally you hurt your friend and you regret it…"

"I'm an honest man. I do him a favour or pay the damage. Otherwise he'll get revenge."

"Father, you're wise and you've said revenge will be retaliated."

"True." Halldór sighed, and looked at his sword and shield which hung above his bed.

When Halldór was young and sailed with Vikings, he had purchased the sword from a verbose merchant who swore it had belonged to a victorious English king. From then on, Halldór cherished the sword and named it Kingsmate. Later, when Halldór rode around Iceland with Kingsmate in its sheath, people knew he was a powerful man.

The last time Halldór had raised Kingsmate was when he threatened Helgi with it. Now the sword was out of his reach.

Shortly after Lodmundur's visit, winter arrived with a blinding snowstorm. During the day Katla tried to teach her father Bible stories which exalted the virtues of patience and tolerance. She skipped stories about Jesus walking on water and others her father would call a fantasy.

117

At night the household members carved and spun in the sitting room. Compared to the workers at Saudafell, the ones at Holl looked solemn. Katla missed Gróa, Garpur, the guests and their stories. Instead of hearing lively chat, Katla sat by her father's bed and listened to him complain about snowdrifts, lack of news, stink from the fire, the scriptures, and the fact that his wife was deliberately starving him to death. Katla was not immune to Halldór's reproaches. He accused her of ruining his reputation and reducing his wealth, all because of the irksome poet.

Katla found it increasingly difficult to maintain her cheer. Often, she was near tears. One day, when Halldór was praising Thórdís's strength of character, Katla decided to play a role not unlike her sister.

While she sewed a belt by Halldór's bedside, she said, "Father, you've been to so many exotic places. Why don't you tell me stories from your travels?"

He was startled and stared at her. "Those stories resemble most Viking stories. I sailed and fought in distant lands, I was considered witty, a sportsman and I became rich. I've never been boastful. — What once was, is now trifling."

"You returned to Iceland."

"Iceland is the only country worth living in. — Here we're independent. We run our own farms and affairs. Or used to."

"You had a lot of foresight."

"Still, we're in decline. Chiefs battle about nonsense. — I've travelled the region trying to make peace, to reason with men, but what do I reap in return but heavy meals and exhausted horses?"

"What are your worries, my father?"

"Maintaining friendships and resolving disputes. How can I respond when friends and cousins fight like madmen over a woman – one fickle woman? How short-sighted and frivolous have men become?"

Katla suspected he was talking about Helga the Beautiful and said, "Who is fighting?"

"Gunnlaugur the Serpent-Tongue, my quick-tempered

cousin and friend of foreign earls. He and Skáld-Hrafn argue like adolescents, making enemies of men who used to live in peace. These selfish poets don't know anything beyond making simple language so complicated no one can comprehend their meaning. They fight without purpose. We banned duels at Althing, but they get around the law by sailing across the ocean just to kill each other. Because of one woman!"

"Helga the Beautiful is unhappy being married to Hrafn because she loves Gunnlaugur."

"Loves! — Quit this childishness. She knows her father has the right to give her to whomever he pleases, and she respects him, as you should respect your father."

Instead of calming her father down, Katla managed to make him angry. Halldór tried to stand up but wailed in pain and fell on his back in the bed again. Two men tried in vain to help him to his feet. The high snowbanks outside prevented men from fetching a doctor.

Halldór wanted Katla to sit by him while she spun and sewed. Katla asked him about the status of each farm in the district.

"It is simple. Men affiliate either with peaceful chiefs or with defiant rebels. — Tell your rebellious mother to give me more food. She's starving me to death."

One night Halldór surprised Katla. He pointed to the belt she was embroidering and said with a gleeful tone, "I should wear such a belt."

"You?"

"Why not? Sew a colourful and exquisite waist belt for your father."

She laughed. "I shall."

Katla measured Halldór's waist with a rope, and sewed the longest belt she had ever done, letting him pick the colours.

On a stormy day in late winter when she sat with her mother spinning, Katla said, "Does Thórdís ever visit you?"

"She has not been here since her wedding."

"Do you think Thórdís is angry with me because Helgi

119

divorced her?"

Oddlaug tightened the knot in her hair. "Thórdís made the decision. Helgi was useless and she wanted to get rid of him as soon as she could."

Katla was hurt by the way her mother spoke about Helgi but said, "Were you disappointed they did not have children?"

Oddlaug shrugged her shoulders. "They were never compatible."

Katla wondered if her parents had ever been compatible. Maybe Thórdís knew.

Later, she asked her father if she could visit Thórdís at Hvammur.

He grinned. "Why not? It's time you two quit bickering about the escaped loser. Tell Thórdís to visit her parents, who have fulfilled all her wishes."

"Have you found a suitable man for her to marry?"

"Even though she is the wisest and the most beautiful of all women, she's too headstrong to obey any man."

"Even you?"

Halldór laughed, and so did Katla.

All summer Katla thought of visiting her sister, but she needed two escorts. The summer was short, and the farmhands at Holl were busy tending animals, fishing and haymaking. The trip had to wait.

Halldór was enraged when he heard the chieftain Snorri had travelled to Borgarfjordur with his men and killed Thorsteinn Gíslason at his farm. Now Halldór was incapacitated and could not help settle the unrest.

Katla tried to calm her father. "If these men were Christian, they would not kill each other in revenge. When are all these killings going to end?"

"They'll end when men quit meddling in each other's affairs. Especially religious matters."

"Maybe Gissur the White will make an improvement."

"What a fool you are. Gissur is responsible for the unrest."

Frost covered the ground in early autumn. Farmhands were busy night and day covering hay and gathering livestock. Katla and her mother filled the pantry hut with sausages, barley and skyr in tubs for the winter.

Halldór accused Katla of ignoring him.

When Katla was no longer needed for farm tasks, she returned to sitting by her father's bed and sewing.

One day Katla said, "Your stomach has gone down. I bet you can stand up."

"My back hurts."

Katla suggested his spine be supported by a brace, as was the custom with a broken leg. Halldór agreed, and three men lifted him up so she could slip a long piece of fabric around his waist. He complained it was too tight.

Katla said, "You're getting thinner every day and soon I'll have to tighten the wrap even more."

After a few days, Halldór could stand up with the help of two men, and walked from his bed to the living room. He announced that soon he would make visits to the troublemakers in the valley and bring a peace proposal. But the snowdrifts grew and men had to shovel their way from one shed to the next. Oddlaug made sure her husband did not get all the food he demanded. If the severe weather continued, she would have to allocate the food in an equitable manner over the winter.

In the evenings, Katla entertained the household with songs and taught those eager to learn. All, including her parents, seemed happier. Perhaps it was Katla's wishful thinking, but did her mother and father exchange affectionate glances at the end of winter?

During the winter, when no one was watching, Katla sewed two mantles. The sky-blue one was for Thórdís. The other, a scarlet red, was for Helgi.

As the snow melted, Halldór ordered twelve men to ride with him to check on friends and relatives. Two men lifted him onto the biggest horse in the valley. Before he rode off, he stroked the colourful belt Katla had sewn, and said, "Now my friends will see what a pragmatic daughter I have." His laughter echoed in the valley.

Katla was pleased to see her father ride away with his twelve men. No one at Holl would miss their master. She hoped he was not hunting for a husband for her.

~~~

On a sunny day in spring, Katla rode away from Holl on her mare Stjarna. Two of the foremen, Aevar and Dagur, escorted her. She was going to visit her sister in Hvítársída. As they approached Hofdi, where Helgi's parents lived, Katla was overcome by longing to find out if they knew of Helgi's whereabouts. She asked the men to ride with her up the path to the farmhouse.

Thórdur and Nidbjorg stood in front of the farmhouse and watched Katla as she dismounted Stjarna. They greeted her respectfully and invited her and her escorts to rest their horses and enjoy refreshments. Katla thanked them, but declined the offer because she was on her way to visit her sister at Hvítársída.

Nidbjorg was a rotund woman and said in a haughty tone, "Thórdís is not the woman she pretended to be."

Thórdur gave his wife a sharp look. "She's not the only one responsible for the dissolution of the marriage."

Katla did not share their discontent, but smiled and said, "Peace is what matters. What others did wrong, we should forgive."

Nidbjorg sniggered. "You are a Christian, I hear."

"Yes, like your son Helgi."

Thórdur said, "Members of Earl Eirikur's court are not Christian."

Katla was overcome by joy. "Helgi is a courtier! Has he earned a good reputation?"

"He has indeed. — He's the earl's right-hand man and is named Skáld-Helgi." Nidbjorg sounded proud.

Katla was surprised. "Is he going to stay in Norway another winter?"

"He plans to sail to Iceland this summer."

"What magnificent news. If he still wants to marry me, I hope he will have your approval."

Thórdur frowned. "Our approval matters less than your father's."

"My father knows I'll not marry anyone else."

Nidbjorg smiled coldly. "That's what the vagabonds say."

"Halldór and I agree that a marriage based on passion alone is ill-advised," Thórdur said.

"Our bond is based on love, not on passion alone. — I'll be a loyal and useful wife."

"It's futile to discuss this matter before Helgi arrives," Thórdur said. "And I'll never offend my friend Halldór without good reason."

Nidbjorg expanded her chest and said, "Helgi is now famous and can pick from eligible and virtuous young women."

"I know he's returning to Iceland because of me."

Oddlaug and Thórdur glanced at each other without responding. Katla mounted Stjarna, bade the couple farewell and rode off. She had never entertained the thought that she was not virtuous enough for Helgi.

The melting snow from the mountains gushed into the Thverá river, causing it to roar as it raced down the valley. Aevar had a difficult time finding a place for the horses to cross the river. The package which contained Thórdís's blue mantle dangled down from Katla's saddle and she feared it would get wet. She asked Dagur to tie it around her waist.

Dagur hesitated. "If you fell into the river with such a heavy package, you would drown immediately. It's better to tie it around my waist."

"I would rather drown than have your life on my conscience," Katla said.

Aevar rode first across the river but not without disaster. The water surged over the horse's back and he lost his footing. Katla gasped as Aevar fell off the horse and the stream tumbled him down the river. She prayed aloud to God, Jesus and Freyja.

Her prayers were answered. Aevar and his horse managed to find footing further down the river. Katla and Dagur rode along the bank across from where Aevar stood, soaking wet. Katla bent over, kissed Stjarna and whispered to her to be fearless and calm because angels protected them. She followed Dagur across the river, the water pummelling her thighs. When she reached the other side, she thanked all gods and angels for keeping them safe.

Even though the ground was soaked due to the melting snow, the trip went well. They rode north of the Hvítá river and passed a couple of farms before reaching Hvammur. A steep ravine with gushing water bordered the farm to the west, and Katla thought how thrilling it must be to climb up the hill beside the hissing stream. The view from there towards the Eiríksjokull and Langjokull glaciers must delight every eye, even Thórdís's. The beautiful landscape was not enough to make Helgi happy at Hvammur. Was it possible that Helgi did not belong in Iceland? What a dreadful thought.

The buildings at Hvammur consisted of a longhouse, a wide farmhouse and several sheds. Gravel and crushed hay covered the areas closest to the buildings to prevent the horses from sinking into the soil.

Labourers greeted Dagur and Aevar and attended to their horses. Katla dismounted and stood there alone, soaking wet, shivering in the east wind, not knowing where to go.

Aevar was removing the parcel from Katla's waist when Thórdís approached her. She looked different. Her hair was tied in a knot at the nape of her neck and her face was brown from the sun. Instead of the customary feminine cloak, she was dressed like a labourer in a blue shirt and men's trousers. The sisters examined each other for a moment.

"What's the reason for your sudden visit?" Thórdís said.

Katla shuddered due to the wet clothes and the icy reception she had received from her sister. She could not control her emotions: the tears flowed and she wailed, "I came to ask you for forgiveness."

"Forgiveness is for the foolish."

No one knew how to crush Katla's spirit as effectively as Thórdís. Katla felt her cheeks burning. This time Katla would not give her sister the upper hand. She wiped the tears off her face with her sleeve and said, "Perhaps you're angry with me."

Thórdís laughed scornfully. "Why should I be angry with you? I pity you."

"Why do you pity me?"

"I hear you're lovesick and crazed from being assaulted by priests."

"Do you blame me for Helgi wanting to divorce you?" Katla said.

"Oh, Katla, you have no power over me nor over Helgi. I profited from the divorce." Thórdís looked down to a field where cattle grazed. "I like it here." Her look became stern. "Helgi was idle and skittish. I just heard from a merchant he's loafing in Norway, surrounded by the earl's harem girls. He takes advantage of their slavery and fondles them whenever he pleases."

Katla looked at her sister with tears in her eyes. "Why do you try to hurt me?"

"I'm not trying anything. You're blinded by fantasies and you refuse to see the truth."

Finnbjorg appeared at Thórdís's side and said without emotion, "Good day, Katla. — Thórdís, why don't you invite Katla inside and get her out of the wet clothes?"

Thórdís shrugged. "Why not? Follow me."

They walked into the clean sitting room, where a fire crackled in the pit. Katla was holding the parcel with the mantle she intended to give Thórdís, but she decided to wait until Thórdís's attitude improved.

Katla undressed, and Finnbjorg put her wet clothes on a bench by the fire. Thórdís handed Katla trousers which had a pouch at the crotch intended for a man's penis. Since Thórdís was dressed in similar trousers, Katla did not find Thórdís's offer humiliating and put the trousers on. How comfortable they were. No wonder men liked them. She grabbed the pouch at her crotch and laughed. Once she started laughing she could not stop.

Thórdís laughed also. "Don't you like these trousers?"

"Yes, but a woman doesn't need a pouch. Why not sew trousers without the pouch?"

"You're a good seamstress."

"Shall I make you such trousers?"

"Why not?"

"Can we be reconciled?"

Thórdís smiled. "As long as you don't mention any Christian nonsense. The priests are driving our father insane."

"I promise."

More relaxed, the sisters sat and discussed the farm. Thórdís talked with enthusiasm of milking cows, fattening calves and pigs and growing green pastures. Finnbjorg brought them a delicious porridge made of grains, herbs and lamb.

Katla described to Thórdís how she coloured wool and linen. Thórdís listened and complimented Katla on her initiative and output. Katla untied the rope from the package, and unfolded the sheep hide and the linen which protected the mantle she had made for her sister.

Thórdís's eyes lit up when Katla handed her the mantle. "Oh! It is beautiful."

They chatted amicably for a bit, until Katla asked Thórdís what man her father intended to marry her to.

"There are plenty of greedy men who want Hvammur but not me, because I'm known as a tyrant. I appreciate being called a dictator." She sniggered. "I've never met a man I like well enough to live with, so I shall not marry in the near future."

They walked outside. Thórdís showed Katla the longhouse, sheds and other new structures. She stressed that Helgi had not contributed to any of the improvements.

Katla noticed female workers doing heavy shovelling and working the charcoal pits.

"Are you going to ride with our father to Althing to meet men?" Katla said.

"Why would I need to meet men? Hermundur at Gilsbakki takes care of voting on my behalf and I give him my opinion on matters before he leaves."

"Don't you want to have children?"

"What for? Girls are sold to bloodthirsty men, and boys leave home to kill other men or be killed. I don't see a benefit in such upbringing."

"Children can be so tender."

"Lustful men entice tender women and priests deceive them with lies."

"I want to be a mother."

"If you want intelligent children then marry a wise and peaceful man. But after your ordeal with the priest, it's difficult for our father to find a rich and respected man who's not put off by your reputation."

Katla looked Thórdís square in the eyes. "I shall only marry Helgi."

"I'm not going to discuss this troublemaker with you ever again. — Your clothes must be dry by now."

They strolled into the sitting room.

When Katla was about to remove the trousers, Thórdís said, "I want to give you the trousers. You can remove the pouch."

"I will." She was glad to wear the trousers on her return trip because her undergarments were still wet. Her cloak was long enough to hide the trousers.

Katla was relieved to know Thórdís did not miss Helgi nor blame her for their divorce. Despite their differences, Katla felt at peace with her sister.

On her way home Katla prayed to God, Jesus and Njordur that Helgi would have a safe voyage home to her.

~~~

Katla was on the hill collecting flowers for her dyes when she spotted a vagabond woman walking up the path to the farmhouse. The woman, called Tora the Tattler, wore layers of tattered but colourful clothing. Katla ran down the hill, caught up with Tora before she knocked on the door, and said, "Good day, Tora. Do you have any news I might be interested in?"

"I do, but my hands are cold."

"Sit down and wait a moment." Katla ran inside, picked up a pair of mittens she had knitted and gave them to Tora, who put them on her bluish hands. Katla waited eagerly.

Tora took her time and said, "A ship from Norway is moored at the mouth of Hvítá river."

Katla said, "Would I know anyone on this ship?"

Tora smiled, displaying a few broken teeth. "A windbag called Helgi is there pitching wares to whoever is dumb enough to pay."

"Thank you, and wait a bit while I fetch a sausage," Katla said.

"Make it a big one."

She ran off and returned with a sausage from Oddlaug. Tora the Tattler put the sausage in her sack and wandered down the path.

Katla could barely contain her joy. She ran up to her elf rock to tell Vonadís the news. Even though her mother, her father and Thórdís thought believing in elves was childish, Katla could not confide in anyone but Vonadís.

One thing was clear. Helgi was not allowed at Holl. Nevertheless, Halldór could not prevent Katla from riding down to the Hvítá river.

The opportunity arose the next day when Halldór and Oddlaug rode east to visit neighbours.

Katla hurried to the hot spring, washed her hair and rinsed it with scented herbs. She dressed in the blue cloak with a colourful woven trim. Over it she wore a matching mantle embroidered with golden flowers. She combed her hair until it fell in waves down her shoulders to the waist, draped a silk veil over her hair and fastened it with a woven hairband. She removed the red mantle she had made for Helgi from her trunk, as well as a belt with gold and silver embroidery, and wrapped them in linen. When she asked Aevar to prepare her horse and to take her down to purchase supplies from a ship docked at Hvítá river basin, Aevar said, "Does your father approve of you going?"

She smiled. "Do not fear my father. I'll take the blame for

making you go. Please also bring Dagur with us."

"It will be our honour to protect such a handsome woman."
He laughed.

Katla had looked forward to this day for years and nothing
could cast a shadow on her joy.

Katla and her escorts arrived at the river basin when the sun
was still high in the sky. Her heart beat faster when she spotted
the ship and she let her horse sprint to the dock. She stopped
beside a couple of men who were tying parcels to horses.

There he was, standing by the river bank, his shoulders
broader, his long hair glistening in the sun. He turned around,
saw her, dropped what he was doing, came running, grabbed her
around the waist, lifted her from the saddle and swung her
around in a circle before putting her carefully down on the
ground. This happened so fast, Katla was speechless and weak.

Helgi knelt in front of her and kissed the back of her hand.
"My dearest Katla, you're the most beautiful, the brightest and
the happiest woman I've ever known. No matter where I am,
you're my first vision when I awake in the morning, and my last
thought when I close my eyes at night." He shed tears.

Katla was astounded by his candour, and a wave of joy
swept over her. She laughed until tears ran down her cheeks.

Helgi took her hand and led her to a trunk. They sat down
and he dried her tears with the hem of her silk scarf. With dreamy
eyes, Helgi told her of the intricate poems he had composed for
Earl Eirikur, and how bored he was as a courtier because he
missed her so intensely.

Katla thought of her sister's claim that Helgi had bedded the
earl's concubines. Of course those tales were fabricated gossip.
No dark thought was going to cast a shadow on her joy.

She told him of her visit to Hofdi and how proud his parents
were. She skipped telling him that his mother had suggested
Katla was an unsuitable match for Helgi now that he was famous
and she tarnished, but said, "Where shall we live when we're
married?"

Helgi laughed. "Near the ocean and far from enemies."

They returned to the ship. Helgi lifted her aboard as if she were a butterfly. He showed her how men rowed, and where they kept provisions amidships. He unlocked a large trunk and removed a scarlet mantle embroidered with gold and silk thread. "A gift for you from Earl Eirikur," he said. He also gave her a headdress fit for royalty.

"This headdress you shall wear on our wedding day."

Katla's eyes swelled with tears. "These are the most beautiful clothes I've ever seen."

"Befitting the most bewitching woman in Iceland."

"I shall cherish your words and these gifts as long as I live."

Helgi held her chin up, smiled and looked her in the eyes. "Now there's nothing to get in the way of our marriage. I'm rich enough to buy a farm and livestock. — I shall pay your father the amount he wants to secure our engagement."

"We have hurdles to face."

"No hurdle is so high we can't jump over it," Helgi said and laughed.

"My father listens to slander, and he would be furious if he knew we had met."

Helgi's eyes flashed when he said, "I'm rich, Earl Eiríkur is my friend, and men will be reluctant to offend me."

Even though others were watching, Katla embraced Helgi. "Why do men not sanction marriage based on love and devotion?"

"They're deceitful, heartless and jealous."

"Men should learn to embrace faith, hope and love… I also brought you presents."

Katla gave Helgi the mantle and belt. He embraced the mantle and kissed the belt. "Now I have a piece of you with me forever. I will call this my Katla-cape and wear it until it's tattered."

"You have to gather your relatives and friends and ask my father for my hand. He won't refuse men he respects."

"I will, my beautiful bride to be."

She smiled and said, "The only true gossip is, I'm lovesick for you."

She called Aevar to come with the horses.

Helgi tied his gifts to her horse and kissed her on the forehead. "Tomorrow I'll visit kinsmen and friends. Before the end of summer they'll vouch for us."

Helgi embraced Katla and she rode off with her escorts. She sprinted ahead of Dagur and Aevar and sang to the sky, "I love you, I love you. I'm yours and you're mine."

~~~

As it was midsummer, the sun was still visible when Katla returned to Holl in the evening. She dismounted in the yard and held on to Stjarna's reins.

Katla's father was outside. Supported by a cane, he waddled towards Katla like an angry swan. "How dare you frolic with my foremen when we trusted you to manage the farm while we were gone?"

Katla would not let his fury overshadow this glorious day. She smiled. "Forgive me, father. The farm was in good hands. Has something gone wrong?"

"Where did you go dressed like a gentlewoman?"

Katla scratched Stjarna's neck and kissed her between her nostrils. "I rode down to Hvítá basin to meet with Skáld-Helgi."

"Skáld-Helgi! — I forbade you to see him."

"He's famous and wealthy and he's going to ask you for my hand."

"And I shall refuse him again and again. The youngest sons of Ósvífur the wise Helgason are sitting inside."

"What are their names?"

"Vandrádur and Áskell."

"They were found guilty of killing Kjartan Olafsson. They're murderers."

"Kjartan is dead and buried and the fine was paid. The sons of Ósvífur are highborn, wealthy and successful Vikings."

"They're close relatives of Skáld-Helgi."

"But not his friends. I've made an agreement with Vandrádur."

Katla handed Stjarna's reins to Aevar. "What arrangement?"

"You'll marry Vandrádur Ósvífursson. Due to your tarnished reputation, it will cost me a fortune to give you away to a decent man."

"Vandrádur is not a Christian and he's a ruthless warrior."

"He's baptised, as men are forced to be nowadays."

"Skáld-Helgi protects my reputation, and he won't demand a dowry. Dear father, please wait to give me away until Helgi asks for my hand properly."

"Absurd! This cavorting jester shall never prance on my property. My reputation is at stake."

"Let's walk inside and talk to the brothers," Katla said. Arguing with her father now was futile.

Katla recognised Vandrádur from his visit to Saudafell. He was tall and muscular and his beard was neatly trimmed. He held the grip of his sword as if he were waiting for an opportunity to draw it. Katla suspected he would rather slice men's throats than settle down. Before he greeted Katla, he examined her as if he were evaluating a cow for sale. "You're extravagantly dressed."

Instead of appearing humble, as young women were taught, Katla stared into his icy blue eyes which reminded her of Thórdís, and said, "Do you dislike it?"

Áskell interjected. "Quite the contrary. You're as beautiful as we've heard."

Vandrádur spat out, "But are you as infamous as they say?"

"Jesus Christ and God have forgiven me my trouble with the priest and therefore I'm free of all sins."

"What about your lovesickness?"

"Is it a sickness to love one man? Your cousin Skáld-Helgi and I have not misbehaved and I shall not lie down with him until we are married."

Vandrádur's face turned red and he said to Halldór, "Your daughter is crazy."

Halldór slammed his cane down. "I'll never permit her to marry Helgi Thórdarson."

Vandrádur looked at Áskell, still angry. "No matter how beautiful Thórkatla is, I want a woman who's all mine. Not a woman who blabbers about matters of the flesh with a stupid priest." He stormed out.

Halldór called out to him, "She'll change her mind!"

Áskell walked up to Halldór and shook his hand. "You're a good friend. It's a shame your daughter is as rebellious as she's beautiful, and therefore an unsuitable bride. I trust you will void our agreement."

"I shall discipline my daughter."

"Vandrádur is joining Vikings in Norway. We'll evaluate the situation upon his return."

"May he be successful. Ósvífur is fortunate to have so many honourable sons and humble daughters. I was not as lucky."

"We have a large and loyal family," Áskell said.

Halldór stared at Katla and said, "Childless, unmarried daughters are of no use."

Áskell bade farewell and walked out.

Oddlaug had been sitting in the corner, listening to the conversation. When Áskell left she stood up, walked to Halldór and said in a firm tone, "Women sew sails enabling you to traverse the seas where you ravage like villains, steal valuables and abduct innocents. Women sew your clothes so you don't have to walk about cold and naked. They sit by the bed of a fat man all winter long, entertaining him while he's immobile due to his own gluttony. Women manage the farms while the so-called chiefs visit their concubines. Why do you then call women useless?"

Halldór yelled, "How dare you talk to your husband this way?"

"Your obstinacy is absurd," Oddlaug said.

"My reputation will be damaged forever if I allow Katla to live here, as deranged as she is."

"Father, I follow my heart," Katla said.

Halldór tried to spring to his feet without supporting himself with the cane. He fell flat on the floor. The boards cracked and creaked while Halldór wailed. Oddlaug called for help. It took four men to carry Halldór to his bed.

Again, it became Katla's duty to attend to her father. After three days a doctor arrived and examined Halldór's spine and legs. One foot was broken. He put braces around Halldór's foot and told him to lie on his back with his head propped up. As before, Halldór had to endure rationed food, but tried to talk his maids into slipping him sausages at night. The keys to the pantry were tied to Oddlaug's silver belt, and since the maids feared her more than Halldór, no one gave him an extra morsel.

Halldór's curses and complaints continued to dominate the atmosphere at Holl. Katla took to praying out loud. When Halldór said, "Shut up," Katla walked out. Since Halldór could not relieve himself in the outhouse, maids put big rags over his bottom and manhood and removed them when they were soiled. The odour was so unbearable that Katla only sat with her father after he was cleaned.

Where was Helgi? Had he heard about her father's injuries? According to custom, it was disrespectful to ask a bedridden man for the hand of his daughter. Katla needed to get her father back on his feet quickly.

A few days later, Thórdís, Finnbjorg and two farmhands appeared without notice. Katla was glad to see her sister wearing the blue mantle she had made for her. Finnbjorg carried a parcel Katla suspected contained healing potion. Finnbjorg's brew might work better than the doctor's worthless prescriptions. Thórdís and Finnbjorg rushed to Halldór's side and asked to be alone with him.

After Finnbjorg and Thórdís had been with Halldór for a while, Thórdís sat down with her mother and Katla in the sitting room and said, "Father's foot is infected and he's burning with fever. If the ointment Finnbjorg has wrapped around Halldór's foot does not work, his foot will have to be amputated."

"He'll not want to live without his foot," Oddlaug said.

Thórdís said, "Right." She looked at Katla. "It's your fault he broke his foot in the first place. Vagabonds and honourable travellers' gossip about your visit with Helgi and his insulting behaviour towards you."

"Helgi greeted me with joy."

"Did you embrace and kiss while others watched?'

"He was just showing me love and kindness. Helgi was

noble."

"Noble men protect the reputation of wellborn women."

"I don't care what others think of me."

Oddlaug stood up and said brusquely, "Thórkatla, this matter is not about your passion. It concerns your family. From now on you must behave like a virtuous well-bred woman."

"Soon Helgi will be here with a group of friends and relatives to ask for my hand. The best way to maintain the honour of the family is for my father to agree that I marry Helgi. "

Thórdís smirked. "Katla, how can you be so naive? I heard Helgi is on his way to Arngeir at Steinar to fetch his concubine. Believe me, he'll be in for a surprise."

Katla stood up and tried not to look hurt. "I sewed trousers for you. I hope you like them." With tears in her eyes and a heavy heart, she walked to her bed and pulled her trunk out. At the top of the trunk lay the cape Helgi had given her. A tear fell on it and she wiped it off with her sleeve.

Thórdís liked the trousers, but Oddlaug found them disgraceful and said, "You'll get a bad reputation for wanting to resemble a man. Who will marry you then?"

"I don't mind being alone, mother," Thórdís said, and smiled. "Hermundur Illugason protects my reputation, and whoever makes fun of me will have to face his wrath."

After Thórdís left, Katla hung Helgi's cape above her bed as her protective shield. When people laid eyes upon the royal cape they would see how precious Katla was to Helgi.

22
Helgi

After Katla's visit to the harbour, Helgi whistled happy tunes while he sold the remaining malt, grain and timber to local farmers. In the middle of a transaction, he felt something nudge his shoulder blade and turned around. It was Sleipnir. Helgi hugged his neck, shed a couple of tears, and whispered in his ear, "You're the best friend I ever had."

His father stood next to Sleipnir, holding the reins of a draft horse, and said, "As you wished, I brought an extra horse."

Helgi grabbed his father by the arm. "Are you proud of me, father? Now I'm both rich and famous."

Thórdur smiled hesitantly. "I hope good fortune will follow."

Helgi slapped his father on the shoulder. "Have faith in my fortitude, father."

When Helgi and his father passed Holl on their way to Hofdi, Katla was nowhere in sight. Soon they would be inseparable.

After enjoying a delicious meal at Hofdi, Helgi gave his father a scarlet cape, his mother a gold brooch and a silver comb. He entertained them and the household all evening with stories of Earl Eirikur and his court.

Early the following day Helgi walked up to his father, who was brushing his horse, and asked to speak to him.

After they sat down, Helgi said, "Dear father, now I'm rich enough to ask for Thórkatla's hand."

"I'm disappointed to hear this trip has not made you wiser." Thórdur stood up. "Halldór is injured and feeble, and you should not insult an ill chief by asking him for his daughter's hand." He walked to his horse. "I have more pressing chores than arguing with a lovesick man," he said as he mounted the horse.

Helgi was devastated by his father's attitude. Did Halldór's friendship matter more to him than his son's happiness? What was he to do? Perhaps Hermundur would back him.

The next day Helgi rode to Gilsbakki.

When Helgi passed Hvammur he thought of Thórdís. Plump cows grazed in a field; calves looked healthy; the structures were well maintained. Thórdís was a diligent farmer, better than he would ever be. She never needed a man. In many ways, the sisters were as different as a fox and a puppy. They had one thing in common: determination. Thórdís did not let Helgi or anyone keep her from capturing Hvammur. Katla was equally determined to marry Helgi. To be worthy of her, he should follow Hermundur's example: be productive and resolute.

When Helgi approached Hermundur about riding with him to Holl to ask Halldór for Katla's hand in marriage, Hermundur said, "You've impressed the earl and others in Norway and I would be pleased to help you get settled in Iceland. But I will not alienate such a faithful ally as Halldór has been to me and my father."

"After Katla and I are married and have children, I'm certain our parents will rejoice."

"Halldór is ill-tempered but a valued friend to many, including your father," Hermundur said.

"If my father agrees to talk to Halldór about a marriage arrangement, will you support me?"

"I might. I heard Vandrádur Ósvífursson has withdrawn his request to marry Katla because of her refusal to marry anyone but you." Hermundur put his hand on Helgi's shoulder. "But malicious talk about Katla is not the only gossip concerning you that's circling the country."

"What else is new?"

"Vagabonds talk about your concubine."

"Hrefna is safe with Arngeir and I'm going there to pay him what I owe and to give her freedom."

"I hear she's with child."

"What! How does Arngeir dare to impregnate my concubine?'

"He claims to own her now, since you owe him money for her upkeep, and that you're busy chasing other women and that you seduce Katla every chance you get."

"Arngeir is a shameless liar." On his way to the door, Helgi added, "He shall be punished for his treachery."

Hermundur stepped in front of him, grabbed both his shoulders and said, "Be careful, Helgi. The law is on his side. He's not liable to pay you damages for violating a concubine because it's now illegal to own them."

"Then he shall pay for spreading lies about Katla and me."

Hermundur let go of Helgi's shoulder and said, "Arngeir is a wrathful drunkard. Try not to insult him, and remember he's related to Halldór and to me."

"I don't care. It's against the law for landowners to defame their friends and relatives."

"Revenge breeds further revenge and I don't want to choose whether I should support you or Arngeir. We're bound by law to pay penalties for injustices our relatives commit, but not those of our friends, unless we choose to do so. I beg you. Don't let Arngeir rile you."

"I shall control my temper."

Helgi bade farewell, mounted Sleipnir and rode out to the Hvítársída valley.

Helgi allowed Sleipnir to sprint along the bank of the Hvítá river until they turned on the path which led to Steinar. The farm was located between two rivers, Thverá and Hvítá. The roof of the farmhouse had holes in it, and the walls of the barn sagged.

Arngeir stepped outside and grinned when he saw Helgi. He smelled of rancid ale and slurred his words. "What a surprise. The woman-chaser has honoured us with his poetic presence. Have you already visited every other whore in the valley?"

Helgi's face got hot. "You have been spreading false rumours about me."

"I only tell the truth. One of the earl's courtiers described your affairs with slave girls. Others bear witness to your flirting with Thórkatla Halldórsdóttir. Her father is my kin. He's ill and near death because you've defiled his daughter in front of honest men."

Helgi yelled, "Slander and lies!"

"Oh, I heard you seduced Katla with empty promises, embraces and kisses." Arngeir blew kisses into the air.

Helgi was enraged. "If it's true Hrefna is with child, then you have deceived me."

"I've not deceived anyone. Don't you know it's illegal to keep concubines?"

"I want to see her."

"You can see her, but you can't take her away."

Arngeir shouted, "Hrefna, come see your former whoremonger."

Hrefna appeared in the doorway. Her belly was broad and looked like she was about to give birth. In spite of her weight, she rushed to Helgi and said, "Why didn't you pay him up? Look at what he did to me."

"What happened?"

"After the year was up, Arngeir said he owned me."

Helgi walked up to Arngeir and yelled, "You shall pay me a penalty for making Hrefna pregnant and for spreading lies about Thórkatla Halldórsdóttir."

"Penalty! I should charge you for leaving her here without paying for her upkeep."

Hrefna said, "Upkeep! I should be paid for keeping house."

Arngeir slapped Hrefna. She grabbed her cheek and stepped behind Helgi, who could not contain his rage.

Helgi drew his sword and brought it down hard on Arngeir's neck. He fell over as blood gushed from the deep wound.

Hrefna cupped her abdomen and called out, "Arngeir is dead!" She rushed past Helgi and grabbed the rope of a horse tied to a rock in the yard.

Helgi was still holding his sword high when a huge man showed up in the doorway, saw where Arngeir's body lay by the door, lifted his sword, charged towards Helgi, and said, "You're a dead man."

Without thinking, Helgi knocked the sword from the man's hand and, in a rage, stabbed the man, who fell lifeless at Helgi's feet.

Helgi stepped away, spun in a circle, holding his sword with both hands, and shouted, "Anyone else want to kill me?"

Labourers and maids who had witnessed the argument and the killings scurried away.

Hrefna rode up to Helgi where he stood with his bloody sword and said, "Am I now a free woman?"

"As free as the mother of a fatherless child can be," Helgi said

He placed his sword in its sheath, took coins from his purse and handed them to Hrefna. She grabbed them, rode by Arngeir's corpse and spat on it.

Helgi mounted Sleipnir and followed Hrefna until he reached her side. "Where are you going?"

"To Hvammur where my mother is."

"If you bounce on the horse all that way, the child will be born."

She looked straight ahead. "No one cares."

"The child will. Go easy."

Helgi turned north towards Thverárhlíd. He was shaking. How could he have killed five men because of women? What kind of an imbecile was he? Hermundur had warned him, but still he had let his temper get the better of him, and killed without thinking.

Sleipnir was still sweaty and short of breath so Helgi allowed him to set the pace.

When a horse neighed, Sleipnir stopped and looked east. Helgi recognised Hrefna's horse in the distance. But where was she?

Helgi turned Sleipnir around and rode to where Hrefna lay by the road, screaming. Her bare knees were bent and wide apart. Helgi dismounted and saw the crown of a black-haired baby appear between her legs. "What shall I do?"

"Take the baby's head and pull like you do when a lamb is born."

Helgi wiped his bloody hands on his trousers, cradled the infant's head and pulled gently. The infant slid out and Helgi held it, not knowing what to do next. A long string extended from the infant's navel into Hrefna.

Hrefna moaned, "Put the baby on top of my stomach. Take a knife and cut the cord close to the baby's navel. Then tie a knot by the navel."

Helgi drew his knife, did as she said, and returned the knife to his belt.

"Hold the baby's feet and lift it up."

Again, he did as she said.

With one hand Hrefna pulled the remaining string from her vagina until the placenta was out. She screamed in pain. A lot of blood gushed out of her. "If the baby is a girl, I will take her. If it's a boy, I don't want to see him."

"Why don't you want to see the boy?"

"Because Arngeir's cursed blood runs in his veins and I have no intention of bringing up an evil monster."

"It's a boy."

"Kill him then."

"Kill! How can I?"

"You just killed five men."

"Five armed men. I cannot kill an innocent infant."

Hrefna sniggered and coughed. "Men are cowards. You use women to entertain you, to bear your children and to raise them. You teach your boys to kill before they're grown up. When they're killed, mothers are left behind, destitute and heartbroken. As I see it, it's an act of mercy to kill an infant boy."

"To wipe out the human race is evil."

"I don't give a damn about the human race. — If you leave the boy here, I'll kill him."

He looked up when he heard the sound of hoofbeats coming from the east. "Men are coming. I must leave."

"I'll rest here and then walk to Hvammur. Take the youngster and do what you will with him."

The boy was slimy, bright red in the face and never let up on his cries. Only a woman could silence such an infant. "Doesn't he need to be fed?"

Hrefna never looked at the boy. "His lips shall never touch my breasts. — Hurry off with him."

Helgi took the boy and wrapped him in a blanket which he

141

had tied to his horse. He secured the bundle to his chest with a rope, as he had seen maids do when they needed both hands to milk cows. He mounted Sleipnir and rode as fast as he could in the direction of Thverárhlíd. The boy quit crying after a while. Helgi stopped to see if the infant was still breathing. Thank God he was.

Hrefna's words about men's brutality popped into his mind.

He called out, "Jesus Christ! Free me of recklessness and woman chasing!"

How could Katla love him when he was so careless? He should know by now that love was more important than conquest.

When Helgi approached the bank of the Thverá river, he dismounted and led Sleipnir across the river. The road passed Holl. He must tell Katla of his blunders before she heard them from others. How could he justify what he had done? Instead of gathering friends and relatives to support him in asking for Katla's hand, he had killed a well-connected landowner, a cousin of Halldór and Katla, and his man, while Halldór was confined to his bed.

Helgi's biggest challenge was no longer asking Halldór for Katla's hand, but staying alive. Arngeir's relatives would seek revenge. As Hermundur had warned, Helgi was not justified in seeking penalties for Arngeir impregnating Hrefna. Arngeir's brothers would summon Helgi to Althing and expect him to pay a hefty restitution. Even worse, those impatient beasts would set out to kill him before the next Althing.

What was he to do with Hrefna's boy?

23
Katla

On a foggy evening, several days after Katla visited Helgi at the river, Katla sat by her father's bedside sewing while he snored. The maid Runa came to her and whispered in her ear that a guest was in the yard waiting for her. Katla wrapped a woollen shawl around her shoulders and went outside. Helgi was at Sleipnir's side, holding a bundle. She hurried to him but stopped when she heard an infant's cries coming from the bundle. Helgi's clothes were muddy and spotted with blood.

"My dear Helgi." She looked at the infant. "Where does the baby come from?"

"I'll tell you, but the boy is hungry and needs to be fed."

Katla took the black-haired boy in her arms. He quit crying and stared at her with eyes which reminded her of the bark of an old tree. She smiled, and the boy cooed while she carried him to the kitchen.

She handed the baby to the maid Runa and said, "Please find milk for him, bathe him and wrap him in linen."

Runa hesitated, then said, "He looks like a Laplander." She took the boy in her arms, but did not hold him close.

"What difference does it make? The boy is robust and hungry." Katla grabbed several rags which hung by the fire-pit and carried them outside.

She led Helgi to a shelter inside an outhouse. How could he have changed so much in a few days? Before he was proud and gallant. Now he looked defeated, exhausted, his shoulders drooping. Tears streamed down his face as he told her the story of the killings, Hrefna's hardships, the birth of the boy, and Hrefna's refusal to accept the child. While he spoke, Katla wiped sweat, blood and tears off his face and hair.

She kissed him on the cheek and said, "God will reward you for saving Hrefna's son. I'll make sure the boy survives."

"My beloved Katla, I don't deserve you. Why do I continue

to break your heart and tarnish your reputation with my misdeeds?" He kissed her on the forehead. "I should have thought of you before I killed the men. Now, I might not survive long enough for us to marry."

Katla stroked his hair. "Surely, they won't kill you for defending the honour of two women and saving a boy."

"To them, Arngeir is more important. I must go to Hofdi and tell my parents of this misfortune."

"Will you be staying there?"

"Arngeir's brothers will seek revenge. If they cannot find me, Althing will decide my fate."

"But Helgi, the next Althing is in many months."

"You shall never lack anything." Helgi untied his purse from his belt and handed it to Katla. He slid a large gold ring on her finger and said, "The ring is your proof of my everlasting love. Keep this ring where others cannot see it."

When Helgi was gone, Katla put the ring in the purse which she hid beneath her clothes.

What should she do with the baby? Katla's mother did not like Hrefna, whom she suspected of promiscuity and sorcery. But Katla remembered how passionate and uninhibited Hrefna had been, making love in the hollow years ago, and she felt sad for Hrefna's fate.

Katla's mother was sitting with two maids by the fire-pit when Katla entered the kitchen. Runa was holding the wrapped infant. The other, Lauga, had given birth recently. Katla said to her, "Please let this baby suck some of your milk."

Lauga said, "Why me? The boy could be ill."

"He looks healthy to me."

Lauga took the boy reluctantly and let him suck.

Katla asked her mother to talk to her in private.

When they were seated in the sitting room, Oddlaug asked, "Where does the dark baby come from?"

"Helgi saved it from death and brought it here."

Oddlaug was angry. "Why didn't he take it home to Hofdi?"

"Helgi's life is in danger." Katla cried, her head on her mother's shoulder, and told her of Helgi killing the men and of

Hrefna having the baby.

Oddlaug lifted Katla's chin, looked into her eyes and said, "Katla, you must sever all ties with Helgi. He's a sinner who will only bring you sorrow."

"Helgi has a good heart and he will be forgiven," Katla said, and looked down.

"He is too impetuous to wield a sword. What disastrous fate you have chosen for yourself, my beloved daughter."

"Dear mother, can we hide the baby boy here?"

"Not for long. But while he's here, let's keep his identity a secret. Hrefna's unbridled ways made her unpopular at Holl."

"What happened to her fiancé, Thórmundur?"

"Your father made him attempt to cross the Hvítá river pulling a draught horse during a flood. He drowned."

"How sad that Hrefna lost the man she loved. I could not go on living if I lost Helgi."

"Women who live for the love of one man are inviting disaster. Better to love Jesus Christ. He never deceives."

"What shall we do with Hrefna's son?"

"My dear Katla, you received him. You must find him a home."

"I promise I will, but you must allow him to stay here until he's well enough to travel."

Oddlaug sighed and said, "You take care of him then."

Rainstorms pounded on Holl for days. Katla stayed inside and attended to the infant who never cried in her presence. He slept by her side and she cooed to him, tickled him and kissed him on the belly. The glint in his eyes reminded her of Hrefna. The members of the household were not as bewitched by the boy and called him Swarthy. The nickname angered Katla. She named him Eilífur and told the maids to call him by his name.

Katla wondered if Eilífur could have a positive effect on her father. She took the boy to Halldór's bedside and told her father that someone had "left" the boy, but not who his parents were. She sat with the boy by Halldór's bedside and sang. Eilífur babbled as if he also wanted to sing. Halldór laughed when "the orphan" punched the air in time to the melody.

"He'll be a strong fighter and a hero," Halldór said.

"I hope he won't kill anyone with his fists."

"The boy could be useful as a guard, but a brown-eyed bastard can never buy land."

"A guard could die for his master."

"To sacrifice your life for a chief is an honour."

"A dead servant is soon forgotten. A man of God brings peace."

"Priests are beggars, living off other men's labour."

"They bring us messages of kindness and peace from God."

"They are worse than vagabonds. At least the tattlers bring news of the district, but priests bring invented tales of foreigners who don't concern us."

As if to object, Eilífur started crying loudly.

"The boy crows like a cock, ready to put up a fight. He's no dupe or priest." Halldór laughed until his belly shook.

Katla stood up and walked away with Eilífur. She did not want him to be influenced by Halldór's heathen opinions.

One evening, a week after Eilífur arrived at Holl, Runa whispered to Katla that Helgi was waiting for her by the cowshed.

Katla felt a stab of pain when she saw how thin and forlorn Helgi looked. They sat down on a rock behind the shed, but Helgi held on tight to Sleipnir's reins.

He kissed Katla on the cheek and stroked her hair as if he were caressing a young child. She embraced him.

"Dear Katla, please forgive me for abandoning you when all I desire is to love you and take you for my wife."

"I know."

He cried. "Now I have to leave the district to protect my father's reputation and safety."

"You were only protecting Hrefna's honour."

"Hrefna's honour! Arngeir humiliated me."

"How?"

Helgi's eyes flashed with anger. "Hrefna was my property

and he took advantage of her without my approval. Much worse, he told men that I had defiled you." His eyes softened when he looked at her. "My dear Katla, you're so innocent."

"How Hrefna must have suffered."

"Hrefna! She trapped me by insisting I take Arngeir's son."

Katla was surprised to hear how callous he was towards Hrefna and said, "You could have made her pregnant yourself."

"Perhaps, but men trust concubines to be careful."

"In what way?"

Helgi patted her on her head. "It's improper to discuss such matters with a noble virgin."

"Poor Hrefna, losing the man she loved. Her tenderness drowned with her sweetheart."

"It pains me to see you so distraught." He kissed her on the forehead.

"I fear losing you like Hrefna lost her beloved," Katla said.

"Hrefna is a free woman, but I'm a hunted man. Hermundur is Arngeir's cousin and he'll have to take sides with Arngeir's brothers at Althing, even if they are brutes. They won't care how insulting Arngeir was to me. How he talked about you. They'll be looking to kill me before the next Althing."

"You must go into hiding until your case is decided at Althing."

"Winter is coming and I doubt if anyone is willing to offer me shelter."

He gave Katla silver coins and rode away into the foggy darkness.

Every night when Eilífur was asleep she shed tears while praying for Helgi's safety.

One day, Arngeir's cousin visited Halldór and told him of Helgi's killings and of Hrefna being the mother of the black-haired boy. Halldór cursed Helgi so loudly that every person outside and indoors at Holl heard it. Katla winced. When the man left, Halldór called Katla to come to him and said, "The bloody butcher has the nerve to prowl my property at night like a thief."

"Helgi was punishing Arngeir for spreading slander about me, your daughter."

"You're still fooled by his gibberish. He throws a bastard boy in your lap without a second thought."

Katla enraged her father even more by defending Helgi. She said, "I'll find the boy a home."

"Children like him should be drowned."

This angered Katla and she said, "If your concubine had a child, would you drown it?"

"How cocky you've become. If Helgi had a grain of decency, he would take the boy himself."

Propelled by his anger and assisted by four labourers, Halldór managed to stand up. He told all the members of the household that Helgi or any bastard children were banned from entering his property. He would fire anyone who went behind his back.

~~~

Hrefna, who was probably now recovering at Hvammur with her mother Finnbjorg, must be longing for her infant. Or so Katla thought. Therefore, she saw it as her duty to return Eilífur to his mother.

The next morning, she asked the nurse maid to feed the boy for the last time and to prepare him for the journey. Halldór approved of her trip, and ordered Aevar and his assistant to escort her.

Eilífur was tied to Katla's chest and remained calm on their journey while she hummed songs. When they passed Hofdi, the farmhouse was invisible because of fog. She prayed Helgi was safe wherever he was.

The Thverá river was much calmer than the last time she crossed it, and their trip went smoothly.

When they arrived at Hvammur, Katla asked Aevar to take care of Eilífur while she talked to her sister.

Thórdís, Finnbjorg and Hrefna were nowhere to be found. In the kitchen Katla met a maid who told her that Thórdís and

Finnbjorg had gone on horseback up the hill along the ravine.

"Where is Hrefna, Finnbjorg's daughter?"

The woman looked down and stammered, "She's not here." Then she scurried away.

Something strange was going on.

Katla walked up the hill along the ravine. The creek cascaded down into the valley with a soothing sound.

She spotted two men ahead who held the reins of several saddled horses. She walked up to them, but they did not notice her as they were staring away to the east, as if they were expecting someone.

"Where can I find my sister, Thórdís?" Katla said.

The men turned around with surprised looks. One man pointed hesitantly to the east. "She's down in the hollow."

Katla walked to the edge of the hollow, where Thórdís, Finnbjorg and several other women stood by a heathen temple built of piles of rock. The women wore hooded black cloaks. Katla did not want to interrupt their ceremony, as they might be concocting sorcery. She sat down and watched them.

A large hole had been dug in the ground and a motionless woman, dressed in a white frock, lay at the hole's edge. Katla gasped. The woman in white was a corpse. Hrefna's corpse. Did she die after giving birth? Helgi said Hrefna wanted to rest by the road before heading to Hvammur. Did those men fail to show her mercy?

Katla sat still, and with tears in her eyes she watched Finnbjorg arrange Hrefna's hair. Thórdís stroked Hrefna's frock until it was smooth.

Two women lowered Hrefna's body into the grave. Another woman held a steaming bowl and moved it back and forth while she chanted a strange poem. Thórdís and Finnbjorg tossed some items into the grave. Each woman said something while she threw dirt into the grave until Hrefna was covered. Then they covered the grave with rocks.

Katla was too upset to linger. She stood up and ran down the hill. When she approached the farmhouse, she heard Eilífur's distressful cries. He calmed down as soon as she took him into her arms. Out of her satchel she fished a feather she had wrapped with linen and dipped into butter and milk before she left. Eilífur sucked eagerly on the butter blend.

What would happen to the boy now that both his mother and father were dead?

Within moments, Finnbjorg arrived, walked straight to her grandson Eilífur, and stared into his steady eyes, which Katla could now see resembled Finnbjorg's eyes.

Finnbjorg reached out for her grandson and took him into her arms. "Welcome, Eilífur the visionary."

"How did you know his name?" Katla asked.

Finnbjorg smiled. "The wind whispered it in my ear."

"I regret that Eilífur will not be able to enjoy his mother's care," Katla said.

"Hrefna did not know he was our kin." Finnbjorg rocked Eilífur, and he did not let his eyes wander from his grandmother's face. "Men took advantage of Hrefna because she was sensual." Finnbjorg looked at Katla. "You're also a passionate woman and you should be cautious around men. Men covet beauty, wealth and power." Finnbjorg walked off with Eilífur.

Thórdís arrived and Katla asked her, "What happened to Hrefna?"

"She walked all the way here alone."

"Were there no men on the road who could help her?"

Thórdís sneered. "One tried to hit her and accused her of being the cause of Arngeir's death. Another said she was a murderer because the child was nowhere in sight."

"How vicious men can be." Katla wanted to say that Christian men were more merciful, but did not.

As if Thórdís had read her mind, she said, "One of them was a priest."

"A priest!"

"Why be so surprised? Was it not a priest who could not constrain his lust in front of you?"

"But he is forgiven."

"Nonsense. Men use women as they please then pitch them

to the wolves."

"In spite of their brutality, you believe in the heathen gods."

"I don't idolise any god or man. I believe in nature. It's as far-fetched for men to think they can control women as it is to control nature itself. We are wiser because our strength comes from nature. Like the prophets Urdur, Verdandi and Skuld, we sense what was, what is and what will be. Therefore men seek our wisdom, but they are too stupid to see they can't obtain it by using force. Wisdom is a gift, as Gunnlodur showed when she gave Óðinn the skaldic mead."

"I believe in love. A man and a woman who love each other, and are allowed to marry, are as strong as nature itself."

Thórdís laughed sarcastically. "When you find a man who loves one woman so deeply he does not desire another one, let me know."

"Helgi is kind. He saved Hrefna's child."

"Don't be a fool. He was so eager to save himself, he left Hrefna for the wolves. You saved Eilífur, not Helgi."

"In spite of these calamities, no one will succeed in keeping Helgi and me apart."

"You have chosen a difficult destiny for yourself."

Katla did not accept any refreshments and bade her sister farewell.

As she rode away from Hvammur she pitied Thórdís, who did not love a man, nor trust any man. Love was the foundation of life. To let go of the hope of love was the same as inviting death to one's door.

24
Thórdís

A week after Eilífur arrived at Hvammur, Thórdís washed her straight hair, rinsed it in Finnbjorg's magic herbs, snapped a silver belt around her slim waist, draped the blue mantle from Katla over her shoulders, and secured it in front of her chest with a gold brooch.

Men would be men, driven by libido like stud horses. It irritated Thórdís, but she took advantage of the fact that powerful men accommodated the women they desired. Her quest was worth her effort.

Thórdís rode on her mare Gydja to Gilsbakki with two escorts. She was angry and let Gydja trot at a rapid pace so her anger would not diminish on the way. Helgi killed a man for taking advantage of a woman, although he had used her himself.

Katla's worst folly was to allow Helgi to dump the child on her. Before Katla brought Eilífur to Hvammur, she should have thought of what consequences were in store for Thórdís for keeping Hrefna's bastard on her premises. Thórdís was now connected to the murder of Arngeir at Steinar, although no one but Finnbjorg, and perhaps Helgi, knew in what way.

Thórdís regretted two things: having hired Hrefna as Helgi's mistress and having suggested to Helgi that Hrefna be boarded with Arngeir at Steinar. Only Finnbjorg knew Thórdís blamed herself somewhat for Hrefna's destiny. Thórdís felt better about it after she saw how fond Finnbjorg was of Eilífur. Now Thórdís had to do her best to secure the future of Hrefna's son.

From day one, Thórdís felt more connected to Finnbjorg than to her own mother. The old woman deserved her grandson to be recognised as Arngeir's son. Who could fight for Eilífur's legal rights but Thórdís? No one. Therefore she took it upon herself to be Eilífur's guardian, even though the boy was in Finnbjorg's care.

Despite Thórdís's low opinion of Helgi, she was opposed to him receiving a harsh sentence for the murder of Arngeir at

Steinar. Due to Arngeir's wicked ways, no one shed a tear over his departure, and most men felt Helgi had done the district a favour by killing him. But even though Arngeir was a villain, his kinsmen were bound to revenge his murder or seek restitution.

Thórdís sought Hermundur's support as he was steadfast, easy going and resourceful. In the past when he had observed her with admiration, she pretended not to notice. She treated him as a friend, but made sure she was never alone with him. Men did not tempt her.

When she arrived at Gilsbakki she was invited into the new longhouse. Hermundur welcomed her sincerely, but he was melancholy.

Near tears, Hermundur said, "Here sorrow reigns."

"Has your father Illugi passed away?"

"He's still alive but my brother Gunnlaugur has been slain."

"Slain? I thought he was in Norway?"

"Skáld-Hrafn and Gunnlaugur continued arguing about Helga the beautiful. They duelled in Sweden and killed each other."

"What childishness," Thórdís said, and shook her head.

"Our father is going to avenge Gunnlaugur's death," Hermundur said.

"Skáld-Hrafn is dead, so who then shall pay?"

"The decision is up to Althing."

"I understand your grief." She padded Hermundur on the arm.

Hermundur sighed. "Gunnlaugur was a daredevil."

"And Helgi Thórdarson is a hot-headed fool. His blunders are mounting up," Thórdís said.

"It's true, and now we're in a predicament. As Arngeir's cousins we must prosecute Helgi for killing Arngeir."

"The next Althing will be complicated for you," Thórdís said. "Helgi considers you his closest friend."

Hermundur's broad shoulders slumped forward. "My position is burdensome. I would rather not get involved."

"You're also related to Katla and to me. Arngeir's lies about

Katla incensed Helgi so he killed the brute."

Hermundur straightened his back and raised his voice. "Uncontrollable temper and woman-chasing ruined both Gunnlaugur and Helgi. Neither one could control their desires."

"Arngeir was guilty of lewdness and slander."

Hermundur looked her in the eyes and said, "I cannot help but admire your loyalty. At your request, I promise to talk on behalf of Helgi at Althing."

"Thank you for your loyalty. Another matter needs to be resolved. Hrefna and Arngeir's son is now dwelling with his grandmother under my roof."

"Men say the boy is the bastard son of a concubine."

Thórdís felt her anger flare up but she tried to speak calmly. "Arngeir announced he was the father of the child in front of many witnesses."

"Then I shall discuss the matter with Arngeir's brothers, but I doubt they will accept the boy as their nephew."

"The boy has the right to inherit his father's assets. Neither Hrefna nor the boy are responsible for Arngeir's death."

Hermundur gave her a determined look. "Your beauty is legendary, and you're one of the most eligible women in Borgarfjordur. Why don't you take a husband?"

"I have not met an unmarried man whom I consider my equal," she said, and smiled.

He looked the other way. "Then you're not meeting the right men. Why don't you ride with me to Althing so you can appraise eligible men yourself?"

Thórdís had to be careful. "Skáld-Helgi's matter will be argued there, and I would rather not be in the thick of it."

"I expect fewer controversies next summer."

"Then I might go." She stood up.

Before she left, Thórdís went to see Illugi the Black to give him her condolences. The stern landowner was grief-stricken, consoling himself with vengeful thoughts, but he was obliged to wait until the next Althing to prosecute Hrafn's father for Gunnlaugur's death. A few years back he would have killed Hrafn. The prospect of remuneration did not console Illugi any more than watching crows gorge on a dead whale.

Thórdís bade him farewell, walked to the farmyard, took Gydja's reins and said to Hermundur, "Gunnlaugur was overindulged."

"Possibly," Hermundur said.

"Heroism and wealth mattered more to him than keeping the peace."

"Too many men are afflicted with such delusion," Hermundur said.

"You are the exception." She stepped on a rock and mounted her horse.

"You know Eilífur's claim is difficult to pursue," Hermundur said.

"But it is a just claim," Thórdís said, and rode home.

Hrefna deserved better than for her son to be left without his father's identity and his assets.

25
Katla

Katla missed Eilífur as if she had lost her own child. She had taken care of the infant from the time Helgi brought him to Holl. She sang for him, stared into his gleaming eyes, and wished she could bring him up as her own child. But because of Halldór, Eilífur was better off with his grandmother.

Autumn came and freezing sleet fell to the ground for days on end. Katla stayed inside.

Halldór's ill-temper increased and Katla avoided his presence. One day he summoned Katla to his bed and said, "Helgi has no supporters in Borgarfjordur and he shall never set foot on my land. He has disgraced his own father and put him in an impossible position. Without doubt, Helgi will be found guilty for the murders and sentenced to exile next summer. I don't intend to anger Arngeir's brothers by allowing you to stay under my roof. You shall return to Saudafell as soon as the weather permits."

Katla looked into her father's grey eyes and said, "God will punish you for holding distant relatives in higher esteem than your own daughter." She walked out.

Even though Katla would miss her mother, she welcomed returning to Saudafell. Gossip about Helgi and her did not seem to bother Gróa and Garpur. At Saudafell she could gather supplies, sell her handiwork and earn enough money to purchase a farm for Helgi and herself.

Before she left, she sewed satchels for her gold and most precious jewellery and hid them under her clothes, next to her skin. She arranged linen, cloaks, capes and larger jewellery in her trunk.

A couple of days later the sun came out. Katla, Aevar, Dagur and two other men set out for Saudafell. As before, her trunk was tied to a sled pulled by two draught horses. The sled glided over the frozen ground and their trip seemed quicker than before.

When they ascended the mountain pass below Baula, rapid hoofbeats caught their attention. It was Helgi on Sleipnir. When her escorts saw him, they lifted their swords.

She called to Aevar and Dagur, "Please drop the swords. Helgi will not harm me. I'll pay you well for keeping his visit a secret."

They lowered the swords but did not return them to their sheaths.

Katla and Helgi dismounted, walked to a hollow and sat down where they were hidden from the road. They kissed and embraced. Katla was aroused so she kissed Helgi with fervour and wanted to lie down with him.

Between gasps she said "I love you" several times.

He kissed her all over her face and said, "Men are vulgar and meddlesome. My honour does not matter to them. I am so angry about the false stories they spread about you, the purest of all maidens." He punched the air with his fist.

Katla stroked the dark locks from his forehead. "Be careful, my love."

"Those men will pay for the slander."

"I cannot bear the thought that your life is in danger," Katla said.

"I have to ride away so you'll not be found guilty of collaborating with me."

"I'll give you money so you can leave the country." She loosened her mantle. "I have it here."

He took her hand. "I have enough. I fear we can never wed."

"Of course we will. Don't give up hope. All you need is to receive forgiveness from the king and the bishop."

"With my luck, I'll need forgiveness from the Pope himself."

She smiled. "With the Pope's blessing, you would be a very free man."

"You're courageous and far-sighted although your nose is pretty short." He kissed the tip of her nose.

They discussed where he should go and agreed he should

avoid all roads and head north, where he could board a ship without being recognised.

Helgi embraced her again. "Never forget that you're the only woman I want to be with."

Katla smiled. "I've been conquered by your love and I shall never grieve for another man but you, whether you're alive or away."

"I'll always remember your words, your smile and your courage."

In the distance a group of horsemen approached. Helgi jumped on his horse and rode up the valley. Katla walked to her horse crying and prayed to God and Jesus to show Helgi mercy.

26
Helgi

Helgi headed north-west along a slippery hillside.

Where could he go? Even though he carried enough silver coins to pay for food and lodging, no one would house a man who killed without considering the consequences. He should have restrained himself, left Steinar and prosecuted Arngeir for defamation, as civilised men did now. In a fit of rage he had squandered the honour Earl Eirikur had bestowed upon him, and dishonoured his father.

Arngeir's brothers would kill Helgi as soon as they could. Even though he owned a bow, arrows and the sword Earl Eirikur had given him, he could never fend off several men by himself.

Famished and exhausted, he turned up the path to Kvennabrekka, hoping the old woman who lived there and enjoyed his stories could house him.

A big sheep dog guarded the front door and barked when Helgi dismounted. The dog sniffed him and wagged his tail while Helgi petted him. A plump young woman with braided chestnut hair opened the door and smiled. He asked for Thórgerdur.

The youngster examined his cape, his sword and his face with keen interest and said, "Thórgerdur is old now and confined to her bed."

"That is indeed sad news. But do you still offer lodging?"

"It depends. Most men stay at Saudafell as they have entertainment. But I will ask Thórgerdur."

The young woman showed him to Thórgerdur, who smiled, reached out her frail hand and said, "The young poet has returned."

Helgi shook her hand.

"He wants to spend the night," the girl said.

"He's welcome here, and he is to pay by telling me stories from foreign lands. Give him a meal first."

After Helgi had eaten, Thórgerdur introduced him as "the poet" to her nephew who now ran the farm. He and the girl sat down and other people entered. Helgi forgot his own troubles as he told stories of the earl, his court and the exotic slave girls. He skipped the part where he fondled them, an activity he was now ashamed of. Thórgerdur laughed until she coughed when Helgi told of poets competing to compose intricate poems no one understood but the poets themselves.

After Thórgerdur fell asleep, he was led to a bed in the corner. He lay there thinking about his grandfather Einar, wishing he were alive so he could give him good advice.

The next morning, Helgi woke before daylight from a dream where his grandfather Einar had said: "Seek advice from a wise man, without delay." Then his grandfather took the reins of Sleipnir and led him up the trail to the farm Tunga in Saelingsdalur valley.

Helgi got up, dressed, saddled Sleipnir, mounted him and rode north towards Saelingsdalur. Did he still have relatives at Tunga? His grand uncle, Ósvífur, had moved to Laugar at Snaefellsnes with his beautiful daughter Gudrun. Snorri was now the chieftain of the district and lived at Laugar.

It occurred to Helgi that his grandfather wanted him to seek advice from chief Snorri himself. Snorri was regarded as one of the wisest men in Iceland, loyal to his friends but vicious to his enemies. As Illugi the Black from Gilsbakki and Snorri were sworn enemies, Helgi was unsure whether Snorri would welcome him.

Helgi rested Sleipnir twice on his way. He passed the Hvammsfjordur shore, not far from where he had met Narfi, the old fisherman. Then, Helgi was on his way to seek support from his grandfather, but ended up grieving his loss instead. Now, he was seeking support again. This time his errand was even more crucial.

Saelingsdalur valley looked glorious in the bright sunshine. When Helgi approached Tunga, two men came riding towards him. They introduced themselves as Snorri's guards. Helgi told them he was the grandson of Einar Helgason the Bowltinkle. The guards took him to the new farmhouse, where Helgi waited while one of them entered the house. He returned quickly and invited Helgi to enter. The guards kept his sword, bow and arrows.

Snorri sat in the seat of honour. He was a man of average height, with blond hair and a red beard. They exchanged questioning looks. Snorri grinned and said, "Why does a man from Borgarfjordur visit me?"

"I dreamed I should seek advice from you."

Helgi told Snorri of the dream.

"Your grandfather and his brother Ósvífur were honourable men. But why don't you seek advice from Illugi or Hermundur?"

"I sought their advice in the past, but failed to heed it, as I should have."

"Why should I give you advice if you won't heed it?"

"I consider your counsel equal to my grandfather Einar's, and I shall heed it."

"You have created more conflict in your district than I've done, and that's no small feat." Snorri sniggered. "Many men would consider it just to kill you."

"This matter will be decided upon at Althing next summer," Helgi said.

"Your killings are difficult to justify and therefore I doubt the decision will be in your favour. You seem like a decent fellow, but short of friends."

"You're a clever man of the law. What shall I do?"

"I have enemies in every district, and I would rather not add enemies without good reason. I shall not interfere when your case is discussed at Althing. But I will promise you one thing. I will not speak against you. Neither shall I speak in support of your enemies."

"I understand. What do you think I should do?"

"Do you want to pay restitution to Arngeir's kinsmen?"

"Why should I? Arngeir abused a woman I trusted him with, and spread rumours about me and Thórkatla Halldórsdóttir."

"Even though he's dead, Althing can decide what fines you should pay."

"I can't go to Althing alone, without supporters."

"If you don't send a settlement offer with your kinsmen to Althing, I advise you to hide far away from Borgarfjordur until your case is decided upon." He smiled. "And far from the beauty at Saudafell."

Helgi thanked him for his good advice. Snorri offered him refreshments and he accepted. They spoke about the laws of the land and Helgi learned a great deal from Snorri. The chieftain seemed to appreciate his curiosity. When they were almost done eating, a beautiful and pregnant blonde woman walked in. Snorri introduced her as his wife, Hallfrídur. She was friendly towards Helgi and their eyes met. Snorri asked Hallfrídur to leave.

Snorri said, "All tales about you are not mere fables. I can tell you enjoy impressing women."

"I only want one woman."

"Thórkatla is loyal to you and I suggest you do not betray her with reckless dallying."

"I promise," Helgi said, remembering Snorri was a womaniser, albeit not a reckless one. "Where do you suggest I go?"

"You decide, but a man riding around wearing a red cape, carrying a sword worthy of kings, and a knight's bow is as easy a target as a lone lamb is to a fox."

"True. I shall buy drab clothes."

Snorri called a maidservant and asked her to bring a brown cloak. After she returned, Snorri gave the cape to Helgi.

When Helgi was leaving, Snorri said, "Your grandfather Einar was a brilliant poet, and a diligent man until the end of his days. A man who catches and cultivates his own food is happier than the one who covets another's bread."

Helgi thanked Snorri for the meal and good counsel.

What a fool Helgi was for not studying law, and becoming a man of the law, as his father had wanted him to be. Now he was an aimless, pathetic criminal who would soon be hungry. How could he feed himself? Where should he go? If he were to go into hiding, how could he be hired as a fisherman?

He turned south looking for Narfi, the self-sufficient old fisherman.

Helgi rode towards the seashore by Laekjarskógur. He was overcome by joy when he spotted the old man rowing his small boat as if it were a limber seal, manoeuvring between submerged reefs and rocks. The tide was high. Narfi waited until a small wave carried the boat on its wings and set it down on the sandy beach.

When Helgi came closer he noticed three small fish wriggling at the bottom of the boat. Narfi stepped out of the boat, unsteady on his feet, smiled at Helgi, and said, "Good day. Why is the poet dressed like a pauper? Are you now one of those silly Jesus followers who gave up on life?" He slapped his thigh and he laughed until he coughed.

"Good day, Narfi. In a way, I have given up everything but my life. Yet, not willingly." Helgi removed the fish from the boat and tied a string through their gills. "Where are you headed, my friend?"

"To my humble cabin," Narfi said, and pointed towards the scrub land behind them.

"I'll carry the fish, or do you want me to gut them here?"

"By the shed."

Helgi pulled the boat up the shore and tied the fish to Sleipnir's saddle. He pulled Sleipnir behind him and walked in step with Narfi until they came to a small and sturdy cabin, hidden in the bushes. A narrow brook flowed nearby, where they gutted the fish.

After they had rinsed the fish and washed themselves, they entered the tidy cabin, where a fire-pit stood at the end and two beds on either side.

Helgi said, "Can I stay with you until next summer and go fishing with you?"

"What trouble are you in, young poet?"

Helgi told him the story.

Narfi shook his head. "I don't know if I can trust a hot-tempered poet."

"I promise to control my temper."

"Your hands are too delicate to do anything worthwhile."

163

"My grandfather was a good poet and a good fisherman. I promise to learn to catch my own food. I'm good at carving."

"My wife is dead and I'm old. Why should I care if bloodthirsty brutes want to kill me for giving a poet shelter. Better to die for a reason than drown or starve to death."

Helgi embraced Narfi. "Thank you for your generosity. I shall be helpful."

He settled in with the old man, who proved to be prudent in many ways. He steered Helgi to the best fishing spots and taught him to tie a fishhook to a greased line and lower it to the bottom until a fish bit the hook. Narfi's lean arms were too weak to haul a large wriggling fish into the boat. Helgi struggled to overpower the fish until he succeeded, even though his hands burned, bled and swelled.

When they returned home they cleaned the fish and cooled their hands off in the creek. Helgi discovered that wrapping fish skin around his scratched and aching hands before he went fishing protected his hands from further pain and injury.

Narfi could sense a change in weather by inspecting the sky and sniffing the breeze. If he thought a storm was approaching he refused to go fishing, even though they were unable to row far from the shore in the small boat.

Helgi felt alive out at sea, where being vigilant of swelling waves, submerged reefs, swimming whales, and shifting wind kept his fear of vengeful men at bay.

Sometimes seals rested on reefs not far from shore. One day Helgi spotted a huge seal who had a difficult time following the other seals as they slid into the sea. Without warning Narfi, Helgi took his bow in hand and sent an arrow into the seal's head.

Narfi hit Helgi on the arm and yelled, "You still murder on impulse! You don't slaughter an old seal any more than you kill an old man."

Helgi was taken aback by Narfi's words. "He was near death."

"His name is Somi and he's been my friend since he was a baby. — When he lingers on the rocks I know it's stormy out at sea."

Even though Helgi admitted to being hasty, he felt they should get the seal, flay it and eat it. Narfi refused and said he would not eat Somi any more than he would devour his brother. They did not speak while Helgi rowed to shore.

Narfi owned one cow that gave plenty of milk. Helgi collected driftwood, made walls out of rock, built a shed for the cow and Sleipnir, and hung fish fillets out to dry.

In late autumn Narfi's neighbour, named Steinmódur, came to exchange grain for fish. Helgi introduced himself as Bardi, Narfi's cousin. Helgi's hair and beard were long and snarled. How could anyone doubt he was a seasoned fisherman and a farmhand?

Steinmódur told them the news. The main case at the next Althing was the burning of Njáll and his family. Both sides had gathered supporters from all corners of the country and big confrontations were expected. To Helgi, this meant that Njáll's fire would dominate the debate. The parliament attendees would therefore not spend much time arguing his case, and decide in favour of Arngeir's kinsmen.

"I have to go and deliver grain to Saudafell," Steinmódur said.

Helgi cheered up and said, "Can I ask you to give a message to Thórkatla Halldórsdóttir who dwells there?"

"Is she the lovesick girl who seduced the priest?"

Helgi felt his face turn red in anger. Narfi pulled on his arm and said, "Vagabonds make up stories to get food. You can't believe what they say."

"A farmer told me everything about Thórkatla and her hot-headed poet," Steinmódur said.

Helgi took a deep breath and tried to appear calm. "What farmer?"

"He lives at Midgardur in Borgarfjordur and was a friend of Arngeir at Steinar." Steinmódur stood up. "What's the message?"

"This message is for Katla's ears only. Tell her a visionary said not to expect shooting stars in the sky any time soon. The wise man said she should pray to the four brightest stars."

Steinmódur gaped at Helgi and said, "Where did the visionary come from?"

"He was a vagabond who could not make it to Saudafell."

"I'll give her the message." Steinmódur repeated the message several times, shook his head and left with the fish.

After he left, Narfi said, "If you're going to punish every slanderer in the country, you'd have to kill half of the landsmen. What use is Jesus Christ to you if you don't follow what he preaches?"

Helgi stormed out, walked down to the creek and splashed cold water on his face to cool his temper. He wanted to jump on Sleipnir, ride straight to Midgardur and kill Arngeir's friend for defamation. Then these words flashed into his mind: "Let all bitterness and wrath and anger and clamour and slander be put away from you, along with all malice."

But these scriptures failed to calm him down. Whoever wrote them did not know Helgi's predicament.

The winter came early with debilitating frost. Glacier-thick ice covered the bay. Helgi picked up bones which had washed ashore and polished them, as he had learned to do in Norway. When the sun shone he tied the bones to his shoes and slid across the ice. The exercise calmed him down, but he missed his skating mates in Norway. Narfi and he spent most days inside the hut trying to stay warm. Narfi told fishing stories and braided ropes. Helgi told stories of knights and the court while he carved arrows, knives and bowls.

In autumn, when the ice melted, Helgi was restless and wondered why he was hanging out on a remote farm with an old man rambling about fish. He was young, healthy and an astute sportsman who had many assets which kings valued highly. Why stay in Iceland where he was haunted, of no use, and could not see Katla?

27
Katla

Katla tried to find peace of mind by staying busy with sewing, weaving and singing.

The guests at Saudafell, who did not know Katla's identity, freely discussed Helgi's vicious behaviour, embellishing as they talked. Some said they had seen him at the west fjords, others up north and one out east. Wherever Helgi went, he slaughtered men for slander. Their laughter penetrated Katla's heart like a sword as she listened quietly.

On an ice-cold day in early winter she was walking outside to get fresh air when four imposing men rode up the path to Saudafell. They dismounted and talked to Garpur, sounding wrathful. Garpur was not given to angry comments unless he was provoked. He raised his voice. She could not hear what they said but they pointed towards her time and again.

Katla walked to the men and greeted them. The one in charge was Hallkell, who lived at Midgardur. He was repulsive with black greasy hair, a broad face and a lumpy nose. He claimed to be her father's friend and related to the murdered Arngeir. Garpur whispered to Katla that she was not obliged to answer their questions.

"I shall find Helgi and make him pay for the murders," Hallkell said.

"Are you so bloodthirsty that you cannot wait until the matter is discussed at Althing?" Katla said.

"We're going to keep this murderer from fleeing abroad and from hiding his assets before the case is settled."

"You're a rude troublemaker for coming here looking for Helgi. My father would disapprove of you involving me in Helgi's legal matters, or have you already discussed this with my father?"

"I have not."

"You show him and Garpur disrespect by implying that Helgi is hidden at Saudafell."

Hallkell seemed surprised at her frankness and his look became even more dour. "Helgi brags about his exploits but runs away like a scared mouse."

Even though Katla was angry, she said calmly, "A wise mouse avoids wild cats." She turned around and walked inside without bidding Hallkell and his men farewell.

Two days later, Garpur came to Katla where she stood by her loom and said a grain trader had brought her a message. She walked outside and greeted the man. His name was Steinmódur.

"You're as beautiful as they say," said Steinmódur. He smelled of fish.

She hoped the purpose of summoning her outside into the cold weather was not just to satisfy Steinmódur's curiosity. "What's the message?"

"I was asked to tell you about a visionary." He laughed. "A visionary said not to expect shooting stars in the sky any time soon. And you should pray to the four brightest stars." He scratched his head. "Maybe they were five?"

At first Katla stared at Steinmódur, not having any idea what the message meant. Then it dawned on her and she smiled. "The visionary, right. He came by last summer." She laughed so hard tears trickled from her eyes.

Steinmódur laughed also. "The message is funny."

"Who gave you this message?"

"Well, it was a young man who said the visionary asked him to give you this message."

"What was his name?"

"His name was Bardi, a relative of Narfi the fisherman. He dwells in a cabin below Laekjarskógur."

She gave him a coin, thanked him for the message and walked smiling into the guest quarters. She did not tell anyone the message.

Hope had returned to her heart.

Now she knew where Helgi was, but how could she visit him? A blinding snowstorm from the north pounded on Saudafell the next day. Ships with goods to trade would not sail into Hvammsfjordur until spring. Even then, she could not run the risk of visiting Helgi, as she would be followed, and if anyone knew of Helgi's whereabouts, it could put him in danger. She was forced to stay away from Helgi until after Althing's verdict. She prayed Helgi would stay with Narfi until then.

28
Helgi

Helgi was relieved when the ice melted on the bay and the sun stayed longer in the sky. Despite Narfi's objection, he dragged the boat to the bay and went fishing daily, except on foggy days.

Every time he went out, Narfi said, "If my boat breaks, I'll be like a bird without wings."

Sleipnir was getting fat from lack of exercise. When Helgi was about to take Sleipnir for a run, Narfi said, "You're as careless as an untamed colt. Are you looking to be killed?"

"No." Helgi sighed. "I'll wait until the men have returned from Althing."

Later in the summer, when the haymaking had peaked in the district, Narfi and Helgi discussed the best way to find out Althing's verdict on Helgi's case. Narfi offered to ride to the next farm bringing fish, and try to exchange it for meat. Helgi made a wagon from driftwood, arranged cleaned fish on it and tied the wagon to Sleipnir. The horse did not like this encumbrance one bit, but calmed down when Narfi mounted him. Helgi was surprised by the ease in with Narfi jumped on Sleipnir. He watched the confident old man on the fat horse until they disappeared on the other side of the woods.

Narfi returned late in the evening with a wagon loaded with meat. He dismounted Sleipnir without uttering a word or smiling. Helgi was eager for the news, but Narfi did not like to be rushed, so he waited. Helgi untied the wagon and led Sleipnir into the fenced area while Narfi washed off in the creek. Then he asked Helgi to sit by him. "Now I'll tell you the story from Althing. Arngeir's many friends and kinsmen said plenty of bad things about you."

"Did no one speak on my behalf?"

"Hermundur Illugason told of how Arngeir used the whore and slandered Thórkatla. He offered to pay your fine if you would not be judged an outlaw."

"He's an honourable man. Was he the only one?"

"Chieftain Snorri then spoke, and said he agreed with Hermundur in this matter."

"I did not expect his support. They're not friends by any means."

"Snorri said you were the grandson of the poet Einar Bowltinkle, whom he admired. You were young and impulsive, but a good poet, intelligent, and capable of being a lawman."

"Did men listen to him?"

"They listened, but more men wanted you to pay a penalty and be exiled."

"What was the verdict?"

"Your penalty was lowered; Hermundur said he would pay to keep peace. You're exiled for three years."

Helgi jumped up in a frenzy and howled, "Three years!"

"They say Arngeir's kinsmen are not satisfied and want revenge. They will find you here. I think you should leave." Narfi sighed. "Even though you have done a useful thing or two here."

"I'll go," Helgi said, but he had no idea where to go. How could he talk to Katla without anyone seeing him? If Arngeir's kinsmen had assembled a team of allies they would be keeping an eye on Saudafell, waiting for an opportunity to kill Helgi.

29
Katla

Katla cried and cried when Gróa told her of Helgi's verdict. "Now all the evil men in Iceland will be looking to kill him," Katla stammered.

"Let's hope he flees abroad."

"I wish I could protect him."

"If he shows up here, you must tell him to stay away from Saudafell."

Gróa was right. The next day, Hallkell from Midgardur and several men arrived at Saudafell. Garpur talked to them and Katla ignored them. When she walked up the hill, she saw them hiding by the road. In spite of her longing to see Helgi, Katla hoped he was up north or on his way to Norway, but she feared he was close to Saudafell.

Could he still be with the old fisherman?

On a sunny autumn day a vagabond told Katla that a merchant ship was moored at Hvammsfjordur near Búdardalur. Katla told Garpur she wanted to go there to buy linen and other supplies. He sent two men with her and they rode off.

Katla stopped at Laekjarskógur and asked her escorts to help her find an old fisherman named Narfi who fished in the vicinity. They had an idea where to find him, but warned her they had to rush if they were to return to Saudafell before sundown.

They followed the coastline until they came upon a rowboat on the shore. From there they followed a trail which led to a small cabin hidden in the brush. One skinny cow mooed in the yard. No hay was in sight, but the pantry hut was full of meat and dried fish.

Katla walked into the cabin. On one of the beds lay the corpse of an old man with a white face and blue lips. She sat on the opposite bed and sobbed. Overcome by grief, she lay down and the faint smell of Helgi's sweat oozed from the blanket. The odour tickled her nostrils as if it were the scent of a flower. She sat up, lifted the blanket and eyed a sturdy carving knife. It had to be Helgi's. She secured the knife in her belt.

One of Narfi's legs was crooked and swollen. He must have broken his leg.

Katla went outside, found hay, fed and patted the cow, while her companions dug a grave for Narfi in the yard, carried the corpse outside, and laid it in the grave.

She sang while the men covered the grave with dirt and rocks.

Katla's companions wanted to kill the cow, but she did not want to. She told them they would save time by not going to the merchant ship, so instead they rode slowly, pulling the weak cow behind them. Soon they spotted another cow in a field and left Narfi's cow with her.

When she arrived at Saudafell, she said to Garpur, "We found the corpse of an old man called Narfi in a cabin."

Garpur was no fool. "You told me you were going to buy goods from a merchant ship. Instead you found a corpse in a cabin. It seems to me the reason for your trip was not to buy linen but to look for Helgi. Do you realise that you endangered my good men?"

"I was foolish. Please forgive me."

"Don't do it again. I'll find out the whereabouts of Narfi's relatives. And I will tell my men to keep your involvement a secret."

"Thank you, Garpur. I do not deserve your kindness."

"You don't deserve Helgi's problems. Stay clear of him while you're here."

Where could Helgi have gone? She had to help him if she could.

On a starlit night she told Gróa she was going to eat her dinner up on the hill so she could watch the northern lights dance up close. Gróa put sausages in a sack for her, and asked her to be careful.

Before Katla climbed the hill, she put Helgi's knife in her belt. When she was near the dense brush, she lay down on the

173

moss, looked up into the sky and asked the stars to make Helgi appear. Then she sang. Before she had to return to the farm, she buried the wrapped sausages in the ground and piled rocks on top.

After seven nights of star watching she heard a whisper in the brush. "Katla, you are the loveliest maiden my eyes have ever beheld."

Her heart leaped with joy and she whispered, "Helgi." Then she crept into the brush.

Helgi lay in a mossy hollow. He was dirty, anxious and his eyes darted back and forth as if the devil were stalking him. She grabbed him, hugged him as hard as she could and whispered, "I love you, I love you."

He relaxed a little. "I'm sorry I'm so tense. Villains who want to make money by killing me are hiding everywhere." Then he told her of his mishaps.

Katla kissed his eyes. "I suffer because you have to roam the hills like a fox in hiding. You must go up north to Gasar and board a ship there."

"Then I won't see you for many years."

"Have faith in the stars. They'll guide us together again, but now you must leave Iceland." She kissed his parched lips.

"I returned to Iceland to marry you, but instead I'm an outlaw. I wish I could take you with me."

"If you abducted me, I would be a happy woman, but you would be an outlaw forever." She smiled through the tears.

"I'm a dead man without you," Helgi said while wiping her tears.

"You will live. Pray to God we'll be as one."

They embraced again. "Can we be intimate before you leave?" Katla said.

Someone called her name from down below.

"I love you too much to rush such a precious act," he whispered.

She sighed, gave him the sausages, told him where the others were hidden, handed him the carving knife, and told him of Narfi's death.

Helgi sobbed. "I failed Narfi too. But you saved him, as you are saving me."

"Get released from your sins in Norway as soon as possible," she said.

He kissed her forehead. "Promise me you'll not abandon your joy, your smile and your singing."

"I promise."

Katla rushed down the hill. With a heart full of hope, she hummed, "I love you. I love you. I love you."

The next day and every day thereafter she dressed in colourful cloaks, held a prayer in her heart, and smiled at every person and animal she met. Some people looked the other way. She suspected they avoided eye contact with her because they had heard gossip about her lovesickness. Others returned her smile and it brightened her day.

Helgi was right: joy was contagious.

30
Helgi

After Helgi left Katla above Saudafell, he crawled down the other side of the mountain to Tunguá river where Sleipnir was tied to a tree. Helgi wept all the way down. What was wrong with him? Wherever he went he left a trail of torment: a weak old man, parents who suffered in silence, and a disgraced young woman of honour. Now he was a lonely outcast, forced to forsake for three years the people he treasured the most in Iceland.

When Helgi reached Sleipnir he hugged his neck and whispered, "I'm troubled, dear Sleipnir. If I'm to become a true Christian I must learn to ask God for forgiveness."

They crossed Tunguá river and followed the canyon until they reached the Haukadalsá river, and headed up the muddy trail, hiding in hollows whenever Helgi spotted horsemen.

After six days without covering much ground, a snowstorm hit them. Sleipnir refused to go on and neighed loudly. Another horse neighed in return. Sleipnir snorted and waded through the snow in the direction of the neighing horse. The horse stood by a hut which contained hay, but Helgi saw no sign of men. What a blessing! Helgi fed both horses and slept in the hut overnight. When hunger plagued him, he took small bites of a sausage. Would the food last until he reached the north?

Next day, Helgi tied a bundle of hay to his saddle and left the rest so the tied horse could reach it. He mounted Sleipnir and rode until the trail reached the bank of a canyon. Below was the Haukadalsá river he needed to cross. But the hill down was steep. As they started to descend, hail pounded them. He dismounted, removed his sword from its sheath, wrapped the sheepskin around himself and stood by Sleipnir's side while the snow piled up all around them.

When the snowstorm abated, Helgi started to descend, with Sleipnir in tow. Soon Sleipnir slipped, pulling Helgi with him down the hill. A powerful avalanche followed, pushing them to the bottom of the canyon. Helgi gasped for breath, holding his sword up high until the snow flood ceased. In time he dug himself out.

He saw a bulge where Sleipnir lay and pulled him to his feet. But Sleipnir had hurt his foot and was limping. The saddle hung to his side. He thanked God the bundle with Katla's cape was still tied to the saddle, hugged Sleipnir's neck and wept once more. The food and money were gone, his bow and arrows lost. Beset by regret, he whispered, "Good God and Jesus Christ, I promise not to kill another man except in your name. To deserve your forgiveness I shall seek to be redeemed and go wherever you send me."

Suddenly the earth vibrated, roared and swayed in waves underneath them. Sleipnir neighed loudly. The earthquake stopped as abruptly as it had started. Shortly thereafter the mountain above them rumbled with sliding rocks.

It took Helgi and Sleipnir two days to walk down the Svínadalur valley.

Then Helgi must have fainted.

Sleipnir woke him with a neigh. Ahead he saw a group of men riding towards him as if they were surrounded by a mist. He clasped his sword and tried to stand up. Instead, he fell to his knees.

A man the size of a troll, wearing a sparkling colourful cape, called out, "Helgi, do not fear your friend Hermundur Illugason."

31
Katla

A couple of days after Helgi left, a vicious snowstorm covered the hillside above Saudafell.

Katla was standing by her loom praying Helgi was safe when Garpur told her Hermundur Illugason was waiting for her in the living quarters and wanted to speak to her in private.

Her heart pounded; she feared he brought her bad news about Helgi.

Hermundur was a gallant looking man, tall with shoulder-length wavy auburn hair. A scarlet cape was draped over his broad shoulders as if it were proud to sit there. No wonder he was one of the most influential landlords in the country.

He walked towards Katla with a curious look. His observant eyes were void of greed and scorn. "You're as beautiful as people say," he said.

"I'm honoured to meet Helgi's most esteemed friend," Katla said.

"I found it unbearable to hear of Helgi's hardships," Hermundur said. "Therefore, I made an agreement with Arngeir's kinsmen and paid Helgi's restitution.

"How generous of you."

"I set out to find him and tell him he was no longer an outlaw. When we came upon Helgi at Svínadalur, he was famished and had lost most of his belongings. Sleipnir was injured. I gave him a spear and some clothes. He begged me to give you his regards."

Katla shed tears of joy and smiled. "You're a true friend and God will reward you for your kindness."

Hermundur smiled. "Helgi is a good man, but too impetuous, as my brother Gunnlaugur was."

"Where is Helgi?"

"He wants to sail to Norway and return once his enemies have calmed down."

Katla wanted to kiss Hermundur on his cheek but held back

as he might misunderstand her friendliness. "Do you have news of my parents and Thórdís?"

"Thórdís is still unmarried."

"Do you disapprove of that?"

He looked surprised and it occurred to Katla he was fond of Thórdís. He said, "I'm concerned on your father's behalf. You and Thórdís look somewhat alike and you both want to decide for yourselves whom you marry. But you do differ in temperament and vocation."

Katla smiled. "Thórdís wants no man and I want one man."

"Your father is unable to travel and he is dispirited by not having grandchildren."

"When I marry Helgi, we'll have children."

Hermundur shook his head. "You have made life miserable for yourself."

"My father made me miserable."

"So be it. — People say you are the best seamstress in Iceland. I want to buy the most beautiful dress you have made for my wife."

Katla jumped to her feet. "You bring me honour with your request." She hurried to the sleeping quarters, opened her trunk and removed a sky-blue cloak, embroidered with gold leaves. When she returned, she said, "I want to give you the cloak for protecting Helgi and enabling him to sail to Norway."

"Thank you. Helgi has paid me himself with a gold ring Earl Eiríkur bestowed upon him. I want to pay for the beautiful cloak." He handed her a small but heavy purse.

She thanked him and when he was leaving, she said, "You're an honourable man and God will bless you for your kindness for the rest of your life."

When she was alone in the sleeping quarters she opened the purse from Hermundur. It contained a large gold coin and a weighty ring, the earl's ring Helgi had given Hermundur before going up north.

She kissed the ring and put it at the bottom of her trunk.

32
Helgi

Hermundur left two men to accompany Helgi to Gásar and loaned Helgi a horse for himself and enough coins to buy a fare to Norway, if a ship should still be sailing from Gásar this late in the year. Hermundur took Sleipnir and promised to find a place for him to heal.

Helgi was in luck. One ship was moored at Gásar and he secured a place on it. Gunnar, the ship's owner, said unrest was spreading throughout Norway, as Earl Eirikur was away in England. The earl's brother, Sveinn, now ruled over northern Norway. His reign might not last as Olafur the Rotund was about to conquer all of Norway, in the name of God.

Helgi said, "I expected a good reception in Norway due to my friendship with Earl Eirikur. Now I could be at a disadvantage."

"We'll sail to south Norway where Olafur the Rotund reigns. It's peaceful there, as far as I know," Gunnar said.

The voyage went well and they sailed along the coast of Norway until they saw King Olafur's fleet. On the shore, Olafur's courtiers approached Helgi, eyeing his gold sword grip and jewelled pommel.

"Is Sighvatur Thórdarson still King Olafur's court poet?" Helgi said.

"He is more than a poet to the king. Sighvatur often speaks on the king's behalf at public gatherings."

The courtiers escorted Helgi to Sighvatur, who greeted Helgi as a long-lost friend. Sighvatur stammered a bit when he spoke, which surprised Helgi, as Sighvatur's poems were articulate and fluid. Sighvatur promised to introduce Helgi to King Olafur once Helgi had made a Christian poem in praise of the king.

Helgi composed a poem inserting God and his will where appropriate. Sighvatur liked the poem and introduced Helgi to

King Olafur.

Olafur Haraldsson was a strongly built man of average height. His broad, pinkish face and his fluttering blue eyes exuded boundless ambition. He listened to the poem and asked Sighvatur his opinion.

"The poem is constructed with skill and it honours both you and God," Sighvatur said.

"But Helgi, you were a courtier of Earl Eirikur. He is my enemy, as is his brother Sveinn."

"Your excellency, I prefer to serve a Christian king."

"You're brave and you have justified your right to fight for Christianity against the heathen chiefs who intend to dethrone me."

"It's an honour to fight for the true religion," Helgi said. "But I am tormented by sins and anguish."

Olafur asked him to explain. Helgi was honest and the king listened.

"Only the Pope can release you from your sins."

Helgi was surprised but said, "Your advice is sound."

"All men who suffer due to evil deeds must be saved by God's grace, and God has trusted me to convert all men in Norway to the Christian faith. It's a complicated task as many landlords would rather idolise the heathen gods and fight those who oppose their vulgar ways."

"The peace of Christ is worth seeking."

"I hear you're an outstanding sportsman. You could improve your place in the eyes of God by fighting for me in the name of everlasting peace."

Helgi did not have a choice. "I consider it an honour to fight for Jesus Christ."

"You're a wise man. For your loyalty I shall finance your pilgrimage to Rome when the right time comes."

Even though Helgi did not intend to kill more men, his position at the court required him to bear weapons and follow the king's commands. He practised throwing the javelin, pitching an axe, fencing and archery. Helgi and Sighvatur became close friends and attended church together. It was Sighvatur's dream to go south on a pilgrimage to Rome, but he promised the king to postpone his trip until the king ruled all of Norway.

Earl Sveinn Hakonarson also wanted to rule all of Norway. Sveinn was at Nidaros in central Norway, and a battle between Olafur and Sveinn was imminent.

Helgi travelled with King Olafur on his ship *Visundur*. The ship's stem was made of gold in the shape of a bison's head. The king's fleet was large, but Sveinn's even larger.

When they came upon Sveinn's fleet, a brisk battle ensued. Olafur was zealous and aimed his bow so his arrows landed on target. Helgi stood by his side and sent one arrow after the other into the chests of Sveinn's warriors.

The battle was fierce, men died, others were wounded, and some ran ashore. In the end, Earl Sveinn and his soldiers fled. Helgi was relieved as he was exhausted and dismayed by the casualties.

King Olafur and his men removed valuables from every ship abandoned by Sveinn's men. The king divided the treasure and Helgi exchanged his share for gold coins. The priest blessed Helgi's heavy purse for one coin and declared the loot a blessing, as the king had doubled God's domain in Norway.

The king was resolute. His spies found out that Earl Sveinn was in Sweden. As Olafur sailed with his fleet west along Vik, he gathered support and promised all men peace would reign in all of Norway when the one true God, with the king's help, was in charge. Blessed by the priest, the fleet sailed to Lidandisness.

Helgi was not as proud as other surviving soldiers of the bloody battle. King Olafur claimed Earl Eirikur and Sveinn were heathens, but Helgi suspected they were Christian. He felt like a traitor for killing Sveinn's men.

Helgi was bewildered. Why was it a sin when Helgi killed evil men, but not when the king ordered killings? No priest had an answer to the question of what murders were justifiable in the eyes of God. Helgi would seek his answers from the Pope in Rome.

With time Helgi's respect for King Olafur diminished. The king preached Christianity but practised cruelty. Men who did not succumb to his rule or cow to priests, the king branded as heathens, and killing such men was thus justified in the name of God.

A king who only appreciated poetry about his own accomplishments and virtues was not to be trusted.

As the snow melted, Helgi was eager to leave King Olafur's court and start his long pilgrimage south towards Rome. The word reached the king's court that one of the king's sworn enemies was gathering troops in northern Norway, and another battle was imminent. Helgi was determined to find a way to go south before the king summoned his troops.

At Helgi's urging, Sighvatur joined him in a meeting with the king.

Helgi addressed the king: "I am honoured to have served you, my king. But my past sins weigh on my heart. I have prayed to God and I feel now is the time to set off on my journey to ask the Pope for forgiveness."

King Olafur responded, "I am reluctant to lose a skilled soldier and an accomplished poet. But since your purpose is inspired by God, I shall allow you to go."

Helgi bowed to the king. "Your highness, I thank you from the bottom of my heart."

"I trust you, Helgi, and I am relying on you to carry out two good deeds on the way."

"I would be honoured."

"Heinrich the Second is now the Holy Roman Emperor, and I want you to bring him a weighty message from me." The king crossed himself and continued, "And you shall deliver another message to Pope Benedict upon your arrival in Rome."

"Where would I find Emperor Heinrich?"

"He could be anywhere in the Roman empire, but he prefers to dwell in Saxony. I expect him to be close to Hildesheim. Sighvatur will prepare the two scrolls in Latin and I trust you to keep them safe. I want to make two things clear to the Emperor: I rule over Norway, and I am his ally."

"I understand. Perhaps I should travel on horseback to the Emperor and to the Pope. Thus I could deliver the messages earlier."

King Olafur laughed so his belly shook. "You are a clever man, Helgi, but I would not insult the Pope by allowing you to take a shortcut to obtain forgiveness from His Holiness. You will wear a cloak like an ordinary monk."

The next day a priest arrived with a long staff, a leather satchel, a big hat, a bottle, and a grey cloak embroidered with a cross.

Helgi wanted to make sure funds were available to him upon return from Rome, so he could head for Iceland without delay. Sighvatur agreed to store Helgi's sword, Katla's cape and half of his money.

On his pilgrimage, Helgi intended to shed his mental distress and become a free man, not subject to the whims of kings. But was freedom possible within the parameters of Christian doctrine? He doubted it. For survival, most men were destined to bend to the will of a more powerful man. The king claimed to follow God's will. Who knew for sure what God wanted? The Pope instructed priests to inform men of God's will, but when the priests were questioned, they declared God wanted men to atone for their sins and believe in Jesus Christ.

Helgi suspected the king was taking advantage of illiterate men by pretending to know God's will.

33
Katla

One evening shortly after Hermundur's visit, Katla sat in a corner of the guest quarters at Saudafell, embroidering and listening to the guests' conversation. Katla had braided her hair and wrapped a scarf around it so men would think she was married.

Three of Ósvífur's sons, Vandrádur, Áskell and Torrádur, walked in. The guests stopped talking and stared at these massive men. They headed straight for the fire-pit and warmed themselves. Some guests greeted them, others ignored them. They sat down and a maid brought them porridge. While they ate in silence, Garpur chatted about the weather and the harsh winter ahead.

Katla recalled that Helgi did not like his cousin Vandrádur, and had called him dull-witted. Katla was amused to think how Helgi would have laughed at Gróa's observation that Vandrádur preferred men to women.

But Áskell saw her, pulled Vandrádur's arm and said, "Are you Thórkatla Halldórsdóttir?"

"I am," she said.

"You look older," Vandrádur said.

"So do you," Katla said, and smiled.

"I hear you sing for the guests sometimes," Áskell said.

She knew the brothers were heathens, and said, "I sing Christian songs."

Vandrádur laughed sarcastically, but when Áskell elbowed him he quit laughing.

"Christian songs are beautiful," Áskell said, and turned to Garpur. "May Katla sing for us?"

"If she chooses," Garpur said.

Katla sang one verse. Áskell complimented her and gave her a gold coin.

She made a habit of being pleasant to people and repeated the words of Christ whenever she could. Because of her resistance to men's advances, she was called Katla Helgi-Maiden, a name derived by combining the name of the Virgin Mary and her devotion to Helgi. Her nickname did not bother her, nor did she let slander get to her. She kept her mind on her work and on accumulating valuables. The wealthiest wives in the country requested her colourful woven woollens with gold embroidery. Men ordered cloaks, dresses, capes and gowns to give to their women.

During the winter Katla taught two maids to spin and sew clothes with more precision, freeing up Katla's time to embroider cloaks, capes and belts. When the stars sparkled in the evening, she dragged a couple of sheepskins with her to the nearest hollow, lay down and talked to Freyja Star and Christ Star. Helgi Star sparkled when she sang, sending her light beams which warmed her body down below. When the Christ Star also flashed, she felt all stars approved of her touching herself while she imagined Helgi making love to her. In the end, when her body relaxed and she sighed, she dedicated her breath to Helgi. Afterwards her face was flushed and she thanked Christ for allowing the stars to illuminate the sky and her path.

Deep in her heart she hoped she would be pregnant like the pure virgin.

In the spring, when she heard of merchant ships moored at Hvammsfjordur, her heart beat faster in anticipation of hearing news of Helgi. When weather allowed, she rode down to the harbour with escorts and bought gold thread and linen. Men greeted her with respect when they eyed the royal cape she wore, which gave her a chance to ask if they knew of Helgi's whereabouts. One merchant told her Helgi was at the court of King Olafur Haraldsson and had fought with him.

A few weeks later, a merchant told her that Helgi was on a pilgrimage, walking to Rome. She was overjoyed.

On her return to Saudafell, she told Gróa and Garpur, "If Helgi is walking all the way to Rome he must be humble already."

"Or angry because he will be robbed," Garpur said, and laughed.

"It's childish to believe a starving, unarmed man with sore

feet is a virtuous man," Gróa said.

"Christ will protect him," Katla said.

"You would do better marrying a noble man here in Iceland before you're too old to have children," Garpur said.

"I shall only raise Skáld-Helgi's child."

"If Helgi returns after the Pope robs him, he'll be impoverished," Gróa said.

"His heart is never poor, and his poetic skills will flow forever like a mountain spring."

"That spring is drying up because few people understand skaldic poetry any more," Garpur said.

"He does not have to compose poems for kings. He can praise chiefs and remarkable women."

"Few men are brave enough to recite poems honouring women," Garpur said, and smirked.

"Too bad," Gróa said, and glared at Garpur. He left.

Gróa said, "If his pilgrimage goes well, Helgi will be gone for at least two years. Who knows what he'll do then? Maybe he'll become a priest. Why don't you let your father arrange for you to marry a decent man until Helgi returns?"

"I want to be an unwed virgin when Helgi arrives."

"He sleeps with whatever woman he wants," Gróa said, and threw her hands in the air.

"After he's saved and we are engaged, he'll never bed another woman."

"He's too adventurous to settle down," Gróa said, wrinkling her freckled nose.

On a midsummer day, when Katla was trading with a merchant at Hvammsfjordur, she spotted a pile of strips made of walrus hide. She asked how much he wanted for the strips.

The merchant said, "What does a beautiful woman want with rough hides?"

"What do men with rough hands do with these in Greenland?"

"They tie them together and make nets to catch fish."

"Do you know how to make such nets?"

"I do."

The merchant made a loop with one strip and slipped another one through. Katla was elated and traded one embroidered cape for all the walrus hides. In the near future, after she had bought a farm for her and Helgi, their farmhands could catch fish in those nets.

Her helpers arranged the strips with difficulty on the sled they had brought with them and tied them down with rope.

On the way back to Saudafell she decided Helgi and she should buy a farm near the sea. Then Helgi could sail and fish as he pleased. She would not expect Helgi to enjoy farming. If poetry, archery and rowing out to sea made him happy, she would see to it that others did the chores.

The workers at Saudafell made fun of her for buying the walrus hides. She laughed, but told no one what she intended to do with all those walrus strips.

34
Helgi

Helgi was ready to set off on his pilgrimage, but he was perplexed. Was the long walk necessary for him to succeed in the future? Was he more of a sinner than most Icelandic or Norwegian men? To find the answers, he went to see an old priest whom he found kneeling in front of a statue in the church.

They sat down and Helgi told him of the men he had murdered, slander, love, concubines, the earl's slave girls, battle and other hurdles he had faced in his short life, and asked, "Which of these are sins in God's eyes?"

"Whatever you do to hurt others is a sin."

"But I've done many good things. Saved a baby, made poems, given expensive gifts and fought with the king for Christianity. In spite of good deeds, bad luck has chased me like a starving polar bear."

"You lack humility."

"Humility is for women and servants."

The priest shook his bald head and crossed himself.

Helgi sighed. "How does a man obtain humility?"

"When you walk to Rome, praise Jesus Christ and God with every step you take. Contemplate Christ's suffering. Little by little, your heart will fill with sincere regret. If you kneel in front of statues of Jesus and the Virgin Mary in all the churches you visit on your way, and if you sleep on bare floors in monasteries with holy men, your heart will overflow with reverence and your actions will be infused with the spirit of Christ."

"But I risk being killed on the way, unarmed with a purse full of gold."

"Then you will die in the name of God and thereby procure rebirth. God will punish the thieves."

"King Olafur believes the Pope will release me from my sins because I have eliminated dozens of heathen men and kept them from harming others."

The priest smiled. "The king's will is one thing, and the truth of God another."

"Why can't I ride on horseback to arrive sooner in Rome?"

"Humility is not obtained in a rush."

Helgi was about to take his leave when two short monks walked in. The priest introduced them as Adam and Josef. Helgi nodded his head at them with indifference.

The priest said, "You're a lucky man, Helgi, because Adam and Josef will be your companions on your journey to Rome." He smiled cunningly. "They know Latin."

Helgi was mortified and said, "I want to walk alone."

"The king commanded that they accompany you."

"The king?" The monks were dressed in worn cloaks, their beards matted. "One would think they were paupers."

The monks looked near tears and the priest said, "As I just said, you lack humility, Helgi."

Helgi tried to ameliorate the situation. "I'll be happy to buy new cloaks for them."

"Fancy clothes attract thieves, but not God," the priest said.

"What about shoes? They can't walk barefoot on rocky roads. Even God can't demand such unnecessary suffering."

Adam and Josef looked at the priest with probing eyes.

The priest said, "Shoes are in order."

Helgi, Josef and Adam took leave of the priest and walked to a shoemaker where Helgi purchased socks and shoes with thick soles for the monks.

Adam asked Josef, "Isn't it shameful to avoid suffering?"

Josef crossed himself and said, "The apostles wore shoes, I think."

While they put the socks and shoes on, Helgi wondered if Christianity made men into nitwits.

God's will was still an enigma to Helgi. He was not prepared to trust God to keep him alive on the journey.

The following day, before he stepped out from under his covers, he tied a knife to his calf and felt more confident right away. His long cloak would cover the knife.

~ ~ ~

The three pilgrims boarded a ship which sailed from Lidandi to Aalborg in Denmark. Twenty other passengers were on board and Helgi looked forward to conversing with normal men. But when he greeted a couple of men, they ignored him and looked away.

"Why do men pretend I don't exist?" Helgi asked Adam.

Adam smiled and said calmly, "You must get used to men treating you like a pauper. They fear you are going to beg."

Helgi chuckled and called, "I'm not a beggar, only a man seeking forgiveness."

"I'll forgive you if you shut up," said a gigantic man with two swords swinging from his belt. He laughed sarcastically.

Adam pulled at Helgi's sleeve. They moved to the rear of the ship and sat there quietly.

"Danes don't like Norwegians," Adam whispered.

Haraldur the second, the brother of Knutur the Wealthy, king of England, then ruled over Denmark. Danes were suspicious of King Olafur of Norway because he was determined to drive Earl Sveinn out of Norway. When Helgi attempted to discuss the king's and the earl's struggles for power with Adam and Josef, Adam whispered, "God's servants don't concern themselves with battles between kings."

The weather was warm when the boat docked at Aalborg.

As the bishop had instructed, the pilgrims contemplated scriptures on their three-day walk from Aalborg to Viborg. Adam and Josef carried with them two well-preserved tomes in Latin. One was the Bible, the other one they called Didache. It contained the teachings of the twelve apostles.

According to the monks, man was a sinful beast. To waste money was sin; to sleep on a bed was an indulgence; to admire beautiful women was lust, and to be tempted by them was a monumental sin. Suffering seemed like the only virtue.

When they walked through a small village, an enchanting woman wearing a red scarf over her long black hair glanced at Helgi. He smiled but she looked away and flitted by. If only he had a scarlet cape draped over his shoulders and a gold sword tucked into his sheath. Then she would admire him as most women had in the past.

Josef seemed to read Helgi's thoughts. "Be not lustful, for lust leadeth unto fornication," he said, quoting the Didache.

"I thought God had created all there is? Can apostles, monks and pilgrims not admire beautiful things?"

"Only those we don't lust after."

Helgi said, "We can admire the statue of the Virgin Mary but not a live woman who looks like the Virgin Mary."

Adam laughed. "When you overcome the lust of the flesh, you'll understand the difference."

"If I don't lust after things," Helgi said, "I might as well be dead. I want to relish being alive."

The heat irritated Helgi. Why could he not shed his cloak and walk in his undergarments? The monks said it was indecent to expose bare legs. Was Jesus not bare-legged in the desert? Was it an act of humility to walk in clothes drenched in sweat?

His mood improved when it started to rain. He removed his cloak and put his knife in the bag which contained the rolled-up scrolls for the emperor and the Pope. It rained all day and his soaked undergarments stuck to his body.

"You don't look like a pilgrim," Josef said.

"When Christ walked into the water, was he soaking wet or naked?"

"It's a good question," Josef said. He pondered everything.

Adam must have memorised every word written in the Bible and in the Didache. While the two monks trudged along the trail, in heavily soaked clothes, they discussed how Jesus must have dressed.

Their socks soon wore out. Large blisters and sores formed on their feet.

"I suspect we were shielding ourselves from suffering by wearing socks and shoes," Josef said. He removed his socks and shoes and put them in his satchel.

"Comfort is as fleeting as felicity," Adam said, and removed his shoes.

While Helgi removed his shoes, he pondered whether fleeting felicity was not superior to ceaseless misery.

On the way to Viborg they rested only when they were exhausted and slept under the naked sky. After three days they arrived in Viborg, wet and hungry. Viborg was an episcopal seat, where two churches were under construction. They located several monks with haggard faces, kneeling by a hut where they said a monastery would soon be erected.

"When are they building it? Tomorrow?" Helgi snapped.

The monks burst out with laughter and one said, "Maybe, if you stay and help us."

The monks gave the pilgrims a loaf of bread and offered them sleeping places on the dirt floor inside the hut. Helgi slept well and woke up hungry. According to the bishop's guidelines, they should beg rather than waste any of the money intended for the Pope. Helgi hated begging. Even though Adam pointed out that it took humility to beg, he bought bread before they resumed their journey.

The walk from Viborg to Ribe took another three days. They ate all the bread and slept outside as it was warm.

When they arrived in Ribe, one of the oldest towns in Denmark, a mass was about to begin in the newly renovated church. Josef and Adam were eager to attend it. Helgi would rather have lingered at the market square but he relented and went to mass.

The grandeur inside the church was blinding. Everything shone like the sun. Gold goblets, statues, chalices, candlesticks, incense holders and crosses. Many crosses. A colourful statue with the face of the Virgin Mary stood next to the lectern, and a large wooden cross hung above the altar. The bishop's gown was embroidered with gold.

The church was full of commoners who could not understand the Latin mass. Many walked in a procession up to the altar afterwards and told the bishop their sins, received forgiveness and paid with gifts. The bishop's face looked sour, the sides of his mouth turned downward. The frowning bishop was a descendant of emperors famous for their brutality. He

193

commanded the young monks in his monastery to labour like slaves to please Jesus. He gathered gold in the name of the church, but kept it for himself.

Helgi could not fake reverence for the bishop and his church. He hurried out.

Their next destination was Hedeby, a trading town in Jutland ruled by Vikings and heathen men.

While they were in Ribe, Helgi saw a beautiful woman with a scarf draped over her voluminous blonde hair. She looked like Katla, and the young woman's beauty captivated him. She was in the company of a gallant man and two children. Could Helgi and Katla be so content in the future? The thought infused Helgi with joy and he walked at a brisker pace in the direction of Hedeby. The monks scurried to keep up with him.

Helgi heard birds singing in the forest and wondered what prompted them to start singing. The sound reminded him of Katla and he called to his companions, "Do you hear the birds singing?"

Adam replied, "God has entertained us with singing birds all the way."

"Right," Helgi said, not wanting to confess that his mental and physical distress had kept him from hearing the tweeting birds. He resolved to quit brooding over his many misfortunes.

At nightfall they stopped by a lake and washed their feet. The buzzing sound of bees lulled them to sleep. When Helgi and the monks woke up, they were covered in bites and itched all over. They cooled off in the lake, but Adam's face blew up. He struggled to breathe and collapsed to the ground shortly after they resumed their journey.

"You go on without me," Adam moaned.

"Adam, I cherish you more than myself," Josef said, "and I shall not take one step without you." He sat down where Adam lay.

Helgi sighed. How could he leave the monks behind after promising the king and the bishop he would look out for them on the way? "I shall carry you on my back like Jesus carried the cross."

Josef stood up, cried and hugged Helgi.

Helgi lifted Adam and draped his limp body over his shoulders, thankful Adam was no heavier than a lamb.

After walking half a day, Helgi was exhausted, had backache and was irritated because now when Adam was awake he wriggled constantly. "Why can't you stay still?" Helgi said.

"Please forgive me, I'm so itchy," Adam said.

They rested by the road in a little village while Adam continued to scratch himself.

A woman with black hair and wearing a long robe stopped, looked at Adam and said, "You need an onion to heal this."

Helgi cheered up and asked where he could find an onion. She said to wait, returned with half an onion, and told Adam to rub it all over himself. Adam hid behind a wall, disrobed and did as the woman said. When Helgi saw Adam was no longer itching, he gave the woman a gold coin and kissed her on the cheek.

The woman smiled and said, "You're a man of amours. It shall torment you until you die, and you'll be long-lived."

The walk to Hedeby took another four days. Adam stank of onion and Helgi avoided being close to him.

The monks were eager to visit the oldest church in Denmark, located in Hedeby, a river town where ships crossing from the Atlantic Ocean to the Baltic Sea sometimes anchored. The church turned out to be little more than a paltry hut. By contrast, a lively market was the town's centre of activity. Helgi would not have minded lingering there for a bit, but the aggressive salesmen scared Adam and Josef, who declared that the devil's greed controlled Hedeby.

They left in a hurry.

Helgi was annoyed and walked at a rapid pace, but slowed down when overcome by hunger and aching feet. He sat down and yelled to the sky, "Why punish me – an ordinary man?"

Adam said, "God is not punishing you. He has given you an opportunity."

"How is suffering an opportunity?"

195

"Whatever happens to you is a blessing, and an opportunity for you to improve. Love your sores for they shall be healed. Look." He pointed. "God has provided you with a cold creek to restore your burning feet." Adam reached out his gentle hand and Helgi took it. As they walked to the creek, Helgi's mind filled with gratitude to God for relieving his suffering, at least for now.

~~~

The smell of fish greeted Helgi, Josef and Adam in Flensborg. They headed to the harbour and watched as boats piled with herring drifted on the calm sea into the harbour. Vigorous men quickly piled the fish into large barrels. Others heaved the barrels onto carts.

They could not find a church in Flensborg. As they left town for Hildesheim, a thick cloud of flies swarmed around them. They attempted to wash the smell of fish off their clothes in a creek but to little avail. Helgi prayed for rain. He never felt a drop.

They walked and walked and Helgi thought and thought, while his feet and body burned and ached. To take his mind off the pain, Helgi contemplated what to do when he arrived in Iceland. The next night chief Snorri appeared in his dream and told him, "You will be a prudent lawman." In the morning he woke up infused with energy because he liked Snorri's prediction.

The next night he dreamed that Katla came to him, healed the sores on his feet and said, "This journey is your gift to God. You're surrendering your will to Jesus Christ. Eat, sleep and behave as he did." She smiled until her dimples became canyons of joy, her eyes sparkled like the stars in the sky, and her laughter echoed like birdsong in spring.

For seven days Helgi and the monks walked to Hildesheim, singing most of the way.

Once in Hildesheim they headed for the famous cathedral. Before entering the church, Adam and Joseph knelt in front of a rose bush and prayed in Latin.

"Why don't you wait to pray inside the church as usual?" Helgi said.

Josef stood up and said, "This bush is famous and holy."

Adam said, "King Ludvik was hunting in the woods when he lost his pendant with a relic of the Blessed Virgin Mary. His attendants found the pendant hanging on this rose bush and no one had enough strength to remove it. Later, Ludvik had this chapel built by the rosebush and dedicated it to the Virgin Mary."

The monks considered relics to be proof of Christ's existence. But Helgi saw no reason to worship anything but Katla. No saint, pope, bush or a cross radiated love the way she did.

Bernward, abbot and bishop of Hildesheim, was supervising the construction of an enormous church in honour of St Michael and Bernward wanted to be buried there. The abbot knew his way around science, construction and mathematics. He painted walls himself and made intricate silver and gold objects. He demanded efficiency of his workers and slaves. Dozens of men transported rocks and laid bricks wherever Helgi looked.

The abbot had also built a monastery where Helgi and his monks slept on a cool floor.

Helgi was eager to unload the scroll from King Olafur to Emperor Heinrich the Second. To his dismay, the emperor was not in Hildesheim but in Bamberg. Adam and Josef insisted on heading to Fulda first because eminent monks gathered there. Helgi relented.

The people they met on their way to Fulda differed from those they had passed on the way to Hildesheim. They were poor, wore tattered clothing, begged and some were too ill to walk, but they wailed prayers to God for mercy.

The gigantic church in Fulda and its precious objects did not enchant Helgi as much as the well-stocked library. Every activity in Fulda seemed to be organised, and focused on education and enlightenment. Outside and inside dozens of monks taught men of all ages reading, writing, science and arts. Inside artists painted

197

and outside sculptors chiselled large rocks into shapes. How Helgi would enjoy staying here and studying. He sighed. The Pope waited in Rome and Katla in Iceland.

The monks of Fulda were obliged to pray for anyone who wanted them to. The names of those seeking prayers were written on large hides and kept inside the monastery. Over one hundred monks knelt there, each with his own stack of names, and prayed for one after the other. Helgi, Adam and Josef added their names to a hide.

God had to be equipped with exceptional hearing to decipher all the monks' prayers.

On their walk to Bamberg, Adam told Helgi that Emperor Heinrich had established a diocese and a cathedral in Bamberg. After ten days they arrived at Bamberg, where Adam spotted a Norwegian monk who understood the language spoken in town. He told them Emperor Heinrich was busy preparing for a crusade to Poland to convert the country's population to Christianity. And to conquer it, Helgi thought.

The Norwegian monk introduced them to a knight of the emperor's court who promised to give the emperor the scroll from King Olafur.

When the knight returned, he said the emperor did not have time to meet with Helgi. He handed Helgi a scroll with the emperor's insignia which should guarantee Helgi's fair treatment wherever he travelled within the Roman Empire. According to the Norwegian, the emperor disliked going south of the Alps because the heat made him miserable. The emperor counted on his friend Pope Benedict the Eighth to ensure peace reigned in the Italian districts.

On their way south, a Danish monk told them that the Pope's army was trying to drive Muslim armies out of Italian territories.

"What sort of men are in the Pope's army?" Helgi asked.

"Volunteers and foreign soldiers. He favours the Christian Normans from France, and pays them for fighting the Muslims in the name of Christ."

"Why does the Pope have an army? Is it not the emperor's duty to fight the Muslims?"

"The emperor is busy preparing to invade Poland, leaving the Pope to protect his territories himself."

What was Helgi doing trudging along like a pauper with gullible fools? Instead of crawling to the Pope, begging him for forgiveness and mercy, he could be a soldier, the Pope's soldier, proud and armed. He should find the Christian Norsemen who were fighting for the Pope.

The thought of riding on a horse reduced the pain in Helgi's feet. He walked to Ulm like the devil was chasing him. The walk took six days. Each day the heat increased and they cooled off by soaking in rivers on the way. Still, the odour emanating from their cloaks was repulsive to all but swarms of flies.

Ulm contained fewer churches than castles. Dark- or light-skinned people strolled about. Merchants and buyers argued on the town square about the price to pay for jewellery, weapons and food items.

Helgi was not shopping, but looking for a man of Norse descent. He was overjoyed when he noticed a blond, armed man, and spoke to him in Norse.

"I didn't recognise you, Skáld-Helgi, with your immense beard and your soiled pathetic cloak," the Norseman said, grinning.

"Who are you?"

"Axel. — I was at Earl Eirikur's court, but I'm sure you don't remember me. You preferred to roam the hills making up poems about an Icelandic damsel than play with your companions." He laughed. "And you, the man who got to enjoy the earl's harem, are now nothing but a plain monk."

Helgi disliked Axel's comment but kept his temper under control. "I'm on a pilgrimage to Rome."

"You must have sinned a lot to take such a demeaning trip."

"Where are you going, so well armed?" Helgi asked.

"Twenty soldiers and I were hired to protect

Constantinople. The midgets who live there don't know how to fight."

"Do you know who's fighting for the Pope?"

"They come from Normandy where they have settled," Axel said.

"How are they doing?"

"I see the glimmer in your eyes, Helgi." Axel smiled. "Would you like to fight with them for your pope?"

"Can I? While on a pilgrimage?" Helgi looked up to the sky.

"Well, if you change your mind, try finding them at the harbour in Genoa or in Pisa – if they can bypass the Muslims."

"I thought those towns were part of the Roman Empire."

"Supposedly, but the chiefs in those territories have a hard time fending off the Muslims because they control the nearby islands. But the Pope is busy assembling an army to fight the Greeks – who don't yield to his rule, although they are supposed to be Christian."

"Is there no peace around the Pope then?" Helgi asked.

"Popes must fight for their cause, not unlike other power-hungry men." Axel looked amused. "Independent soldiers like me can make a bundle from these wars." He showed Helgi a long and sharp knife, decorated with jewels. "Whoever tries to steal this from me will lose a hand – or his head."

After Axel left, Helgi wandered around the square looking at spices, honey, fruit and grains. He stopped by a merchant who sold bows, iron swords and knives like Axel owned.

Adam walked up to Helgi while he was examining a bow. "Are you going to buy a weapon?"

"A bow could come in handy for killing a deer," Helgi lied.

"Jesus did not kill animals to eat," Adam said.

"Others killed for him," Helgi said.

"We should beg for our food. It teaches us humility."

Helgi put the bow down. "Would it hurt to change course and head for Genoa?"

"It's risky. I heard men are fighting there."

"The poor Pope. How can he protect the Christian faith if heathen men, Muslims and Greeks are closing in on him?" Helgi sighed in defeat and glanced at Adam from the corner of his eye.

"Isn't it the emperor's business?" Adam said.

"The emperor is up in the far north."

"He will protect the Pope and the churches with his army."

"It appears that the Pope's army consists of begging monks." Helgi smirked, eyed the bow with regret, turned around and they trudged south, out of town.

~~~

At the start of the pilgrimage Helgi was driven by guilt and hope for retribution. Now, he envisioned another way, a shorter and more satisfying way to compensate for his missteps.

It took them thirteen days to reach Lake Konstanz, where Helgi and the monks bathed, swam, and prayed in a round church built in the honour of St Mauritius. Helgi was in a rush to find the Pope's soldiers. They walked towards the Alps.

After passing Lake Bodensee, they headed up into the mountains, slowing down to catch their breath. Helgi welcomed the cool air, and after walking uphill for two days he felt a sense of elation. The trees no longer obstructed the view, the ground was rocky, and the pristinely white mountain peaks penetrated the sky with sharp points which reminded Helgi of swords. With each cool breath Helgi felt infused with joy and optimism.

They slept in huts on the way and woke up early as it was difficult to sleep during the chilly nights. Helgi dreamed of God who lived in the clouds and told him to hurry to Iceland. The following nine days they trudged uphill at a steady pace and ate little. Helgi could no longer distinguish between hallucination and awareness.

"Men have built remarkable things, but nothing is as miraculous as the mountains," Helgi said.

On the Septimer pass which cut through the mountains, they came across a spring dedicated to St Mauritius. The monks were eager to drink the spring water as it was reputed to heal all ailments.

"What did this Mauritius do to become a saint?" Helgi asked

Adam.

"He was a black man from Egypt."

"A Christian from Egypt?"

"He was a leader in the Roman army at a time when many Roman rulers felt threatened by Christians and wanted to attack them. The emperor demanded that Mauritius and his army fight the Christians. Due to his strong faith, he refused. The emperor became enraged and had every tenth man in Mauritius's troop killed."

"Did Mauritius then change his mind?"

"On the contrary. He said that they would rather die innocent than live in sin."

"Were his men faithful to Mauritius?"

"So the story goes."

"Then Mauritius sanctioned the murder of troops due to his own convictions?" Helgi said.

"His convictions were God's convictions."

"Is God therefore not opposed to wars?"

"Soldiers should above all serve the only true God, and then the state."

Euphoria swept over Helgi. He drank and drank from the spring and said, "Saint Mauritius is my man, my saint who understands me. I'm destined to fight for the Pope and the Emperor in the name of God." He laughed.

"If you are so destined, I shall ask God to protect you from the tragedy of war," Adam said, and crossed himself.

Which one would God listen to? Helgi pondered and gloated. He knew that violent and power-hungry men still outnumbered the passive ones.

The Septimer pass lay between two giant mountain ranges. Despite their exhaustion from ascending the Alps for days, Helgi skipped with delight when they reached the peak of the pass. Ahead and below lay a magnificent landscape bursting with colour. They walked down into a broad valley where apples fell at their feet as if the fruit trees were inviting them to a feast. They bypassed fields of yellow grain, purple grape orchards and meadows with glorious flowers in all colours of the rainbow. Workers with dark hair laboured here and there and waved to the three pilgrims.

Smiling from ear to ear, Joseph said, "Have we come upon heaven on earth?"

The sun shone day in and day out but they never lacked water. Despite the delightful surroundings, Helgi was preoccupied with his plans. The Pope's enemies should be driven away so these cheerful residents could cultivate their fields in peace.

The Pope was a holy man, who should reserve his energies for saving souls from evil, unencumbered by commanding an army. Experienced soldiers, like Helgi, should protect the Pope's domain in the spirit of Saint Mauritius. God had sent Helgi on this pilgrimage to help the Pope deal with his enemies. By his selfless sacrifice, Helgi would have a chance to cleanse his soul.

But where could he find those Norse soldiers?

Helgi and the monks arrived at Como, a long lake surrounded by mountain ranges on all sides. They headed for Piona, a small monastery located on a peninsula by the lake. The resident monks received them well and offered them accommodation overnight. Although it was peaceful inside the monastery, the road outside bustled with travellers.

Helgi asked Adam to find a monk who knew both Latin and the Lombard dialect.

"Why?" Adam said.

"I must find out where the Pope's soldiers are."

Adam's eyes grew bigger. "Why do you want to locate them?"

"The Pope has hired them to drive away Muslims and other heathens from the Roman Empire. He selects his soldiers carefully."

"You're no longer a soldier."

"I'm experienced. When I drank from the spring of Saint Mauritius, God told me Mauritius was my saint and I should fight for the conversion of all heathen men to Christianity."

"God must have meant for you to talk them into converting. Didn't he?"

"Priests and monks can turn simple men into believers by teaching them the scriptures. I have learned to bring sense to men with the help of weapons. The Pope knows weapons are more effective than talk when dealing with violent men."

"God told you so himself?"

"He whispered this to me. Or was it Saint Mauritius? One of them."

Adam crossed himself. "What can I say? I'm aghast."

Helgi crossed himself also. "God's ways are unpredictable."

"What's next for you?"

"To find the Pope's army and join them."

"But you may die."

"Then I shall die in the name of God. Won't men who lose their lives during a pilgrimage go to heaven?"

"I gather. At least according to tradition." Adam scratched his nose. "But we're close to Rome and should not be in danger the rest of the way."

Helgi patted Adam on his back. "I accept that I shall either go to heaven or to the Pope's quarters."

The thought of applying his fighting skills to driving the heathen dwarfs out of the country filled Helgi with joy. As Saint Mauritius did, he could keep his faith while fighting. Why should he be ashamed of the skills God had bestowed upon him? The Pope was not an ignorant man. He knew his adversaries would rather flee than fight fearless and courageous Vikings.

Helgi, Adam and a local monk sat down by the route frequented by the emperor's army. The local monk asked a passing soldier about the Norsemen. He said they should be in Pavia.

Helgi hurried south toward Pavia.

35
Katla

In late summer Aevar the foreman at Holl arrived at Saudafell with several men to speak to Katla. She welcomed him and asked for news.

"Your father Halldór is ill and he wishes to see you before he dies."

"Does he want to ask me for forgiveness?"

"He didn't say. One thing I know, your mother misses you," Aevar said, reserved as usual.

Katla's eyes filled with tears. "I shall honour my father and mother."

Garpur invited Aevar and his men to stay overnight. Katla packed her trunk and the next morning Aevar, assisted by his helpers, carried the heavy trunk outside and secured it to a wagon. Katla put presents into a sack, hugged Gróa and Garpur, and rode with Aevar to Holl in Thverárhlíd.

On the way she wondered how Thórdís and Eilífur, the son of Hrefna, were getting along. Could Eilífur's sweetness melt her sister's heart? Katla recalled how delightful it was to squeeze the newborn baby to her chest. If Eilífur's grandmother Finnbjorg was still alive, she would dote on him. If not, he was under Thórdís's supervision.

When Katla and her escorts rode up to Holl she was alarmed by how many horses were gathered by the stables. Her mother stood with several men outside the farmhouse and Katla feared her father had died. She ran to her mother and embraced her while tears flowed down her cheek. Her mother pressed Katla to her chest for a while and then they examined each other's faces. During the two years they had spent apart, Oddlaug had gained weight and her braided hair was the colour of silver. They walked into the farmhouse holding hands. Oddlaug was limping. Katla's heart ached to see her mother suffer.

"Wash yourself before you meet your father," Oddlaug said.

"He's still alive!" Katla pulled her hood down and adjusted

the scarf which protected the hair from the road dust.

"He has guests. Why do you cover your hair?"

"I promised God I would cover my hair so it won't ignite lust in the men I meet."

"Your father will want to show off your beauty."

"Who are the guests?"

"Vandrádur Ósvífursson and his kinsmen."

"Back again? What's their errand?"

"Trade, I suppose. Go wash the dust off."

"I will uncover my hair if it pleases you." As Katla splashed water on her face, she wondered why her mother was now concerned with pleasing her ill-tempered husband.

Vandrádur and two other men sat on a bench near Halldór's bed and drank ale. Vandrádur stood up when he saw Katla and greeted her with the same indifference as when they last met. Or was it repulsion?

Katla walked to her father's bed and was taken aback by Halldór's swollen face and mountainous midsection. His smile seemed kind. He said, "How young and beautiful you look. Your hair is still the thickest in the land." But when he saw her mantle his smile faded, he grimaced and asked Vandrádur and his men to step outside for a moment.

After they had left, Halldór said, "How dare you wear an outlaw's mantle under your father's roof?"

"Helgi is not an outlaw. He is a free man."

"In Iceland he has enemies hunting for him."

"The mantle is a gift from Earl Eirikur and the most elaborate in this land. I wear it with pride wherever I go."

"You shall forget this vagabond as I have betrothed you to Vandrádur Ósvífursson."

"Vandrádur? Why did he change his mind?"

"Coerced by his brothers, I suspect."

"I thought he didn't want me because men know I love Helgi."

"Men know Helgi is a lost cause."

"Vandrádur has never cast an eye of desire on any woman."

"You are no longer young and not a coveted bride."

"Helgi will marry me."

"Nonsense. Helgi would rather ramble barefoot from one church to another and beg strangers for handouts than marry you. Why can't you see his lack of courage and loyalty? If he betrays his father, he'll betray you, as he has done already."

"He's a Christian and you don't grasp his deep faith."

"His faith is nothing but a flight from reality."

Katla said, "Vandrádur is an unkind brute."

"What impudence from a homeless woman! You and Vandrádur seem a perfect match, both so selfish and arrogant." Halldór laughed loudly until he could barely breathe. "Your children will be more adamant and independent than those who kiss the ground kings and bishops walk on." He coughed and spat blood into a cup. Katla did not move but a maid entered, took the cup and left.

When he had caught his breath, Katla said, "You cannot force me to marry Vandrádur, no matter how lavish the dowry is. By the way, what is my dowry?"

"All of Holl. The greenest land in the valley."

Katla was surprised. "Where should my mother live?"

"She'll stay here as before."

Katla walked back and forth contemplating whether she could promise to marry Vandrádur on her terms. Her father was on his deathbed and she should be practical. "I promise to marry Vandrádur if Helgi does not arrive by the end of next summer."

"Then I'll be dead."

"Even so, I will keep my promise."

Halldór smiled, lifted his head, reached for the beaker and drank. He was about to call for the guests, but Katla stopped him.

"I agree to marry Vandrádur on two conditions," Katla said.

"How audacious you are. What conditions?"

"My mother is ailing and I want to move to Holl right away."

"I agree. And what is the other?"

"If Vandrádur is killed before the wedding, I want to inherit the property."

"Are you plotting to have Helgi murder Vandrádur?"

Katla smiled. "I am not. Vandrádur has an abundance of enemies, and I suspect he'll be killed while pillaging with Vikings abroad."

"Vandrádur is a brave soldier. He won't be killed."

"Do you agree to the conditions?"

"If you promise never to mention Helgi again."

"I promise, unless you mention him first."

"You're tougher than I suspected," Halldór said, and smiled.

After Vandrádur and his companions had come in, Halldór told them that the wedding would not take place until late the following summer.

Vandrádur seemed relieved and grinned. "I agree. I'll sail abroad in the meantime to make us even wealthier."

The betrothal was made official without Katla and Vandrádur ever looking at each other.

Katla walked out to tell her mother the news.

"What made you agree to marry a man whom you despise?"

"Three reasons. I will stay here at home with you and help you out. Helgi will have returned home. If Helgi does not show up and I marry Vandrádur he will be absent most of the time. He's not fond of keeping company with women and I doubt he intends to lie down with me."

Her mother smiled. "You and Thórdís are more alike than I thought. You're both determined to get your way."

"Dreams diminish as you age."

Oddlaug sighed. "I hope to embrace at least one grandchild before I die."

"I promise to do my best," Katla said.

"Just be sure the child is born after you are married," Oddlaug said, and pinched Katla's cheek.

36
Helgi

On the five-day walk from Lake Como to Pavia, the three pilgrims passed colourful fields where the locals picked fruit and vegetables. Sometimes the workers threw fruit and bread to them, or at them. Helgi discovered that if he smiled when he picked up the food, the locals laughed. Not allowing disrespect from others to rouse him to anger brought him a sense of accomplishment. He could indeed be humble, or at least friendly, and grateful.

As they rested by the river Po, Adam said, "It brings me infinite joy to see you laugh at sullen men pitching food."

Helgi said, "Isn't each morsel of food a gift from God himself?"

"Indeed it is."

"Even though the morsel is given with reservations, it's a gift nonetheless," Helgi said.

"It is."

Helgi tore a piece off a loaf of bread and said, "You are faithful companions. God will protect you all the way to the Pope's domicile."

"Where are you going?" Adam asked.

"As I've said before, I feel obliged to fight for the Pope."

"If it's indeed a true calling from God, we must honour it," Josef said.

"But you don't speak the native language," Adam said.

"I know who the unbelievers are, although I don't understand their words," Helgi said.

Suddenly the earth shook like an earthquake in Iceland. They jumped to their feet. The sound of hoofs pounding on rocks grew louder and a cloud of dust approached them from the north.

"My prayers are answered. Here they come!" Helgi yelled.

"Who is coming?" Josef called, his eyes wide. "The Pope's troops."

The soldiers dismounted by the river and led their horses to drink. The troop consisted of over two hundred men, all clean shaven, light skinned, muscular and well armed.

Helgi approached them and called out, "Is there a Norse-speaking man among you?"

Several looked up and one tall, red-haired man with muscular arms walked to Helgi.

"Who are you?"

"Helgi. Skáld-Helgi Thórdarson from Iceland."

"The womaniser and soldier of repute?" the redhead said.

Helgi laughed. "I'm an accomplished soldier but a retired womaniser. Are you the soldiers who are fighting for the Pope?"

"We are a Norman troop. My name is Frederik."

"I have been called by God to help you drive off the enemies who have invaded the Pope's territory."

Frederik introduced Helgi to Robert, the leader of the Norman troop. His hair was blond, his mouth wide and he talked nonstop. Helgi did not understand a word he said. Frederik said Robert was a descendant of the Norseman Gongu-Hrolfur, baptised Rollo, the first Duke of Normandy.

Soon Helgi was dressed in the army uniform. In private he gave Adam and Josef half of his gold coins for food or for the Pope, and then hid the rest of the money inside his undergarments.

The soldiers gave Helgi a bow, arrows and a steel sword. He felt like a new man, a useful man, and he thanked Saint Mauritius and God for appreciating his skills and for helping him face his destiny.

Robert, the Norman troop leader, was impressed by Helgi's archery and fencing skills, and made him his right-hand man. The soldiers were accustomed to fighting with sharp axes and some could hit their targets from thirty paces, but few could throw a spear faster than Helgi.

On their way to Rome, they were approached by one hundred armed men wearing garish clothing. The leader bore a crown made of leaves. He introduced himself as Melus and spoke even faster than Robert. Melus was a Lombard nobleman from Bari on the east coast, where he had ruled until Byzantine soldiers invaded his territory and pushed him out. In short, Melus was petitioning the Normans to help him conquer the Byzantines and recapture Bari.

"I only fight in the name of the Pope," Robert said.

"I understand you're Christians and so am I," Melus said. "The Pope wants nothing more than to eliminate Byzantines from Italy." Then Melus offered to ride ahead of the Norman troops to ask the Pope to bless the alliance.

Helgi watched Melus turn his gaudy soldiers around. Even with the assistance of this Norman army, Helgi doubted they could defeat the Byzantines.

He called out to Frederik, "Is Bari now part of the Byzantine Empire?"

"It is."

"They believe in Christ, don't they?" Helgi asked.

"They're not Roman Christians like the Pope," Frederick said.

"They'll crush us. As soon as we invade Bari, they'll ship thousands of men from Constantinople."

"The crossing will take them too long. Don't worry. They can't beat us." Frederik laughed with confidence.

But Helgi had not marched for months in order to become an easy target for Byzantine Christian men. What was he to do?

Rome was a whirlwind of activity. They rode on streets laid with stone, by ornate churches, ruins, imposing forts, spacious amphitheatres, palaces with massive columns and temples built to honour fallen kings. What amazing efficiency and skill these workers displayed.

They stopped by a round plaza in front of Laterno, a three-storey palace where the Pope resided. Next to the palace stood the Church of John the Baptist where the Pope held his masses.

Robert dismounted, and walked to the palace to find Pope Benedetto.

While Robert was gone, Helgi walked around. Clean water

flowed to the area down stony tunnels. Bare-chested, stocky men worked nearby. They blended sand, ash, white powder and water, and made walls from this muddy mixture by splashing it on layer by layer with remarkable speed and accuracy. Each layer hardened quickly and somehow the walls did not lean. Why could they not build using this method in Iceland?

When they returned from their meeting with the Pope, Robert looked worried but Melus was smiling. The Pope approved of the Normans joining Melus and his troops in driving the Byzantines out of Bari.

Helgi asked Frederik to warn Robert about the skilful Norse Varangians, hired mercenary soldiers who fought for the Byzantine emperors.

Robert raised his index finger and shook it at Helgi with fury, while uttering a flood of angry words. Frederik translated. "He says you lack faith in his leadership. If you doubt he's the most victorious commander alive, he insists you return the horse and the weapons."

Helgi said, "I believe in God and Saint Mauritius. I will ask the Pope for advice in this matter."

Robert agreed, and Helgi walked unarmed to the palace, hoping he could communicate in Latin.

When Helgi saw at least a hundred pilgrims waiting in a long line to gain an audience with the Pope, he thanked God for not having to stand there under the blazing sun.

The Pope's assistant brought Helgi straight to Pope Benedetto VIII, who was dressed in a white cape with an embroidered cross on the front. He sat on a throne. Helgi fell to his knees, bowed to the Pope and then stood up. The Pope was a few years older than Helgi, with a handsome, somewhat feminine pale face, straight nose, prominent cheekbones and a cleft in his shaved chin.

Helgi said in Latin, "God has led me across fields and mountains to your holiness, so I could be released from my sins. When I drank from the spring of Saint Mauritius on the way, his spirit consumed me. I sensed the saint wished me to fight for the holy Pope because I'm a skilled soldier. Next, I was led to the

Norman troop and joined them, believing I could fight for your holiness and for all Christian men to expel the enemies of our faith, even though the Byzantine army is much larger than the Norman and Melus's troops combined."

"What do you fear?" the Pope asked.

"Accumulating more sins and not obtaining forgiveness from God and your holiness."

Helgi handed him two scrolls. "These are messages to you from Olafur, King of Norway, and from Emperor Heinrich."

Pope Benedetto handed the scrolls to his assistant and asked him to read. While the Pope listened, his dark-brown eyes never strayed from Helgi's face. Could the Pope decipher his thoughts?

When the assistant finished reading, the Pope took a deep breath and said, "God almighty has blessed you. You received a revelation when you drank from Saint Mauritius's spring. By God's grace, the saint is now your guide. As matters stand, you shall not join the Norman troop to fight in Pavia. Emperor Heinrik has not sent enough soldiers here to protect our domain. The Lombards are the Pope's allies but they have trouble defending their lands from Saracen invasion." The Pope wrinkled his black eyebrows so furrows formed between them. With an authoritarian tone of voice he continued, "In the name of God, I want you to do the following. You are to select forty soldiers, Norsemen or Romans, and take them to Salerno. You will be provided with a guide, horses and clothing for all soldiers. Prince Guaimar of Salerno has trouble with Muslim Saracens who invade his shores and pillage his district. In the name of God, you are to drive these heathens out of Salerno. When it is done, you are to return to me and I shall release you from the burden of your sins." The Pope knocked on the floor with his pastoral staff.

Two men dressed as soldiers guided Helgi to a side door, and along a corridor to an immense hall piled with swords, spears and bows. He was invited to select the best weapons.

His guides carried the weapons he chose, and showed him where to bathe and where to sleep. The following morning, the guides would accompany him to select his soldiers. He asked how he could learn more about Salerno. Soon thereafter, a short, smiling Norse monk called Johannes entered his room. Helgi embraced him as a long-lost friend.

Johannes told Helgi Salerno was south of Rome and bordered the sea. The long and unprotected beach enabled the black-skinned Saracens to moor their ships and rampage through the area at will. The Saracens ruled all the islands near the Italian peninsula, including Sardinia, Corsica and Sicily.

"Then it is all about controlling the shore," Helgi said, deep in thought.

"I expect so."

Before he went to sleep in the soft bed, he thanked Saint Mauritius and God for the honour bestowed upon him. Even though the assignment was dangerous, it was his best, or perhaps his only, chance for retribution.

He promised Katla he would stay alive and return to Iceland as soon as he could.

The next morning, Johannes walked in carrying a tray with fruit, cheese and bread. While they ate, Helgi said, "Do many Norsemen come here to be absolved of their sins?"

"They do. Most of them are gigantic men who regret having robbed and killed innocent people."

"How can I find such pilgrims?"

"Some are waiting for the Pope outside, some are resting in monasteries and others are praying in churches."

When the guards asked Helgi how he wanted to assemble an army, he said, "One of you shall go with Johannes to monasteries and churches to find Vikings who are on a pilgrimage and bring them to me. The other shall go with me to the plaza, where we'll gather experienced soldiers."

"Don't you want any men from the Pope's guards?"

"I would like two to guide us to Salerno," Helgi said.

The Pope's men and Helgi succeeded in assembling forty fit Vikings. As Helgi suspected, they were eager to serve the Pope and to obtain a quick release from their sins.

Helgi inspected the troop as if he were a king. Self-assured, with sarcastic smiles, the pilgrims-turned-soldiers looked more threatening than any of Robert's Normans, even in their tattered cloaks. Helgi named them the Pope's Army and announced, "This mission is inspired by God and mandated by the Pope himself. If we are successful, we'll bring peace to a crucial ally of the Pope, and each of you will be honoured and admired. On your return, you'll receive absolution from your previous sins."

The Pope's soldiers cheered and punched their fists in the air. With a glint in their eyes, they selected their weapons. Once they had mounted strong horses, they laughed as if they were headed to a joyful feast.

As the Byzantines ruled over Naples, it was too dangerous to ride by the shoreline from Rome to Salerno. They travelled for two warm days through Capua and Benevento in Lombardy, where green valleys lay between tree-covered mountains. They slept in a monastery on the way.

Helgi and his troops dismounted in front of an imposing castle perched on a hill facing west and south. They were guided to an elaborate dining hall where Prince Guaimar III greeted them. Behind the prince stood several beautiful dark-haired maidens wrapped in silk scarves and smiling sweetly. The longing for the soft embrace from submissive women flared up in Helgi. He pushed away the thought and turned his gaze to the prince, who sprang to his feet and kissed Helgi on both cheeks. As the prince talked, he frolicked about the floor and waved his arms. He reminded Helgi of a colourful butterfly.

Helgi asked the prince in Latin, "How many ships do you have?"

"None. The bastards robbed them, burnt them, and now we can't defend our shores. They harass our people, rape and abduct the women into slavery."

"Are any of the villains here how?" Helgi asked.

"Let's see," the prince said, and led Helgi to an opening in the palace's wall. He pointed to a ship out at sea and another one moored in the harbour.

Lightning flashed near them, thunder followed, and relentless rain fell from the sky as they watched. The prince invited them to eat, drink and spend the night because visibility was poor in such horrendous weather. Helgi convinced the prince that it was easier to surprise men when it was raining.

Helgi told his troops to eat quickly and then go down to the beach on foot, well armed.

Most of the soldiers hid while Helgi and five men sneaked down to the harbour. They came upon two Saracen guards who were crouching under a canopy, approached them from behind, and killed them. Helgi and his men jumped on board the unmanned ship. Using their axes, they hewed several holes in the bottom of the vessel, then went ashore, cut the ropes and pushed the ship away. The high tide would soon recede, carrying the ship out to sea where it would sink.

Helgi put five men by each house the Saracens occupied. He sent the rest of the soldiers down to the harbour, where they hid. When Helgi blew his war horn, the Saracens rushed down to the shore, but when they saw their ship adrift, they looked bewildered. After the Norsemen had killed all the visible villains, they searched the houses, one by one.

Wet to the core, Helgi's men walked up the hill and looked out to sea. The other ship was not visible due to a dense fog. When they arrived at the castle, the prince gave them elegant clothing and delicious food.

"Honourable prince, I must ask you to keep beautiful women away from the Pope's soldiers, as we must resist the lusts of the flesh."

The prince laughed. "Perhaps the beautiful women are the reason our soldiers lose to the Saracens." He came close to Helgi and whispered, "The Pope himself is not chaste, but he expects his priests to be celibate." He fluttered away, singing, "Passion softens the heart."

During the next few days, Helgi and his troops inspected the long Salerno shoreline and saw no ships. The prince was confident that Helgi's troops had scared the Saracens off forever. Helgi disagreed and suspected they would return in force.

Prince Guaimar invited them to stay for the winter. Helgi was eager to gain the Pope's absolution and to travel over the

Alps when weather permitted. He needed to board a ship in Norway by midsummer if he was to reach Iceland by the end of the summer.

After Christmas, Helgi and the Pope's army prepared their exit. Prince Guaimar offered them money, which they turned down, but they gladly accepted horses, equipment and plain brown cloaks to wear on their return to Rome.

~ ~ ~

Once at the Laterno palace, Helgi and his troops were led into a large hall where a bishop clad in a white robe sat on a platform. As instructed, the soldiers knelt in front of the bishop, confessed their sins and promised to be virtuous. Helgi was first in line. He told the bishop about fondling many women, having a concubine and murdering some men for good reason, killing heathens to protect Christianity in Norway, and killing Saracens to protect the Pope from heathen invasion.

As if reciting a boring poem, the bishop said, "Do you promise God you'll be chaste from now on and be faithful to the woman you shall marry?"

"I promise."

The bishop laid a hand on Helgi's head and said, "God forgives you." He asked Helgi to step aside and summoned the next man in line.

Helgi was perturbed. He had travelled all this way to obtain forgiveness from the Pope, not his dispirited assistant.

The bishop stood up and stepped aside.

Helgi was relieved when Pope Benedict walked in and the bishop ordered the soldiers to kneel once more.

The Pope said something very fast in Latin which Helgi could not comprehend. Then he changed his voice and talked slower so Helgi understood. "You were willing to risk your life in the name of God and secured peace in a land plundered by heathen men. You have paid for your sins and are now free of them. It is still up to each one of you to atone for your sins in your homeland, be peaceful and serve the will of God and your church. All of you who agree shall come to me for my blessing. Helgi, you shall be last."

When it was Helgi's turn, the Pope thanked him for his service, blessed him and asked him to stand. Helgi thanked the Pope and asked his permission to ride home instead of walking, as he and his companions had been delayed in Salerno. The Pope agreed and offered two men from the Emperor's army to guide them north through peaceful territory.

Helgi and his troops stayed in the Pope's palace and dined with monks in an elaborate setting. Helgi assumed the white linen and the gold bowls were bought with hard-earned coins, donated by poor people, in exchange for the absolution of their sins. The excess did not sit well with him.

His fellow soldiers and sinners ate with vigour. Helgi chuckled. He was not the only one with limited humility and reverence.

On the return trip up north, Helgi and his cohorts sat on their horses like proud knights. Each carried axes and knives under their cloaks. They had plenty of provisions, crossed the Alps without trouble, and arrived in Denmark at midsummer, where the group split up.

Helgi and six of the men sold their horses in Aalborg and boarded a ship to Nidaros.

The poet, Sighvatur Thórdarson, greeted Helgi in Nidaros. Helgi was not sure what made him happier, receiving his sword or draping over his shoulders the cape Katla had given him.

Sighvatur said, "King Olafur plans to invite you to stay at his court through next winter."

"The king shows me great honour, but I want to sail to Iceland without delay. Will you help me to find a ship I can buy a share in?"

"I happen to know of two experienced seamen, both named Illugi, who are sailing for Iceland soon."

"I'm a lucky man. God's mercy has followed me from the time I first met the Pope."

Helgi stayed with Sighvatur and told him the details of his

trip. Sighvatur was a devout Christian and wanted nothing more than to go on a pilgrimage. He was waiting for permission from King Olafur to depart.

"But Sighvatur, you haven't sinned enough to justify going through the hardships involved in a pilgrimage."

Sighvatur smiled and said, "I'm still an ambitious poet and I could be humbler."

The next morning, they rode to the harbour where Sighvatur introduced him to the two giant Illugis, strong men but aloof. Helgi hoped their lack of conversational skills indicated that they were diligent sailors.

The ship, a sturdy knarr, named *Falki*, sported a tall mast and a large rolled-up sail tied to the spar. "I hope the ship lives up to its name and moves as fast as the falcon, but it's wide in the centre, which could slow it down," Helgi said.

"The more cargo we carry, the more we'll sell in Iceland," the younger Illugi said.

"I hope God guides us to Iceland quickly," Helgi said.

"Njordur will see to it," the older Illugi said, and sniggered.

For two years, Helgi had been in the company of humble and Christian men. Now, he had to count on strong men who could control the sail in stormy weather, but these men repulsed him. Were all strong men aggressive? Muscles grew by fighting, fencing and swinging swords. Helgi sighed, hoping he would not have to fight again. He could stay strong hewing wood, fishing and building rock walls.

37
Katla

At the peak of summer Katla rode with Aevar from Holl to Hvammur. Thórdís's farm seemed larger: more buildings, more cows, more horses. Thórdís carried herself like a nobleman, dressed in trousers and a white shirt. Her golden braids sat in a circle at the top of her head, which reminded Katla of Queen Astrid's crown.

Thórdís's sarcasm was familiar. "I see you're still wearing the old cape from Helgi," Thórdís said, laughing.

"After Helgi returns, he'll keep me warm." Katla smiled.

"How many women do you think he'll seduce on his pilgrimage?"

"I never think about it."

Katla resolved to toughen up and ignore Thórdís's cutting remarks.

A young, spry woman, dressed like Thórdís, walked out of the farmhouse and introduced herself to Katla as Ásný.

Thórdís looked at Ásný with unusual kindness. "Ásný lives here and helps me to run the farm. She is more efficient than any man I know." Thórdís smiled.

Ásný and Thórdís showed her the new outhouses with pride. They spoke as if they were of equal status, saying "we" when they described the improvements, as if Ásný owned a piece of Hvammur.

Finnbjorg was still alive and Katla went to see her where she sat sewing. She thanked Katla for keeping her grandson Eilífur alive.

"Eilífur must be seven or eight by now. How is he doing?" Katla said.

"He has inherited the best from his mother and father. He is an agile sportsman like his father and cheerful like his mother, but a bit of a dreamer. He is haymaking with the farmhands." Finnbjorg sniggered. "Only two male workers remain at Hvammur."

"But the chores require strength."

"Thórdís hires only women. Strong and unmarried women. They do most of the work around here."

"It's probably easier to tell women what to do than men," Katla said.

"Staying outside and handling animals suits women. We live in harmony with nature, and we understand animals."

Eilífur walked in. He was tall, and had an abundance of black, curly hair which resembled Hrefna's.

"You must be Katla, because you're the most beautiful woman I've ever seen." He squeezed her hand. "I thank you with all my heart for bringing me to my grandmother."

Katla was unaccustomed to such kindness and she laughed. "You were so sweet and alert for a baby, it was a delight to hold you."

"Please tell me the story of how I was born."

Katla told him the story, omitting that his mother did not want to see him. Katla also told him joyful stories of Hrefna while she was at Holl.

"May I visit you at Holl?"

"If your grandmother and Thórdís permit."

Later Katla asked Thórdís if Eilífur could spend the rest of the summer at Holl.

"If our father agrees," Thórdís said. "He's not fond of children born to concubines."

"I'll get his permission before Eilífur comes."

"I don't remember seeing you this happy," Katla said. "Are you going to marry again?"

Thórdís shook her head. "I've not met a man who I want to be intimate with."

"I hope God will bring you such a man," Katla said. When Finnbjorg and Thórdís glanced at each other, she added, "Or perhaps Freyr."

They all laughed.

"I'll pray to Freyr for peace," Finnbjorg said.

"And prosperity," Thórdís said.

"But not fertility?" Katla asked.

Thórdís and Finnbjorg sniggered as they used to when Katla was young. They never shared their secrets with Katla or anyone else.

Now, Katla did not care.

~~~

How could Katla talk her father into agreeing that Eilífur stay at Holl all summer? She needed to figure out how Halldór could benefit from Eilífur's presence.

One day, when her father was less agitated than usual, Katla said, "I know how disappointed you are by not having a son or a grandson."

"If Thórdís and you had married virile men, young boys would be running around here."

"I have remedied the situation," Katla said.

"It's hardly a remedy to have a bastard grandson," Halldór said. "Are you expecting a child?"

Katla laughed. "I'm not."

"Why are you scaring your old, sick father once again?"

"I have invited Eilífur Hrefnuson to come here and stay for a while."

"I don't want a bastard child in my house."

"Eilífur is not a bastard. You knew his parents. His father Arngeir from Steinar, our relative, was a robust man, and you used to like Hrefna when she worked here."

"What can the boy do while he's here?" Halldór asked.

"He can learn carpentry and fencing. Unfortunately, there are no sportsmen at Hvammur, as women run the farm."

"Thórdís must be careful. I hear some powerful men covet her land. She's defenceless without armed men."

"I don't doubt men covet all things others own. But Thórdís has many allies in Hvítársída. The chiefs at Gilsbakki would defend her," Katla said.

"Well, she's cunning and ambitious."

"Eilífur is cheerful like his mother and strong like his father, talented and handsome. But he's being short-changed." Katla brought tears to her eyes.

Halldór lifted his brows in surprise. "What do you mean, short-changed?"

"Boys need to learn from experienced and valiant men how to conduct themselves." Katla sighed. "Although Eilífur has abundant potential, he has not been privy to the guidance normally provided by a knowing father. If he only had a mentor who could teach him bravery and sportsmanship."

"Vandrádur, your fiancé, could teach him."

"I gather he could, but he's still out at sea and is not expected until next spring."

"How does Vandrádur dare stay away when your wedding is to take place before autumn?"

"I cannot answer the question without mentioning Helgi."

"What does he have to do with Vandrádur?"

"Vandrádur heard of Helgi's return to Norway and him sailing to Iceland," Katla fibbed. It was only a dream.

"Helgi will not make it to Iceland by the end of summer."

"It remains to be seen. Of course, Helgi could teach Eilífur many useful things, such as fencing, woodwork and Christian scriptures."

As Katla hoped, this angered her father.

"Christian scriptures!" Halldór roared, then coughed. His belly shook the blanket so it wiggled down to the floor. "Helgi can only teach the boy twisted words and lechery."

Katla picked up the blanket and covered Halldór's middle. "Who then shall teach the boy?"

Halldór tried to sit up. He called out, "I will. I'll teach him. When I was his age, I was the sharpest and most agile boy around." He dropped back down.

"It's a shame you're too ill to teach him, dear father." Katla tried to look sympathetic. "How can you fence from bed?"

"I'll get up. You'll see. This farm is now run by incompetent women and Vandrádur Ósvífursson has deceived me."

"Vandrádur has never stuck close to home. He wanted to betroth a woman to save his reputation. People say he prefers the affection of men."

"Men! Gossip and jealousy. If his father Ósvífur were alive, no one would dare call his son a pervert."

"People still gossip about Vandrádur's sister, Gudrun," Katla said.

"Because she's beautiful."

"And cunning."

"Now she is marrying Thórkell and I'm unable to attend the wedding," Halldór said.

"I'm to become her sister-in-law and I was not invited," Katla said.

"You're as beautiful as Gudrun but not as desirable due to your lovesickness."

"If women were allowed to marry the men they love, animosity would decline."

"Nonsense. Peace is achieved by wise alliances and family ties. My agreement with Vandrádur is solid. You should be content at being betrothed to man who has demonstrated great valour and loyalty to his kin."

"Perhaps. But not one woman of good or ill repute has ever kept him company. He travels with one friend."

"Pure defamation! Why have I never heard such gossip?"

"You have not visited other farms in two summers."

"Thórdur tells me all matters in our district."

"He does not go to Saudafell or Dalir," Katla said.

"Get Eilífur here and I shall teach him how a boy becomes a skilful man."

"I'll send for him."

On her way out, Katla felt a sense of triumph because she had managed to approach her father with a clever blend of reasoning, challenge and compliance.

Halldór called behind her. "We need brave chiefs to regain the honour of Holl, my hard-earned property."

~ ~ ~

Eilífur turned out to be a blessing to the bland life at Holl, where few men visited, due to Halldór's notorious temper. The boy was good-humoured and preferred to sit by Katla and practise carving while she wove. Thórdís had taught him how to engrave runes and Eilífur carved Katla's name on a spindle wheel that he gave to her. When Katla kissed him on the cheek to thank him, he seemed embarrassed. She suspected he was unaccustomed to affection.

He also accompanied Katla on her hike up above Holl where they collected dead branches for Eilífur's carving projects. Katla showed him the elf rock and told him of her friend Vonadís, whom she believed lived in the rock. Eilífur was mesmerised by the rock and kept stroking it as if it were a person or an animal.

"Perhaps it's a figment of a girl's imagination that elves live in the rock," Katla said and laughed.

Eilífur wrinkled his brow. "Can't you see they are listening to us? Vonadís was near tears when you said she was imaginary. And the small red-haired boy quit smiling."

"What boy?"

"Your brother, Kollur."

Katla thought Kollur must be an elf, laughed and stroked the rock. "Forgive me, Vonadís, my best friend. I know you exist."

Eilífur laid his ear to the rock as if he were listening and closed his eyes. "They're dancing for us," he said.

"Dancing! Show me."

Eilífur took her hand and danced with her in circles. "They also sing."

Katla hummed a song as she used to do in childhood, and Eilífur mimicked her.

At dinner time they carried branches down to Holl. Katla stopped by the hollow where she had once seen Hrefna making love to her boyfriend. "Your mother loved a young man who drowned in the Thverá river. After I saw them embrace, I decided to save myself for a man I loved. I met Helgi the same day, and I have loved him ever since."

Eilífur's eyes widened. "But Helgi used my mother as a concubine. How can a man who says he loves you marry your

225

sister and use other women for his pleasure?"

"He's affectionate, and I love him. Promise me, when you're of age, you'll marry the woman you love above all."

"But I was told I'll never be permitted to wed the daughter of a chief, even if she loves me."

"If you're wealthy and you own a farm, you can."

"How do I become wealthy?"

Katla kissed Eilífur on top of his black hair. "My father is wealthy. He'll teach you."

"Halldór! He's sick and grumpy."

"In his youth, he learned fencing, joined the Vikings, selected his friends carefully, and in spite of overeating he's one of the most respected landowners in the district."

"If he finds fault with me, what shall I do?"

"Thank him for his guidance. Then he'll be reluctant to ridicule you when you make mistakes."

~ ~ ~

Katla eavesdropped when Eilífur first sat by Halldór's bedside. Eilífur did not waste time gaining an ally in Halldór. He said, "What a marvellous sword! You must be strong and important to own such a sword," probably referring to Halldór's sword which hung over the old man's bed.

"I shall let you see the sword up close," Halldór said, then shouted, "Dagur, come here!"

When Dagur arrived, Halldór said, "Get the sword down and lay it on my stomach with the handle pointing at my chin." Halldór laughed, and continued, "Be careful not to kill me."

When Dagur left, Halldór said to Eilífur, "This sword is a trusted friend and it comes from far out east in a place called Gardaríki, where the strongest iron swords are made."

"Did you sail all the way to Gardaríki?"

"I sailed with the Swedes on the rivers and I became a wealthy man."

Katla could hear Halldór straining to lift the sword. "I'll keep the sword close and before the week is over I shall be able to lift it."

"You're a brave man," Eilífur said sincerely.

Within a week, Halldór could lift the sword and showed Eilífur the basics of wielding a sword. Katla kept eavesdropping.

"I wish I could have seen you swing the sword when you were younger," Eilífur said with awe in his voice.

"I was the quickest in my troop."

"Thórdís called you a champion."

One day Halldór let Eilífur attempt to hold the sword. Katla gasped and peeked through the doorway. Eilífur tried to lift the sword until he was red in the face before he let it drop. Halldór laughed.

Eilífur sounded sad. "I'm too weak to wield this sword. I must practise with a lighter sword."

"You're pragmatic and cautious. Valuable qualities in a man."

The following nights, Eilífur stayed awake late, carving a sword out of a long branch.

When he showed it to his mentor, Halldór said, "Behold. Your sword is the same size as mine! You're a competent carver, little Eilífur."

"I intend to practise with the wooden sword until my hand, wrist and elbow are strong enough for a real sword."

By early winter Eilífur could lift Halldór's sword, point it forward and hold it still until his forearm shook. He did not attempt to swing it.

Then Halldór said with pride, "This is precisely how you learn to master the sword."

In the evening, Katla saw Halldór practise bending his arm while holding the sword. She smiled. Now her father had a reason to recover.

With time, the miracle happened. Halldór's stomach shrank and he gained enough strength in his arms to raise himself and sit up on his bed.

"Old age often benefits from youth," Halldór said.

Eilífur was so elated to see his teacher sitting, holding a

sword, and wielding it like an adroit sportsman, that he stayed awake all night chiselling. He kept what he was carving a secret.

The next day Eilífur carried two staffs to Halldór, each staff with a rounded long piece of wood across the top. The boy explained that these were crutches for Halldór, to help him stay on his feet. Two strong workers supported Halldór while he got used to the crutches. At first, Halldór's legs trembled like a newborn calf's, and walking unassisted was still far off. From where Halldór sat in his place of honour, he chatted with Eilífur about sportsmanship and conquests. Katla and her mother welcomed the break from Halldór's cranky comments, and hoped he would soon be walking.

38
Helgi

Before they departed Nidaros, Helgi arranged his trunks full of treasures midship on *Falki*, and tied a worn sail over them to prevent them from sliding about during a storm.

Within a matter of days, Helgi would walk on Icelandic ground as a wealthy, Christian and admired man. How happy Katla and his mother would be when he presented them with silk scarves, rings of gold and brooches made of rare jewels. His father's gifts included a king's sword and Muslim axes.

When Helgi, the two Illugis and ten oarsmen were about to set out to sea, a wretched old man approached them and introduced himself as Thórgils. He carried a sizable leg of mutton.

"Have mercy on an old man and bring him to Iceland with you."

Illugi the younger said, "Go away, you old fool."

The older Illugi said, "We don't have room for a useless old man on our ship."

"I have wealthy kinsmen in Iceland," the bald man said. "A priest told me I was bestowing upon you, noble Christian men, great honour by trusting you to carry an old man to his homeland. If I could only die in Iceland with Christ's words on my frail lips and eternal peace in my worn heart."

"You'll be dead long before you ever see Iceland," Illugi the younger said, and laughed.

Thórgils turned to Helgi and said, "I trust you to take me with you, Skáld-Helgi."

"Shut up, you old devil," Illugi the older said.

Thórgils ignored the two Illugis and said to Helgi, "You're blessed by the Pope himself, and capable of performing the work of the saviour, or have you turned your back on the kind-hearted teacher who died on the cross for your sins?"

Helgi wondered if God could have sent this wretched man to test his faith.

Thórgils must have sensed Helgi's weakening resolve and said, "I trust you to carry me home on the waves of the Lord as you are pure of heart. I have enough food in my parcel to feed my tiny stomach. Besides, I'm a skilled and experienced sailor."

"We must leave at once if we are to take advantage of this tailwind," Illugi the older said.

"Thórgils." Helgi tried to sound stern. "In the name of God, I'll take you if you promise to be useful."

From the time Thórgils set foot on board, he never strayed far from Helgi, chatting incessantly, attempting to entertain Helgi with fictitious stories of his heroic feats in foreign lands. Helgi found it difficult to concentrate on navigating the ship with this blabbering wretch next to him.

Finally, Helgi asked Thórgils to shut up.

Three days later, gigantic roaring waves battered *Falki*, like a pod of whales intent on devouring the ship. Every sailor but Thórgils held the rigging tightly. The Illugis and Helgi attempted to lower the sail, but the storm overpowered them. The ropes gave way and the sail ripped from the yard. The wind whipped the sail back and forth while the sailors cowered. Soon the wind carried the sail into the abyss while old Thórgils wailed loudly and then stopped. Helgi crawled to him. The old man had quit breathing. Helgi wrapped the corpse in a hide, secured it by ropes, and with the help of a sailor, threw the bundle out to sea, where it was gulped by the waves.

Helgi regretted not having crossed and blessed the old man.

When the weather cleared enough for them to see stars, they pointed the ship west. The journey went well for two nights but then fog engulfed the ship, followed by a violent storm. A lump the size of a large fish was thrown from the sea and landed on the deck, scaring the oarsmen. The lump was Thórgils, unwrapped and deformed, resembling a ghost. He howled incessantly.

Fear gripped the sailors at the sight of the lifelike corpse. They lost control of the oars and threw themselves down on the deck. Helgi did not panic at the sight of Thórgils as he suspected the old man was possessed by the devil. He picked up a sharp axe and hewed Thórgils between his shoulder blades. The screaming ceased. Illugi the younger wrung the devil's neck and threw him overboard.

The sailors praised Helgi for his valour, thanked him profusely, picked up their oars and began rowing. Their newfound peace did not last. A blinding hailstorm battered the ship and stung their eyes, preventing them from seeing ahead.

They only had enough food for a day.

Illugi the older said to Helgi, "We have to reduce the crew. Let's make the weakest oarsmen fight each other until the strongest men remain."

"What an idiotic idea—to encourage good men, who have battled storms together, to fight each other to death over food. We shall say our prayers and trust the Lord with our sincere hearts to bring us ashore."

Helgi said his prayers aloud, but no one joined him.

Shortly thereafter the hail stopped, the water calmed, and he glimpsed the enormous white glaciers of Greenland. They followed the rocky shoreline until a dense fog surrounded them and the land was invisible.

Suddenly, *Falki*'s starboard was struck with such force that men and merchandise were thrown in the air and dumped overboard. Helgi grabbed the side of a small boat as it was dislodged into the sea. He managed to hold onto the boat as a giant wave carried them away from the sky-high iceberg that had shattered *Falki*. Helgi called to the sailors but the only sound he heard came from the rocking iceberg. He removed his sword from its sheath and used it to row as fast as he could. More icebergs approached him and he paddled with all his might to avoid hitting them. Out of nowhere, a sandy beach appeared ahead. Using his last bit of strength, he paddled towards it. The boat hit a rock, and water gushed in through a hole. Helgi cursed and removed his sheepskin shoes, stuffed them in the hole, dislodged the boat from the reef and paddled towards the beach. The fog was too dense for him to see far, but he gathered he was in a narrow fjord, as hills rose on both sides and a few icebergs floated away to sea. He thanked God he was still wearing the

Katla-cape, even though it was soaking wet and heavy.

The boat filled with water and he swam towards the shore until he was able to stand up. He took a few painful steps along the beach, collapsed in the sand, rolled over on his back, and lay there, shivering.

He called out, "God, what have I done to deserve this? Did you take all my possessions because I didn't give the Pope all the gold. What about my poor shipmates? Could you not save them? Must I die a slow death, frozen and starving in Greenland?"

Where in hell was he?

He was losing the feeling in his feet, and struggled to get up, but his legs did not obey. Despite his attempts to stay awake, sleep overtook him.

~~~

A man's voice woke Helgi up. "What is your name?"

Helgi opened his eyes. Over him stood a middle-aged man wearing wool trousers and sealskin boots. "Helgi Thórdarson is my name." He coughed and spat out salty phlegm.

"From Iceland? I am Forni." He reached his hand out to Helgi. "Could you be Skáld-Helgi?"

Helgi took his hand, sat up and remembered he was in Greenland. "I am." He tried to stand up but his feet were numb.

"You're frostbitten. My men will carry you." Forni called out to two men who stood near, by a boat pulled up on the shore.

Four men carried Helgi to the boat and laid him down. They gave the boat a gentle push and then stepped aboard. Forni followed.

Forni's men rowed the boat out of the fjord to the sea, following the coastline northwards. Forni fed Helgi seal meat and while Helgi ate, Forni talked. In spite of his aching legs, Helgi tried to listen. Forni was a farmer, lived under Sólarfjollum in Eiríksfjordur, and was best friends with Leifur the Lucky who discovered Vinland. He was born in Reykjadalur in Iceland, the grandson of Tin-Forni. "I've heard various stories about you, Helgi, some positive, others disturbing, but you're welcome to stay with me while you recover."

Helgi was broken-hearted and mumbled, "Finally when I'm a free man and rich enough to marry Thórkatla Halldórsdóttir, what happens? A bloody storm! My ship is wrecked by an iceberg. All my men gone—my fortune swallowed by the icy sea."

"Your misfortune is akin to that of many seafarers. Perhaps God has blessed you by bringing you to the shores of Greenland."

"Blessed me. How?"

"Merchant ships come here from Iceland with freight and news. Powerful men oppose your marriage to Thórkatla. God must have sided with them."

"God? Who knows his will?"

"God wants men to honour their fathers."

"Katla's father is a heathen."

"Heathen or Christian, Halldór found a respectable groom for Katla."

"Katla? Betrothed? To whom?"

"Vandrádur Ósvífursson."

Helgi warmed with anger. "He's an ignorant, deviant man—she'll never marry him."

"She can't marry you—your reputation in Iceland is beyond repair."

"How so? The Pope pardoned all my sins."

Forni took Helgi's hand and said, "I believe I was sent by God to save your life."

"After all these years I cannot break my promise to Katla."

"If you defy Halldór's will once again, you'll have no friends in Iceland."

"My beloved Katla will grieve until the end of her days."

Forni patted him on the shoulder. "You do not have the means to ask for her hand in marriage."

"But my heart still aches for her." Remorse and hopelessness overtook Helgi. He hid his face with his hands and cried so his body shook.

"Do not lose courage. You're still an educated Christian

man, loyal to King Olafur, and you could become an important man in Greenland. "

"How?"

"We'll talk about it once you have regained your health. Now we are in Eiríksfjordur and you should look around."

Helgi observed the shore as they sailed by countless islands and reefs which reminded him of Iceland. Imposing cliffs rose from the ocean to the sky. Below them, rust-coloured moss and shrubs in autumn hues covered the rocky hills. As they sailed farther into Eiríksfjordur, the wind calmed and a few small icebergs drifted towards the sea. Eirikur the Red gave the land he discovered a name it deserved; at least the ground by Greenland's shores was green.

On their left stood the land Eirikur the Red had settled and named Brattahlíd. Fat sheep wandered in the field. The large farmhouses were built with rock walls and turf roofs. Behind them rose green hills, dotted with boulders. A small church stood apart from the cluster of houses.

"Who built the church?" Helgi asked.

"When Leifur returned from a visit to Norway he converted many Greenlanders to the Christian faith. Among them was his mother, Thjódhildur, who wanted a church. Hence the church was built and named Thjódhildur Church."

"Is there a priest here?"

"He came with Leifur the Lucky from Greenland, but he's so old now he has forgotten all the scriptures. He still blesses everyone who approaches him." Forni laughed.

"Does Leifur still live in Brattahlíd?"

"He took over the farm when Eirikur the Red died twelve years ago. Sad to say, Leifur is now getting old. He's a great man, peaceful and Christian. His son Thórkell is now in charge of Brattahlíd.

Forni lived at the end of Eiríksfjordur on a farm called Under Sólarfjollum. His farm was as well kept and as imposing as Brattahlíd. Forni's wife Aesa greeted Helgi. Geirlaug, a plump and cheerful maid, massaged Helgi's feet and clad them in warm socks.

The longer he stayed with Forni, the more Helgi's mood improved. He felt welcomed, and in the evenings he entertained the household members with stories and poems.

Leifur the Lucky, the head of Brattahlíd, was a widower who carried himself like a statesman. The chief welcomed Helgi at Brattahlíd and he visited often. Leifur's son, Thorkell, and Helgi discussed spreading Christianity in Greenland and strengthening the bonds between Greenland, Iceland and Norway. With them, Helgi felt respected, and in the company of equals. He thought of chief Snorri Thorgrímsson's remark that Helgi would make a good advocate of the law. Greenland's law, and lack of it, became the subject of his conversations with the chiefs. If they passed laws similar to those of Iceland and Norway, they could eliminate infighting and prevent pillaging by lawless pirates.

Helgi ended his visits by praying for Katla in Thjódhildur Church.

Even though Helgi could barely walk, he wanted to be useful by carving wood. But driftwood was scarce in Eiríksfjordur. Instead of wood, the Greenlanders made tools from a soft rock they called carving-stone. Helgi borrowed a knife and carved bowls, spoons and other objects.

When he could walk, Forni showed him a wrecked ship which lay on the shore of his farm.

"Why don't you have this ship repaired?" Helgi asked.

"No one nearby knows how to build ships and we don't have the iron needed to secure the boards."

"Maybe I can carve nails from walrus tusks and whale bones. I saw shipbuilders use wool and fat to seal the wood."

"If you can make it seaworthy, I'll give it to you," Forni said, and grinned.

Helgi worked day and night to repair the ship he named *Mauritius*, in honour of his saint. In six days, after the ship was fully repaired, Helgi smeared tar made from seal fat on the outside and inside of the ship to prevent it from leaking. The broken yard and the missing sail did not bother Helgi. Because of the wandering icebergs by Greenland's shores, it was safer to row than to use sails.

The ship was Helgi's vessel to freedom.

Three of Forni's workmen helped him push *Mauritius* to sea. They rowed the length of Eiríksfjordur and the ship glided with ease. Helgi felt he was reborn and called to the sky, "Thank you, Forni, Mauritius and holy God!" The shipmen laughed.

That evening Forni said, "You shall marry a substantial woman here in Greenland."

"I would like to send for Katla."

"I thought you were intelligent, but now you sound like you're out of your mind."

"Perhaps I'm being unrealistic," Helgi sighed. "Katla may be betrothed or married."

"You're poor, and you have powerful enemies in Iceland. You have nothing to offer Katla."

"Or any woman," Helgi said. He felt like giving up.

"You're still a man of many talents. A wealthy widow might welcome a man like you."

"A wealthy widow, in these empty fjords?"

"I happen to know a young widow by the name of Thórunn. She was married to Skeggi the Proper. Shall we go for a visit?"

"A visit?"

"Yes."

How could he refuse Forni, who had given him his life and a ship? Even though Helgi's heart did not warm to the idea, he needed to increase his assets and gain respect by marrying a woman of means.

A week later, Helgi, Forni and ten oarsmen sailed south to Herjólfsnes, to pay the prospective bride a visit. Before the trip, Helgi carved a drinking horn out of a walrus tusk to give to Thórunn.

The oarsmen rowed with vigour while Forni and Helgi kept them advised of reefs and icebergs to avoid.

Forni kept glancing at Helgi as if something was bothering him.

"What is on your mind?" Helgi asked.

"While the sea is calm, I shall tell you about Thórunn's

misfortune."

"What misfortune?"

"When you first see her, you might be startled… But you're a man of courage and you won't look away, I suspect," Forni said and chuckled as if he were embarrassed.

"What? Isn't she beautiful?"

"Her face is beautiful, if you don't pay attention to the tooth."

"What tooth?"

"A front tooth which extends out and down between her lips."

"Are you saying Thórunn is ugly." Helgi had lain with many women, but never an ugly one.

"Just the tooth. Skeggi the Proper adored Thórunn. He didn't let one tooth prevent him from taking pleasure in his wife."

"How long has she been widowed?"

"A while," Forni said and looked away. "Every man she was betrothed to, and whom she hired to help run her farm, has died."

"Is her tooth a murder weapon?"

"She didn't kill them or want them dead." Forni wiped sweat off his forehead. "Although there's something dubious about how the men died."

"Before you put my life in danger, tell me what you know about her."

Forni sighed. "A sly farmer lives on a farm called Hellir located at the mouth of Helliseyjarfjord. His name is Thorvardur and people believe his wife Gríma is a witch. The couple have two vicious sons, Eyvindur and Thórir."

"Where is Helliseyjarfjord?"

"It's the next fjord west of Herjólfsnes, where Thórunn lives. Icebergs fill Helliseyjarfjord all year round, making it impossible to get round in a boat. In summer, they must manoeuvre between dangerous reefs to reach the sea. Because no one sails into Helliseyjarfjord but this family, we don't know what goes on in the fjord. Men suspect they hide their loot there."

"What kind of loot?"

"Several calves and lambs have disappeared from Herjólfsnes and Thórunn believes the treacherous family hankers after Herjólfsnes because it's easily reached by sea."

"I have no interest in fighting barbarians here in Greenland or anywhere," Helgi said.

"Herjólfsnes is worth it. The inlet provides shelter from the wind and the pastures are green. Skeggi the Proper had a fast longboat and made many trips north-west to Greipar to fish."

"Why all the way to Greipar?"

"The best fishing is found there. Skeggi would return with his ship full of seal meat, walrus tusks and sometimes whale meat—except for his last trip, when Skeggi and his men disappeared…"

"Disappeared?"

"We think the evil brothers, Thórir and Eyvindur, set Skeggi's ship on fire when it was out at sea."

"How has Thórunn managed to get by?"

"She is a force to be reckoned with. After Skeggi's death, Thórunn ran the farm at Herjólfsnes with the help of her brother Ornólfur, a good man. One autumn day, when he was sailing with two oarsmen by a reef close to the mouth of Helliseyjarfjord, he noticed a capsized ship. The oarsmen told Ornólfur to sail on, as the evil brothers owned the ship. But when Ornólfur saw the brothers standing soaking wet on a small reef, waving to him, he went to save them. The devils rewarded this good deed by killing him and throwing his body out to sea. Before the brothers could jump into the boat, the oarsmen pushed out to sea and fled, living to tell the story of Ornólfur's murder."

Helgi was astonished. "Don't tell me those brothers are still alive."

"They are. It's not the end of the story. After Ornólfur's death, Thórunn hired a foreman. After working for three days, he became ill and fell over dead. Later, Thórunn became engaged to a man, who also died mysteriously.

"Are you implying the woman is under a spell?"

"Most men think the old witch Gríma, the evil brothers' mother, is to blame. Due to this so-called spell, no one wants to marry Thórunn, even though her farm is valuable and she's hardworking."

Helgi was angry. "I thought we were friends. Why do you lead me into the devil's den?"

"I trust you above all men, as the Lord shows you his mercy."

"I think you're a bit overconfident in my abilities," Helgi said, and sighed. Yet his curiosity and promise of adventure were aroused. "If you want respect from decent Greenlanders, you need a wife of substance. "

Without Thórunn's assets Helgi would be a poor and powerless man, dependent on others. If he agreed to marry Thórunn, he would only have to sleep with her once to legitimise the marriage.

39
Katla

Katla appreciated the harmony Eilífur brought to Holl. But gloom descended on the farm with the first frost in the autumn when Oddlaug took ill with fever and was confined to her bed. Katla was surprised how distraught her father was by his wife's illness. He refused food, but ordered the staff to feed his wife well and to attend to all her needs. Each morning, he stopped by Oddlaug's bedside and said, "Get healthy, my wife," and every night he said to her, "Sleep well, my wife." Halldór could walk unassisted and spent the day in the longhouse where Eilífur kept him company. He recited Hávamál to Eilífur and made sure every verse was lodged in the boy's memory.

Katla heard Eilífur recite one.

"The halt can manage a horse,
The handless a flock,
The deaf be a doughty fighter;
To be blind is better than to burn on a fire:
There is nothing the dead can do."

Katla sat by her mother's bedside most of the day, sewed, sang, told stories and dried the sweat off her mother's brow. Oddlaug did not improve and had difficulty breathing.

On the tenth day of her mother's illness, Halldór said to Katla, "I've sent Dagur to fetch Thórdís. Maybe Finnbjorg can cure your mother."

Thórdís arrived the following day, bearing a potion and plants from Finnbjorg. She forced Oddlaug to drink the potion, but Oddlaug frowned, spat out the murky mixture and said to Thórdís, "My heart and my head have caused me enough suffering. I don't intend to die with a rotten taste in my mouth."

"I was trying to help," Thórdís said, her voice cracking.

"You're a resourceful and wilful woman, but I trust God to determine the time of my death," Oddlaug whispered.

"I understand," Thórdís said, and put down the potion. "I'll leave you alone to do as you please."

"My dear Thórdís, although I have failed to demonstrate it to you, I do love you."

"I know that I resemble my father in temperament, and you never liked that," Thórdís said with a bitter tone.

"I only dislike cruelty and selfishness," Oddlaug said and closed her eyes.

Thórdís patted her mother on her arm, walked out and rode off.

After Thórdís left, Oddlaug said softly, "Tell me Katla, was I a good mother to you?"

" I've never doubted that you were fond of me, my dear mother," Katla said with tears in her eyes.

"I disappointed you because I did not think you should marry Helgi."

"You did, but I understand."

Oddlaug coughed. "My dear Katla, help me to sit up because I want to tell you something."

Katla helped her sit and propped her up with blankets.

Oddlaug took a few breaths and said, "I was trying to protect you from disappointment. Helgi is not worthy of you. He's a rambling adventurer who puts his needs ahead of those of his family. You are kind, loyal and beautiful."

"But you agreed Helgi should marry Thórdís," Katla said.

"Thórdís did not care what kind of a man she married."

"I cannot recall seeing you and father kiss each other and be joyous together."

"Man's heart is complicated, my dear Katla. I'm responsible for our unhappiness."

"You? You always tried to please him."

"Not always. I have not lain with him since Kollur died."

"Kollur? Who is he?"

"When you were a year old, I bore a son whom we named Kollur. He was a large boy and the birth was difficult. Halldór was so proud and wanted to take the boy with him everywhere he went, even before he was a year old." Sweat formed on Oddlaug's brow and Katla wiped it off. "One day, Kollur had a fever and cried because he did not feel well. In spite of my objection, Halldór said Kollur would calm down on the ride and took Kollur with him. When they returned home, Kollur was sweating and short of breath. He died three days later."

Katla cried, stroked Oddlaug's hair and hugged her tight. "My dear mother. Nothing is worse than losing a loved one."

Oddlaug cried and trembled in Katla's arms. She moaned, "Halldór and I have never discussed Kollur since."

"You've missed out on so much. Where is Kollur buried?"

"He is buried on the other side of the boulder you call your elf rock."

"Eilífur saw him."

"Although I'm a Christian woman, I've never forgiven Halldór." She coughed and spat blood into a rag. "Put me down again."

Katla did as she said and washed her face. "You have endured many hardships. What can I do for you, dear mother?"

"Call a priest to bless me before I die."

"The priest shall come."

Katla asked Dagur to ride to Borg to get the priest. She did not tell Halldór.

The priest arrived the next day and Katla met him outside. He was clad in a tattered cloak and had a long beard. He said shyly, "Where is chief Halldór?"

"He is weak, praying in the longhouse, but it's my mother who wants to receive God's blessing before she dies."

Katla led the priest to her mother's bed. Oddlaug asked to be alone with the priest.

Katla walked to Halldór and said, "My mother asked for a priest and he is now with her."

Halldór mumbled, "How dare you leave her alone with an idiotic priest?"

"What harm is it to fulfil your wife's last wish?"

Halldór's eyes filled with tears. "Her last wish. Impossible! She was as robust as a wild stallion."

"She is out of breath."

He looked at Katla with sorrowful eyes. "Is the end near?"

"I think so," Katla whispered. Seeing her father so hurt

made her weep.

"I should talk to her instead of the wretched preacher." When he stood up, he fell forward, smashing the bench in front of him. He landed on top of it, his head touching the hearthstone.

Katla ran to the door and screamed for help. Dagur and several men came and helped Halldór to sit up. Blood trickled down his face from a cut in his forehead and he tried to wipe his eyes with his sleeve. His shoulders drooped and his lips quivered.

"Are you in pain, father?" Katla asked.

Tears trickled down his beard. "I want to say something to my wife."

Dagur said, "We'll help you to her bedside."

"Excuse me," said a voice by the door. The priest walked closer, looking petrified. "Oddlaug has passed on. I have given her God's blessing and crossed her."

Halldór spat in his direction and yelled, "Out of my house, you inept dimwit. You've killed my wife with your despicable lies. Get out!"

"My mother is gone," Katla cried out and ran out after the priest.

The priest turned around and said, "I shall never come here again." He disappeared.

Katla rushed to her mother's side. Oddlaug's face was as white as the linen which covered her body, but her mouth seemed to form a smile. Her arms were crossed over her chest. Katla kissed her on the forehead, squeezed her hand and knelt by her side crying until she sensed a hand resting on her shoulders.

"Oddlaug was a good woman," Eilífur said behind Katla. "But she was weary of this life. Now she can rest in peace."

Katla stood up and hugged Eilífur. "In spite of your youth, you understand everything."

"Halldór is broken-hearted," Eilífur said. "He needs love."

Dagur and three men placed Halldór in his bed and laid his sword by his side. The sore on his forehead was washed, but

243

Halldór lay limp as a wounded bull in his bed, quiet, with closed eyes.

A relentless snowstorm struck the farm and men could barely trudge between the farm and the outhouses. All the workmen's efforts were spent saving the animals from suffocating under snowbanks. Eilífur built a coffin for Oddlaug in the longhouse. Four days later Oddlaug was put in her coffin, and Dagur and his men dragged it on a sleigh to a shed where it would stay until she could be buried.

After Oddlaug was placed in her coffin, Halldór refused to eat. The following day, Katla sat by his side and sewed.

"Why don't you sing?" Halldór said.

"I thought you didn't like my singing."

"It stirs the heart," Halldór said.

"Your love for my mother is still in your heart."

Halldór sighed. "I suffocated our love with ill temper and criticism."

"Love never dies. It's like an ember which needs kindling to keep burning. Or it turns to ash and the joy of life withers with it."

"In spite of all your adversity you have managed to maintain your joy of life," Halldór said.

"How can I help being overcome with delight when I see lambs and calves burst out into the light and start sucking, running and calling for their mothers?"

"Perhaps the joy of life dwindles in the autumn when we slaughter the animals," Halldór said.

Katla giggled. "Maybe men think they can ingest the animals' vitality."

Halldór laughed weakly. "Could we be yearning for the calves' vivacity and the lambs' tranquillity when we tear the flesh apart with our teeth?"

"You think so?"

"I think I ingested unhappiness with every bite I swallowed. If I had only followed the advice of our forefathers: 'A gluttonous man who is not mindful will eat himself to death.'"

"My mother told me about my brother Kollur."

Halldór's lips quivered. "She held me responsible for his death and hated me until her last breath."

"She told me she felt partly responsible for your joyless relationship."

"I never tried to make it up to her."

"Were you in mourning?"

"Of course... I kept it to myself."

"Did the grief lessen with time?"

Halldór scratched his beard. "The other day when I was teaching Hávamál to Eilífur and he kept repeating over and over, 'Grief devours the heart if you do not tell another all of your mind's malady,' it occurred to me I never discussed Kollur's death with anyone, not even Oddlaug... Do sing your mother's favourite song for me."

Halldór lay with closed eyes and cried silently while Katla sang. Then he went to sleep and Katla resumed her sewing.

When he awoke, he said, "Send for my friend Thórdur."

"It's a north-easterly outside. The ground is covered with snow," Katla said.

"Vicious weather never kept Thórdur and me from helping a friend in need."

Katla asked Aevar to go to Hofdi to fetch Thórdur. While his horse was being saddled, to Katla's surprise, the storm subsided.

When she told her father of the change in weather he said, "Njordur is faithful to his followers."

Thórdur arrived later in the day and spoke with Halldór in private. Then he summoned Katla, Eilífur and Dagur to come to Halldór's bedside.

Halldór said, "Soon I will die and I want to tell you my wishes."

"Eilífur, I will bequeath to you my sword. You are not to use it unless your life, or a friend's life is at stake. When chiefs realise how competent and reliable you are, you will obtain loyal friends."

"What will happen to Eilífur?" Thórdur asked.

"Next spring he should go to his relatives at Steinar."

245

Thórdur grimaced. "I don't think it's a good idea. Those men are violent. Eilífur's presence will remind them of Arngeir's death."

"Hermundur and his friends have paid for your son's recklessness," Halldór said.

"Deep wounds heal slowly, if ever," Thórdur said.

"What's there to do, then?" Katla said.

"The boy is a good worker. I will take him in," Thórdur said.

"You are a man of honour, my friend," Halldór said. "Katla, you shall dwell at Holl and own the property with the following stipulations. Helgi shall never live on my land. Thórdur agrees. If Vandrádur does not return by spring and you don't want to live here alone, then you shall sell the property to a friend or an ally."

"Thank you, father. I promise," Katla said.

"I'm fortunate to have fathered beautiful and wise daughters. Nevertheless, I have been cursed with their failure to bear children. Katla, if you give birth to an heir while you live at Holl, he shall inherit the land when he's eighteen."

"I agree."

That night, Halldór went to sleep with his hands crossed over his sword on his chest and never woke up again.

Eilífur built a long and deep coffin for Halldór's corpse, and the workmen placed it next to Oddlaug in the outhouse. The coffins would stay there until the spring.

What was Katla to do now?

40
Helgi

Helgi's heart sank as he eyed the immense glaciers which soared above the farmhouses at Herjólfsnes. How could he survive a winter locked in by icebergs and glaciers, far away from his new friends in the Eastern Settlement?

A cow and a few sheep lingered in the marginal pasture in front of a sturdy longhouse.

Thórunn greeted them with a wide smile. Her walrus-like tooth extended from underneath the upper lip and bent over the lower lip down to the middle of the chin. Helgi was so repelled, he had to avert his gaze for a moment. Why did she not have the ugly tooth pulled?

Instead of risking insulting her, Helgi forced a smile and looked into her deep blue eyes, which reflected both sorrow and suspicion. Her thick auburn hair was tied into a knot at the nape of her neck.

Forni and Helgi followed Thórunn into the orderly longhouse. To Helgi's surprise, she offered them ale. Where did she get the grain for ale making? Could it be a potion like the one Finnbjorg and Thórdís had given him years ago? He took the horn and sipped carefully. The drink tasted like Norwegian ale.

When Forni told Thórunn of their errand, she sniggered and said to Helgi, "Don't you fear you will suffer the same fate as all the men in my past?"

"I doubt sorcery is enough to kill me," Helgi said, and laughed.

"You laugh," Thórunn said. "Christian men have not succeeded in eliminating witchcraft, at least in Greenland."

"Sorcery is nothing but delusion propagated by unwitting women," Helgi said.

Thórunn giggled. "Although you have travelled widely, you're as short-sighted as other Christian men. Are you sure you don't fear the effects of witchcraft?"

"I don't fear anyone," Helgi said.

Forni looked at Thórunn. "For you to marry, someone has to cast aside the black cloud which hovers over you."

"I doubt if any man is capable of removing it," she said, glaring at Forni.

"Helgi has many skills," Forni said.

"Pretentious poems about kings and dead chiefs do not carry any weight in these parts," Thórunn said. "What does Skáld-Helgi offer me more tangible than convoluted words?"

Helgi looked down. Forni came to his rescue and said, "The farm at Hornes in Einarsfjordur."

"I don't plan to move away from Herjólfsnes, even though this farm is infected by tragedy," Thórunn said.

Helgi gathered that Thórunn's will was as solid as her tooth. Before she took total control, he needed to assert himself. "I will not live here. It's too isolated. Forni has made a generous offer."

"The land at Hornes is fertile," Forni said.

Helgi clapped and smiled. "There you are, I prefer to live there."

"We shall see," Thórunn said and licked her tooth.

"Then shall we make your engagement official?" Forni said.

"Only if Helgi promises me two things."

Helgi looked into her eyes. "What shall I promise?"

"You shall promise to avenge the murder of the two men I loved the most, my husband Skeggi and my brother Ornólfur."

"I'm a Christian man and I no longer kill without good reason."

"The murderers were heathen," Forni said.

"They were neither Christian nor heathen. They only believe in evil deeds," Thórunn said.

"Are you sure the brothers from Hellir murdered Skeggi and your brother?" Helgi said.

"I am sure. And they are sworn enemies of King Olafur, and of all rulers," Thórunn said.

Helgi had served the Pope as a soldier of God. Could Saint Mauritius have sent him here to secure peace and Christianity in Greenland? He should not baulk.

"I promise to avenge the death of your men, if the

248

murderers are indeed atheists," Helgi said.

"I will only share my home with a man if I bear at least two of his children," Thórunn said.

"You already have two sons," Forni said.

"Two sons? Where are they?" Helgi said, surprised.

"Skeggi fathered my sons, Steingrímur and Jokull, who are now coming of age. They shall dwell in Herjólfsnes and run the farm until you have fulfilled our agreement. When we marry, I'll bring to Hornes in Einarsfjordur two maids, two workmen, all my goats, two cows and two horses."

Thórunn was as clever as his ex-wife Thórdís. She did not trust Helgi and she seemed repelled by his past. Nevertheless, in a dark bed on a cold winter night he could lie down with her, after drinking an ale or two.

"I agree," he said.

Forni sealed the betrothal. His oarsmen bore witness.

The wedding would be held when the farm at Hornes was ready for occupancy.

When they took leave, Helgi asked God to bless this decision, even though he found his prospective bride repulsive.

On their return from visiting Thórunn, Forni made a detour into Einarsfjordur to show Helgi Hornes, the farm he had given him. Steep cliffs rose from the sea where the Hornes land bordered the north-west shore of Einarsfjordur. Farther up the fjord was an inlet with a rundown dock. On a slope above the dock stood a small farmhouse and one outbuilding surrounded by a modest field.

Helgi commented to Forni, "A horse would be useless here. I could not go far."

Forni said, "On the contrary, in the summer you can ride up the ravine."

Helgi returned the next day with tools, food and a couple of workmen on loan from Forni. They collected driftwood from the islands at the mouth of Einarsfjordur. Helgi did not want to be beholden to Forni for long and intended to pay him once Thórunn sold Herjólfsnes.

Even though he now owned a farm, Helgi felt more like a laborer than a landowner. He was keenly aware that his prosperity in Greenland was subject to Thórunn's whims. It was his own fault. He could have married Katla but was too proud to live off her assets. Now, he was even more destitute, dependent on a repulsive woman for his sustenance in a foreign land. Still, he was grateful to Forni and to God for keeping him alive. At night he fell to his knees and promised God to serve Greenland, and the Lord, to the best of his capability.

At the end of autumn he sailed his ship south with six oarsmen to fetch his bride and livestock from Herjólfsnes.

Thórunn's sons, Steingrímur, sixteen winters of age, and Jokull, a year younger, carried their mother's belongings from the farmhouse and stacked them by the Helgi's ship. They avoided Helgi's gaze but he was impressed by their strength and reserved manner. The oarsmen loaded the ship and pulled the animals aboard.

A few days after Helgi and Thórunn moved to Hornes, Forni and Thorkell brought the old, forgetful priest to Hornes. The priest performed the simple ceremony in jumbled Latin. No one understood.

The only female guest was a brusque woman named Valgerdur, Thórunn's cousin, who lived on a farm nearby. After the ceremony, the two women seemed content to sit in a corner by themselves while the men ate and drank.

Helgi's first wife had ignored him unless she needed something from him, and so did his second wife. He was relieved and stayed out of Thórunn's way.

41
Katla

After her father's death, Katla asked Thórdur of Hofdi if Eilífur could stay with her for the winter and he agreed. She felt he was part of the family and treated him like a son. Eilífur missed Halldór more than anyone. Eilífur's kind and attentive presence had cracked Halldór's tough demeanour and exposed the chief's generous nature.

When most of the snow had melted but the nights were still frosty, Thórdís arrived on horseback, accompanied by a muscular woman.

They walked into the living quarters and Katla said, "You are brave to ride all the way here in this cold weather."

"I intend to stay until our parents are buried and the farm is in good hands."

Katla resented being treated like an ignorant child. "The farm is in good hands and it was our father's wish I would inherit it."

"If Helgi should show up, he cannot live here."

"I know. When I marry Helgi, I'll sell the farm."

"You are a vulnerable woman, and I expect some greedy man will attempt to force himself upon you."

"I've successfully refused the advances of men up until now," Katla said.

"You have, and so have I." Thórdís smiled.

"We're both strong, in our own ways," Katla said.

"Maybe," Thordis said. "Back to the matter at hand. Our parents didn't want similar burials and we must abide by their wishes."

"Our mother wanted a typical Christian burial and our father wanted earth to be heaped over his grave," Katla said.

"I think it best to have a private burial first. Later, the priest can perform his ritual over their graves to keep the Christians in the valley quiet." Thórdís sneered.

"I don't want any guests at the funeral," Katla said.

"I agree."

Thórdís's maid or workhorse was called Herdís. She scrubbed walls and floors and the beds Halldór and Oddlaug had slept in. She burned all the couple's clothes, bed linen and covers. Katla was grateful.

After the cleaning ordeal, Thórdís asked Katla to come to the sleeping quarters. On the floor by Halldór's bed stood a large locked trunk that Katla had never seen her father open. Thórdís opened the trunk with a key and Katla gasped with astonishment when she saw its shiny contents. There lay treasures made of gold, coins, buttons, brooches, knives, belts and more.

Thórdís laughed wholeheartedly. "Our father was cunning, and greedy."

"In spite of all his wealth, he wanted a substantial dowry for me," Katla said.

"He was proud."

"What shall we do with all this?"

"We'll divide it between us and keep it a secret. If we need money, we'll sell one item at a time. Do you agree?"

"I do."

They divided the treasure evenly. Thórdís kept her share in her father's trunk. They wrapped Katla's share in a sheet of linen and placed it in Katla's trunk, on top of all her other treasures.

"Now your trunk is full. You sure have a lot of valuables in there," Thórdís said.

"Yes, I've been working hard." Katla did not want her sister to see the gold and silver that Helgi had given her, and the treasures she had earned with her singing and sewing. She locked her trunk. Now, Helgi and she could afford to buy the biggest farm in Iceland and all the animals they could feed.

When Thórdís was ready to leave, with her trunk tied to the sled, she said, "Promise me not to tell Helgi about your inheritance. Father would not approve. And if Vandrádur should show up, don't tell him."

"I promise."

Before they separated, Katla said, "Did you know our

mother gave birth to a boy when I was about a year old?"

"Of course I knew. After his death our parents were grief-stricken and did not speak to each other. Our father ignored me until I figured out that he might like me better if I tried to be more like a son to him."

"It worked. You were good to him," Katla said, and Thórdís's eyes seemed mistier.

"And you were good to mother," Thórdís said.

They embraced, and when Thórdís rode off, Katla wondered why it was so difficult for people to talk about their disappointments, their pain. No one understood the hurt she felt from loving Helgi because they thought her pain was self-inflicted. Did she have a choice whom she loved? She doubted it.

~~~

When the snow had melted and the ground above the elf rock was soft, Katla asked Dagur to have the workmen dig graves there for her parents' coffins. Thórdís arrived after the coffins were placed in the graves but before they were covered. One of Thórdís's horses carried a large sack up the hill with items Halldór had wished to be buried with. Katla was glad Thórdís kept the contents of the sack a secret.

Katla crossed her mother's grave and said the Lord's Prayer.

As the workmen filled the graves with dirt, Katla felt Vonadís bless the graves of Kollur's parents.

The spring brought all its gifts, and Katla renewed her joy with each blooming dandelion, kicking calf and bleating lamb that caught the light of day.

Thórdur arrived to pick Eilífur up. Before he left, Katla gave Eilífur all her father's weapons that had not been buried with him. Eilífur embraced Katla and told her she was like a loving mother to him. Thórdur heard it and looked away. Katla was eager to ask Thórdur if he knew how Helgi was, but she kept her mouth closed.

The next day one of Vandrádur's relatives came by to tell

her Vandrádur had been killed in a battle in Sweden. That night, she fell to her knees and thanked God for saving her from marrying Vandrádur. She doubted if any of her cousins would attempt to marry her off, due to her age and to her obsession with Helgi.

For the first time in her life, Katla was free to go as she pleased and to dispose of her assets without asking anyone permission.

Eilífur arrived for a visit in late summer and told her that Helgi had returned to Norway from his pilgrimage and sailed to Iceland. She gave Eilífur a big hug and kissed him on the cheek. He blushed, and she could not stop laughing. She sang over and over, "God is good. God is good."

When Katla heard that a ship was moored by the mouth of the Hvítá river, her heart jumped, and she ran up the hill to see if anyone was riding towards Holl. When Helgi did not show up for two days, Katla dressed in the cape he had given her and asked Dagur to accompany her down to the harbour. She took a couple of colourful mantles with her to exchange for goods.

The ship was a merchant ship from Ireland, and the captain did not know of Helgi's whereabouts. She held back tears while she bought linen, golden thread and other supplies she needed for embroidery.

On her way home, she made up her mind not to think about Helgi lying lifeless at the bottom of the sea. Instead, she envisioned him arriving on shore and walking around. The thought calmed her mind and her hope resurfaced.

Katla was not as skilled as Thórdís in giving farmhands orders. But when she pretended to be as decisive and direct as Thórdís, workers heeded her. She thanked people more often than her sister did, and she never wore trousers.

The clothes she made were still in great demand and she kept saving the coins she earned. She was perhaps the only woman in Iceland who could dye cloth red. It took a large wooden bowl and an inordinate amount of cow urine and mountain grass to bring out the red colour. The proportion of the ingredients and the length of time the cloth sat in the urine blend was Katla's closely guarded secret. The wealthiest women in Iceland coveted her embroidered scarlet capes.

After the sheep were sheared in the autumn, the wool collected, lambs slaughtered and the sausage preparation was under way, Katla was exhausted and depressed. Winter approached, but where was Helgi?

As if summoned by her, Eilífur paid her a visit to tell her Thórdur and Nidbjorg did not know where Helgi was.

42
Thórunn

After their wedding, Thórunn learned that the upkeep of the house at Hornes was not Helgi's priority. His ship, the dock and his rowboat captured most of his attention, and he was more concerned with impressing the chiefs at Brattahlíd than with honouring her.

They slept in separate beds. Some nights he crawled under her covers, stroked and kissed her breasts—never her mouth—and inserted his erect manhood when she separated her legs. She could not help but grasp his buttocks. He got up as soon as his member went limp, leaving her baffled. Was he only performing his duty to impregnate her or did he enjoy it? They never discussed their relations.

After Helgi's work preferences became clear, Thórunn told her workers to take orders from her, and Helgi did not object.

Helgi was accustomed to adulation. Men complimented him on his ship repairs, and women responded to his looks. Thórunn saw no reason to join this ignorant group.

One day, without warning, Helgi was beset by pain, lost his appetite and could not get up. Once he fell asleep, his body went limp, but his eyes moved under his eyelids. Thórunn suspected he was under a spell.

On the third day of this madness, Helgi called out, "Katla, I promise, I promise."

"What do you promise?" Thórunn asked.

"I promise to eat and drink."

"Then keep your promise," Thórunn said and held a cup to his lips. She knew of his obsession with Katla Halldórsdóttir. Perhaps his illness was Katla's fault.

After twenty days, Forni arrived at Hornes with six men and one priest. They went straight to Helgi's bed.

"No, no, no!" Helgi screamed.

Forni said, "What's ailing you?"

Helgi did not respond.

Forni turned to Thórunn and said with an accusatory tone, "Men are calling you a witch who wants to kill Helgi."

The priest added, "Someone suggested you should be stoned to death."

Thórunn seethed with anger. "What kind of idiots are you, listening to tattlers? I want Helgi to stay alive. Someone has put a spell on all of my men, and I suspect it is the witch Gríma."

The priest stammered, "You don't believe in Christ, or you would have married in a church."

"But a sorceress I'm not. Do men of Jesus and God now believe in witchcraft?"

Without looking at her, Forni said, "Helgi's condition seems incurable. What is there to do?"

The priest said, "Evil spirits roam around this place, and I cannot do anything but pray to God to remove them."

"Do as you please," Thórunn said, and walked outside.

In a short while Forni and the priest joined her.

"Is he recovering after receiving God's blessing?" Thórunn sneered.

"In God's time," the priest said and walked away.

Thórunn went in to see Helgi. He still lay motionless in his bed.

"Ignorant men with authority. The worst kind," Thórunn said.

Thórunn's interest in Helgi's recovery was not inspired by love or fondness. If he died, she would be persecuted. In spite of her attempts to serve Helgi, he refused to eat or drink. He squirmed with pain, and his face looked beastly. While he slept, his face relaxed and his lips seemed to smile. When he awoke, Thórunn asked him about his dreams, but he claimed not to remember anything. He lied. Was he dreaming about Katla?

What should she do? She waited for the full moon and sat outside licking her long tooth, the tooth which others called a walrus tusk.

When Thórunn was a young girl, the front tooth grew

beyond her other teeth, causing her immense pain. This started shortly after Thórunn's father refused Gríma's proposal that Thórunn marry the witch's son, the mischievous Eyvindur. Thórunn's mother knew that Gríma was responsible for the spell and told her daughter it was easier to live with a walrus tooth than an evil man. She was right. Thórunn was grateful to her parents for not giving her to Eyvindur, even though they had been subject to Gríma's revenge ever since.

The protruding tooth was no doubt intended to repel men, which it did. She found a good man anyway. Skeggi the Proper did not let one tooth keep him from adoring Thórunn. He was a great man. Helgi was not.

As Thórunn matured, she discovered that if she licked the tooth during a full moon, her mind filled with clarity. From then on, she asked the moon to lift the spell which grew the tooth. After Skeggi and her brother died, she asked her tooth and the moon for revenge.

Now, she needed to put Helgi's predicament in perspective. Looking at the moon, she licked her tooth as if she were licking the last drop of butter from a bowl and prayed for Helgi to be healed.

The next day, someone knocked and Thórunn opened the door. Outside stood a strange woman wearing a black sheepskin cape decorated with various bones, animal tails and pins. Her skin was dark and her hair hidden under an enormous hat.

"My name is Hjordís."

The ground was covered in snow. "Where did you come from?"

"Over the mountain." Hjordís was calm and courteous. "The maker himself directed me to you." She stepped aside. "You may not come close to me."

"Why not?"

"You're under a spell. I must cure Helgi to lift your curse."

"As you wish," Thórunn said, and stepped aside while Hjordís walked inside. "I think he covets women in his sleep."

Hjordís walked straight to Helgi's bed and asked to be alone with him.

Thórunn walked into the kitchen, thinking the strange woman could either cure Helgi or kill him. Either result was acceptable.

43
Helgi

Helgi woke up from deep sleep when he felt a cold hand press against his forehead. Through a haze he saw the outline of a woman with frizzy hair. She stared at him with dark reflective eyes as if she were deciphering his thoughts. A maid stood by her side holding a candle.

"My name is Hjordís," the woman said with a seductive whisper. "I came to heal you of your maladies."

Helgi whispered, "Please help me. I need to confess, but I can't remember any scriptures. I must cross myself, but my arms are limp."

"I can neither read nor sing and I don't cross myself. But I do offer other solutions."

She was holding a folded piece of rawhide. "This hide contains the name of the creators and their blessings for men. Clench it between your teeth until your mind clears."

After a while of clenching the hide, Helgi remembered his dreams and wrongdoings. He was horrified, removed the hide, and said, "Each night I dream the same dream."

"Tell me the dream," Hjordís said.

"Every evening a woman seduces me. She's as fair as the peaks of Greenland's glaciers."

"Do you know her name?"

"Mýrídur."

"Can she cross herself? Does she sing?"

"I don't know. She speaks like an angel, and when she smiles, she evokes fervent passion in me."

"You're lovesick, and beautiful women tempt you."

"They have done."

"I suspect Mýrídur is a witch in the guise of a beautiful woman to prevent you from embracing your wife. If you agree, I'll teach you a trick to find out whether she favours Jesus or sorcery."

Helgi was perplexed. Mýrídur was bewitching indeed, but he

could not subsist on dreams alone. "What trick?"

"You shall compose three obscene and libellous stanzas and recite them to her. If she does not disappear, you can copulate at will."

That night Mýrídur came to him and embraced him fondly. He gave himself permission to delight in carnal pleasures before reciting to her the sexually obscene and derogatory poem. As soon as he finished, Mýrídur transformed into an ugly old witch and accused him of being a traitor who took advantage of her affection. Suddenly he remembered his Christian creed and said it out loud.

Mýrídur hissed and said with a shrill voice, "Thórunn is guilty of poisoning you."

He recited a bawdy poem out loud.

"How beastly of you to reward me with such vulgarity," the witch said.

"Go away, you old shrew. You can no longer tempt me with your vulgar ways."

When the beast tried to bite his neck, he made the sign of the cross over his face. With his heart filled with the power of God and the goodness of Jesus, he called out loud, "God, my Lord, Jesus!"

The witch fled and took Helgi's illness with her.

Helgi opened his eyes, expecting to see Hjordís. Instead Thórunn sat by his side. She appeared beautiful and he asked her to lie down with him. He treated her with tenderness, kissed her on the mouth, and filled her with his manhood.

As soon as the ice in the fjords had melted enough for Helgi to row his boat, he fished and visited farmers. Even though the spell no longer plagued Thórunn or him, his lust for other women did not diminish. Geirlaug, Forni's maid, who had massaged his frostbitten feet when he first arrived in Greenland, was still drawn to him. He delighted in watching her milk the cows in the shed with her thighs spread wide apart. As she pulled the cow's nipples, he sneaked up behind her and lifted her skirt. She giggled, put the bucket aside, stood up and led him to a pile

261

of hay where they played.

Even if he shared carnal acts with other women, his heart belonged to Katla. To keep her close he went outside on a starry night, talked to the Katla Star and asked her to protect her namesake.

44
Katla

When Katla did not receive news of Helgi for two months, she feared he had drowned on his way to Iceland. She lost her appetite for food.

Thórdís arrived on a brisk day and said to Katla, "What is the matter with you? I heard all the way at Hvítársída that you looked like a ghost and had abandoned sewing, eating and even chatting with elves."

"No one has heard from Helgi since he left Norway."

"It's your responsibility to keep your farm Holl prosperous. You are crazy to allow a useless vagabond to ruin your life. Helgi must have managed to wreck his ship and has settled down on the bottom of the sea."

Katla wiped her tears with her sleeve. "How can you be so cruel to your sister?"

"I don't pity you for your obsession with Helgi. But I'm relieved to learn that, despite your whining, you have enough smoked meat and sausages made for the winter months. Or so Aevar tells me."

"What is the reason for your visit, other than adding to my heartache?"

"How long are you going to wallow in your misery?" Thórunn said.

"If I don't hear from Helgi, I'm going to Norway next spring."

"To Norway?" Thórdís said scornfully. "Do you want to become one of the king's concubines? Because nothing awaits you there but lecherous men."

For the first time, Katla screamed at her sister, "I'm the best seamstress in the country and I am rich."

"And who wants to sail with a single woman who has never been on a boat?"

"I've dealt with many merchants throughout the years and I'm certain I can pay a respectable one to take me to Norway."

Katla was fed up with Thórdís's brutality. "You've never been fond of me—why do you concern yourself with where I go on land or on sea?"

"What will happen to Holl while you're on your manhunt?" Thórdís said.

"I shall hire a manager."

"Have you found a capable one?"

"I will as soon as the winter is over."

"Too late then, because he has to prepare for the summer chores. It's crucial the farm is left in capable hands before you chase Helgi to Norway."

Katla sighed. "I guess you're right. Maybe we should talk about finding a manager."

Thórdís smiled. "Wise decision."

Katla should have known Thórdís had a plan, but said, "Do you know one?"

"Our cousin Bjorg and her husband Flosi are having a hard time taking care of their family."

"I thought they had a good farm at Snaefellsnes."

"Last winter one snowstorm after another hit their farm. The ice was so thick, the grass never recovered for the summer and their fields were ruined. They had to sell the surviving livestock before it starved to death."

"Where are they?" Katla asked.

"They have not succeeded in finding a home, because they have three young children," Thórdís said with quivering lips.

"It breaks my heart, and yours too, it seems," Katla said.

"They have worked hard, and have done nothing to deserve such a destiny," Thórdís said, looking stern again.

"Right."

"Once upon a time, you were cheerful and people called you jolly Katla."

"Once upon a time, I was hopeful."

"Then restore your hope," Thórdís said. "Maybe Helgi is alive after all." She walked out.

Two weeks later, Bjorg, Flosi and their three children came

to Holl. The youngest girl, Aldís, was three and had wild blond curls. She ran back and forth, clapped her hands, and laughed at everything. She reminded Katla of herself as a young girl.

While Katla spun and sang, Aldís danced and twirled in front of her.

Bjorg oversaw the cooking, making skyr and cheese, and managed the maids. Flosi oversaw the farming and managed the workers. He and Aevar became fast friends. Cows were milked on time and the sheep was gathered and placed in the sheds before winter reared its snowy head. Katla kept busy weaving and sewing clothes for the family, and they were grateful.

Before Christmas, Flosi and Bjorg made ale from malt and grain they found in the pantry shed. Katla practised songs and taught the children. Even the five- and seven-year-old boys tried to sing along.

All of Holl's residents were invited to the guest lodge for the Christmas celebration.

"We rejoice in the rising sun because Christ is the true light of the world," Katla announced.

Candles were lit and ale served. Katla could not remember a happier time in the Holl household.

Eilífur came to Holl before Christmas and stayed for several days. He helped Flosi make fish nets during the day. The nets, made from the sealskin strips Katla bought from the merchant, looked durable. Flosi expected them to sell well to fishermen in the spring.

Since Holl was now in good hands, Katla could sail to Norway in the spring.

When Bjorg and Flosi tried to persuade Katla not to sail to Norway, she said, "My life is worth nothing without Helgi. God whispered to me the sea has not swallowed him. Helgi might still be in Norway, and is better there until his enemies in Iceland are dead. I'll find Helgi and stay with him in Norway."

~~~

In the spring, when ships sailed into Borgarfjordur, Katla

sent Flosi and a workman to the dock to see if they could buy a fare for her to Norway. After three trips, they succeeded and paid her fare with the sealskin nets.

Flosi and Aevar accompanied her to the dock. A couple of horses dragged a wagon with a new trunk Eilífur had made her. The trunk contained food for the trip, mantles, capes, frocks and men's trousers. She left her other trunk, with most of her treasures, at home. For the trip, Katla dressed in the cape Helgi had given her, freshly washed. She also brought a sheepskin cape with a hood to protect her cape from the rainstorms at sea.

The merchant who owned the ship was named Konáll, the same man who had sold her the walrus strips a few winters back. He gave Katla admiring glances, received the fish nets with glee, and had them piled by the trunk under the ship's mast. The weight at the centre of the ship made it steadier and prevented the ship from capsizing in a bad storm. An old sail was stretched over the cargo. Katla feared the cargo could shift in a rough sea and asked Konáll if he should not use the nets to tie the cargo down. The ship's captain liked the idea and the sailors spread the nets over the cargo and tied them to beams. Konáll gave Katla the best seat in the centre of the ship and ordered all sailors to let her be.

Before they set out to sea, Flosi cautioned Katla about Konáll. "Beware of the pushy merchant."

Katla was the only woman on board. She avoided the sailors but moved often to dodge the flapping sail. She grasped the nets firmly when the waves heaved the ship from side to side. To avoid seasickness, she ate only a few pieces of dried fish.

At first the sea was rather calm. The sail caught the breeze and the ship moved smoothly over the sea. During the short nights, Katla leaned back, gazed at the sky and tried to locate the stars. The constant movement made it impossible, and she fell asleep. The dilemma of urinating in front of twenty men worried Katla. She avoided the potential embarrassment by swirling her cape around her while she relieved herself. A sailor threw the pan's contents overboard.

When a rainstorm pounded the ship, she wrapped the

sheepskin cape around her and grasped the walrus nets until her muscles ached. Konáll kept busy trying to secure the merchandise and Katla welcomed a break from his incessant chatter. When the weather calmed, Konáll asked her about the reason for her trip.

"I'm going to meet my fiancé."

"Who is the lucky one?"

"Helgi Thórdarson, named Skáld-Helgi."

"So you are the famous Katla?"

"Do you know Skáld-Helgi?"

"He's well known in Norway."

"For his poetry?"

Konáll smirked and said, "Who understands his poetry these days? He's better known for his sportsmanship, pilgrimage and lovesickness."

Katla looked down and said calmly, "Do you know where he might be?"

"He bought a share in a ship and set off from Norway, the last I heard."

"Where did he sail to?"

"Towards Iceland."

"When?"

"At the end of last summer."

Katla's heart pounded. "But he never arrived in Iceland."

Konáll smirked. "Therefore I suspect you are no longer betrothed."

"I doubt the sea has swallowed Helgi," Katla said, and turned away from Konáll.

~~~

After fourteen days at sea, the Katla's ship glided into the fjord by Nidaros. Tall trees covered the steep mountainside on both sides of the fjord, and as the ship approached the shore, she was greeted by a field of magnificent flowers in countless colours. She could not contain her delight and called out, "Look at the flowers!" What magnificent dyes she could make using

267

these flowers.

Several ships blocked the pier at the head of the fjord. Konáll cursed as he could not find a space close to the pier and moored his ship a short distance from shore. Katla and her possessions were hoisted into a boat, which two men rowed to the shore. Workers, women and well-dressed men lingered to watch the boat gliding into a small dock. Katla marvelled at the diverse clothing they wore and wondered who she should ask about Helgi.

She asked the oarsmen to put her trunk down by a group of women, then stood by it as if nailed to the ground, mesmerised by the sweet fragrance of the air and the brightly coloured linen sold by loud men with black beards, wearing white tunics. At their side sat Southern women wrapped in silk scarfs from top to toe. When Katla made eye contact with their coal-coloured eyes, they averted their gaze. Some sewed silk clothing, manoeuvring fine needles with expertise. Katla longed to approach them and to learn their sewing techniques, but she did not dare abandon her trunk, afraid it could be stolen.

Where should she sleep? As she sat down on the trunk, it dawned on her that she had failed to make plans for her stay in Norway. Since Helgi was a famous poet, she assumed people would know his whereabouts. But Nidaros was crowded with strangers, foreigners, peasants, the young and the old, the rich and the poor. When Katla eyed the beautiful silks and other fabrics, a sense of worthlessness descended on her. The mantles she made appeared rough and dull compared to the ones for sale around her. Some men stared at the ornate mantle Katla wore, and she felt ashamed for being dirty. She had to find a place to wash before she met Helgi. But where? How could she abandon her trunk?

A group of priests or monks clad in robes stood not far from her, and when one of them glanced her way, she stood up and waved to him to come to her. He looked perplexed but then walked to her with another monk.

She made the sign of the cross before asking the monks, "Do you know a man by the name of Skáld-Helgi who went on a pilgrimage to Rome?"

One monk said, "I've heard of him. Joseph went with him on the pilgrimage."

She jumped with joy. "Where's Joseph?"

Joseph turned out to be close by. When Katla introduced herself, his eyes filled with tears. "God has allowed me to meet the Christian woman whom Skáld-Helgi loved as much as many love Madonna herself. So you are Skáld-Helgi's virgin?"

Katla could not help crying too. "Tell me, tell me about Skáld-Helgi."

"I walked most of the way to Rome with Helgi." He told Katla of Helgi's bravery, of Helgi receiving a calling when he drank from the well of Saint Mauritius, and his fighting in the Pope's army.

"Did the Pope have an army?" she asked, surprised. She could not imagine the Pope as a warrior.

"Helgi chased away the Saracens who raided the Pope's territory."

"Did the Pope forgive his sins?"

"He did indeed, but Helgi said his happiness depended on marrying his virgin in Iceland—the beautiful maiden he left behind because of his sins. Neither King Olafur, the court poets nor the bishops could sway his determination."

Katla smiled and said, "Helgi has made many sacrifices to be free of his sins."

Joseph dried his tears and said with a solemn expression, "But why have you travelled all the way to Norway?"

"My father is dead. I can marry Helgi now, but I wanted to warn him he still has enemies in Iceland."

"I thought he sailed to Iceland last autumn," Joseph said. "How sad you're here alone."

She drew a kerchief from her pocket and blew her nose.

Joseph looked like he wanted to console her. "Of course, he could have travelled with the king south to Sarpsborg."

"Who knows for sure?" Katla asked.

"The king's courtiers, I assume."

"Where can I find them?"

"They're everywhere, but most of them are with the king."

Katla looked around as a well-dressed woman, followed by three escorts, walked towards Katla.

The woman was tall, a redhead with freckled face and moss-green eyes. "Greetings. My name is Signy and my husband is Sighvatur Thórdarson, court poet to King Olafur."

"Sighvatur Thórdarson. He is Skáld-Helgi's friend."

"Who are you?" Signy asked.

"Thórkatla Halldórsdóttir."

"Welcome. I've never seen a woman with a more beautiful smile."

Katla was embarrassed. "I'm so dirty after the voyage."

"If you agree, you can stay with me until we find out Helgi's whereabouts. I live on an island called Saela, north of here. Only Christians live there, and they are building churches. We can stay in Nidaros tonight and then travel to Saela tomorrow."

Katla cried—this time in gratitude. "What a generous, kind woman you are and so beautiful, Katla said.

Signy's escorts lifted Katla's trunk onto a wagon hitched it to the biggest and strongest horse Katla had ever seen.

They walked to an assemblage of cabins, large and small. On the way, Signy said, "I am Celtic and I feel at home on Saela. When all of Norway was heathen, a Celtic woman called Sunneva lived there, and when the heathens invaded the island, she hid in a cave and died there."

"What a sad story," Katla said, and cried once more, this time because of Sunneva's tragic fate.

"Now you can stop shedding tears because joyful days are ahead here in Nidaros. Preparations for King Olafur's wedding are in full force. The king has been down south in Sarpsborg since Candlemas. My husband, Sighvatur, is with the king and they are on their way to us."

"Could Helgi be with the king?"

"I have not heard. He could be with the courtiers here in Nidaros. They are defending the territory from the intrusion of hostile farmers who live north and east of here. Soon we will find out where Helgi is." Signy patted Katla on the cheek. "You'll enjoy your stay in Norway in the meantime. Magnificent festivities are ahead, and then we shall dance."

"Dance?"

"Olafur the Stout is travelling with his wife Astrid, who was just crowned the Queen of Norway, even though she is Swedish. King Olafur of Sweden is her father." Signy laughed. "Our Olafur is cunning. He married Astrid without asking her father permission."

"Isn't the king of Sweden angry?"

"Furious and jealous because Olafur the Stout wins more wars than he does. The Swedish king was in a precarious situation because he fathered Astrid with an enslaved woman named Edla."

"Did Astrid's father mistreat her?"

"Quite the contrary. She's beautiful and eloquent and the king adored her."

"Did Olafur the Stout marry Astrid in Sweden?"

"Too risky. The wedding took place in Sarpsborg in southeast Norway last spring. Their journey from there to here is taking longer than usual because the new queen travels with an entourage of one hundred men and the king with even more." Signy laughed. "He could not have fewer courtiers than his wife."

"I hope they don't argue on the way. It could start a war," Katla said, and laughed.

Signy and Katla enjoyed inventing reasons for the king and queen to bicker.

Instead of going to Saela Island, Signy and Katla settled into a small guest cottage near Nidaros and prepared for the arrival of the king, the queen and Signy's husband.

Katla felt invigorated after bathing in a large wooden tub. She dressed in a long, sky-blue dress and tied around her waist a gold belt she had inherited from her father. Over her shoulder she draped a blue scarf and tied it with two gold brooches. She covered her hair with another scarf to symbolise her betrothal to Helgi.

Signy said, "You're the most beautiful woman I've ever seen."

Katla draped an embroidered green mantle over Signy's shoulders and said, "The colour enhances your mossy eyes and red hair."

Signy stroked the mantle. "Thank you, Katla. These are both gorgeous and unique. If you continue sewing clothes like these, you'll become rich and popular among the noblewomen in Norway."

"But the silk clothes at the market are more beautiful and expertly adorned than the clothes I have woven and sewn."

"We can't wear those silks in the winter. Your material is more suitable for Norwegian weather," Signy said.

Even though the king was absent, Signy and Katla were invited to dine in the king's lodge. Katla asked the chief courtier, who sat between her and Signy, if he knew where Skáld-Helgi was.

"He sailed towards Iceland last summer."

Katla said, "He could not have."

Signy said quickly, "I bet he's there. We'll find out soon enough. Let's drink to the new queen."

Katla lifted her horn and forced a smile. She did not want to upset Signy any more, but she found it difficult to think of anything but Helgi's whereabouts.

After dinner, Katla and Signy walked to their abode where Konáll the merchant and another man were waiting for them. Konáll introduced the man as Skúli, the brother of Illugi, who had sailed with Helgi.

"I heard my brother Illugi and my cousin Illugi drowned at sea by the coast of Greenland. We assume the same fate befell Skáld-Helgi," Skúli said.

Katla rushed inside and cried for what was left of the evening. Her wailing kept Signy awake.

The next morning Signy was so angry her face was bright pink and her freckles more pronounced. She said, "Helgi can't be the only man on earth whom you can love. Now it's time you accepted his fate, became useful, and served King Olafur, who was generous to Helgi. There's a shortage of clothes fit for the king's men and women here."

"Should I not return to Iceland?"

"Returning now serves no purpose. Nothing awaits you in Iceland," Signy said. "Here, you have a remarkable opportunity to serve the king and the queen, and to accumulate valuables."

Signy turned out to be right, and Katla was hired to sew a gold embroidered mantle for Queen Astrid. The commission brought Katla to her senses.

"I have to find the dark people who sell the silk, and buy their needles," Katla told the courtier who hired her to make the queen's mantle.

"They are about to sail away."

"Can we go now?" Katla said.

They rode down to the harbour. Katla bought silk the colour of redcurrants, golden thread, silk thread in various colours and sewing needles. The courtier paid with exotic coins.

When she sewed, she avoided thinking of Helgi lying at the bottom of the ocean. She feared soiling the priceless fabric with her tears.

In time, her reputation as the best seamstress in Nidaros lessened the gossip about her obsession with Skáld-Helgi. People did not giggle when she passed them any more, but smiled. She returned all smiles, remembering Helgi's wish for her to keep smiling and spreading joy wherever she went. It was her way to honour Helgi.

~~~

Queen Astrid, King Olafur and their entourage entered Nidaros, causing a commotion. Men and women vacated lodges and cottages and others moved in. Loaded merchant ships sailed into the harbour. Goods were unloaded and transported by horse to the lodges, while dozens of muscular armed men guarded the houses and the harbour.

Seeing the mayhem, Katla stayed inside and sewed while

Signy went to meet her husband Sighvatur.

When Signy returned, she said, "The king doesn't want to settle down in Nidaros before his men have built a large lodge, fancy enough for the queen. Until then, they intend to live in Lofoten."

"Lofoten! But it is so far from Nidaros," Katla said.

"The king wants to control all men, including the heathens whom he ousted from Lofoten. Some are the queen's friends who now live up-country, and the king wants to prevent them from visiting her."

"I guess it's easier to guard an island. But why does Queen Astrid have so many escorts? I thought the king's men would guard her too."

"A man with a large entourage is a powerful man. The same goes for women."

"A woman without escorts is therefore a woman without power," Katla said.

"You're amusing," Signy chuckled. "I doubt if we'll ever see the day when Astrid is outmanoeuvred by the king."

"I hope they'll live in peace."

"The queen is baptised, but she still keeps in touch with her heathen friends, much to the king's annoyance," Signy said.

"It's a miracle your husband is friendly with both the king and the queen."

"Sighvatur finds it easier to compose poetry than to make peace between those two." Signy's demeanour was serious now. "No one must hear the way we talk about them. The good news is that the queen's private maid told me Astrid was so impressed by the mantle and veils you sewed for her that she's going to wear them this evening."

"Will I get to see the queen?"

"You're invited to the banquet, and you'll be one of the honorary guests."

"But I don't know how to behave with royalty."

"Your beauty is so captivating, we have to make sure you don't outshine the queen."

"I'm older, but I'll dress modestly and braid my hair, so men won't stare at me."

Signy sighed and said, "Sighvatur is dealing with a predicament."

"What?"

An Icelandic poet named Ottar, who once served the king of Sweden, wrote a defamatory poem about Queen Astrid. King Olafur was furious because he felt the poem was derogatory, and when Ottar came to Norway, the king had him thrown in a dungeon, intending to have him beheaded.

"Why is this Sighvatur's problem?"

"My husband and Ottar are childhood friends. Three days ago, Sighvatur went to the dungeon and asked Ottar to change the parts of the poem which upset the king, and to compose a poem honouring king Olafur. The next day, Ottar asked to recite both the revised poem about Astrid, and the new poem about Olafur, in the king's presence."

"Did the king allow it?"

"Thanks to Sighvatur, Ottar will be escorted from the dungeon and allowed to recite both poems at the dinner tonight."

"Tonight! I am so honoured. How clever your husband is."

"He's a peaceful man, a good Christian, and he plans to go on a pilgrimage to Rome like Helgi did. It's up to King Olafur to choose the time."

When Katla walked into the king's lodge, she was too shy to look around and kept her eyes fixed on Signy's veil in front of her. After they were seated, she heard the sound of music and looked around. A woman was playing a harp so beautifully that Katla wanted to sing, but she resisted.

The king and queen walked in and sat down on their respective thrones. All eyes, including Katla's, rested on the beautiful queen, who held her head high and her chest lifted as if to greet the sun. Her large brown eyes darted about as if they wanted to catch everything. When the light caught her voluminous shiny brown hair, red sparks appeared to dance around her crown. Her bright red lips parted in a faint smile. Did the queen assume ownership of everything around her—the courtiers, the servants, and her stocky king, who reminded Katla of her own father? The king seemed strong, his gaze steady and imposing.

Maids, as numerous as the guests, served reindeer meat and soup made with mysterious ingredients. As soon as the guests finished eating, the maids whisked the bowls away.

Two huge men led the poet Ottar in front of the king. With his hands tied together, Ottar was ordered to sit on the floor in front of the king.

Queen Astrid winked at Katla and smiled, while the king stared down at Ottar.

Ottar did not look like a humble man, and without being asked he started reciting his ode to King Olafur. Some courtiers shouted, "Shut up, you shammer."

The king, now even angrier, yelled, "Quiet!" When all were silenced, the king continued, staring with an evil eye at Ottar, "Before you are beheaded, you will recite the rude poem about my honourable queen, so she can hear it."

Sighvatur, who stood behind the king, said, "Your excellency, only you can decide when Ottar will die. Therefore, it's of no consequence if the honourable king hears both the poems."

The king allowed Ottar to recite both poems. Katla could not grasp their meaning, but after Ottar was done, Sighvatur praised the latter poem for its accurate content and skilful construction.

King Olafur said, "Because of my merciful nature, I'll let you keep your head in exchange for the poem."

"Your gift is indeed merciful, even though my head is rather ugly."

The courtiers laughed. Olafur pulled a gold ring from his satchel and gave it to Ottar.

Queen Astrid followed suit by sliding a gold ring to Ottar. "Take this sparkling band. It is now yours."

King Olafur said to the queen, "Why are you rewarding Ottar?"

In a sweet voice the queen said, "My honourable king, sure you're not going to reprimand me for rewarding a man who pays homage to your queen, in the same way you rewarded him for the homage paid to you." She looked at the king, half smiling.

When the king beheld his wife's radiant face, his demeanour softened. "I shall not reprimand you this time, but I do not sanction your friendship with Ottar."

The king allowed Ottar to stay in his court. As Ottar had received his head in exchange for praising King Olafur, his poem was called 'The King's Ransom'.

Katla admired the queen for the clever yet subtle way in which she influenced the king. Thórdís was as shrewd. Unlike them, Katla had never learned to use trickery to get her way. Or maybe she did when she talked her father into giving her Holl. The farm would provide her with a safe abode when she returned to Iceland.

45
Thórunn

Thórunn stood in the doorway at Hornes in Greenland and watched her husband and a workman row out into the bay. Helgi was going to visit his friend Thorgrímur the Giant at Langanes. Thorgrímur was Thórunn's cousin, and a rich self-appointed chief. Like Leifur Eiriksson, who had passed away recently, they deemed themselves superior, due to their friendship with King Olafur of Norway and their so-called Christianity. At their meetings, they invented rules of conduct for the common Greenlanders, which they referred to as laws. Thórunn was not fooled. Their alliance was based on their shared craving for control.

Thorgrímur the Giant had a sister named Valgerdur who also lived at Langanes, and was Thórunn's best friend. When Helgi visited Thorgrímur, Valgerdur used the opportunity to visit Thórunn.

Before long, Thórunn spotted Valgerdur's boat approaching. Her spirits lifted as she was eager to discuss her dilemma with her friend. Thórunn went inside to warm up her special brew.

Valgerdur was a stocky woman. Due to her size, deep voice and shrewdness, men listened to her.

Once Valgerdur was seated and drinking the ale, Thórunn said, "Cousin, I'm furious because Helgi has not kept his promise to avenge Skeggi and my brother's murders."

"What is keeping him from fulfilling his duty?"

"He claims there's no evidence Eyvindur and Thórir murdered Skeggi and my brother, and that he could never gather enough fit seamen to join him on the long and dangerous trip to hunt down the brothers."

"Coward," Valgerdur said, and sipped the ale.

"Helgi claims the evil brothers stay either in the iceberg-covered Hvalseyjarfjordur or in Greipar, where they have many allies."

"My dear Thórunn, you are too subservient to Helgi." Valgerdur shook her head, swirling her black braids. "I'll offer you my four sons, who are all able swordsmen. Tell Helgi they'll assist him in giving those murderers their due."

"You're my best ally," Thórunn said, smiling.

After Valgerdur departed, Thórunn finished her brew and rubbed her protruding tooth, as was her habit when she needed to be stoic and wise. She was fed up with Helgi's irresponsibility. She resolved to make his life miserable as long as Eyvindur and Thórir were still alive.

When Helgi returned from Langanes, Thórunn said, "You paddle about the fjords boasting of your exploits, so you can become a chief in Greenland. Tell me, what honourable chief breaks the promise he made to his wife?"

"What's on your mind?"

"When we were engaged, you promised to avenge the death of Skeggi and my brother. You act as if you have no responsibilities but to chat with other slothful men. I'm demanding you keep your promise."

"Does Thórdís at Langanes have nothing to do but to criticise me?"

"Our agreement has nothing to do with Thórdís."

Helgi averted her gaze. "I'm concerned with the lawlessness in this land, and I find no reason to kill men who have not been judged."

"No reason! Greenland has no laws to honour, so murderers pillage where they please. Don't you care that Eyvindur and Thórir rule the Western Settlement with other murderers. Soon they'll control both Greipar and the Northern Settlement?"

"I doubt if they can."

"Someone must have the courage to fight for control of Greipar, the best fishing grounds off the coast of Greenland. Soon enough, the villains won't let men from the Eastern Settlement fish there."

"True."

"As long as the villains are alive, they'll neither bend to church rules nor the laws you men of the Eastern Settlement make. Why is it not in our best interests to eliminate these lawless murderers?"

"Where do you think I can find boatmen who can fight?"

"Thórdís at Langanes has offered her four sons to assist you in finding Eyvindur and Thór."

"I need thirty strong and armed fighting men."

"Although my two sons are young, they're strong and they know how to swing swords. My cousins will join forces with you to fight for my reputation, as should be your priority."

"I don't want to be responsible for the death of innocent young men. Don't you fear that Gríma, the villains' mother, will put a spell on us? "

"Valgerdur and I, with the help of Hjordís the sorceress, will take care of Gríma and her so-called sorcery."

Helgi stared at Thórunn with a fiendish look in his eyes. "I shall do it, but don't blame me for the loss of precious lives."

As he stormed out, Thórunn thanked her tooth for giving her the wisdom to deal with Helgi.

46
Helgi

Before the autumn freeze, Helgi, with Thórunn's prodding, assembled thirty men, equally skilled at sailing and fighting. They loaded the largest ship in Einarsfjordur and sailed north-east towards Greipar. In calm weather, the journey to the Western Settlement took about six days, and to Greipar about ten days.

The ship glided with ease out of Einarsfjordur, and passed Lambey and the islands west of Breidafjordur. On the fifth day, as they approached the Northern Settlement, pouring rain, dense fog and swelling waves made it impossible for them to look ahead.

Steingrímur called out, "It's Gríma the sorceress. She's trying to wreck us, so we can't kill her sons."

Valgerdur's son called back, "Don't worry, we have some magic on our side."

"Anything can happen when witches fight each other," Helgi answered. "Let's sail out to sea until the storm has subsided."

When the fog left and the waters calmed, they headed north until they reached Greipar, where Gríma's sons had a lodge. They sailed towards the shore, where Jokull spotted the brothers talking to a few men. When the villains saw Helgi's ship, they hurried up towards the lodge.

Helgi's crew moored the ship next to the brothers' vessel. Helgi boarded their ship, holding his sword high, and then he jumped ashore. The evil brothers ran into the lodge. Steingrímur and Jokull and the rest of the crew followed closely. When Helgi and his stepsons burst inside the lodge, Eyvindur charged at Helgi holding a long-hooked spear. The blade came close to Helgi's eye.

Eyvindur laughed loudly. "You're better at whoring around than fighting."

Helgi's temper flared. He ducked, ran towards Eyvindur with his sword straight ahead, and rammed it into Eyvindur's chest.

Eyvindur's brother, Thórir, swung two axes, trying to fend off the blows coming from Thórunn's two sons. Jokull was quick, and knocked the axe from Thórir's hand. Then Steingrímur dealt him a death blow with his sword, and Thorir fell to the floor.

Helgi was surprised by the agility of Thórunn's sons, and said, "Well done."

The two villains were now dead. Helgi, Jokull and Steingrímur searched the lodge, and did not see other men inside. But they found Gríma the witch crouching on a bed.

Jokull said, "There has never been a worse witch alive than Gríma. Let's stone her to death."

"It's a sin to kill an unarmed woman," Helgi said.

"Sorcery and an evil heart are Gríma's weapons, and she'll keep killing until she's dead," Steingrímur said.

"We won't be affected by witchcraft," Helgi said on his way out. He asked two men to collect all valuables inside the lodge and load them onto their ship. The last man out of the lodge carried a stack of weapons, but suddenly he dropped the load and fell on the ground, stone-dead.

Steingrímur screamed, "It's Gríma! The witch has sent a spell."

"Never again," Jokull said, as he lit a torch and threw it into the lodge. He walked to his brother and watched with a grin while the lodge burned.

After Helgi returned from Greipar, he was praised as a hero by all but Thórunn, who said, "It's a good thing I have brave sons and cousins. You could never have eliminated the evil brothers without my family and friends backing you up."

"Right you are. I hope the days we kill each other for revenge are over," Helgi said, and sighed.

"Men will continue to kill for land, fish and whatever they lust for," Thórunn said.

"If we have good laws, there will be less fighting."

"I doubt it," Thórunn said, and walked away.

Helgi rowed to Brattahlíd to visit his friends and the church. The old priest forgave Helgi's sins and soothed his regrets. Despite the praise he received from the chiefs of Greenland and the progress he had made constructing laws, Helgi still suffered from loneliness, which only Katla's soothing hand could cure.

47
Katla

The day after the grand royal dinner, Astrid made Katla her private seamstress.

Signy said, "The queen wants to prevent other women from wearing more beautiful clothes than she does." She laughed.

"I'm thrilled. Now I can choose the most expensive fabrics and trim the queen's mantles and gowns with gold and silver."

"And you get four assistants."

"First, I'll send them to collect flowers, but I shall never teach anyone my colour secrets."

"Clever woman," Signy said.

Late that autumn, Katla moved with Queen Astrid and her entourage to the main island of Lofoten, where many lodges stood with high, sloping roofs on each side. The steep mountains and many narrow inlets made it impossible for the queen's heathen friends to visit her.

The king was constantly on the lookout for any threats to his kingdom. He sailed up and down Norway's coastline, visiting each community to make sure every chief was his ally.

Katla felt that, for a Christian man, the king was too eager to kill, but she kept her opinion to herself. She was too busy to ponder the king's business, and even too busy to think of Helgi. No longer besieged by grief and depression, Katla began singing as she sewed.

Queen Astrid was as clever as she was beautiful, and her servants did not dare keep secrets from her. Somehow, the queen discovered every potential threat to her dominance, and noticed every sign of loyalty. She could surprise her servants and courtiers with reproaches or compliments, ostracism or friendship. Katla was awed by the queen's ingenuity.

One cold winter day, the queen summoned Katla to her quarters. Katla was apprehensive, as she had no idea what to expect. Perhaps the queen disliked some of her sewing.

The queen invited Katla to sit.

"News from Greenland has reached us. Skáld-Helgi's ship was wrecked there. A man named Forni found Helgi lying on the beach, cold and incapable of walking, but with the help of good people, Helgi is recovering."

Katla could not contain her joy. She called out, "Thank you, my God!" She cried with joy and hugged the queen. "I'm so grateful to you for the wonderful news."

The queen chuckled. "I sense the fire of bliss and the flame of love burning in your breast."

"Forgive me, your highness," Katla said, and sat down.

The queen's smile faded. "I understand that Helgi does not intend to go to Iceland any time soon."

"Then I shall sail to Greenland."

"Would you not be better off marrying here? I know a noble and gallant earl whom the king wishes would marry a beautiful woman, and you immediately came to mind."

"My dear queen, I have loved one man since I was fourteen years old. I travelled to Norway for the sole purpose of marrying Helgi, only to discover he had sailed for Iceland to marry me. Due to his love for me, he has faced unspeakable hardships and it's a miracle he's alive. I shall not turn my back on him, even if he's destitute and debilitated."

"Your loyalty is commendable."

"May I have your permission to sail for Greenland in the spring?"

"Others have failed to cool the love you have for each other. Such love is too exceptional to oppose."

The queen promised to find a space for Katla on the first ship which sailed to Greenland. In return, Katla resolved to sew the queen's attire with love and devotion in her heart, and she did. For some reason, Astrid was generous to Katla and gave her presents made of gold and ivory. "Embrace all your treasures, because gold and jewellery reflect a woman's worth."

Katla figured out which earl Astrid wanted her to marry. Everyone but the king knew the earl was the queen's lover. To repay the queen her favours, Katla set out to find a suitable bride for the queen's earl. Katla's beautiful assistant, named Inga, wanted to stay at court instead of marrying the man her father had chosen for her, who lived in Bergen. If the king married Inga to the earl, she could stay at court, and so could the earl.

Inga knew of the earl's relationship with the queen and sanctioned it before their wedding.

Astrid repaid Katla with a golden pin. At court Katla learned men were prone to infidelity, but women who married for status also had a weakness for dalliances.

Katla learned that ships heading to Greenland did not leave until midsummer owing to the treacherous icebergs, which plunged out to sea from the glaciers and closed off Greenland's fjords in the spring. They did not melt or drift to the ocean until mid to late summer.

The queen told Katla, "You must be patient, dear. Love like yours will outlive the icebergs."

After King Olafur arrived at Lofoten, he summoned Katla to his lodge. Queen Astrid sat by his side and a man with gentle-looking eyes stood by the king.

The king had a grim look on his face when he addressed Katla. "What's the purpose of your trip to Greenland?"

"I'm a Christian woman and I have loved only Skáld-Helgi since I was a girl. He loves me equally. Destiny has prevented us from marrying. Now he's ill and destitute in a foreign land. I would like to take care of him and marry him if the honourable king permits it."

The king sighed and said, "Your desire is fuelled by lust rather than common sense."

Queen Astrid laid her dainty hand on the king's arm, looked in his eyes and smiled seductively. "Love can also include common sense."

The king cheered up and said, "We have not received news of Helgi for months, but the last we heard, he was ill. Since Helgi is destitute, his best choice in Greenland is to marry a rich widow." The king laughed. "Therefore, he could be married when you reach Greenland's icy shore. What then?"

"I doubt if a rich woman would marry a sick and impoverished man, or have Greenland's glaciers rendered them feeble-minded?" Astrid said, and winked at Katla.

The king looked at the gentle man standing next to him. "What is your opinion, Skúfur?"

Skúfur smiled softly. "Rich farmers outnumber unmarried widows in Greenland, as far as I know."

"Are many Greenlanders still heathen?" The king said.

"They are."

The queen said, "It seems to me a Christian woman would be useful in Greenland, or what do you think, my lord?"

The king addressed Skúfur. "Are you willing to take on the responsibility of sailing with Katla, and to make sure she's brought to Skáld-Helgi, should he be alive in Greenland?"

"I'll do my best. But what if Helgi has died or departed for Iceland when we arrive?"

"Then you shall have her brought to Iceland when the next ship sails."

Katla bid a happy farewell to the king and queen, put all her belongings in her trunk and rode with Skúfur and his entourage to Nidaros, where his loaded ship was moored. Katla spent one night in Nidaros and early the next morning she paid a visit to the monks she had befriended. They walked with her to the ship. To her amazement, men were carrying four goats aboard the ship. If these animals could survive a rough sea voyage, so could she. She resolved to take care of the goats, keep them calm and make sure they did not starve.

Skúfur's ship moved fast. Before she knew it, they were way out at sea. Katla liked Skúfur and they made pleasant conversation on the way. Skúfur lived at Stokkanes, across the bay from Brattahlíd, where Eiríkur the Red, the discoverer of Greenland, had settled. After Eiríkur's death, his son, Leifur the Lucky, took over running Brattahlíd. Leifur was famous for having discovered the enormous land of Vinland to the west. When Skúfur last saw Leifur, he was suffering from old age. Leifur's son Thorkell had taken over Brattahlíd and ran most of the affairs of the Greenlanders.

On the fourth day of their journey, Katla and Skúfur were chatting near the front of the ship. She asked Skúfur, "Do you know where in Greenland Helgi is?"

"He was staying with my neighbour Forni, who lives under Snjófjollum."

One of the sailors overheard them and said, "Are you talking about Skáld-Helgi?"

"We are," Skúfur said.

"I heard he was engaged to Thórunn, the widow of Skeggi the Proper."

Skúfur was surprised by this news. "How dreadful. All the men who were close to Thórunn met mysterious deaths."

"She's wealthy and she expects Helgi to avenge the murders of Skeggi and her brother," the sailor said, laughing.

Katla broke into tears. "I should never have allowed him to leave Iceland. He must be miserable after his harrowing shipwreck."

Skúfur asked the skipper, "Do they live at Herjolfsnes?"

"It's possible, but Forni gave Helgi Hornes in Einarsfjordur."

Skúfur turned to Katla. "If Helgi has married, you can stay with me until you can sail for Iceland."

"Thank you. I want to stay with Helgi. I'm not going to desert him again."

"Few wives will permit their husband's consorts to live on their premises," Skúfur said.

"I am no one's consort. We'll have to see Helgi before I make a decision."

Katla was quiet the rest of the journey, watched the seagulls which swarmed around the ship, hugged the goats, gathered their turds and threw them overboard. When time came to relieve herself, she squatted among the goats.

Helgi must have heard of her engagement to Vandrádur and assumed she was married. Even if Helgi was married, they would make love, in spite of the derogatory names they might give her. No one in Greenland was strong enough to keep them apart.

On clear nights, Katla lay back, stared at Helgi's star and hers, and asked them to guide her. She wondered if Helgi would have children with his wife even if he lacked affection for her. What was Thórunn like and why were all the men she cherished killed?

48
Helgi

One day in early autumn, Helgi was preparing his boat for a trip to visit Brattahlíd when he spotted Skúfur's loaded ship sailing up Einarsfjordur and turning towards his dock. Helgi called for his men to go down to the dock, as he expected Skúfur to be offering goods for sale. Thórunn appeared in the doorway as his workmen hurried down to the shore.

When the ship pulled up, Helgi was surprised to see a woman on board. She was wearing a mantle just like Earl Eirikur had given Helgi years ago. Could the woman be a figment of his imagination, as Katla was constantly on his mind?

As he walked down to the dock, the woman disappeared from Helgi's sight. She must have been a hallucination.

Skúfur greeted him and stepped onto the dock.

"Welcome, Skúfur," said Helgi, "You've been gone a long time. What are you offering for sale?"

Skúfur smiled and said, "I am bringing you other cargo than Norwegian goods."

"What cargo?"

"A woman."

Helgi laughed. "I'm a married man and I have no use for another woman."

The woman removed her hood and approached him. Her light, wavy hair flowed over her shoulders. She smiled as she stepped ashore.

Helgi froze for a moment, then ran to her, put his arms around her, squeezed her and whispered in her ear, "Katla, you're the most beautiful woman my eyes have ever beheld." He felt her tears on his cheek. "I hear you singing in my ear every night," he whispered.

Katla loosened her embrace and looked at him, her blue eyes glistening, and whispered, "After I heard you were a free man, I had to find you."

Helgi stroked her hair. "Can you forgive me? I foolishly

wrecked my ship and ended up here with nothing."

"You still have your life, and you can whisper words of love in my ear."

Thinking of the mistreatment they had endured in Iceland, Helgi's temper flared. "Our families never understood how deep our bond was.."

"Even so, you were pardoned. And now you have married another woman."

They looked around and were met by many sets of prying eyes.

Helgi addressed his workers. "Don't stare at us. Fetch drinks for Skúfur and his men." He took Katla's hand and led her to a rock where they sat, and each told of their experiences during the last ten years.

"When I was washed onto the shores of Greenland, I was ill and impoverished. Later, I was told you were engaged to Vandrádur. In desperation, I married Thórunn, whom I have no fondness for. And, I'm ashamed to say, I am guilty of keeping a concubine in Eiríksfjordur."

"History repeats itself. You marry frigid women and seek warmth in fickle arms."

"And yet you're the only woman I desire."

"It's time we ignored what others say," Katla said.

He took her in his arms and kissed her lips until she needed to catch her breath.

49
Thórunn

Thórunn watched the ship approach the dock at Hornes, saw the sailors jump ashore, and a woman embrace Helgi for an indecent amount of time.

How did they dare? In front of her?

Thórunn wanted to run down to the dock and throw the woman in the ocean. Her condition kept her in place. The child she carried weighed her down and her swollen legs made it difficult for her to walk. She wobbled back inside, sat down and told her maid, Hallbera, to find out who the visitors were.

Hallbera returned and said, "Skúfur sailed here from Norway with a ship full of wares and goats." She giggled.

"Who's the woman?"

Hallbera looked down. "Her name is Thórkatla, but people call her Katla, and she's Helgi's friend from Iceland. She's wearing a king's mantle."

How did this flirtatious woman dare to set her defiled foot on Thórunn's ground? Wearing a king's mantle! Helgi's selfish lust for this Katla was legendary in Iceland, Norway and Greenland. People mocked Helgi's womanising in general, and his obsession with Katla in particular. Unfortunately, no one had had the courage to tell Thórunn about Helgi's lecherous pursuit of women until after she married him.

Helgi had humiliated Thórunn by fondling another woman in her presence, and in front of her household. How did they dare flaunt their carnal greed in broad daylight? Katla must be half-witted for wasting her youth on the sluggard that was Helgi.

Helgi and Katla deserved punishment for the insult.

Everyone knew Helgi kept a whore in Eiríksfjordur, and visited her often. When he sailed there, he pretended to be visiting Forni and Thorkell in Brattahlíd. Helgi pretended to be a lawman who wanted to shape Greenland's law after the Icelandic law. Would he uphold the Icelandic law prohibiting men to keep concubines? Thórunn hissed.

The embarrassment was enough. Thórunn rubbed her protruding tooth and asked it for a clever solution.

Ever since Helgi avenged the death of Skeggi and Thórunn's brother, he had been defiant and disrespected her. Few men knew that she had coerced Helgi to hunt down the villains, and that she had gathered the warriors who went with him. Without her, Greenland would not be rid of the worst murderers and derelicts in the country. Now, Helgi was revered as a hero for chopping the head off one or two villains, while swinging the sharpest sword in Greenland.

What kind of a hero would dishonour his wife in the presence of her staff and strangers?

After they were married, Thórunn had to endure hearing him recite over and over the love poems he had concocted lying on his back, staring up at the sky. Did Helgi think this deranged behaviour had escaped her? Did he think she cared about the frivolity men called poetry?

In spite of Helgi's indiscretion, Thórunn was not conquered. Sorcery and adversity had not defeated her yet.

When she was a girl, she wanted to have her long tooth removed to be prettier. Skeggi was the only man who thought she was beautiful despite the tooth. After his death, she was grateful that the tooth was embedded in her gum forever. The tooth was her weapon and reminded men she was capable of biting. Even though people called her a witch, she did not try to change their opinion. She was a rich and influential landowner. The fact that men feared her gave her more control than any beautiful woman could wield by exploiting a man's fleeting adoration.

Thórunn's power was everlasting. She held the reins now as in the past. She rubbed her tooth and contemplated how she could control Helgi and his whore. Thórunn was not a sorceress, but she could be shrewd when needed.

She laughed as she rubbed her belly to calm down her kicking baby. Only a strong boy could fight this hard to burst out of his confines. This son would be her ally and not his father's.

One thing Thórunn knew. Helgi's ambition mattered more

than his lust. Had he ever fought to marry Katla? Would he fight for her now? Thórunn resolved to test his courage.

Katla was the daughter of a respected chief with powerful friends. Since Katla had probably never married, Thórunn should avoid treating her like a concubine.

Thórunn told Hallbera to fetch Helgi, and to invite the merchant and his crew to a banquet. She wanted to make sure that the temptress was never out of her sight.

Helgi looked subdued when he entered the living room, and she asked him, "Who are the people down at the dock?"

"Skúfur from Stokkanes just arrived from Norway with goods for sale."

"Why is he docking here instead of at Eiríksfjordur?"

Helgi looked down. "He wanted to talk to me."

"You are lying to me and it's not the first time. I don't intend to engage in a guessing game, so tell me the identity of the woman you embraced so lewdly."

"Thórkatla Halldórsdóttir from Holl in Thverárhlíd, my neighbour and former sister-in-law."

"Katla the lovesick. You insult me with your misconduct."

"It was not my intention, but Katla and I have not seen each other for ten years."

"Let me make one thing clear, you'll never enjoy intimacy with her while we're married."

Helgi sent Thórunn a hateful look. It did not affect her, as he had never ignited the tiniest flicker of affection in her heart.

"Why don't you introduce your friend to your wife?"

"I'll bring her in." Helgi hurried out.

He returned with Katla. The woman was no longer young. Fine wrinkles surrounded her swollen eyes, but she was still beautiful.

"Thank you for wanting to meet me," Katla said. "I'm Thórkatla Halldórsdóttir."

"Please take a seat, Thórkatla." Thórunn looked at Helgi and said, "Go outside and entertain the guests while we chat."

When Helgi was gone, Thórunn enquired about Katla's journey and Katla told her of King Olafur, his queen, and her sewing.

Thórunn gathered that the woman had some talents. It was time to get to the point. "For an unmarried woman, you've led a productive life in popular places. What brings you to Greenland?"

"I came to see Helgi. I did not hear of his marriage until we were out at sea."

Thórunn was relieved to hear how honest Katla was. "You still wanted to visit him in spite of his marriage?"

"I did."

"I shall never allow you to be intimate with Helgi."

"I understand. Men and circumstances have prevented us from marrying." Tears swelled in Katla's eyes. "You'll be the final person to deny us the intimacy we have yearned for since we met."

"You shall leave with Skúfur and get passage on the next ship to Iceland."

"According to Skúfur the last ship this autumn has already sailed to Iceland. Skúfur has invited me to dwell at his farm in Eiríksfjordur over the winter."

Thórunn licked her tooth, then said, "I'll not permit you to leave here and go to Eiríksfjordur."

"Why not?"

"Because Helgi is deceitful. He'll dishonour both of us by visiting you."

"What choice do I have?"

"I invite you to stay here at Hornes and be well taken care of over the winter."

Katla's sky-blue eyes were as round as the moon. "You surprise me. I'm overwhelmed."

"Do you accept the invitation?"

"I do, with gratitude."

Thórunn smiled, and Katla stared at her protruding tooth, her shrewd tooth, her warrior tooth. Good. Thórunn called for Hallbera and asked her to fetch Helgi.

When Helgi arrived, Thórunn told him to sit, and she addressed both of them. "This will be the last time I permit you to speak to each other until Katla leaves for Iceland with the first ship next spring."

"In other words, you want to keep an eye on her," Helgi said, trying to contain his anger.

"To keep an eye on you. I don't trust you, Helgi, but if Katla promises not to attempt to talk to you, I shall take her word for it. If you fail, I shall send her to the East Settlement—to my cousins, who'll never allow you, Helgi, on their premises."

Katla said, "I've endured many years without communicating with Helgi. I accept your invitation to stay here and I promise not to speak to him."

Helgi looked at Thórunn with ice-cold eyes. "How wicked of you, my wife."

Thórunn smiled. "My wickedness will never match yours."

Helgi jumped up and rushed outside.

Thórunn said to Katla, "You shall stay in a comfortable, well-heated hut, situated up the hill. My maid, Koltorfa, will stay with you and make sure all your needs are met."

Katla thanked her politely and said she was going to bid Skúfur farewell. She stood up and walked to the door carrying her head high. Thórunn could not help but admire Katla's composure and resolve.

50
Katla

Katla thanked Skúfur for the journey. She told him of her agreement with Thórunn, and said that she would stay at Hornes for the winter.

Skúfur's eyes flashed with anger. "The arrangement is an insult. She wants to isolate you from the community. You don't have to accept it."

"If I stayed with you in Eiríksfjordur I would never see Helgi. Here I can see him without bringing shame upon him or me, as a Christian woman should."

"You are honest and pure of heart."

"Even though my love for Helgi has not diminished over the years, I don't intend to damage his reputation or his position as an important leader in Greenland."

Skúfur shook his head and ordered two sailors to unload Katla's belongings.

Helgi's workmen brought Katla's trunk to a cabin up the hill. She followed them with her new maid Koltorfa, a dark, stocky and strong woman who trudged along beside her.

When Katla reached the front door of the cabin, she turned around and looked downhill at the farm and the bay. The prospect of watching Helgi come and go filled Katla with joy.

The cabin was clean inside, and a fire pit stood in the corner. Koltorfa told the workmen what supplies they would need and not to forget to stack firewood close to the door.

Once Katla and Koltorfa were settled in, Katla pulled the needles, yarn and cloth from her trunk and showed it to Koltorfa.

"Tell me, Koltorfa, who needs clothes at the farm?"

Koltorfa scratched her head. "Each of us has a woollen cloak, but not as fancy as yours."

"What about the baby?"

"Oh, it just gets what's cut off from the worn grown-up clothes, I think."

"Maybe I can make something for the little one."

"Oh, it'll be a big baby."

Katla laughed.

Thórunn was an enigma to Katla. She did not let her ugly tooth, her pregnancy or Helgi's preoccupations interfere with her status in Greenland. What would Katla have done in Thórunn's situation? She would have thought of the baby first, and Thórunn did exactly that. As far as Katla knew, the baby growing in Thórunn's belly was Helgi's first child. Katla felt that a part of the child belonged to her.

Every time Katla spotted Helgi in the distance, he must have sensed her stare, because he turned around and smiled at her. Then he pointed to the sky. After he had given her the sign twice, Katla understood what he meant. The stars. Their stars. Helgi Star and Katla Star still glistened in the sky. The next night when the sky was clear, Katla dressed in her sheepskin mantle with the big hood and told Koltorfa she would be outside watching the stars. She would be praying to Jesus Christ who owned the brightest star in the sky, the Jesus Star.

Outside, she spread a sheep's hide over the frozen grass, lay on her back and gazed at the stars. Her first prayer was directed at Jesus, who she asked to protect Helgi from all evil. Could she have been sent by God to be Helgi's guardian angel? When she turned her head and looked down the hill, she saw where Helgi lay behind the farmhouse, staring toward her. Katla's heart beat faster, she felt warm all over, and thanked the stars for giving her and Helgi a united mind. The Freyja Star was brighter than usual, and Katla asked her that in some one, one day, she and Helgi could be joined. Then the Northern Lights danced around the stars and Katla was sure the elves and the angels were now lining up the stars to unite the lovers in time.

On every starry night, Helgi and Katla would lie outside, far from each other, yet so close they could see and feel each other. When Helgi went inside, Katla went into her cabin, slept deeply and dreamed of the dancing lights in the sky.

One morning she watched Helgi go down to the dock. Koltorfa told her he was going to Eiríksfjordur to fetch a midwife because Thórunn was about to give birth. He was expected to return the following day.

Katla watched the boat until it disappeared around the point. She looked up to see if the sky was clear for Helgi's trip. A black cloud approaching from the west gave her a reason to be concerned.

Most days the weather in Einarsfjordur seemed calmer than it was in Thverárhlíd, Saudafell and even in Nidaros. But the following day she woke up with hail pounding on the roof. It was still not daylight when the workman, Loftur, burst in the door with a loud bang and ordered Katla and Koltorfa to go with him down to the farmhouse because Thórunn was giving birth.

Katla and Koltorfa dressed in heavy mantles, strapped sheepskin around their feet and legs and followed Loftur down the hill. Once inside the warm house, they removed their outer garments while listening to Thórunn's moans coming from the end of the house. Katla hurried to her.

Thórunn's hair and face were wet with sweat. "My child will be born shortly," Thórunn said. "Do you know anything about childbirth?"

Katla thought about Eilífur and said, "Not much but something. You've had two sons and therefore you know more than I do."

"I was young then and had only men around," Thórunn moaned. "Tell the maids what to do."

Katla asked Thórunn's maid, Hallbera, to wash Thórunn's thighs and birth opening well, with warmed water, "to decrease the danger of sores". She told Koltorfa to wash the sweat from Thórunn's face with cool water to ease her fever.

"The baby is so active. He's trying to kick his way out," Thórunn groaned.

"Take deep breaths and relax," Katla said, and began singing a rhyme that women in Iceland hummed while children made their way into the open air.

"Why are you singing?" Thórunn whispered.

"It calms the infant," Katla said and continued singing.

Soon black hair appeared in Thórunn's birth opening and a

huge head followed. Thórunn's skin ripped, and she screamed in pain. Blood spurted out. Katla continued humming and grasped the child's head. The body followed and she laid the child on Thórunn's belly.

"There you are. A sturdy boy," Katla said as Koltorfa cut the umbilical cord. Thórunn went limp, and Katla worried she had fainted. She asked Hallbera to wash the baby well with warm water and wrap it in linen. The boy cried while Koltorfa cleaned the blood and slime from Thórunn.

"The boy is starving," Koltorfa said.

Blood kept running from Thórunn's birth opening. Katla pressed bundled linen tight up to Thórunn's crotch and asked Koltorfa to fetch a bowl of snow quickly and wrap it in linen. Once it was done, she removed the blood-soaked linen she had held to Thórunn's birth opening and Koltorfa pressed the linen-wrapped snow to Thórunn's crotch.

Katla laid her ear to Thórunn's mouth, detected a faint breath, and said, "We have to wake her up." She took a handful of snow and pressed it to Thórunn's forehead. Thórunn opened her eyes. Katla put sheepskin under Thórunn's shoulders and raised her up while Hallbera exposed Thórunn's breast and laid the boy in Thórunn's arms. The boy calmed down and sucked eagerly.

Thórunn said, "The boy is observant, and he shall be named Skeggi, after my first husband."

"And he will be modest like his namesake," Katla said.

The storm continued and the snow piled up so high that Katla and Koltorfa could not return to their cabin. Katla worried about Helgi sailing in the storm, but she did not let her anxiety show. With each stormy day, Thórunn improved. She seemed to be at peace with Katla's singing because it calmed people. The sheep and cattle stayed in an outhouse attached to the farmhouse. Sometimes, when the animals were loud and restless, Katla went to the outhouse and sang for them until they calmed down.

Katla did not initiate conversation with Thórunn without a reason. She longed to hold little Skeggi, but Thórunn held tight on to him. The boy stared at Katla while she hummed.

A loom was stored in the corner of the workers' wing. According to Koltorfa, no one used it. Koltorfa must have told Thórunn of Katla's interest in the loom. Thórunn said, "Would you like to use the loom?"

"May I?"

"By all means, and I'll tell Loftur to bring it up to the cabin for you when the weather allows."

When it stopped snowing, Loftur announced that Helgi's ship was approaching. Katla tried to hide her joy. Loftur left to clear the trail up to the cabin and light a fire for Katla and Koltorfa, who entered the cabin as Helgi's boat arrived at the dock. When their supplies and the loom were safe inside, Katla stepped outside, climbed up a snow mound, and watched Helgi walk from the dock to the farmhouse. He kept looking at Katla, not watching his step, and slipped on the ice, where he lay without moving. Katla gasped, worried he was hurt. But he stood up, and both of them laughed.

Katla felt at home in the cabin and was relieved not to be under Thórunn's watchful eye any longer. Koltorfa wanted to learn to sing and Katla enjoyed teaching her. Without doubt, their singing could be heard down at the farm.

To Katla's surprise, Thórunn invited her to the farmhouse whenever Helgi sailed away. They told each other stories. Katla learned of the fate of Thórunn's men, and she sympathised with Thórunn for losing Skeggi the Proper, whom she had dearly loved. She also learned of Helgi's illness, witches and revenge.

Katla gained a deeper understanding of Helgi's predicament. His choice was limited. In Greenland, he had assets, respect and influential friends. In Iceland, he would have been poor and without allies. Most of Helgi's misfortune stemmed from his love for Katla. Because he wanted to marry her, Helgi divorced her sister Thórdís, forfeited his father's trust, killed men, collected enemies and lost all his assets. He even embarked on a difficult pilgrimage to be relieved of his sins. How could she demand more sacrifices from one man?

She still yearned to be intimate with Helgi, and she was determined to get her wish fulfilled before she left Greenland.

How could she and Helgi be intimate without Thórunn and the household members knowing?

At the peak of winter, the sun never shone, the snow piled up around the cabin and Katla did not see Helgi for two months. When Loftur and his men arrived with a sled loaded with supplies, Katla and Koltorfa received them as if they were their saviours. Besides dried fish, meat and eggs, the men brought wool and sealskin. Koltorfa taught Katla to scrape the fat off the sealskin, clean it and stretch it. They made shoes for all the household members at Hornes.

Even though Katla missed Helgi, she dreamed of Holl; playing with Bjorg and Flosi's children; watching newborn lambs and calves; talking to Eilífur and Vonadís at the elf rock. Was Eilífur still at Hofdi and how was he getting along?

At long last, the sun stayed in the sky a little longer each day, melting the thick ice and converting it to streams which gushed down to the bay. The icebergs in Einarsfjordur split, rolled over, crashed into each other and flowed out to sea with cracking sounds.

The workmen broke up the remaining ice between the hut and the farmhouse at Hornes.

With spring, Katla's heart filled with hope. When the moon shone, she wrapped herself in sheepskin, lay down on the wet ground and stared either at the stars or down to the farmhouse. Sometimes, she saw Helgi raise his arms, stare at her and make a circle with his arms as if he were hugging her. How could she leave Greenland without them embracing in private?

One day when the ice on the ground had melted, Loftur arrived with a message from Thórunn. Katla should prepare for her departure as a boat would fetch her the following day.

Katla had to make the time count. She asked Koltorfa to heat water for a bath. She opened her trunk and removed a pouch with a mixture of herbs which Queen Astrid had given her. The queen had insisted the herbs made the skin as soft as on a newborn, and the scent would make her irresistible to the man she desired. Katla did not doubt Astrid's promise. The queen was as clever in the matters of passion as the king was in matters of conquest.

As Katla opened the pouch, a sweet scent floated into every corner of the cottage. The smell reminded Katla of the wares the Palestine men sold at Nidaros harbour. Katla wrapped linen around the herbs and rubbed her body while imagining Helgi's hands performing the task. Her skin felt tingly as her blood rushed from the tips of her fingers down to her loins and tickled her toes. Her skin took on a shiny pink tone.

"I didn't know a woman could stir the senses like you do," Koltorfa said. "A wonder you never married."

"For some reason, God did not want me to be married. Neither has he blessed me with children."

"Perhaps there's still time."

Katla smiled and bathed by the fire while she sang all the love songs she had learned in Norway and imagined Helgi was listening to her. Only he knew their meaning. She dried off in front of the warm stove and combed her waist-long hair.

Helgi was nowhere in sight. Was he going to let her leave without talking to her? She fell to her knees and begged God to let Helgi come to see her.

In the evening, Loftur told Katla that Thórunn wanted to speak to her. Katla dressed quickly in a plain frock and a mantle, wrapped her hair in linen, and picked up the moss-green tunic she had sewn for Thórunn.

The chilly air pricked her nostrils as she walked down the hill.

51
Thórunn

Thórunn was relieved that Katla was leaving Hornes. Even though Katla and Helgi had not spoken to each other, as they had promised Thórunn, they lay outside on moonlit nights like dull-witted dogs, staring at each other or at the sky. Their lunacy was the fuel for mockery by the workers at Hornes and it irritated Thórunn more than Helgi's lust.

Helgi approached Thórunn, and without looking in her eyes he said, "Katla has suffered long enough from my misdeeds. She sailed to Greenland not knowing I was a married man, and I want to bid her a proper farewell."

He looked miserable, as if he were fighting back tears. To her own surprise, she felt pity for him, as she would for a helpless child. "A married man bids an unmarried woman farewell with a handshake," Thórunn said.

"Katla is my first love. It will never change."

Perhaps Thórunn did not have anything to lose by allowing them to spend a moment together without prying eyes, even though they would be groping each other indecently. Why should Thórunn care whether Helgi whored around with his concubine in Eiríksfjordur or with Katla one time? She said, "Your pathetic lovesickness has been a nuisance long enough, as has your infidelity."

"It's true I have bedded a few women and not enjoyed them as I should have. But my love for Katla has never diminished."

"Do you want to feast on her until your death?"

Helgi looked at her as if caught off guard. "What do you mean?"

"If she agrees to take you with her, you are free to leave me, Greenland, your child and all your possessions."

"Will you permit it?"

"Only if you promise never to set foot on Greenland's ground again."

"How can I? It's inconceivable. No one in this country can

304

inscribe runes like I can. The chiefs in Greenland have entrusted me with shaping the laws of this land in accordance with Icelandic laws. I have responsibilities."

"I hear your family is excluded from this list of your responsibilities."

Helgi looked down. "You are very self-sufficient."

"I have to be. As is your nature, you'll forsake your duties."

Helgi waved his hands in exasperation. "We're close to establishing a parliament."

"And a bishop's chair, so you can uphold your perverted kind of Christianity and your peculiar rules of conduct."

He stopped pacing and looked at her. "Good, solid Christianity."

"Since Katla appeared, you have not visited these self-appointed chiefs as you used to. Instead, you've been a layabout and the source of ridicule."

His shoulders fell. "The winter was harsh."

"I'm no fool. Your lust for her kept you here." She pointed to the door. "Go with her."

Helgi paced around like a bewildered lamb. "I have to think."

"Here you only have what others have provided for you. You're free to go."

"I have a son here."

"And another child on the way."

He lifted his brows and stared at her belly. "I'll be branded an outcast if I abandon a son and a wife with a child."

"Right you are. But when have you been concerned about your reputation?"

"It would bring me shame and dishonour to desert Greenland like a fugitive."

"A lovesick man, fleeing. Is your honour then weightier than your lust?"

"My duties are weighty."

From the time Katla arrived, Thórunn had been sure Helgi would not forsake his adoring friends and lofty aspirations for Greenland. Ambition is the curse most men carry to their grave.

"Your duties!" She laughed with scorn.

"I cannot go with good conscience. Instead, I want to stay with Katla for a while this evening."

"Do you promise not to move to Iceland as long as I'm alive?"

"I promise."

"I'll give you permission." Thórunn believed that, as fires turn to ashes, lust will burn out if it is satisfied. "I'll tell Loftur to light three fires outside. When the last fire is out, you are to return home."

"Load up the firewood," Helgi said.

"That I will control." Thórunn called for Loftur and asked him to fetch Katla and to have his men collect firewood.

"How much wood?" Loftur asked.

"Enough to light three fires outside."

Helgi kept pacing the floor while Thórunn waited for Katla's arrival. Thórunn gloated at the thought of Helgi's anguish.

When Katla walked in, she did not notice Helgi, put a frock next to Thórunn and said, "I've made a frock for you, and I chose a colour which resembles your eyes. I want to thank you for your hospitality."

"Thank you for your gift."

Helgi walked to them and said, "Good day, Katla."

Katla turned to him and said, "Helgi."

Helgi looked down.

Thórunn decided to be matter of fact and said, "Helgi has asked me permission to visit you tonight, before you sail for Iceland. Do you want him to come to you?"

"If you permit."

"I'll allow it for a short while, if you promise never to return to Greenland."

"I promise."

"I shall then let three fires burn outside. When they have turned to ashes, Helgi shall return home and you are to stay in your cabin until Loftur fetches you and takes you aboard the ship."

Katla said, with tears in her eyes, "Oh, Thórunn, I know how much this pains you, but I'm grateful for your favour."

The poor woman did not know how small the favour was compared to the offer Thórunn had made to Helgi and he had rejected. "Another thing, you shall never discuss your last meeting," Thórunn said.

"I promise. Are we then reconciled?"

"I am," Thórunn said.

Katla rushed out the door and Thórunn wondered if Katla would be disappointed by Helgi's lovemaking.

Helgi lingered and said, "Let the fires burn for a long time."

"You'll be quick to steal her virginity, but for how long will the theft haunt you?"

Helgi hurried outside.

52
Helgi

On the way up the hill to Katla's cabin, Helgi wondered if he was man enough to take Katla's virginity. Was he robbing her of a prosperous future? If word spread about her impurity, could she marry a good man? Her father was dead and wealth did not seem to matter to Katla. She was free to marry the man she chose. He should be delighted she had chosen him, even though he did not feel he measured up to her virtue and loyalty. Still, his desire for her defied all reason.

When Helgi walked into Katla's cabin, Katla was standing by the stove, stark naked. Reddish light played around her firm breasts and soft abdomen. He was paralysed by the vision he had dreamed about since he first saw her naked. "You're just as you were when you stepped out of the spring at Holl."

Katla smiled. "Three fires burn swiftly. Since I was fourteen years old, I have dreamed of seeing you naked. May I undress you?"

Helgi undressed, but did not approach her. The thought of her virginity was like Christ himself standing between them.

She looked at his flaccid penis and said, "Do you not desire me?"

"I'm reluctant to rob you of your virginity."

"Who else should do it but you?"

"A husband."

"I promised you once that my virginity would be my wedding present to you."

"I am indeed a fortunate man." Helgi removed a gold ring from his finger, walked to her, and said, "Here is the ring King Olafur gave to me." He slid the ring onto her middle finger. "Consider it my wedding present to you."

"The ring shall be with me as long as I live."

"I hope it will protect you and keep other men from violating you. The ring shall be a reminder of the joy we shared."

Katla touched Helgi's member and it rose, not as high as in

his youth, but it rose nevertheless.

They stroked each other and lay down on the sheepskin in front of the stove. Despite his excitement and eagerness, he tried to slide his member in slowly, because he could sense how painful it was for Katla. She did not flinch although blood ran from her opening.

"I love you," Katla whispered and sighed.

"I love you more than any woman on this earth." Before he knew, or could control it, his manly fluid mixed with her virgin blood.

She did not want him to pull his member out before the last drop had escaped.

Afterwards they lay entwined, caressed each other, purred and whispered words of love to each other. His member rose again and they made love, and again for the third time. In lieu of the poems Helgi intended to whisper in her ear, he muttered, "I love you now and will until the end of time." Katla seemed content.

Someone knocked on the door and Loftur called out, "Three fires have burned to ashes."

Helgi stood up and got dressed, and Katla wrapped her body in linen.

Another knock on the door.

Helgi kissed her gently on the mouth and said, "We possess a love like no other and it shall never depart from my heart."

"Will we never see each other?" Katla said.

He could not bear the thought of not seeing her again, and said, "I'm a free man. I could go with you."

"And leave your family and your work behind?"

He blurted out, "Yes, Thórunn gave me a choice." Tears ran down his cheeks.

Katla embraced him. "I know you better than anyone, and you would not be happy in Iceland without friends and important work. Here, you have a son, and you are working to shape Greenland into a lawful society."

"But you are what I love, more than anything. How can I live without you now?"

"You can, and you have."

Another knock on the door.

"And I have been miserable."

"You have also made hasty decisions. Stay here for one year, and if you want to leave then, come to me in Iceland."

He squeezed her tight. "One more year without you is an eternity."

"The stars in the sky will keep us connected."

He dried her tears with his fingers. "Don't think tragic thoughts but rejoice in the hope spring brings, as you used to." He kissed her on both eyes.

Katla smiled and said, "I almost forgot your present."

She gave him a colourful mantle made from exotic silks. He held it as if it were a precious child, turned around without speaking, carried it outside, walked to the farmhouse and laid it carefully on his bed.

As he sat beside the mantle on the edge of his bed, Thórunn arrived and said, "The pleasure you have enjoyed appears minuscule."

"On the contrary." He stroked his hair.

Thórunn said, "The king's ring is missing. Her virginity was expensive."

"Her damage was greater."

"How did she like the love poems?"

"In the past I composed poems with joy in my heart. Now, my thoughts are bitter and my heart aches."

He lay down on his bed, turned on his side facing the wall, and covered his body with Katla's mantle.

53
Katla

Katla stayed awake the rest of the night in the cabin. She caressed her sore groin while recalling every gesture, every gaze and every word Helgi had uttered. She resolved not to wash until she arrived in Iceland.

At this time of year, the sun never sat. Katla dressed in a frock and the king's mantle Helgi had given her. The ring was too large for her finger. She slipped it on a walrus strap and tied it around her neck. If she should drown, the ring would go with her to the bottom of the sea.

Loftur arrived with another man to carry her trunk down to the dock.

Katla walked down the hill. Thórunn stood by the door holding little Skeggi, who was crying madly. Thórunn waved to Katla, who took it as a sign to calm Skeggi down by singing to him. Katla sang as loud as she could. It calmed her mind, and when she reached the dock, Skeggi was no longer crying. Helgi was nowhere in sight.

The ship belonged to Skúfur from Stokkanes and he waited for her by the dock. She greeted him with a faint smile.

Skúfur said, with a grave look on his face, "I regret you were so isolated while in Greenland."

"Getting to know Helgi and Thórunn was enough for me," she said, and looked at Skúfur with tired eyes. She sat down on a sheepskin at the keel next to her trunk. She looked for Helgi when the ship drifted from the dock but could not see him. As Hornes disappeared from her sight, she leaned on her trunk, hung her head and went to sleep.

Katla woke up with rain pounding on her back. The waves swelled up high and flung her to the ship's bottom. The water slapped her face, and the sheepskin was soaking wet. She began sneezing and her face felt as if it was on fire. She prayed to Jesus Christ to bring her to heaven, because on this earth she had accomplished what she had longed for, except for having a child.

Hope had kept her alive but now she felt her future was hopeless. What could she look forward to? How could she be joyful without Helgi and without the hope of ever seeing him again?

~~~

When the ship moored at the mouth of Hvítá river, Katla was too weak to walk ashore, and a sailor carried her. Because of the swelling in her loins, she was unable to sit on a horse without moaning in pain. When she urinated, tears sprang to her eyes. The pain was bittersweet as it reminded her of Helgi's affection. Could the pain be her punishment for having relations with a married man? She could withstand it.

Katla was placed on the wagon next to her trunk for the trip home. On the way, the wagon bounced her up and down on the uneven road. When she arrived at Holl her back was as sore as her groin and she fell over when she tried to stand up.

Bjorg ran to her and said, "Don't try to walk. Flosi will carry you inside."

As Flosi picked her up, she noticed the children, all much taller, standing side by side looking at her.

"How grown and beautiful the children are," Katla said, and managed a faint smile.

"Would you like a bath?" Bjorg said as they entered the farmhouse.

"I would rather lie down on my bed," Katla said.

After Flosi laid her down on the soft bed, she sighed with relief. Bjorg brought her lamb broth, which Katla slurped slowly.

Katla fell into a deep sleep and did not leave her bed for many days.

In one dream she saw Helgi surrounded by starlight. He smiled at her and said, "Life beckons below your breasts, keep it full of fodder. Fill your heart with joy and spread it."

Katla woke up with a jolt. At first, she did not delight in the dream. But after repeating Helgi's message several times, she stroked her abdomen. Could she be pregnant? If so, she should bathe, eat well and regain her health.

She called Bjorg and told her she wanted to bathe and start sewing. She suspected the family had been quiet for days just to please her. Now, she summoned the children and sang for them. As time passed, Katla started to feel nauseous. She was delighted and wandered outside to spew. Her monthly bleeding stopped, and her waist swelled. She made a larger frock for herself and stroked her belly with delight.

Bjorg and Flosi were amazed that she was with child, and she did not keep it from them or anyone else that the poet Helgi Thórdarson was the father.

Joy carried Katla and her growing belly through the summer. She sang while she sewed.

One day in late autumn, her sister Thórdís arrived at Holl with five men, including Hermundur Illugason from Gilsbakki. Hermundur had aged since she had last seen him at Saudafell many years before when he brought good news from Helgi and bought a gown from her for his wife. Hermundur oversaw all the valley's affairs, and he looked the part, composed, with the bearing of a commander.

Katla greeted them with joy. She suspected their visit concerned the fate of her unborn child.

Even though Thórdís was dressed in trousers, she reminded Katla of Queen Astrid. When Hermundur looked at Thórdís, his eyes reflected affection, but Thórdís pretended not to notice his adoring gaze.

Once Hermundur and Thórdís were seated inside the enormous guest lodge, Thórdís enquired about Katla's stay in Norway and they listened to Katla's stories without interrupting. Hermundur lifted his eyebrows in awe when she said King Olafur and his queen had arranged the trip to Greenland and given her farewell gifts.

"When I sailed, neither the king, Skúfur or I knew that Helgi was married."

Katla told them of her stay in Greenland and showed them the ring from Queen Astrid, and King Olafur's ring that was a present from Helgi.

"You must own more rings from kings and earls than any other Icelander," Hermundur said, and smiled.

When Thórdís heard of Helgi's wife in Greenland, she laughed sarcastically and said, "There, he finally got what he deserved."

Hermundur said, "Judging by his accomplishments in Greenland, I doubt if Helgi will move to Iceland."

Thórdís got to the point. "Now you are with child and again people gossip about your immoral ways."

"What's the gossip?" Katla said.

"That you're lovesick and you are deluded about who fathered your child."

Katla smiled. "Why does it matter whether Helgi or someone else is the father of my child?"

Hermundur said, "It matters to me and to your sister, Thórdís. Helgi is not in Iceland and cannot be reached to confirm that he fathered the child. Due to our kinship, and my friendship with Helgi, I see it as my duty to protect your reputation."

"Hermundur is thinking of your prosperity and of keeping peace in our district," Thórdís said.

"What advice do you have?" Katla asked.

"The best solution is if Helgi sent word from Greenland about being the father of the child," Hermundur said.

"No one is sailing for Greenland until next spring," Katla said. "What then?"

"A priest," Thórdís said.

"A priest? Despite believing in Jesus Christ, I doubt the priests in Iceland uphold Christ's teachings. Priests smeared my reputation before, and I'm sure they still do."

"I agree those nitwits interfere too much in private matters," Thórdís said, and looked at Hermundur.

"A priest has to absolve you to free you from your sins." The way Hermundur smiled indicated he did not believe his own words.

"If a priest assures me he can save me and my child from

314

the wrath of God, and of Jesus Christ, he's welcome here."

"We've heard Thórdur and Nidbjorg at Hofdi are offended by your claim that their son has fathered a child outside marriage," Hermundur said.

"They have been displeased with Helgi and his affairs for a long time," Katla said. "But do they intend to ignore their grandchild and the grandchild of my father, Thórdur's most loyal friend?"

Deep in thought, Hermundur examined her face. "This is how I propose to resolve this matter. I shall declare that I believe this is Helgi's child, but that I cannot confirm it before he sends a message from Greenland. We shall therefore wait until next summer to verify the father's identity."

Thórdís looked at Hermundur with a smile and said, "Thank you, Hermundur, for your clever words." Katla knew Thórdís's admiration was a pretence. Without doubt, Thórdís had put the clever words in his mouth.

They stood up.

"I shall summon the priest to visit you," Hermundur said.

As Katla watched them ride away, she was certain they had made the trip to save their own reputation.

~~~

The snow began piling up outside Holl in early winter. Katla stayed inside, spent much time in bed, stroked her belly and imagined the starry sky with a new star she named The Child's Light. Katla believed that Helgi knew she was with child as he had pointed out her pregnancy in her cherished dream. The thought kept her in high spirits.

Two months after Christmas, Katla gave birth to a child with dark hair, white skin and Katla's eyes. Before Katla went to sleep at night, she asked Helgi to let her know what she should name their girl. On the third night, Helgi came to her in a dream and said, "She's your divine reflection and shall bear your name."

The mother held little Katla most of the time, washed her and let her suck her breasts as much as she liked. Helgi's and

Katla's loves were united in their delightful daughter's body. Even though Katla suffered from abdominal pains, she tried to eat as much as she could. Little Katla seemed content with her mother's care, and she never cried.

In early spring, a priest knocked on the door and Bjorg brought him inside where Katla sat feeding her daughter. The priest averted his gaze when Katla handed her daughter to Bjorg. She covered her exposed breast without rushing.

Katla decided to treat the priest with deference, as he controlled her daughter's destiny more than any other powerful man. How could she obtain his mercy?

In King Olafur's court, Katla learned that wealthy men bribed priests with gifts. She pondered what in her possession the priest might cherish. Before she left Norway, the court's bishop gave her the Bible and a book in Latin about Christan doctrine, which she could not read.

The priest was a middle-aged man, sullen and self-important. When Katla welcomed him with the warmest smile she could muster, his demeanour softened. She told him stories of monks, bishops, the king, the queen and several of her influential friends in Norway. With each story, the priest's eyes got bigger and eventually reflected reverence.

She said, "His excellence, the holy King Olafur, wanted nothing more than for Helgi and me to unite in marriage. But unbeknownst to us, Helgi was already married when I arrived in Greenland. He married because he thought I was betrothed to another man." She sniffled and smiled through her tears. "We loved each other as we loved Jesus Christ who dwells in heaven."

"Your destiny has indeed caused you suffering."

Katla removed the old book from her trunk and showed it to the priest. "Grimkell, King Olafur's court bishop, gave me this Bible."

The priest stared at the Bible in awe.

Katla fell to her knees in front of the priest. "Now, I want to ask for your forgiveness." She laid her right hand on the Bible and looked up to the priest. "On behalf of the bishop, the loyal friends of the church and the reputation of the innocent child, I humbly ask God to free me from the sins Helgi and I indulged in to give life to this glorious child. In the name of God, can you forgive us?"

"I can, but—"

Katla cut him off. "This child must have entered this world with God's blessing. Little Katla is my gift for all the misfortune I have endured."

"Helgi's wife could bring you to justice," the priest stammered.

"She is a heathen woman, and she was responsible for the act, when Helgi and I… became intimate."

The priest indicated that he did not want to hear more, made the sign of the cross in front of himself and then in front of Katla.

Thus, mother and daughter received God's blessing and the priest obtained ownership of precious holy writ. Katla asked him to baptise little Katla and he acceded to her request.

On a sunny day at the end of summer, Katla was outside arranging flowers to dry when Thórdur, Nidbjorg and their two escorts arrived at Holl. They dismounted and the older couple walked up to her. Thórdur looked tired and frail, but his manner was still congenial.

Nidbjorg commanded more space than her husband but was livelier. She said, "I shall not keep the reason for our visit a secret. We have received a message from Helgi. He claims to be the father of your daughter and he wants us to treat her as our granddaughter."

Katla laughed with joy. "I hope your granddaughter will bring you as much happiness as she has brought me."

Bjorg arrived with little Katla in her arms. The girl laughed when she saw her mother and held out her arms. Her grandparents cheered up. Katla took her daughter in her arms and introduced her to Helgi's parents. Little Katla stared at them and then smiled sweetly.

Katla handed her to Nidbjorg, who hugged her granddaughter, teary-eyed.

After that, Nidbjorg and Thórdur made frequent trips to Holl.

~~~

Eilífur, the son of Hrefna, now a tall and handsome thirteen-year-old, had worked hard for Thórdur at Hofdi, owned his own horse and often rode to Holl after little Katla was born. He adored the girl and called her Dimple because of the dimple in her cheek when she smiled. On every visit, Eilífur gave Dimple a tiny wooden animal he had carved. Dimple spent hours trying to learn the sounds each animal made and arranging them on her little "farm".

Dimple resembled her mother except for the silky and straight auburn hair. She begged her mother to sing all the time and dragged her up the hill to the elf rock where Katla told her stories.

One day Eilífur said, "Dimple is like my little sister." He kissed her on the cheek. Dimple liked it and pinched his nose.

"I hope both of you will live in this valley until the end of your days," Katla said.

Eilífur said, with hesitation, "I don't know."

Katla felt he knew. "What else would you like to do?"

Eilífur blushed. "I want to be like Helgi."

"In what way?"

"Go to Norway, be in the king's court and protect the king from his enemies."

"It could put you in harm's way. But a young man must follow his passion."

Eilífur embraced Katla. "You understand," he said.

"I understand that men are driven to achieve greatness, although I have often disliked it."

Katla told him about the king's court, full of competitive men he should be cautious around.

"I want to be daring. How can I meet King Olafur?" Eilífur said, his eyes glistening.

"You cannot be aggressive with him. He values poems

about his virtue, receiving gifts, watching skilled swordsmanship, and above all loyalty."

Eilífur looked down. "But I'm no poet and I've nothing to give."

"You must understand court poetry, but I'm sure Sighvatur Thórdarson, the king's court poet, would teach you."

"Thórdur taught me Hávamál."

"Hávamál is a set of heathen poems, but they contain some useful wisdom. I would advise you not to recite those in the king's presence unless he asks you to. Do not despair, dear Eilífur, because few of the king's men are as skilled athletes as you already are. Neither do they own swords equal to the one you inherited from my father Halldór. Demonstrate your swordsmanship to the king, swear him loyalty, and I shall help you with the presents."

Eilífur kept smiling and asked, "How long should I stay with the king?"

"Until the king releases you from duty."

Three years later, when Katla learned a ship was headed for Norway, she purchased a fare for Eilífur and gave him an embroidered mauve mantle.

Before he left, Katla pulled from the bottom of her trunk the most beautiful mantle she had sewn. She asked Eilífur to give the bright red mantle to the queen and to tell her it was from Katla, the Icelandic seamstress. She also gave him the name of Astrid's closest confidant. "Tell him that you are a relation of Skáld-Helgi and you are bringing the queen a gift from me."

Katla taught Eilífur how to bow when paying respect to the queen and the king. "When you speak to the queen, tell her the magic herbs she gave me worked, as she said they would."

"Magic herbs?"

"She'll know what I mean."

"Is that all?"

"If she asks you for news about me, tell her I had a daughter whose father is Skáld-Helgi."

"Are you sure she'll not condemn you for bringing up a

319

child outside of marriage?"

Katla laughed. "I doubt she'll condemn others for love and lust." Then she turned serious. "But when in the company of the king, you shall behave like a Christian man. You must learn Christian beliefs, befriend monks and priests."

Eilífur was baffled by such contradictions, but he repeated everything she said. He wanted to remember every word.

"Be candid and fair, earn a good reputation and collect gold. Then return to Iceland, buy a farm and marry the girl you hold dear. Whatever others say about your choice, let it not affect you."

"Thank you for being like a dear mother to me."

When he was gone, Katla wept. Not just because she would miss Eilífur, but because of the hurdles he would face. Why did all young men want to leave the ones they love behind?

She thanked God for having a daughter.

54
Helgi

After Katla left Hornes, Helgi used her cabin on the hill as a retreat, where he carved walrus tusks and recited poetry. He took daily naps on Katla's bed. Covered by the mantle Katla gave him, he dreamt of her and of starry skies.

Six months later, Thórunn gave birth to a plump girl who gazed at Helgi with round inquisitive eyes. One day, after Thórunn had breast-fed the baby, she handed him to Helgi, who squeezed her to his chest and said, "She reminds me of my mother, and we shall name her Nidbjorg."

Thórunn did not show the same affection for her newborn daughter as she did for her son, Skeggi. The boy did not seek attention, unlike little Nidbjorg, who cried when anyone but Helgi held her.

Thórunn said, "She wants to be your daughter."

"Can I take her up to the cabin?" Helgi said.

"By all means," Thórunn said, and sighed.

He looked into Thórunn's swollen eyes and realised that she was exhausted from lack of sleep. "You are tired. Take a nap," he said.

"So, you are not blind, after all," Thórunn said, and tucked sheepskin around her daughter.

As he walked up the icy path to the cabin, holding little Nidbjorg tight, he thought Thórunn had a point. He was blind to the needs of his family. Blind like his grandfather had been to the needs of his wife and children, whom he left to fend for themselves in Iceland for long periods of time. For this negligence, Helgi's mother resented her father, and did not share Helgi's admiration for Einar's poetry and fame.

Once inside, Helgi sat down by the warm stove, rocked little Nidbjorg and said, "I'll never leave you to fend for yourself, but I hope you never tire of my poetry, as some have." He kissed his daughter on the cheek and she cooed, yawned and went to sleep.

He laid her down on Katla's bed and recited to her a love poem.

Little Skeggi seemed content in the company of his mother and Koltorfa, who sang to him as Katla used to. Helgi left his son's care entirely to the women, hesitating to become attached to the boy, in case it prevented him from moving to Iceland to be with Katla.

The following summer, when Skeggi could walk, he made a habit of running down to the dock, even in the rain, with the heavy-set Koltorfa on his heels.

One day, when Helgi was getting his ship ready to sail, Koltorfa said, "If Skeggi keeps this up, he's going to slide into the sea and drown."

Skeggi pointed at Helgi's ship just as Thórunn approached.

Out of breath from rushing, Thórunn said, "Skeggi wants to go out to sea and be a fisherman like his namesake. You must teach him how to swim."

"I will," Helgi said, and picked his son up. The boy grabbed Helgi around his neck and squeezed. "Can I take him with me to Brattahlíd? I will return tomorrow."

"If you promise he'll never be without supervision."

"I promise," Helgi said, and handed the boy to an oarsman who was already on board.

As the boat glided out of Einarsfjordur, Helgi sat in the stern, holding Skeggi. Before Katla left for Iceland the summer before, he had promised her to wait a year before considering moving to Iceland. Katla understood him better than anyone. She knew he could not leave his children behind. Helgi kissed his son on the top of his head, consoled by the thought Katla did not expect him to abandon his children.

Once at Brattahlíd, Skeggi was entrusted to the care of Thorkell's wife, while Helgi listened to Thorkell telling him news from Iceland.

"Thórkatla Halldórsdóttir gave birth to a girl she named Katla," Thorkell said.

Helgi stood up. "Who is the father?"

"She claims you are."

"I am. I am!" Helgi cried out and ran to the Thjódhildur

church, where he fell to his knees, wept and prayed for his daughter and her mother until he felt drained, and an immense sense of peace consumed him. An inner voice told him, "Now it is time for you to secure harmony here in Greenland."

~~~

Helgi took his divine order seriously. His mission became to ensure that Greenlanders ratified equitable laws, and he was appointed the lawman of Greenland.

A few years after Katla left, Skúfur of Stokkanes returned from Norway, where he dwelt with King Olafur. Helgi sailed to Eiríksfjordur to visit his friend, and there he learned that unrest had taken hold in Norway, brought on by Knutur of Denmark, who sought to overturn King Olafur.

A tall and dark-eyed young man walked into the lodge and stared at Helgi, who felt he recognised his demeanour.

Skúfur said to Helgi, "This boy came with me from Norway. His name is Eilífur Hrefnuson. He says he knows you."

Helgi jumped up and hugged the boy. "Eilífur, I have not seen you since you were a newborn. How handsome and noble you look."

Eilífur smiled. "You saved me from death, but Thórkatla Halldórsdóttir kept me alive and provided me with the wisdom needed to survive in Norway."

Helgi's eyes flooded with tears. "Katla, my angel." He examined Eilífur's clothing. "She must have sewn this mantle because I have seldom seen one as magnificent."

"She did."

Helgi stroked the hilt of Eilífur's sword. "I've seen this sword before."

"It was a present from Halldór, Katla's father."

Helgi laughed. "The stubborn bull. The ways of the Lord are unpredictable."

They sat down and Eilífur told him of Helgi's cheerful daughter, whom he called Dimple, and of her mother, Katla.

Helgi was moved. "You were brought up without a father,

and I feel responsible because I killed him for fathering a child with your mother. The Pope forgave me and I hope you can also forgive me."

"I do."

"Now I see God himself ordained your birth and I'm grateful to him."

Helgi invited Eilífur to stay with him at Hornes for the winter and Eilífur accepted.

Thórunn received Eilífur with suspicion. Helgi did not let her mood affect him and put Eilífur in the cabin that Katla once dwelt in and Helgi used as his refuge.

Even though Eilífur had a gentle demeanour, he was versatile and a diligent worker. His fingers were long and agile, and he performed most tasks with remarkable speed.

A year after Nidbjorg was born, Thórunn gave birth to a boy they named Thorbjorn. He was shy, but after Eilífur arrived at Hornes, Thorbjorn wanted to be by his side.

Eilífur taught both boys, Skeggi and Thorbjorn, to carve, tie nets, and to fence. He cut down firewood with the workmen and taught them not to hew young trees, and to allow the wood to dry out fully before they used it for firewood. Eilífur borrowed a boat and fished, using nets he made with Helgi's sons. Hornes never lacked fish as long as Eilífur stayed there.

Thórunn said, "What a gift that a useful man is finally a member of the household."

Their daughter Nidbjorg heard this and said, "My father is the most useful man in Greenland."

"How so?" Thórunn asked.

"He is making laws so we don't have to fear villains who could kill us and take our things."

Helgi laughed and kissed his daughter on the cheek.

~ ~ ~

After dwelling in Greenland for two years, Eilífur secured a place on a merchant ship headed to Iceland with a cargo of walrus tusks and whale meat. Before he left, he asked Helgi for advice about buying the farm Steinar, which had belonged to Eilífur's father Arngeir.

"You're a prudent young man and I admire you for it," Helgi said. "I've heard that few things happen in Borgarfjordur without Hermundur Illugason's approval. You should seek his counsel."

Helgi ferried Eilífur to Eiríksfjordur, where a ship was docked at Brattahlíd. He bade Eilífur farewell and added, "You're an honourable and diligent young man. After you have bought a farm, secure the most noble young woman in Iceland, and make sure her father is agreeable."

"I shall marry the girl I love more than others."

"I must warn you that a betrothal based on lust is not a sound basis for marriage."

"It seems to me your advice does not reflect your experience. Or would you not have married Katla?"

Helgi stared at him in silence and a tear trickled down his cheek.

Eilífur said, "Katla told me love and lust were not the same. I shall heed Katla's advice and marry the girl who loves me and whom I love."

Helgi patted him on the shoulder and said, "How did you become so wise?"

"I observe and learn what I deem desirable. From my grandmother Finnbjorg I learned to trust my instincts; from Halldór, Katla's father, I learned that practising skills is essential; from your father, Thórdur, I learned diligence; from Thórdís, Katla's sister, I learned to be my own master; and from Katla I learned affection and loyalty."

Helgi smiled, and said, "Did you learn anything from me?"

"Passion. Passion for life, passion for creation, passion for improvement."

As Eilífur's ship sailed away, Helgi pondered Eilífur's observation. Each man had unique talents, which could be harnessed for the good.

What about passion? Could it be learned? In turn, could a passionate man learn to restrain himself and keep himself from causing suffering? Could he learn to direct his passion towards the good?

He resolved to use his passion to unite men in bringing about change in Greenland.

55
Katla

Katla's monthly bleeding increased as the years passed. Her abdomen swelled and she felt a hard lump under her navel. She tried to sew but had to stop as she lost strength in her arms. She was exhausted and eventually succumbed to lying in bed night and day, suffering from abdominal pain.

Her daughter sat by her bed at night, sang for her, and told her what was happening at Holl and around the district. Dimple had inherited the art of storytelling from her father. She was funny and imitated others by contorting her face, altering her voice and changing her posture. When Katla laughed, Dimple kissed her on the forehead. As Katla had done in fair weather in her youth, her daughter ran around the fields and hills and befriended the animals. When Dimple grew breasts, Katla worried that greedy men would try to take advantage of her daughter, but Dimple was too strong-willed to submit to powerful men.

Katla slept off and on and awoke with foggy memories of dreams where Helgi rode over the sea on his horse Sleipnir and kissed her softly on the mouth. She took up praying to her elf friend Vonadís to help her remember her dreams when she awoke. After a few days, her dreams became so vivid it seemed that the people in them were alive.

One night, Katla dreamed her mother asked her to make arrangements for young Katla's upbringing, because "greedy friends want to ensnare her and capture our farm, Holl".

Katla's sister Thórdís arrived. She sat down at Katla's bedside.

When Katla told her their mother's concern in the dream, Thórdís's eyes filled with tears and she said, "We have often been at odds, but I don't want to see you go."

Katla took her sister's hand. "Thórdís, you are resourceful, and in recent years you've been loyal to me."

"What do you want to do with Holl?" Thórdís said.

"I want Dimple to inherit the farm, but she's too young to run it."

"And the men in our family are greedy," Thórdís said with a sardonic tone.

"Dimple is strong-willed like you are. Although you're a woman, you've managed to hold your own and I admire you for it."

"As our father said, 'You conquer with money and determination.' I would add negotiation skills," Thórdís said.

Katla looked into Thórdís's eyes. "Have you ever loved a man, or did you love Helgi?"

"I never loved Helgi, and I've never loved a man," Thórdís said, smiling.

"Then I pity you."

"You have no reason to pity me. I've never desired intimacy with men. What did your lust for Helgi bring you but misery?"

Katla stroked Thórdís's arm. "Love made me feel alive."

Thórdís squeezed Katla's hand. "What shall become of little Katla? Do Bjorg and Flosi want to take care of her?"

"When she's thirteen, I want her to go to Helgi in Greenland so she won't become the victim of men's greed here in Iceland. She shall decide whom she marries, and I'm confident she'll charm her father into agreeing to her choice."

"If you leave soon, where should Katla go?"

"To Helgi's parents, if they can take care of her. They'll oversee her education and bring her up as their own daughter."

"You're too generous to people who were so obnoxious to you."

"My daughter has the right to enjoy others in the family, which includes spending time with you, dear Thórdís."

"As you know, I'm not fond of children."

"She's no longer a child."

"She is not mature yet. But I'll make sure Katla is well educated and well taken care of."

Thórdís returned a few days later with Hermundur, Thórdur, Nidbjorg and a lawman. Katla articulated her wish for her daughter's care, and said that she wanted Flosi and Bjorg to continue managing Holl. They would receive all profits from their farming as long as they did not diminish the farm's value. Katla then dozed off, content with the arrangements.

56
Eilífur

Eilífur arrived in Iceland during a rainstorm. He bought a horse on the dock in Borgarfjordur, and rode straight to Hvammur, eager to embrace his grandmother Finnbjorg and tell her what he had learned in Norway and in Greenland.

There was a new longhouse at Hvammur. Inside he was surprised to find Thórdís carving runes on a large column which held up the roof. She was wearing trousers, with her hair tied back, still as graceful as Queen Astrid.

When Thórdís saw him, she said, "Welcome, Eilífur. Your grandmother was expecting you."

"I gather she is as keen as ever."

"She's blind, but she's still astute. You'll find her in the kitchen. You can stay with us as long as you choose." Thórdís returned to carving.

Finnbjorg sat by a fire in the kitchen, her grey braids hanging down to her waist. When he approached, she looked up with closed eyes, sniffed the air, and said, "My dear grandson. You have returned, and I can tell by your scent you're a healthy young man, but your clothes are drenched."

He changed his clothes, gave his grandmother a brooch made by a Finn in Norway, and told her about what he had learned overseas, and that he was going to buy a farm in Iceland.

"You have the foresight of our ancestors. Tomorrow morning, you must go to Holl and visit Katla. She is not well."

Eilífur awoke early the next morning and rode to Thverárhlíd. He first stopped by Hofdi where Thórdur and Nidbjorg greeted him. After telling them about Helgi and his children in Greenland, Nidbjorg, still plump, said, "I have a granddaughter named after me in Greenland. I will see her before I die."

Thordur was still spry, and said, "We shall send for all of them when the youngest is twelve."

Eilífur rode on to Holl. Katla was asleep when he arrived,

and his heart filled with sorrow to see her so feeble.

Dimple was up on the hill. The last time they had met, she was a child. When Eilífur called for her, she came running, her auburn hair floating behind her like the mane of a galloping horse, and her breasts bouncing up and down with every step. She was already twelve years old! Her beauty made him gasp, and as she came closer, he was speechless.

She said, "Eilífur, is it you?" She stretched out her arms, but when he stepped back her smile faded, and she stared at him with her mother's bright blue eyes and her white cheeks turned rosy.

He stuttered, "Good day, Katla."

"You can still call me Dimple," she said, blushing. "Tell me all your travel stories."

They sat down in the grass, and he told her of her family in Greenland. She listened and was overjoyed to learn that she had siblings.

Eilífur had to avert his gaze when he spoke, as looking into her eyes made him forget everything.

"Are you a poet?" Dimple said.

Eilífur laughed. "King Olafur and Queen Astrid assumed all Icelanders could compose poetry as quickly as an arrow flew. I could only disappoint. But I memorise poems and stories I enjoy."

"I would rather have you here to tell me stories than far away with the king making up boring court poetry."

Dimple was candid and spontaneous, different from the young women at court, who made it their mission to befriend Queen Astrid and to snatch the richest man available.

"My mother loves stories. Let's go inside, and you can tell her stories of the court."

"But she's so ill."

"She understands what we say."

They went inside. Katla woke up, smiled when she saw him and whispered, "Handsome Eilífur."

He blushed and told Katla how happy Queen Astrid was when he brought her the mantle Katla sent her, and that she laughed for a long time after he told her how well the herbs had worked. The queen was generous to Eilífur, both with her advice and her friendship.

Ignoring her debility, Katla attempted to sit up. Dimple put a folded blanket under her mother's head while Katla pointed at her trunk and whispered, "Herbs, on the bottom."

Dimple opened the trunk and Eilífur described what the herbs looked like. They both bent over the trunk, and found the herbs under clothing, linens, gold, needles and jewellery. Their hands touched and Eilífur's body trembled.

Dimple put the herbs in her mother's hand. Katla grasped one leaf, raised it to her mouth and tried to take a deep breath. She smiled and whispered to her daughter, "Wash yourself using these herbs on your wedding night." Then she closed her eyes and went to sleep.

57
Katla

Katla's abdomen kept swelling. It was so painful that she was always nauseous and unable to eat.

One night, Katla felt a bright light shining on her face. She opened her eyes and saw where Vonadís floated in the air. White silk covered her face and body and fluttered in the breeze. With a crystal-clear voice, Vonadís said, "Katla, my dear. The stars are twinkling in the clear sky. The time has come for you to lie down by our home where your brother Kollur and your parents await you. Wrap yourself in Helgi's mantle and do not fear the journey."

Katla was wide awake, and her pain had evaporated. She pushed her covers aside and tried to stand up. But her legs wobbled as if she were standing in the middle of a storm. She reached for her mantle, which hung on the wall, wrapped herself in it and grasped the cane Eilífur had made for her father long ago. She did not bother putting on shoes and limped out into the corridor, unfettered by cold and pains. When she made it outside, she looked up and saw the moon brighter than ever. She was entranced by the brilliant sky, spotted with shimmering stars which reflected magic. Her heart filled with boundless joy, and she yearned to dwell among the stars which had consoled and inspired Helgi and her in difficult times.

The lovers' souls had united where they belonged, in the infinite sky.

She wanted to rush to the elf rock where she could recline and marvel at the splendour above. Yet when she began walking, her cane slipped, and she fell to the ground. It did not discourage her. She stayed on all fours and crawled like a lamb heading for its mother. The lump in her stomach weighed her down, but it no longer pressed on her spine.

When she looked up the hill, Vonadís was standing by the rock, waving to her and lighting up the path. Katla pulled her mantle so it rested on her back and crawled to Vonadís. When she reached the mossy tussocks, she stopped long enough to inhale the fragrance from the earth. No wonder the dogs sniffed the ground so eagerly. Thus, they could decipher the secrets hidden in the earth. Humans were not as discerning. They could not perceive the past by sniffing, unaware that the truth dwelt beneath their noses.

She continued crawling. The mantle slid off her back. Even if she did not need it for warmth, she could not leave it behind any more than she could shed her love for Helgi. She grasped the mantle and held it in one hand as she crawled the rest of the way, careful not to get it caught under her knees.

When she arrived at the hollow she stopped and looked down at where she once saw Hrefna and her lover embracing. They looked as vivid now as they were then, and Katla was suffused with gladness. She laughed. How delightful love was. Why did a couple in love delay the pleasures of touching each other?

Katla crawled on and every time she took a deep breath, she sensed for a moment something new: the worn-out sheepskin shoes on her dainty feet; little Eilífur; blueberry heather with huge berries; hidden mountain grass; and the soft moss that permitted men and sheep to tread on it, year after year, while seeping their secrets into the earth.

When Katla arrived at the elf rock, she wrapped herself in Helgi's mantle and lay down on her back. The bloody sores on her knees did not diminish the joy she received from the glorious sky.

The Northern Lights in every shade of green danced around the stars, filling her heart with yet more joy. As always, Katla felt the stars guided the Northern Lights so they could communicate with each other. How illuminating their language was, compared to the insensitive exchanges practised by men.

After a while the Northern Lights took on the shape of persons Katla knew. She recognised Finnbjorg, who guided Eilífur and little Katla to each other. They held hands, and it dawned on Katla that their fate was sealed when they found Queen Astrid's herbs in Katla's trunk. She smiled and thanked the Jesus Star for blessing the children's union.

Katla's father and mother appeared in the Northern Lights, smiling and reaching for each other. Peace reigned in heaven.

She stared at the Helgi Star, which became brighter as she gazed. Helgi jumped from the star and said to her in a subdued tone, "My dearest Katla, even though I loved you more than any other, I failed to bring you happiness. You forgave me and the Pope forgave me, but notwithstanding your mercy, my heart is filled with regrets."

"My beloved Helgi, the one who is besieged with regret is unable to enjoy life. Do not regret, love much and enjoy your children. Even if men call the union of our Katla and Eilífur foolish passion, do not listen to them, and give your approval. Hrefna and I agree, and now the mothers decide."

The bodies formed by the Northern Lights turned into green, dancing and flashing ghosts. Katla began singing to all of them, "I love you. I love you all. Love is all." Her heart felt warm, as if it was expanding.

When the elves echoed her singing, she closed her eyes. In her mind a bright light emerged, first in the distance, but then it wrapped itself around her like a loving mother and she quit breathing, relieved she no longer needed to.

Appendix

List of characters in Elf Rock

Map of Western Iceland

Map of the Eastern Settlement in Greenland

Characters in Elf Rock

At *Holl* in Thverarhlíd
  Halldór, farmer
  Oddlaug, his wife
  Thórdís, daughter of Halldór and Oddlaug
  Thórkatla (Katla) daughter of Halldór and Oddlaug
  Jónsi, farmhand
  Vonadís, Katla's imaginary friend at Elf Rock
  Thórmundur, farmhand (Jónsi's son)
  Hrefna, maid
  Finnbjorg, maid and herbalist (Hrefna's mother)
  Dagur, farmhand
  Aevar, farmhand
  Bjorg, manager later
  Flosi, Bjorg's husband, manager later

At *Hofdi* in Thverárhlíd
  Thórdur, farmer
  Nidbjorg, his wife
  Helgi, their son

At *Steinar* in Thverárhlíd
  Arngeir, farmer

At *Gilsbakki* in Hvítársída
  Illugi the Black
  Hermundur, Illugi's son
  Gunnlaugur, Illugi's son

At *Hvammur* in Hvítársida
  Thórdís, after marriage
  Finnbjorg, maid, moved from Holl
  Hrefna, her daughter, moved from Holl

Eilífur, Hrefna and Arngeir's son
Ásný, farmhand

At **Saudafell** in Dalir
Garpur, farmer
Gróa, his wife

At **Kvennabrekka** in Dalir
Thórgerdur, farmer

In **Saelingsdalur**
Einar, poet, Oddlaug's father, and Helgi's grandfather
Gudrún Ósvífursdóttir, Helgi's 2nd cousin
Vandrádur Ósvífursson, Helgi's 2nd cousin
Áskell Ósvífursson, Helgi's 2nd cousin
Snorri Thorgrímsson, a chief

By **Laekjarskogur** shore
Narfi, a fisherman

In **Norway**
Eiríkur, Earl of Norway
Ólafur, King of Norway
Astrid, Queen of Norway
Sighvatur, court poet
Signy, wife of Sighvatur
Adam, monk
Jósef, monk
Ottar, poet and prisoner

In **Saxony** and **Italy**
Heinrich, Holy Roman Emperor
Pope Benedetto VIII in Rome
Bernward, abbot and bishop of Hildesheim
Axel, a Norseman
Robert, leader of a Norman troop

Frederik, member of the Norman troop
Melrus, leader of a troop from Bari
Johannes, a Norse monk in Rome
Prince Guaimar III of Salerno

In Greenland
Forni, a farmer at under Sólarfjollum
Aesa, Forni's wife
Geirlaug, Forni's maid
Leifur Eiríksson the Lucky, chief in Brattahlíd
Thorkell, Leifur's son, lived at Brattahlíd
Thórunn, a widow/Helgi's wife, lived at Herjólfsnes
and Hornes
Steingrímur, Thórunn's son from her marriage to
Skeggi
Jokull, Thórunn's son from her marriage to Skeggi
Thorgrímur, farmer at Langanes, Thorunn's cousin
Valgerdur, Thorgrímur's sister, Lived at Langanes
Thorvardur, owner of Hellir
Gríma, a witch, Thorvardur's wife
Eyvindur, son of Gríma and Thorvardur
Thórir, son of Gríma and Thorvardur
Mýrídur, a witch
Hjordís, a seer
Koltorfa, a maid to Katla

Seamen:
Thorsteinn, a shipper
Illugi 1, a shipper
Illugi 2, a shipper
Konáll, a captain
Thórgils, a trickster
Skúfur, a captain

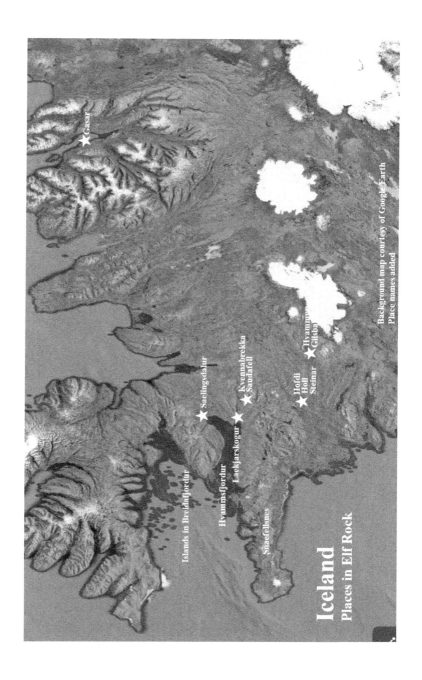

Gásar

Saelingsdalur
Kvennabrekka
Saudafell

Hvamm...
Gilsba...
Hofdi
Holl
Steinar

Islands in Breidafjordur
Hvammsfjordur
Laekjarskogur

Snaefellsnes

Background map courtesy of Google Earth
Place names added

Iceland
Places in Elf Rock

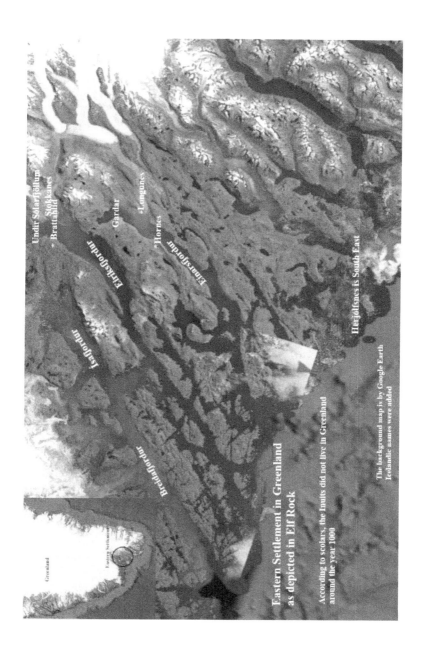

**Eastern Settlement in Greenland
as depicted in Elf Rock**

According to scolars, the Inuits did not live in Greenland
around the year 1000

The background map is by Google Earth
Icelandic names were added

Greenland

Eastern Settlement

Breidafjorthur

Isafjorthur

Eiriksfjorthur

Undir Solarfjöllum
Stokkanes
Brattahild
Gardar
»Langones
»Hornes
Einarsfjordur

Herjölfsnes is South East